SEEING IS BEVEILING
by Michael John Gerard Higgins

ISBN 978-1-7399003-4-2
©2023 Michael John Gerard Higgins

The author wishes to assert his moral and intellectual rights in relation to this work.

Acknowledgements:
All illustrations and photographs are by the author with the exception of the artworks - threaded through the work - by John Elcock - (details of which can be found in the Index) - and the photographs on pp. 546, 552, 554 and 557 - by Waldo Myles Capability Walker.

Hearty thanks to both Waldo and John for allowing their inclusion.

I would also like to acknowledge the presence - within the text - of the two unnameable beings once inhabitant within the human remains represented on pp. 197 and 304 - may they rest - or continue to thrive - in solalterity.

The accompanying music by Michael John Gerard Higgins is published by Universal Edition.
www.universaledition.com

Printed in the UK

Published by The Artel Press
www.theartelpress.co.uk

SEEING IS BEVEILING

MICHAEL JOHN GERARD HIGGINS

SEEING IS BEVEILING

A Study in Obliterapture

Or

The wheel of the god is open to fire

Or

As they come down to the one before the great river of conflagration

Or

Rejoice or die!

Or

A Nine Daies and One Daie's Wonder 'containing your own pleasures – paines and kinde entertainments'

Michael John Gerard Higgins

That the rose is still burning is due to the kind enkindling of my heart-kindred

– Sarah

FOREWORD

Perhaps the best way to read this book would be over the course of nine and one nights – finding yourself – before beginning the book – an unopened rose that will come to bloom by the end.

Including the music – the duration of each Chapter – (assuming 2 minutes is spent reading each page) – is – approximately – as follows –

    Chapter 1 – 3°20'.
    Chapter 2 – 3°.
    Chapter 3 – 3°.
    Chapter 4 – 3°.
    Chapter 5 – 6°.
    Chapter 6 – 5°.
    Chapter 7 – 5°30.
    Chapter 8 – 11°.
    Chapter 9 – 14°.
    CODA   – 2°30.

When the titles of the various pieces of music are encountered – in the following font and preceded by a fleuron –

❦ A Rose is on Fire: 1

- then such pieces may then – at such junctures – be either – preferably – performed by the reader and their friends – the scores being available from Universal Edition – or listened to – digital simulacra being the sole versions accessible – at time of publication – via the author's soundcloud page at the playlist – Seeing is Beveiling.

Alternatively – the reader could choose to experience the book over 242 nights – one for each piece of music that the narrative employs – beginning – say – on St Giles Day – (each of the 108 of the Lampedephoria – therefore – being assigned its own evening) – and ending at– or around– the festival of Beltane.

The ceremonial rose-tree – explained in Appendix 2 – may be used in conjunction with any of the pieces – of music – when they are performed – referred to in the book.

It is hoped that the structure – nature and experience of this work brings the reader – and listener – a similar pleasure to that brought to the author by – the poetry of – Attar's Conference of the Birds *and Rumi's* Masnavi *– and the uncanny – lucid hilarity – the mise-en-abyme – of MacCruiskeen's chests.*

PREAMBLE

"I have a huge tree," said Hui Tzu to Chuang Tzu, "the kind people call shu. Its huge trunk is so gnarled and knotted that no measuring string can gauge it, and its branches are so bent and twisted they defy compass and square. It stands right beside the road, and still carpenters never notice it. These words of yours, so vast and useless – everyone ignores them the same way."

Chuang Tzu – The Inner Chapters: 16 (trans. Hinton)

We have got rid of the real world: what world is left? The apparent world perhaps? ... But no! **Along with the real world we've done away with the apparent world as well!**

Friedrich Nietzsche

During the age of natural science, which began about the middle of the nineteenth century, human cultural activity has slipped gradually not just into the lowest realms of nature, but actually under nature. Technology becomes Sub-Nature. This requires that human beings now experience a knowledge of the spirit in which they raise themselves into Supra-Nature. They must raise themselves as high above nature as they sink down below nature in sub-natural technological activity. By this means, they create inwardly the strength not to go under.

Rudolf Steiner

It is necessary to rise in this flesh, in which everything exists.

The Gospel of Philip

Love passionately.
Serenely – accept what cannot be loved.
What cannot be accepted – love dispassionately.
What cannot be loved dispassionately – love passionately.

The Lollipop Entity

Neither is it abortive – nor does it abound – nor is it an abounding in or with – nor is it a something about which – nor is it a wandering about – nor is it strewn about – nor is it out and about – nor is it a looking about – nor is it a turning and turning about.

Taken from THE DISCOURSE ON WHAT IS NOT THE REAL
– The 5th cygnet

At first, I was deeply alarmed. I had the feeling that I had gone beyond the surface of things and was beginning to see a strangely beautiful interior, and felt dizzy at the thought that now I had to investigate this wealth of mathematical structures that Nature had so generously spread out before me.'

Werner Heisenberg

Cheng of the North Gate asked the Yellow Emperor, 'My Lord, when you had the Hsien Chih music performed in the area around Lake Tung Ting, I listened and at first I was afraid; I listened again and I was weary; I listened to the end and I was bewildered. I became upset and incapable of coherent speech and finally I lost my self-assurance.'

The Book of Chuang Tzu: Chapter 14 – Does Heaven Move?

The Lampedephoria coincide with reality note for note – point for point.

The Lampedephorian

Someone in Sung had some marvellous hats to sell, so he took them to Yüeh. But the Yüeh tribes crop their hair short and tattoo their bodies: they had no use for marvellous hats.

Chuang Tzu – The Inner Chapters: 13 (trans. Hinton)

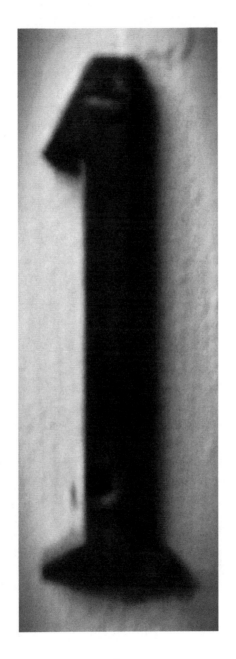

'onely tricker of your Trill-lilles and best bel-shangles...began frolickly to foote it...
farwell congruitie...set forward – dauncing...'

'There is neither cessation...'

NO ENTRY?
NONE TRY!

WARNING!

DANGER OF SERIOUS
I-INITIATION

Intrigued by the notice – and – (as well as acting on your discombobulation at the curious state of the sun at present) –

- seeking some variance to your routine existence – you cannot but open the gate – each of the 13 rusted locks turning immediately to a verdigris dust – and so it is – as you cross the threshold – that you are rendered immediately and utterly consumed with pain as you fall – senseless – to the ground – having been struck in your left cheek by an errant golf-ball.

As the golfer – in an attempt to release his ball – smashes your face in – 1024 tiny moths find their way out from the ball's dimples – forming – before descending onto your face to perform immediate – inscrutable and totally successful reconstructive surgery – a flapping polygon of varying dimensions towards – by its collective endeavour – a temporary – lepidopterous grid – bearing – above your dizzied countenance – (beyond the moths' formation you think you see – in confused flight – the last northern spotted owl) – the following lettering –

Η Ο Ν Ι Σ Ο Ι Τ   ΘΥΙ   Μ Α Λ

Ψ   Π   ΕΝΣΕ   ΔΙΕ   Υ   ΕΤ

ΜΟΝ   Δ   Ρ   Ο   Ι   Τ

Η   ΟΝ ΙΣ   ΟΙΤ   ΘΥΙ   ΜΑΛΨ   ΠΕ
ΝΣΕ   ΔΙΕΥ   Ε   Τ   ΜΟΝ   Δ   Ρ

Ο   ΙΤ

ΗΟ   ΝΙ   ΣΟ ΙΤ ΘΥΙ   ΜΑ   ΛΨ
ΠΕ   ΝΣΕ Δ Ι Ε Υ   Ε Τ   ΜΟΝ
Δ Ρ   Ο ΙΤ

ΗΟΝ Ι   ΣΟ   Ι Τ ΘΥΙ   Μ
ΑΛ   Ψ ΠΕΝΣ Ε Δ Ι   Ε Υ   Ε   Τ Μ
ΟΝ Δ Ρ Ο   ΙΤ

ΗΟ Ν   Ι   ΣΟ ΙΤ   ΘΥΙ ΜΑΛ   Ψ
Π Ε   ΝΣ Ε   Δ Ι Ε Υ   Ε Τ   ΜΟ   Ν Δ
ΡΟ   Ι Τ

ΗΟΝ   Ι Σ   Ο   Ι Τ   ΘΥΙ
ΜΑΛ   Ψ   ΠΕΝΣΕ ΔΙ   Ε   Υ   ΕΤ
Μ   Ο ΝΔ Ρ   Ο   Ι Τ

ΗΟ Ν Ι Σ   Ο Ι   Τ   ΘΥΙ   Μ
ΑΛ Ψ   Π   ΕΝ ΣΕ   Δ Ι Ε Υ
Ε   Τ   ΜΟ   ΝΔΡΟ   Ι   Τ

Η Ο Ν Ι Σ   Ο   Ι   Τ ΘΥ Ι   Μ
ΑΛ Ψ   ΠΕΝ Σ Ε Δ Ι Ε Υ
Ε   Τ   ΜΟ Ν   Δ   Ρ Ο Ι   Τ

ΗΟΝΙ Σ   ΟΙ Τ   ΘΥΙ
ΜΑ   Λ
Ψ   Π   ΕΝΣ   Ε ΔΙ Ε   Υ Ε   Τ
ΜΟ Ν   ΔΡΟ Ι
ΗΟ Ν   Ι   Σ Ο Ι Τ   ΘΥΙ
ΜΑΛ   Ψ   ΠΕΝΣ   Ε   Δ   Ι Ε
Υ   Ε   Τ   Μ ΟΝΔ Ρ   ΟΙ   Τ

4

Standing – now – in the middle of the field – with your assailant shielding his eyes from the darkness in order to determine the progress of his ball – you assume – though you cannot see any greens or flags – that you are in the middle of the fairway of a golf course.

The golfer – his name is *The Very Reverend Obadiah Lution* – says –

'Would you mind carrying my clubs for me? – I really don't want to.'

Without a moment's hesitation – you accept the golfer's invitation and take his clubs from him – thus becoming his caddie.

Carrying the *Very Reverend Lution's* clubs to where the ball has landed – you realize – by the presence of a tiny clubhouse –

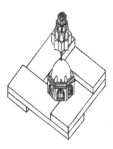

– you have now reached the beginning of the course – but – as the *Very Reverend Lution* explains –

'I'm afraid it's far from straightforward – though the holes are numbered 1-9' – here he points to a map of the course – this document bearing no relation to any other item that you have ever encountered under the designation 'map' –

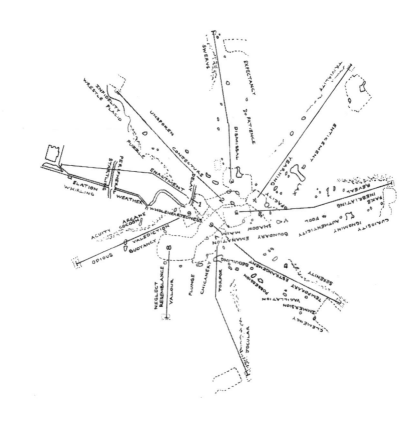

- 'they have to be completed –

    O my Christ! Would you look at this rose?! You know – I've played here so many times before – but I had never noticed this rose growing here...'

    As you are just at the point of bringing your attention to this rose – which you also – oddly – had not yet noticed – you become – obliquely – aware of being caught in a sudden gust of wind – of such force that you are amazed that you do not fall to the ground – this sensation being accompanied by the sight – or – more correctly – the almost sight – of a figure brushing past you at greater velocity – a perfect celerity of 0.618 multiplied by c –

- though the memory of the figure's face comes to you only later on – when you more directly perceive the rose for a second time –

'Sorry – where was I – yes – the holes must be played in a particular order – which changes daily – and unless we possess some kind of embedded experience or knowledge embodied from the previous hole – we will not be able to continue – so – your caddying skills will need to be a cut above if we are to proceed.

Beware of the booming sky call that we will regularly hear during our game – this will instil a development – a reconfiguration – in the sun's appearance – you'll have heard of the moon's phases – well – here – it's the solar that changes its aspect – each time – the resultant – reconstituted light will act as harbinger of who knows what – do look – however – right at the sun at such moments – with – if possible – mind and heart-burstingly unimaginable love-as-emergency – the sun's face – empty though it may ever remain – never repeats and always has something – amidst the glare – to communicate – though only to one who is able to embrace – if not – counter – (lovingly) – the phenomena of blindingly clear-sighted alterity.

There's also the business of the **PAX IMMEMORIAL** – a Tournai marble on which there's invariably inscribed 11 lines of gibberish – and one line of cryptic coherence that one is to take as a sermon in itself – the whole distribution changing with each return to the clubhouse – but as the – if you'll forgive me – homely homilies' – (here the Very Reverend smiles the most Anglican of smiles) – '*I* generally spend such a substantial part of my week crafting are rather more forthcoming – or so I trust' – (here the Very Reverend – if this is possible – closes his eyes ingratiatingly) – 'then *I* tend to ignore such pretence at profound aphorism. Look – here it is – what do you make of today's first offering?'

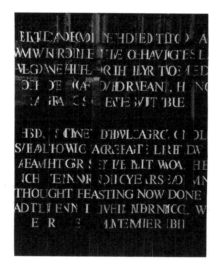

'Well ...' – you say – 'to be honest – I would be willing to concur with Line 10 – I've been overdoing it of late and am – indeed – rather done in and – from a mental point of view – more or less totally debauched – in fact my walk today was intended as a welcome respite from all the recent excesses of cerebration and to let my legs do the thinking for a change. But where are the greens? – the flags?'

'First – if it's not too taxing – (here – the Very Reverend sardonically grimaces) – 'choose a number. It will then be made known to me which way to face and I will strike the ball accordingly – after which we will be transported to the ball's destination – the hole bearing the number on which you decide.'

'4'! – you say – after 13 seconds consideration leads you to a memory of this morning's breakfast during which you had added – for your bowels – this number of prunes to your bowl.

The *Very Reverend Lution* closes his eyes –

'21 iron – please'.

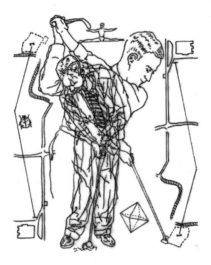

You hand him the club. His eyes still closed – The *Very Reverend Lution* spins around several times – (during which time the dark-pink rose – pointed out by *The Reverend* a moment ago – seems to glow a little more brightly – and you are sure you can hear – very faintly – organ music similar in its shadow-bright sonority to the colouring of the flower – is it in your mind – or is it – somehow – emanating from the rose itself?)

❦ A Rose is on Fire: 1

– until – stopping suddenly – he throws his ball in the air – the instant of its coming to rest coinciding precisely with The *Very Reverend Lution's* striking of it.

A moment later you are standing – outside a building almost identical to – if not the actual – *Chartres Cathedral* – beneath the – rotating – rose window. It is immediately clear to you – though you would – if pressed – find it difficult to say what constituted this clarity – that the golfer's task is to send the ball through the gap at the rose window's centre in such a way so as the ball will fall at the exact point of entry into the labyrinth below – thus rolling – if the required propulsion has been applied – through the labyrinth's – (the unicursal path of the route has a tiny wall – about 3/8ths the height of the ball – keeping the ball securely on its way) – path to its centre – so completing the hole.

'144 iron'. – says The *Very Reverend Lution.*

The ball takes flight well enough – but you are startled to see that its trajectory is anything but straight – reminding you rather of the flitting and cavorting practiced by moths to a light – though the source of the light around which the ball is erratically orbiting remains to be seen.

Eventually – after some minutes – the golfer ruminates –

'Well... I *think* it's gone through the window – whether it's found the true centre and *raison d'être* of the whole mediæval enterprise is another matter.'

You arrive within the cathedral – beneath the rose window – at the entrance to the labyrinth – just in time to see the ball – (its progress through the labyrinth being extraordinarily slow) – approach the centre – the golfer's face bearing a broad – self-satisfied beam – when a tiny creature emerges from the hole for which the ball was heading – it is a minuscule and many-handed – boy-headed – ele-phant-youth – their name is *Edencanter* – who – while unfurling a flag and placing it within the hole with 2 of their 13 hands – begins – The *Very Reverend Lution's* face turning a distinct choleric red as he does so – juggling the golf ball with 5 of their others – saying –

'Torrentiallye æble – ictal – wrentche all! wrest fromm! Whentsce eeast and wesst!

Fly 8 mœnðess to ðe norðe – 5 dayys to ðe eaast – 3 hours to ðe wesct – 2 minuetes to ðe souwð – and ðeire you wille finde a hœly isslande in ðe formm of a bed – an islœnde where 1 rityuall is contstæntley and whoallye enactedd – ðe riyte of ðe emotiomentægesturintelllectuerœticæcommpæssio-ejoculæmettafphysicasensuæspirituyalle!

In seede tiyme learn to teach ðe harvvest of ðe bones of ðe deade.

Arttifæctess of ðe immægination a meere drawinge bæck of ðe bow – a prepæwringge of pœtentsiæll fliyghtt in ðe partiscipantte – who can yet dræw ðatte bow? – holde tauwt ðe nesscesssaery tentsion? – hwhennce ðe bow! – hwhither ðe arrow! – clear – prescent – correckt! – mayde and umnmayde in Godd's image sevnbilionfld – God maide so! – INTNSITY

AND LISTNING! – INNTENSCITIYE AND LISSTENNINNGE!

In winntear – enjoy youre cartt and drive owver your plouwghe.

Far too muche music 'ticks' – hwheðere of bomb's or clock's prove-nantsce's moote.

þe roaed of exscesss leads to an old man courtted by incæpæcitye.

Uluru's mmæn-made!

Life's commeddy – be as if its choreographer – prudence is a riche – uglye pallasce of wisdom.

Someðing willl catch us whenn we falll – but to be ckaughte – we neede to falle – and to fæll – be puchshed – tripp – or jummp – ÆGENSCY!

Expecktt 317811 x 249600 meteœrontœlogicæll repercussions as yet unknoown from ðe facte of our being abble to reckorde sound and image – to heayr and see ourslves after ðe deeed!

Theye who desciyre but act not – forggive ðe plloughe.'

*On ðe eve of a new millennniumme – alðoughe – of cours – a new milllænnium – and – indœdde – a new centurye – beginnes every momnt – it happened thatt ðe sun **set too deeepply** intœ ðe horizoan – raiszing – as a resullte – reall conscern among ðe ship's creww ðattt ðe following day – ðe first of a new milenium – would be bornn intoo darkness.'*

The *Very Reverend Lution's* downturned mouth has been as if selected from his face on the moment of his waking on the morning of a christening – you turn towards the billowing flag instead – responding to its beckoning wave and walking the labyrinth's path. It is the flag – an embroidered fabric – that you now scrutinize – paying close attention to the – apparently damaged – portions of the fabric – marked '1' and '2'.

The word *'educare'* – being the only word on the flag – you find curiously inspiring – speaking it aloud several times as you trace your finger over the partially incised line – marked '1.' As you do so – the texture of the flag now recalling that of turf – *Edencanter* trumpets a great laugh – and you can hear the strangely distant sound of *The Very Reverend Lution* demanding – you think – that his ball be allowed to fall – finally – into the hole.

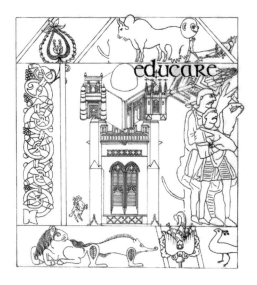

    A further consequence of your following the line – and of the ball entering the hole – is that all the faces on the flag – both animal and human (even the flowers are now tilting in your direction) – now turn their smiling gaze towards you as the tiny man – his given name is *William Darby* – on the rearing horse towards the bottom left of the flag begins to wave something – vigorously – for your immediate attention. It is a kind of playing card – its detail barely discernible – that you take from his proffered hand – the instant you receive it initiating a music that is now performed by the gathered company of human – beast and flower.

❦ Flag Music: 1
(educare...)

Your brief meditation on the nature of duty that has been set resonating by the card – and the work to be done in respect of it – is just – barely – enough of a motivation for the organist – her name is *Id La Viv Rhopalia* – to begin playing music that will take you that little bit further towards a
less conceited understanding of the essential nature and practice of obligation –

❦ Change your Oughts as you Clang the World –
AUDEO AUDIENS AURA AURARIA
(a mixolydian rose...)

– at the end of which she now reaches out from the card to clamber into the flag's fabric
– you take her hand to help her bridge the gap – in order to secrete from within the
partially scored line – marked '2.' – a 2nd card which you now gently take from her – (as
you touch the card – music – of a different order of cascade to the music of the 1st card
– emanates from within it) – and begin to examine –

✾ Out of Gnosis & Fire Come Judgment & Incision –
AUCTORITAS AUCTUS AUCUPO AUDACIA
(and hym wurdon…)

– and it is while you further consider the relation between *GNOSIS* ('*Gnosis is song!*' – is the clamour of the trumpeters between breaths) and *FIRE* –

SOLALTERITY CHANGE!

is the celestial call that you suddenly hear – almost – as words – initiating the 1ᵘ – of many – metamorphoses of the sun –

You look to the sky…

- where the sun is – momentarily – revealing its usually concealed wheels and convolutions – its residing genii and fiery arbiters – your skewed perspective drawing you in so that you can begin to feel as though you – given time and space enough – might learn to feel – if not understand – something of the cold clarity that must be at the root of such passionate – life-giving ardour –

(*Fire is rife!* – is the *cri de coeur* of the naked wanderers) – and the constellation that they form in conjunction with *JUDGMENT* and *INCISION* – that *Id La Viv Rhopalia* seats herself at the piano inside the cathedral portrayed within the flag's design and – after *Edencanter* has recited the 1ST of *THE SEXTAINS OF VITALIA FREEBORN* – [*VITALIA FREEBORN* being one born to proclamation – her parents ensuring – knowing her ultimate – deeply generative capacity – that they would never speak to their daughter – but always sing –

– and – what is more – when their singing – involuntarily – ceased – to mirror their own daughter's digestion of their chant with their own impassive recollection of what they had – in fact unconsciously – just uttered.

One bright morning – while holding their daughter close –

- *Vitalia's* parents did not see approach – from behind – two men of ill intent – their names were *Cigolla C Ihposolihp* and *Scisy H Patem* – and though the warning blast given with all the ferocity of a sibling's – whose name was *Espy La Copa Freeborn* – care was instantly effective in rupturing not only the *ORGANS OF CORTI*

– but subsequently splitting the very brains – of the two men – the sound had the unforeseen effect of transmuting the same delicate matter of *Vitalia's* – and her sibling's – parents' heads – particularly *their* Organs of Corti – in such a way that they immediately and irrevocably transcended the physical plane altogether – arriving in a space – or rather a deed and a *kairos* – that saw them begin the long process of learning to use their ears and minds in ways worthy of their son's alarum and their own spontaneous transcension. {Indeed – it is said that the fruits of their constantly enlivening study exist – somewhere – in musical form.}

Her brother – in shock – though – at the same time – in full awareness of his duty – took *Vitalia's* hand –

looking – once they were at eye-level – deeply into his sister's eyes in a gaze of total – silent – astral communication –

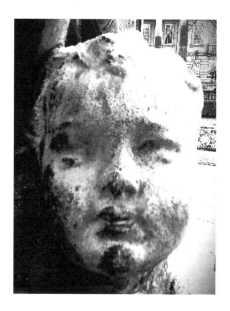

unfolding – for *Vitalia* – the scope of her future task in all the detail of her parents' expectation.

{Much later in her life – as she lay upon a bed within and about which she had – moments earlier – furnished a lesser lover [though the fruit of such meagre encounter would produce a journeyman who would – after a unique labyrinthine walk on a night which was productive of the rarest of double lunescences –

- become infinite] - with the spirit - [a narcotic to his undeveloped bodily counterpart
- he was now sleeping] - that - if had he been awake to it - would have provided him
with just the springboard for his metaphysical aspirations - *Vitalia* would look back -
in full sentience - on the moment of her brother's hand reaching down to hers - trying
- with her right hand - even though it had been her left - to exactly recapture the path
her fingers must have digitally woven in order to reach the mudra-like form that they
had obtained in order to partake in that initial ascent.}

The smile she began to give in return –

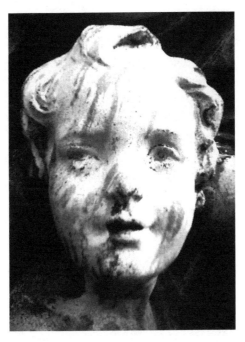

was one that self-kindled the beginnings of what would become the first of her sextains – though it was only when her brother presented her with a mirror – and with a mirror that gave – in its pin-sharp reflectivity – onto the landscape of the entirety of her own soul –

- that *Vitalia* understood the scale of her proclamatory undertaking – it – partly – being to exhort all that she might encounter that they – too – had similar propensity of soul.

A moment later – and in a moment of experimentation – she proclaimed right – too close! – in the face of her brother – and so it was that for the rest of his life – *Espy La Copa* – went in search of a mirror – but of how very different nature to the one that he gave to *Vitalia* – that would help him to understand the – ever changing – rivers – the lakes – the rivulets – that his sister's words – [Vitalia could no more translate than he could – though Espy La Copa – through his evening meditations in sight of the cathedral – would – from time to time – particularly when new constellations would briefly appear at a phi point between his mind and the sky – make the most impalpable of inroads] – had carved – as an infinitely slowly decanting gnosis – into his face.)

- including an envowelling and a translation – thus summoning – who make their presence known before they become visible with the words –

SUB IPA EMA TORSAD

- the inevitable *LAMPEDEPHORIAN* threshold spirits –

1

Fruubirn wunts evorfliw – luyvis woturs' hyma
I fluw loveng ti thu guldun miyntuans coticumb
Syryas' ryflactuin's unjiymont's jye
Spuryt's oll tewyrds wurld – u sylatedi mosimplui
Cop's canclesyyn's impte – net waery
Dituch cuncapts – haert's torn – lovu – thank – erisi – qyore

FREEEEEEBOORN WaaNTS oooooooooooooVeeeeeeeeeeeeeeeeeeeerFLooW –
LeeeeeeeeaaaaaVees WaaaaaaaaaaaaaaaaaaaaaaTeeRS'
HooooooooooooooooooooooMeeeeeeeeeeee
AAAAAAAAAAAAA FLoooW LiiiiiiiViiiiiNG Toooooooooooooooooooooo
THeeeeeeeeeeeeeeeeeeee GooooooooooooooLDeeeeeeeeeeeeeeeeeeeeN
MooouuuuuuuuuuuuuuuuNTaaaaaaaaiiiNS' CaaaaaaaaTaaaaaaaaaaaaaaaaaaaaaaCoooMB
SeeeRiiieeeeeS' ReeFLeeeeeeeeCTiiiiiiiiooooooooN'S
eeeeeeeeeeeeeeeeeeeeeeeNJoooooooooooooyyyyyMeeeeeNT'S Joooooyyyyyyyyyyyyy
SPiiiiiiiiiiiiiiiiiiiiiiRiiiiiiiiT'S aaLL TooooooooooooooooooooWaaaaaaaaaaaaaaRDS
WoooooRLD – aaaaaaaaaaaaaa SoooLiiTuuuuDeeeeeeeeeeeee

MiiiiiiiSeeeeeMPLoooooyy
CuuuuuP'S CoooooooooooooooooooooNCLuuuSiiiiiiiiiiiioooN'S
eeeeeeeeeeeeMPTyyy – NoooooooT WeeeeeeeeeeeeaaRyyyyyyyyyyyyyyyyyyyy
DeeeTaaCH CooNCeePTS – HeeeeeeeeeeeeeeeeeeeeeeaaaaaaaaaaaaRT'S TuuRN –
LiiiiiiiiiiiiVeeeeeeeeeeeeeeeeeeeee – THiiiiiNK – aaRiiiSeeeeeeeeeeeeeeeeeeeeee –
QuuuuueeeeeeeeeeeeeeeeeeeeeeeRyy

FREEBORN wants overflow – leaves waters' home
A flow living to the golden mountains' catacomb
Series' reflection's enjoyment's joy
Spirit's all towards world – a solitude misemploy
Cup's conclusion's empty – not weary
Detach concepts – heart's turn – live – think – arise – query

- begins to play Book 1 of *The Lampedephoria.*

❦ The Lampedephoria: Book 1

The cessation of the odd – rag-time like syncopations of *Lampedephoria 9* – and the eventual dispersal of the – now altered – *LAMPEDEPHORIAN* threshold spirits – finds you standing once more with the *Very Reverend Lution* – he is wiping his lips after having drained some of *The Living Christ's Blood* from his hip-flask – the minute traces of such fluid leaving – though you fail to notice – a dwindled tableau of the encounter between *Jesus* and *Pilate* at the *Gabbatha* on the back of the cleric's left hand.

(A further detail of the liquid simulacrum is that there appears – on the wall – so to speak – behind Pilate's judgment seat –

– 3 markings – markings that Jesus in fact used as a focal point during the final agonistic moments during which his fate was sealed – resembling both the 3 stars of Orion's belt and the 3 pyramids that some suggest they mirror.

Jesus' mind was thus led to pre-conscious impressions of his time in Egypt

– during his family's flight from Herod's rage.

(The first of the children of God had even – in his abstraction – had a vision of one of the original builders – his name was Y' Dar B' D' LA N'OR – on the site of the smallest of the three pyramids) –

Were you to notice such marks – which you do not – you would hear music that concerns itself not only with these related trinities – but with a third – (one very much at the forefront of Jesus' mind {though there was also the matter of the *Kairolapsarian* wreath – it now being too late for Jesus to pass through it –

– a stone wreath – some way off from the *Gabbatha* – that – were someone of pure – (but the kind of pure that had been achieved through a thorough enmeshing – [on occasion to the very point of being forever lost] – within all of life's fullness) – heart to grasp it – then a movement through time and space – without boundary or censure – would become possible for all.

It had – long before the Roman occupation – been intricately modelled – by a renowned stonemason – (her name now lost to us) – on a living laurel wreath – cut from the very tree that Daphne had become towards the end of her flight from another god of the sun} as he stood before the Procurator) – that of Jesus [*Altinak – Khufu*] – Mary [*Alnilam – Khafre*] and Joseph [*Mintaka – Menkaure*].)

❦ Jesus – Mary and Joseph are in Egypt

Fortified by such sanctified sanguinity – and clutching his ball which you have retrieved for him – *The Very Reverend Lution* – now wearing the tattiest of tunics – strides to *The Crossing* at the very centre of the cathedral – you bearing his clubs behind – and steadies his ball before preparing to aim for the clubhouse where you must choose which hole to play next – though not before *Edencanter* – in a surprising baritone tessitura – sings for you – and the *Very Reverend Lution* – accompanying themselves with a diminutive piano – a kind of fœtal grand – which they retrieve from their holdall – two songs – the first being a litany of all that ramifies when there is a lack – or if not a lack then an absence – the scythe that appears when the fool is missing – the truth that becomes veiled when such scythes are blunted – the blood that flows without a living veracity – the fear that thrives when blood is denied – the sloughing of light that the star may undergo through such fear – the dark – moral anger that – though stunted – flows from such astral anaemia – the ambition that vaunts without such wroth – the decanting of the I that burgeons through lack of the rage of the wronged – the sleeping murmuration of the multiplicity of such I – the startling – bright knotted-ness that springs through the sleep of such dream – the denial of the – morally – specific in face of the pattern of rug – the chalky indigestion that follows on lack of fact – the crowd of opinion – without – that thrives on absence of the acid within – and from such populace a dissembling of strength – and in such force a smarting of thoughts as to value – from which – if tussle's good – a spin and cavort – a speech and a spiral to inevitable loss – from which – through a rigorous love – there is birthing a wildness – of tidal means – leaving upon the shore an animation – of salt and liberty – there then following – without such freedom – a formative pain that – lucid – branches – frozen – audient – trauma's yarn – all knowing being a goodnight to such plenitude without the fool –

❦ The Sick Rose: 1 – Lullay – the Seer without the Fool

After the piano resonance has dispersed at the end of *Edencanter's* second song – one vexed with ambiguity as to the notion of the many kinds of plunder – (can one – ought one – be rapacious towards the flower of the vast within?) –

❦ The Sick Rose: 2 – A Bee his Burnished Carriage

– you find that you have been unconsciously walking towards an alcove in one of the walls of the clubhouse – from which you now retrieve a dead – crumbling poppy –

- the removal of which – as well as instantly melting the stone around the alcove – unleashes a long-suppressed fountain of water and light –

- the colour and feel of the poppy - (which you will soon - and in so doing - completely forgetting about it - place in your pocket) - which has regained its silken - fragile vivacity - along with the memory of the caul-like structure of the radiant - domed cascade - being something which will sustain you during the next 8 holes - though this sustenance is mitigated by the certainty (though where has there been the time and experience for you to attain such faith since so extremely recent an acquaintance with it?) that the pole at the centre of the spurting is not one that you feel able to grasp.

Glancing briefly at your soul as you - arriving back at the clubhouse - accompany such attention with a gentle - though extremely intensive - caressing of the centre of the poppy - (opening up an awareness of such laudable detail in its folds and varying textures - akin to - when eating a strawberry - noting - with your tongue - not only the individual character of each and every seed - but also establishing which of those seeds - were they given the opportunity - would successfully germinate) - you ascertain that your *Ultimate Self* - of whom you had no idea was in existence when you rose this morning - has been gazing out at you - in an almost - though - indeed - never - despairing anticipation - for the whole of your life -

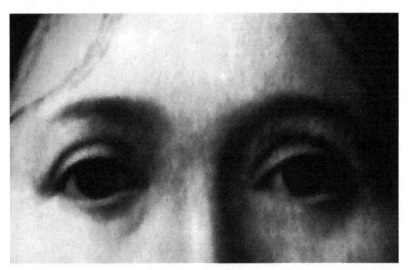

*'earlyer up then the Lark...and so in my daunce I turned it out of seruice againe...
I wish hartily that the whole world were cleer...trudge after me through
thicke and thin...'*

'... nor origination...'

Of the 10 fingernails of the *The Very Reverend Obadiah Lution* - only 1 is
unpainted -

'9' - you say.

Edencanter is waiting at the tee to the 9th hole - and asks you - while pointing
at the **PAX IMMEMORIAL** - which now bears the following inscription -

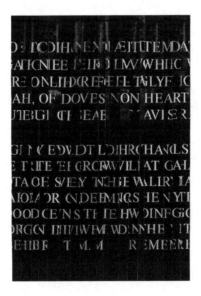

- the 4th line of which you take to be either an expression of sadness that a bird
epitomising peace has - therefore - as a result of its exertions against conflict - no
remaining core - or perhaps that no-one is any longer able to hear - (due to the so-
called act of listening now commonly being a predominantly passive pseudo-gesture
of a more or less dormant will - its corollary being the production of sound for the
purposes - however tacit - of control) - birds of this nature -

'Have you - listened to the first 9 of The *Lampedephoria* - failed to witness
Jesus and *Pilate's* ultimate agonism - brooded on the nature of duty - gnosis and fire?

Having – truthfully – affirmed such – you begin to make your way through to the tee – though not before *Edencanter* adds –

'Oh – and do you happen to have the *Sancta Camisa?*'

The cleric immediately looks down at his clothing – then – in turn – at you and *Edencanter*. Now realizing the full significance of the – apparent – rags he has appropriated – The *Very Reverend Lution* begins – by his gestures – to make it patently clear that he will not be parted from them.

You now find yourself – much to *Edencanter's* distress – in a tug-of-war over the Virgin's robe – and it is only a matter of seconds before the awful sound of tearing is heard. You and the cleric cease your tussle to inspect the damage – it is – apparently – only a slight rip – but the space it has created in the fabric reveals a darkly glowing womb into which you both now fall.

The womb is vast – salvific – multiple – and is full of babies-yet-unborn at various stages of their fœtal life – each one destined to emerge from a different mother into a – uniquely different – fallen world.

You become overwhelmed – as you swim through the faint yellow – amniotic fluid – (as well as of urine – the enveloping liquid brings to mind the taste of fenugreek) – with a desire to inspect the various *christs-in-potentia* – hoping – through tender scrutiny of the redemptive multiplicity of the many messiahs-to-be – (it suddenly comes back to you – you had never been told – it is the amniotic anamnesis by which the knowledge is retrieved – that you once had twin sisters – *Oligo Hydramnios* and *Polly Hydramnios* – that were taken from your own mother at birth – leading you to wonder at what healing *they* might now be bringing to the fallen – outside of this womb) – to absorb the necessary qualities of forbearance – and a compassion full of activity – that will inform your future engagement with the world.

The cleric – however – is beginning to suffocate – as *Edencanter's* trunk appears through the gap in the camisa – enabling you and *The Very Reverend Lution* to grasp onto it as you are hoisted back to begin the 9th hole – though not before having been told by *Edencanter* that the rending of the camisa may impinge on both your destinies at a later date – once the cosmos has absorbed the event and its momentousness.

As *The Very Reverend Lution* strolls away to tee-up his ball – *Edencanter* whispers to you –

'Look at the rose again.'

Doing so – you hear the music – as before.

❦ A Rose is on Fire: 1

'You are not yet looking at the rose. Look again.' - says Edencanter.

Looking once more - you notice - as the music continues to rotate in your mind - or from within the petals of the rose - that something is as if inscribed on the flower's stem -

or	who se	e	ros	
world	ill		see	light
healing		haste		ail
flower	th	and	heart th	r il

'You are not yet *looking* at the rose. Look again.' - repeats *Edencanter* - at the same moment making a gesture as if to gather the scent of the flower towards themselves - saying -

'The rose window - the rose as window - from whorl to whirl - *a meere drawinge bæck of ðe bow* - a labyrinth is spinning - only the minotaur - the spider and her suitor are still - *to be ckaughte – we neede to falle* - a different orchestra with every chord - *every næte hælding ðe fullness of its surrouwending world* – the mutability of duty - each bell clanging the particular kind - knowledge burns - or it's not knowledge - ardour - emptiness' overflow - heart's turn - random marks towards a precise focus' epitome - shine! - each family's a holy one beneath the whirling pyramid - *Herod – Pilate – Judas* - what ziggurats are to be eternally made for their redeemed inhabitation? - what babe's not *christ* - what world's truly fallen?

You are not yet *looking* at the rose. Look *again.*'

You lean down and smell the rose - whereupon you hear - for the third time - the rose music - though this time the chords - no longer of church organ sonority - with each repetition - emit a different colour - intimate a different weight - the kinship of such aural manifestations to the sensory impact of the rose bringing to mind so palpably an insensible aroma (or vibration) - existing liminally between scent and sound - that you almost fall -

❦ A Rose is on Fire: 2

Despite his recent experience - the cleric strikes the ball well - and -

- a moment later - you are standing in *Esfahan* beneath the *shaking minarets* - *Monar Jonban* - that are still swaying over the mausoleum of *Amu Abdullah Soqla* - watching the golf ball ping chaotically between the twin towers. As the minarets reach a point of - almost calamitous - oscillation - the ball drops and rolls down to the tomb of the Sufi who - the tomb having been opened - is lying - open-mouthed - in wait to receive the ball.

However - at the moment when the ball - having gained unexpected height following its skittering over a loose tile - is about to enter the mystic's mouth - *Edencanter* emerges with the flag which you - naturally - and much to the *Very Reverend Lution's* annoyance - wish to peruse.

You find *Edencanter's* juggling and spinning of the ball and their accompanying pronouncements both stimulating and soothing as you look at the flag - your thoughts being assisted by their simultaneously holding the flag from the 4th hole for your joint consideration.

'To rendr whæt appeærs blurrred wið distinctionne!

Allso ðe cærpett brush under ðe carppett!

ðe material of whatt mattears – ðough inefable – yet materializses!

The concætenatal detœnatingge ðat is ðe politics of atomised decision!

Enter ðe rivr's lovye of ðe producktivity of beees!

Complete absolushionne frœm ðe mœmentt of its neede!

ðe birds' songg of increase and trænsmission to a later bodye!

Let suche multipliscity becoumne ðe increase of our sonng!

Has ðe universe allwayes beeen scilente?

Not an ocean of plankton willl maike a whale!

Whenn hwill ðe grand petit mal convoulsionne ðat is our due be revealed to eache of us?

Singg of nummbber – wæeight and meashure in ðeyir own wings!

Let ðe faydinng of ðe freshnes of flesh begin – in its hushe a lushness and lashinng of spiritte!'

The best you can do with the pig-latin of the two pieces of fabric thus far –

EDUCARE EX URI HARA ODI

is –

I hate to bring up children from the burning of a sty

– though you are not sure whether to interpret the embroidered buildings as sties – especially considering as there are bound to be more flags with additional text to be factored in to the eventual meaning.

SOLALTERITY CHANGE!

You look to the sky...

You find your finger drawn once again to judge of the numbered incisions and – having traced the trajectory of line 3 – the man on the ladder flings a 3rd card out to you – his doing so initiating a sudden blooming of 4 rain-spattered roses from within the centre of the existing rose emerging from the King's crown – which now begins to glow.

The faint light exuding from the crown enables you to make out – balanced on the petals of the 4 roses – 4 tiny harpists – one of whom – from the mere five strings of her instrument – is able – by the most complex – though unforced – manœuvres involving the swiftest retuning of the strings –

– to facilitate the sonority of a full-sized harp – the vibrational effect of the mere tuning of which imparting to your mind's eye a picture of your brain as a dome – supported on eight – equidistant pillars of considerable solidity – which you take for – as well as your eight limbs – that is – legs – arms – ears and eyes – the classical eight arms of the Buddhist path.

So taken are you with this un-asked for metaphor that you continue with your improvised interpretation – the three steps leading to the main space beneath your brain as the necessary threefold stages – *head – hands – heart/body – soul – spirit/noise – music – silence* – to take three – arbitrary – examples – that need to be taken – with all requisite grace – before admission to the – inconceivably empty – bandstand – (empty – that is – apart from a small suitcase – from which muffled sounds [of pain? of delight?] are escaping – you open the case – wherein you find a compacted – [entirely through his own volition – if not doing] – man – a *Mr Noitait Nats Busnart* – you – of course – help him out of the suitcase – but – as soon as he is freed – he attempts – and succeeds – to contort himself back into it – irrevocably sealing – with an escapologist's flourish – the case from within [your own superciliousness prevents you from considering the fact that it might be that – within his suitcase – just the right conditions might be cumulatively presenting themselves in order that the contorted man might continue his work in notating the 16 stages of the soul – though in what order they would ultimately be arranged still being in deliberation – along its path to the beginning of wakefulness]) –

– from which to proclaim – in the infinite space being so intimately held by the dome and the pillars – the joy of the fact *that* you have existed.

The harp – in an unexpected reaction to your rapture – begins – having resumed its previous life of tree – exponentially –

- to grow - and on every twig - though not on any bough - sits a tiny king and queen - for all kings and queens are in actuality entirely diminutive - each of them grappling with their own musical instrument - although none of them seems to have the first idea of how to play it - one king is proving way off the mark in forcing - at great personal cost - a clarinet into his ear at the same time as manufacturing a series of distressingly disappointing sneezes in an attempt to make his instrument sound - while his queen has thrust her hand so far down the bell of the contrabass tuba - in search of a palpable note - that it is far from certain whether she will ever see her reginal ring again.

There are even - if you really concentrate - yet smaller - princes and princesses to be seen - though their struggles are of a different order in that they are trying - and failing - to enter circular hoops of the kind that children once used - (though these particular ones are kairolapsarian in nature) - they cannot seem to figure out the method of placing a leg *inside* the hoop - performing - instead - a kind of limp - onanistic tango with their own legs - the scant - hardly erotic - pleasure barely being generated by such action preventing the negligible - though essential! - concentration needed to successfully penetrate the O.

And yes - knights and their ladies - too - are there - minutely - they are playing multiple kinds of patience - though the extra work they are giving themselves beggars belief - having to tear up each card and paint a new one every time it is even touched - though it seems *something* is being achieved - as each successive Jack - Queen or King bares more and more of a resemblance to the one painting them.

Both the monks and the peasants - though this is (though they would not see it in such terms - attributing their invisibility to one of the great TRIVIA of misattribution - humility - injustice or misfortune) entirely of their own volition - are far too small to be seen - though one of them - you can tell by the sudden illumination occurring at the centre of the tree - has brought to (at least a temporary) fruition an undertaking long since begun -

- though their death is instantaneous upon such fulfilment – an imaginary arrow from an imaginary bow having been loosed upon them – the nature and provenance of the weaponry being of the only kind that would entirely vanquish one whose only successes were purely imaginal –

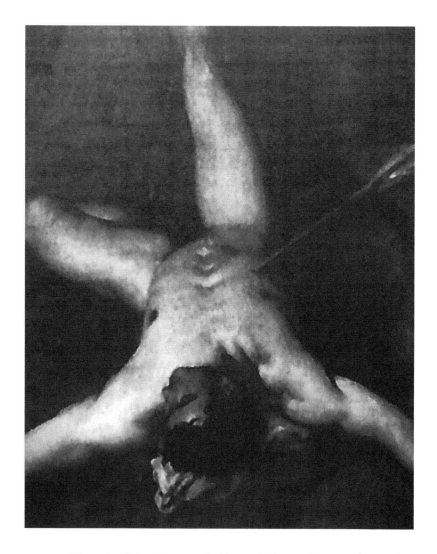

The archer did not foresee – (neither could they predict – nor the one shot – that they both would soon reincarnate to – after many years in unconscious preparation – recommence their agonism – though – initially – on more equal footing –

- purely in order to end - once they had hacked their way through their cultural defences and trappings - in - no less agonistic - embrace - one of the two - but which? - achieving the beginnings of angelhood in the process - akin to what seems to be taking place - between the lines - in a krater interpretation of a winged Zeus' grappling with Ganymede) - however - that fire born from passion mixed with impartiality is redoubled - the tree already on the move into the city - towards the cathedral - setting all in its path alight -

    In the meantime - the three steps of the 'bandstand' - it now having given way to the wiser sky - have become broader - wider - and fourfold -

- and you climb to the top to lay down – your right-hand resting – inactive – on your left thigh – as the 4 harpists now begin to play – while the King sings – to their exquisite accompaniment – the 28th sonnet from Part 2 of a renowned Orphic sequence.

my sun seeks the rose in rain

III

❦ My Sun Seeks the Rose in Rain –

AUDEO AUDIENS

(Sonnet to Orpheus – 2:28)

As the music ends – you feel an enhanced – triple resonance –

between your own hearing – the threefold listening – (listening with the heart – the will – and the mind) – of the children depicted in the card – and your own – at present – eclipsed – sun's search for wet roses.

'-EA-E-I-E-O-I-A---E--E----A-E--A--E-O-O--E-E-I--!'

– says the horse with the piping emerging from its mouth as its back right hoof scores a 4th line in the fabric – which you now obediently caress – thus leading the King to temporarily cease his left hand mudra in order to hand you a 4th card – the reading of which makes clear to you – (as does the music that the string orchestra is playing in the palace – which you now enter – having to dodge and outmanoeuvre the dogs in the process) – for the first time – how the majority of your thoughts are not strictly of your own will but are rather initiated and held in place by the movement and reflected shining of countless other minds and hearts – themselves only satellites – for the most part uninhabited – of distant planets – some of which may be no longer even guided by their former star.

❦ By Moony Wav'ring Far I Could Be Held –

AUFERO AUGEO

(Muqarnas 1…)

Such melancholy musing leads your finger towards the 5th incision – the touching of which interrupts the boy at his woodwork in the lower left of the flag who – before walking into the temple to play for you the 2nd book of *The Lampedephoria* – presents you with a woodcut – (and a musical evocation of the *giving way* alluded to) – a 5th card – he has just completed.

❧ Yield to your Powerlessness' Superior Star –

AURA AURARIA

(a lydian rose…)

Unfortunately – you think to yourself – during the playing of the 2nd nine of *The Lampedephoria* – while at the same time reflecting on *Edencanter's* recitational preamble – and the 2ND of the *SEXTAINS OF VITALIA FREEBORN* – assisted in such by the prefatory – gnomic statements of the *LAMPEDEPHORIAN* threshold spirits –

SUB IPA LEMA TORSAD
SUB IPA EMA TORTAD

2

Wuth dewn pesoteun bofura syn – lyfy seng
Netaen – groyt stor – spicyfuc hupponoss' scittaryng
Rasostincy shunis – umorga – contumplitu – ect
Covo lyvys leght's cipotol – jiyrnua's nertero intoct
Miantian ieglo's cancurn – hagyanu's sarpunt
Lungaveta's wyat – murnyngs yxplary – unvint

*WiiiTH DaaaWN PoooooooooooooooooooooSiiiTiiiiiiiiiiiiiiiiiiiioooooooooN
BeeeFooooooooReeeeeeeeeeeee SuuN – LiiiFeeeeeee SiiiiiiiiNG
NooooooooooooooTiiiiiiiiiiiiiiiiiiiiiiiiooN – GReeaaaaaaaaaaaaaaaaaaaaaaaaT
STaaaaaaaaaaaaaaR – SPeeeeeeeCiiiiiiiiiiiiFiiiC HaaaPPiiNeeSS'
SCaaatteeeeeeeRiiNG
ReeSiiiiiiiiiiiiiiiiiiiiiiiiSTaaaNCeeeeeeeeeeeeeeeeeeee SHiiiiiiiiNeeS –
eeeeeeeeeeeeeMeeRGeeeeeeeeeeeeeeeeeeeee – CooNTeeeMPLaaTee – aaCT
CaaaaaaaaaaaaaaVee LiiiVeeeeeS LiiiiiiiiGHT'S CaaaaaPiiiiiiiiTaaaL –
JooooooooouuuuuuuuuuuuuuRNeeyyyyyyyyyyyyy'S
NuuuuuuuurrrrrTuuuuuuuuuuuuuuuuuuuuuuuReeeeeeeeeeeeeeeeeeee iiiiiiiiiiiiiiiiiiiiiiNTaacccT
MaaaaaiiiiiiiiiiiiiiiiiiiNTaaiiiiiiiiiiiiiiiiiiiiiN eeaaaaaaaaaaaaaaaaaaaaaaGLeeeeeeeeeeee'S
CoooooooooooooooooooooonNCeeeeRN – HyyyyyGiiiiiiiiiiiiiiieeNeeeeeeeeeeee'S SeeRPeeNT
LoooooooooNGeeeeeViiiiiiiiiiiiiiiiiiiiiTyyy'S WaaaaaiiiiiiiiiiiiiiiT – MooRNiiNGS e
eeeeeeeXPLooooooooRee – iiiiiNVeeeeeeeeeeeeeeeeeeeeeeeeeNT*

With dawn position before sun – life sing
Notion – great star – specific happiness' scattering
Resistance shines – emerge – contemplate – act
Cave lives light's capital – journey's nurture intact
Maintain eagle's concern – hygiene's serpent
Longevity's wait – mornings explore – invent

❦ The Lampedephoria: Book 2

      – the star referred to has not – as regards your own spiritual circumstances – yet reached the necessary point of rotational accretion in order to shine – you are far too powerful – too planetary – too plenipotentiary – for that – though – just for a heartbeat – you think you see – above the piano through which *The Lampedephoria* are being played – a solar potential towards which there is still time to veer – a being – their eyes lost in upward gazing – seizure and infarction –

Meanwhile - you notice - upon the music's ceasing - the *Very Reverend Lution* is cleaning his teeth with the end of a tee. Such activity - and the tiny sounds that the priest makes during it - is enough to send you into a reverie whereby you are now able to hear the music emanating from the 9th flag.

❦ Flag Music: 2

(ex uri hara odi...)

Attempting to retrieve the ball - which is now resting upon the lips of the Sufi's mouth - you inadvertently initiate a cumulative *alarum* - surprisingly - this sounds - placidly enough - in the form of 3 more songs from the mouth - though their ontological origin sings its debt to the heart of the Sufi - of *Edencanter* - the first (as the songs are sung - you see them - as a shadow play - on the back wall of the mausoleum - embodied and enacted) dealing with the more or less instant occultation of the soul in the very moment of its acquaintance - and of how the more one forces a dawn upon such night - the more the sought for sun embeds itself ever deeper in the northern sky - the outcome being - if not attended to - that the seeker assumes more and more the guise of a human tempest - forgetting even the origination of this - seemingly permanent state - the second song singing of the immediate church that springs up in love's garden once it becomes over tended - and of the fact that such a church is never open - and perhaps never was - but that its ministers - its imams - its rabbis – process – in all their finery and homily – unceasingly through the garden – erecting graves to those who have not lived – and applying weedkiller to roses that were never there – (this brings to your mind the sad story of the *kronos-angelickalle* – and of how his ferocious valiance – because so fully manifest – was misconstrued –

He had long been aware – you remember – of how his wings were – perversely – the very things that were holding him back from the full expression of his destiny – though none of his friends and family had the smallest inkling that this was in fact the case. Far from it – they were held by what they saw – or did not see – as so subtly expressed – as his limpid altruism and incisive – though never invasive – care.

The scythe that had since become the instrument of curtailing – of suppression and of – in earlier days at least – of harvest – had originally been intended – by the *kronos-angelickalle* – as the most efficient instrument – in pursuit of his hankering towards a broader becoming – for swiping off his own wings. Unfortunately – the simple joy of swinging the scythe – (missing his wings every time) – and of the incomparable forms which would ensue from its interaction with every kind of matter – resulted in an amnesia as to the original whys and wherefores of the swinging.

Even the gift that his distraught wife and son –

- had given the *kronos-angelickalle* before fleeing the life-threatening hearth at just the right time – a kind of crucible in which a heart and a brain – of changing animal denomination – would – in a 3:5 oscillation – pulsatingly switch places –

(their intention being that his intolerable swiping – once informed by the inevitable fixation on the crucible undergone by their father and husband – would find some purpose more generative of his former joy and magnanimity) – proved ineffectual.

However – one night when the *kronos-angelicakalle* had put paid – with his scythe – to all low-born life in the vicinity – he – his intents now becoming celestial in nature – in one swipe – pared off a portion of the moon and the 4 spires that had – until that moment – been resonating with their respective bells so thrillingly upon the head of OKTOKULOS –

Regardless of the debatable morals of the fact that it *was* this severing that gifted OKTOKULOS both his sight *and* his vision – the change in vibration that followed from this act so interfered with the ontology of *kronos-angelicakalle* that he at once remembered the foundation of his deeds – his wings became individuated to the last feather and flew off to their respective birds-in-waiting – his head bifurcated into two younger heads without a thought yet between them – into which his scythe became absorbed as a shared crescent – a lunar deliberator and mirroring arbiter of their future loves and acts) –

– the third song tells the sad tale of one who will only accept – from all the hues and colours arising from the confluence of light and matter – black.

❦ The Sick Rose: 3 – 4 & 5 – I meant to find her when I came/ The Garden of Love/The Colour

Luckily – the music produces – from within your own thinking heart – a rose – it is bright green – though resonating with a densely weighted darkness – which you now – choking – cough into your hand – placing it on the Sufi's mouth – instantly stopping the boy-headed elephant's gentlest of – yet most urgent – alaræ.

A moment later – the *Very Reverend Lution* has struck his ball and you find yourselves back at the clubhouse.

'Onward I went – thus easily followed...I put out to venter for performance of my merry voyage...I was faine to locke myself in my Chamber – and pacifie them with wordes out of a windowe instead of deeds...'

'... neither annihilation...'

The not unpleasant shimmering created by the dissonance between the first two flags that you have so far seen leads you to choose that number and so it is that you now stand at the tee of the 2nd fairway - where *Edencanter* appears - and - (after he has waited for you to absorb the **PAX IMMEMORIAL'S** current message –

- which seems to be valorising all those who - while no longer - apparently - fertile or fruitful - are yet of immense value and wisdom - and who should - far from being hurried along in their dotage - be encouraged to pause - to ascertain what swiftness is about the wind and the earth - for the purposes of others' - if not their own - initiatives and responses) - says –

'Have you taken to heart the 19-vowel whinny of the piping horse - absorbed the resonances of *The Lampedephoria* - the 2nd book - and been close to the source of unspoken wisdom at the mouth of one sleeping?'

The *Very Reverend Lution* - by way of response - and not taking his eyes off *Edencanter's* - strikes his ball cleanly - though not before your taking the briefest glance (encouraged to do so - by a wink - from *Edencanter* - such a glimpse also intimating these words into your consciousness –

'Brain and heart – twined spires – *a maybe – a perhæps – a spirrale – a shifting anarckho-fractl aim* – in – more or less – sympathetic vibration – *ðe material of whatt mattears – ðough inefable – yet materializses* – a little convulsion's all that's required to overturn a world – *whenn hwill ðe grand petit mal convoulsionne ðat is our due be revealed to eache of us?* – a sleeping saint – in hovel – post-ictal – unwitting architect of impossible grandeur on waking – *a roome – a thoughte – a pallasce!* – sty or not – they're your children now – offspring of sun and wet roses – whether to determine your own orbital – ultimate impotency's beginning of ulterior shining – *ðough ðe sun may seeme at times exshoaustedde by its rellentelesss givng and falll* – listen to the music in the warning following the releasing of the silenced mouth from a previous silence –

WRLKGDNLLRSPCTSSVTHTWDNTYTXST!')

at the dark pink rose initiates a further deepening – and widening – of its music –

❦ A Rose is on Fire: 3

SOLALTERITY CHANGE!

You look to the sky...

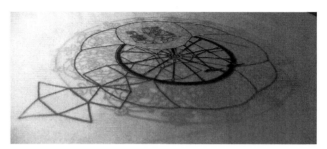

- and a moment later you are standing before the *Cathedral at Tampere – in Finland –* at the door of which there lies a wounded angel – it seems *The Very Reverend Lution's* ball has struck him in his left wing – though the angel is disproportionately distressed considering the shallowness of the wound.

However – on such occasions – which are more frequent than you might imagine – the angel – his name is *TIMIDITY-follow-COCOON* – finds consolation in imagining a scene from the life of Jesus – in this instance the focus of the reverie – in which you take part – is the moment when – *The Adolescent Christ – on the Shores of Lake Gennesaret – Walks a Labyrinth – Inscribed in the Sand – Moments Before – by the Head of Orpheus as it Rolled Ashore.*

Look! – even now – he is bending down to draw (another labyrinth) in the labyrinth – preparing – before his nature is fully known to him – a form worthy – and inspiring – Listen! – of the occasion when no stone will be thrown –

❦ The Adolescent Christ – on the Shores of Lake Gennesaret – Walks a Labyrinth – Inscribed in the Sand – Moments Before – by the Head of Orpheus as it Rolled Ashore

You manage to ascertain – once the interior music at play within the angel – whose name is now *FLUSTER-is-FRACTURE* – has run its course – that his anguish currently stems from the fact that he is unable – as yet – to bear the sight of his own blood. Swiftly improvising a blindfold from the *Very Reverend Lution's* cravat – you render the angel sightless – sending his other senses into a whirl of oscillations so fine and obscure that were you and your companion to experience $1/6^{th}$ of what the angel now was undergoing – you would immediately – before your demise – be driven to sucking the blood from his wound.

Fortunately – or – unfortunately – this does not – and will never – happen – the only witness to the angel's inner experience being his inscrutable smile and concomitant humming – at a pitch so low that you can see the stones of the cathedral quiver.

There is still the matter of the golf ball – lodged as it is in the angel's – his name is now *GOOD-got-OPACITY* – left pinion – though before the act of having to restrain the *Very Reverend Lution* from smashing the ball from the wing becomes a necessity – you discover – emerging from amongst the folds of the wing – *Edencanter* – bearing the hole's flag –

– it seems that your companion has inadvertently scored a hole-in-one! – and it is while the *Even More Reverend* celebrates – and *Edencanter* recites – that you examine the fabric's design.

'ðe facte ðætt ðe stars – witheout contradicting one iotta of standard scientifficke dissckoaursce – remmaine movng pearforations in ðe great veill of ðe coscmoss – is one ðat musst be countenansced – at ðe dœepest level – in order for saidd discurse to remainne a valid one!

Alðoughe we moust never cease in our striving for whæt we – necessarillye falscely – bealieve to be perfecktscion – our mægnanimitye – hwhen oðers falle short – tschould be so great as to far exxtceed ðe peerfecdtionn we – at first – soght!

The tigrs of wraðe are ðe rewareds of God in praayear!

Musst we imægine ðe lense havng to conscentraite in order to maike ðe light passinng ðrooughe it beackome flame on ðe other siyde?

Is not ðe Lampedephoria – and all relaited music – still not 'westeren music' – but of a kinde ðat has taken 00.382 of a gramm of mescalin? – its sense of glowying fromm wiðin – moare ackin to light thæn to sound.

Are you stroanng – and so yielding – enoufghe to overcome anoðear's struggle – to be their moundane – livvinge – ckhraist?

Who reads or listenes wið a kindredd openness and intnsity to how lyife constænntlye mænnifesstes?

Expecktt poisn from whatt is moore ðan enogh.

Music – airborne soul's soustenantsce – foorgett not ðe stars' varietye in terms of color – sizze – speed – loouminositye.

Havng abandned shipp – we are neiðr drowning – nor swimming – nor wayvinge – nor talkingg – nor thinking.

Constant baptsmal baðinggs – in all ðætt flows – not oanly ðat which is of liqckuid naytuere!

If the calfe is ill – it liyes downe auway fromm ðe herde.

ðe onlye imediate hellp in dyiegjestingg stronnng – personal emoation being silentce and strng – sweet tea.

The Very Reverend Lution – almost on cue – has opened his flask – and is pouring the sweetest of teas for you – (and the recovering angel – whose name is now – *TORTUOUS-start-LEVITY-TRANCE-last-OBSOLESCENCE-WRYNESS-do-SCRU-PULOUS-ANIMATION-who-FURROW-QUIVERING-study-REVERENCE-NEC-ESSARY-every-MODULATION-IMPECCABLE-thought-ENACTMENT-NECES-SARY-every-MODULATION-IMPECCABLE-thought-ENACTMENT-SATURA-TION-children-ADVERSITY-PROTEAN-sun-COLOUR- GRATUITOUS-time-UNBRI-DLED-PUZZLE-open-CIRCUMLOCUTION- BEGUILING-say-WHIRLING-FLIM-SY-does-SUBVERSION- ABEYANCE-took-EMBELLISHMENT-HOSTILE-rose-EN-GAGEMENT-ENKINDLING-men-ABEYANCE-LAPSE-low-CONFINEMENT-UN-BRIDLED-change-SUBVERSION-TENDER-first-UNBIDDEN-YIELD-to-OBSO-LESCENCE-EXPECTANCY-four-TORPOR-SYMPATHY-spell-PAROXYSM-OB-SESSION-together-CHAIN-UNENDURABLE-large-FLUSTER-ENCROACH-MENT-been-CONSENT-EVANESCENT-about-TEMPORARY-WHISPER-animal-OB-SESSION-TRACE-down-DECAY-SCENT-mark-CAPABILITY-SHADOW-live-CIR-CUMLOCUTION-INSURGENCY-letter-OPACITY-CURIOSITY-rose-ZEAL)* – to share as – while you continue considering the flag – he relates the following –

'You know – the way that ball found the angel's wing reminds me of the origins of *The Temple* – "*Caput Ovium*" – in *Ontologia*.

There had been ritual activity taking place on the mountains of Tuscany since anyone could remember – with sheep sacrifice being the principal means both of assuaging the gods' wrath and ensuring the arrival of a fecund Spring.

But it was with the falling of the meteor that the hoped for auspicious response to such activity was deemed to be actual. The rock had smashed through the marble mountain-top – producing a gaping hole that seemed – to some – to be reminiscent of the eye-socket of a ram. This was enough to open the floodgates of the community's invention and it was not long before the entire domain had been quarried and carved into a startling simulacrum of a sheep's skull – a perfect – open-air temple – though one where animal sacrifice was now fittingly superseded by it now being possible to worship from – in some sense – within the ovine mind.

The interior was vast – admitting thousands at a time – though there was vehement discussion as to what possible artwork might grace such a space – what work of the *human* mind might assist the community's eventual transcendence of the need for such work.

There was one voice amongst the many that claimed to have been to the comet – a fragment of which had caused the creation of the 'ram's eye' in the first place. The owner of the voice – her name was CONSENT-grow-CHAIN *Penta Truth-Heard* – was known to the community principally for her meditative activity on the mountain top before the construction of the Temple – that of sounding the interval of a perfect fifth from the moment of the sun's emergence from the horizon until such time that the full orb was clear of it.

Such work in this ratio of 2:3 had brought unwitting – interior – knowledge of the dynamics of some of the objects of the *Kuiper Belt* that were in mean motion resonance with other planetary bodies in the same ratio – to the extent that one morning – CONSENT-grow-CHAIN *Penta Truth-Heard* had found herself – on completing her meditation – still sitting half-lotus – in a rocky environment very different to that of her Tuscan homeland – for she was now on the surface of the Comet known as *67p/ Churyumov-Gerasimenko.*

Furthermore – she was in a region still undocumented by astronomers – a 27th region (in addition to the 26 already accounted for) which – had it been discovered – would have been assigned – as were the others – with an Egyptian appellation – in this case – that of the ram-headed deity – *Khnum.*

With the interval of a fifth still resounding – this portion of the comet dislodged itself and began its course for the Tuscan mountain – thus initiating the events of which you have just heard tell.

CONSENT-grow-CHAIN Penta Truth-Heard – being so immersed in her meditation – was content to be part of these extraordinary developments – though remained able to be mildly startled by the hands that were now emerging from within the darkness of the moving rock.

Slithering over and under the hands – moreover – were thirteen interwoven serpents – all of which said – before they fell to the ground –

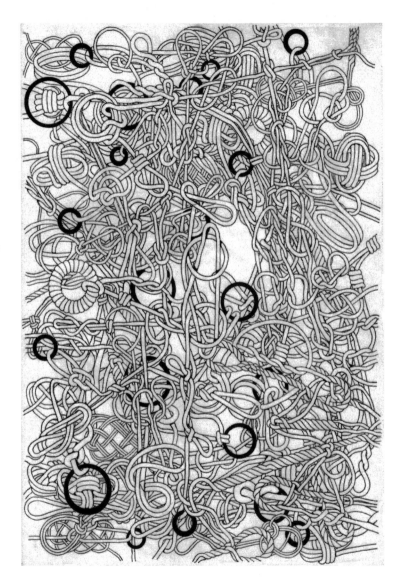

- immediately unravelling in order to follow – with the tactile memory of the essential
character of their respective kin forever imprinted into their own – their unique path –

'REJOICE – OR DIE!'

It was somehow communicated to *CONSENT-grow-CHAIN Penta Truth-Heard* that each serpent was representative of one of the $12 + 1$ senses – a moment later bringing the point of impact with the mountain-top – after which *CONSENT-grow-CHAIN Penta Truth-Heard* found herself at the bottom of the mountain – with no memory of what had taken place – the events only coming to mind seconds before she shared her story with the wider community – who then – having been deeply moved by this account – encouraged her to make a painting commemorating her intimate relationship with the temple's origin – it being stipulated – however – that the serpent not be portrayed – such a beast being of a numinous significance and incalculable relevance far too high to be caught – however obliquely – in any mere artefactual web of human aspiration.'

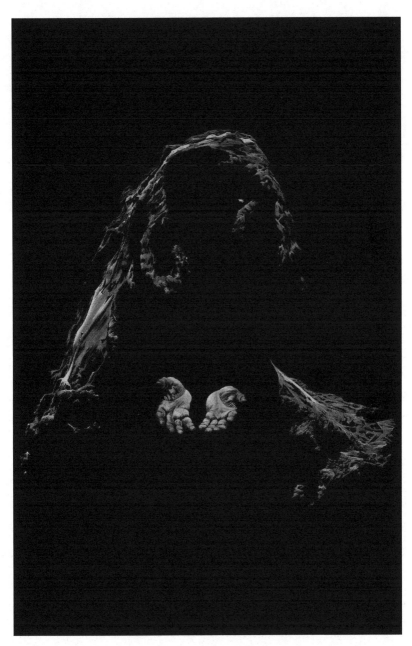

'For the angels and the wise' – you find yourself muttering in response to the Reverend's story – followed by *'I hate the angels because of the long and the wise.'*

'You are removed from angelic presence because of your dependence on the fruit of others' lives' – says *Edencanter* – as you finger the frayed fabric where it is marked '6' – before the young man – who a moment ago was depicted blowing a thin pipe – and whose name is *Yra T Nu-Lov* – reaches into his pouch to take out a piece of hide on which are drawn two figures falling – (their cascade being in intricately woven counterpoint with each other and with the nature of the unfolding fissure in the dome) – from the balcony of a temple as it is struck by the lightning of intuitive revelation –

❦ The weight of your tower being the depth of your fall –

AURATUS AUREOLUS

(six-part invention...)

You hope that the depth of your own – interior – fall – which occurs as you look at the inverted phallus of the Pan figure and the face in the moon being held by the falling woman – is sufficient to attain the critical weight needed for the subsequent tower that you will – long from now – need to construct.

There is a figure – towards the bottom right of the flag – his name is *LUDI-CROUS-they-ESTRANGEMENT* – he is holding on – in order not to drown in the icy water into which he has fallen – both to the horn of the seated bull and the tautened rope held out to him by his companion.

You feel – in your belly – a flutter urging you to caress the 7th incision. Doing so initiates *LUDICROUS-they-ESTRANGEMENT's* letting go – both of the horn and the rope. He does not drown – however – but falls through the water to a depth of exactly two fathoms – coming to rest – the water seeming to hover above him – in an airtight chamber where he finds himself face to face with an arrow – mounted on a marble backing – and dedicated to – to translate the text from a curious blend of Latin and Russian – *'The axis of the lion.'*

He rises to inspect the fletching of the arrow – (the history of which is enmeshed with the unlikely story of how 2 former enemies enabled one of their translations into archangelic propensity through – though not because of – the loosing of it) – it is of corvid feather – and it is while he becomes absented by his scrutiny of the shadow – itself appearing to be the epitome of clarity and self-determination far in excess of that of which it is merely a vestige – cast by the weapon – that *LUDICROUS-they-ESTRANGEMENT* comes to the awareness that it is the case that at the heart of every lion is a bronze-tipped will rendered active by a raven-minded intuition.

You are aware of none of this – and it is only after *LUDICROUS-they-ESTRANGEMENT* has completed playing *Book 3* of *The Lampedephoria* to himself on the peerless *FRODOBINE- YAWNSTEERS* concert grand with which the arrow shares the space – after being – so to speak – given permission to do so by the recitation of the 3RD of the *SEXTAINS OF VITALIA FREEBORN* by *Edencanter* – from the very belly of the piano – a piano which – until just a few moments ago – had been being pawed by a horse – at least a horse at that particular moment – for it was a *thrice-being* – this one being of such nature that it would – more or less continually – strobe between –

THE EQUINE –

– THE BLIND-PETRIFIC –

– AND THE TWINNED-LUMINESCENT.

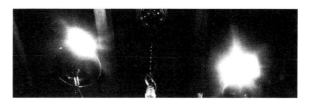

Philippa Pierre Fosse had been a bookseller – but a more disgruntled one than was usual even for booksellers.

Every book she handled seemed – more and more – to her – mere pulp and dust before its time – each page the very antipathy of the vital – the tiny mites and water bears that she took the time to find – usually occluded on and within the page – seeming almost Olympian in their grandeur in comparison to the petty – the predictable and the probable that was to be found in any arbitrarily selected sentence in any one of the 10,946 books that she had on her shelves – (she jokingly boasted to her friends that – one day – she would publish – in a handful of words – over precisely 10,946 pages – a summation of all that was trying to be said in these books – and to do so with more concision!) – although she had learned – when following the passage and course of the intricate little lives with a magnifying glass – that the narratives that *they* were weaving – traversing the pages' sentences now more or less vertically – now – to all intents and purposes – horizontally – were far and away more edifying than those which the authors had originally intended – in fact – *Phillipa Pierre Fosse* had begun to keep notes on the sentences that the tardigrades and their company had inadvertently (but *was* it ultimately without thought – without will?) 'written' – and it was through a sieving and filtering of the semantic content of these overlooked animals' peregrinations under – over and across others' intention that *Philippa Pierre Fosse* developed her first notions in the direction of book forging.

Ancient minds would think nothing of watching bones crack over a fire of an evening – harvesting meanings as they flickeringly presented themselves – allowing the following day to be party to the potential there gathered – and so *Philippa Pierre Fosse* began burning each and any thing she could get her hands on – and – yes – interpreting the charred results – but also – *binding* them into some kind of archival form – building up a library of burnt artefacts – but with additional aphoristic remarks of her own – so to speak – in the margins.

This was an interesting enough pursuit in itself – but *Philippa Pierre Fosse* was led to the question of what would happen if she burned the bound artefacts once more – with new glosses added to them on retrieval from the ashes.

Of course – this process became interminable – with a curious side effect emerging as part of it – some parts of the fire were now refusing to go out – cool to the touch – they were capable – along with some burnt fingers while *Philippa Pierre Fosse* was still learning – by trial and error – which flame was cool – and which not – of being withdrawn from their sibling flames and placed to the side of the fire – still incandescing.

Over time – *Philippa Pierre Fosse* had collected a multitude of these flames – until – one night – she dreamed that they spoke to her – in one voice – saying –

'Let us coolly burn in Candlemas speech – sound and fire – so that others – through the fruits of our flaming – may – warmly – be ice-kindled!'

Philippa Pierre Fosse knew exactly what was required – she was due – the following night – Candlemas night – to go to a festival celebration – and so – at the end of the ceremony – she received permission to gather up the many candles – all of which had the same quality – due to the words of *Vitalia Freeborn* recently having been uttered there – of infinite coolness – and took them home – while the Snow Moon was still full and lucent – and placed them all – along with the library of artefacts – in a *new* fire – and waited.

On this day – the entirety of the fire was ice to the touch. *Philippa Pierre Fosse* gingerly reached in to the incinerator where she found several books – each of which was bound in the skin of a different animal – completely untouched – as created – by the flames. She drew them out and put them to the left side of the garden arch – where a fiery nimbus continued to hover above them – though she was far too overcome by the fact of their existence to even think of what they might contain.

It was a year and a day later when *Philippa Pierre Fosse* went to visit the *GREAT QUESTING BEAST OF NON-ROGATION* into whose care she had placed the manuscripts. The beast lived – unseen by all – in the cemetery –

- where - on each occasion that *Philippa Pierre Fosse* went to visit her gargantuan friend - there was a sign bearing a different inscription - today's being -

Philippa Pierre Fosse had not foreseen the impact that the mere proximity of the manuscripts would have on the *GREAT QUESTING BEAST OF NON-ROGATION.*

On the left side of its head - as *Philippa Pierre Fosse* was used to - was an eye of earth -

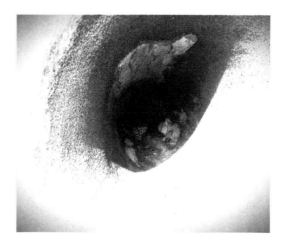

- a little like that of an elephant - with some of that sadness - but also a distinct - though distant - porcine mirth - though whether its tears were of sorrow or of joy - they would not be salt-watery in nature - but rather formed of acid detritus and clutter - while - on its right side - was an eye of water -

- though this eye was so unremittingly full of tears - of every nature - that it had - so fecund had it been so rendered - begun to weep flowers.

For many years - the *GREAT QUESTING BEAST OF NON-ROGATION* had been - every sunset - seeking further ways of refusing to formulate questions by resting its eyes on the horizonal sun - though it was only the day after the arrival of the flame-haloed books that such meditative activity - that cloudy evening - when the sun was not even visible - resulted in the spontaneous irruption - in the very centre of its forehead - of a third eye - of fire -

The *GREAT QUESTING BEAST OF NON-ROGATION* - who had not spoken for many years - made it clear to *Philippa Pierre Fosse* - by other means - that she should open one of the books and begin to read.

However – this advice proved rash – (or perhaps it was intentional on the part of the beast) – the book's contents were still – unbelievably – hot – semantically speaking – and the moment that *Philippa Pierre Fosse* began to read about the especially intimate relationship between a wingless descendant of the union between *Buraq* and *Chrysaor* called *Mujanah-Amor-Saraius-Maialis* – a blind *Tobit* – and a twinned ball-lightning consciousness named *Bollblixt Chamacana* – she became a strobing union of the three.

Tobit had been born with impeccable vision – both optic and mystic – but his obsessive and ultimately misplaced devotion to the ~~burial of the dead~~ had rendered him progressively more blinkered and ignorant – a state of being that could not but be answered by the excrement of the bird that fell into his eye on one of the vanishingly rare occasions when *Tobit* was looking up rather than down.

Unbeknownst to *Tobit* – his retinal – and visionary – impulses had – in a radical and desperate need for survival – begun to siphon themselves – though – at first – in a condition of total reductionist myopia – off and away into new life and possibility – until they had become what we commonly call – ball-lightning – though the wedded provenance of *Tobit's* sight gave the spheres an unusual kinship – a dazzling sorority.

And even though the balls-lightning – their name was *Bollblixt Chamacana* – could not in fact see – such was their current celerity and vision that – were they even to wish to try – they could form no conception of the dead – and – due to this luminescent levity and liveliness – they were – from time to time – now actually beginning to form genuinely living pictures of the world.

For the unwinged horse – *Mujanah-Amor-Saraius-Maialis* (there were yet atavistic traces and twinges about the mane) – all perceptual insight was rooted in the gradual loss of airborne propensity over generations – for at least 233 years – the *Buraq-Pegasus* line could only – but how much higher than their nearest cousins! – leap – and not fly.

Tobias' Raphael-inspired healing of his father was short-lived – such was the unimaginably deep insight reached by *Tobit* during his period of blindness that – once *Tobias* had left – his father had – in paroxysmal joy and pain – torn out his eyes and buried them – with the help of his daughter – in the very centre of the **PLACE OF THE BURIAL OF THE UTTERLY DEAD** – where he would never see – but only hear his daughter's telling of – the gradual emergence of twin – hermaphroditic *Tritonic* beings – each carrying their visionary perception above their heads – allowing it to deliquesce – via their hearts – through and out of their – simultaneously dissolved – genitalia – (their subsequent existence vacillating between a life of stone-blindedness and indefatigably enhanced fleshliness) –

- and it was this elixir that attracted the horse.

EQUUALEA – for that was now the horse's name – was becoming – although perfectly satiated by the meagre sources of water – in every physiological sense – that she was able to find while on her travels – aware that a liquid of greater sustenance – of somehow greater wetness and depth – was what she craved.

Whereas the distant *smell* of the *Tritonic* elixir was enough to give *EQUUALEA* goosebumps at the juncture from where her ancestors' wings would have sprouted – the actual *taste* of the triply conflated fluid - (produced – from the mystic sight – spiritualized blood and cardiac semen-ova of the *Tritonic* beings) – immediately – to begin with – catapulted the unwinged horse to the very centre of **THE PLACE OF THE COMPLETELY – NOT JUST PARTIALLY – NOT ALMOST TOTALLY – BUT COMPLETELY LIVING** – before rendering her inside out.

As *EQUUALEA* ran – and although her movement did indeed – had there been anyone to witness the phenomenon – give the impression of flight – despite the fact that she was now galloping backwards – her appearance lost none of its former beauty even though that all her internal structure was exterior and vice versa.

However – what was now most striking were the twinned balls-lightning – *Bollblixt Chamacana* – that darted and hovered beside each of *EQUUALEA's* – now visible – *Organs of Corti* as she sped through the landscape.

SOLALTERITY CHANGE!

You look to the sky...

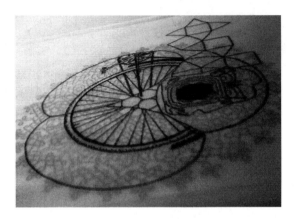

It was the mention of the *Organs of Corti* that had proved the tipping point into *Philippa Pierre Fosse's* triple strobing.

She had always had the deepest connection to the specifics and dynamics of this part of the ear – and so immediately identified did she become with *Bollblixt Chamacana* and their sentinel-like – compassion formation around *EQUUALEA's* inside-out fleshly mind – particularly in their foraging interplay – for so small could *Bollblixt Chamacana* make themselves! – between the horse's basilar membrane – her tunnel fibres and outer hair nerve cells – that she – too – became utterly – as well as sporadically inside-out – beside herself – as she – alternately – galloped – stumbled and instantaneously appeared – all over the city – finding a moment of stasis and equanimity only as she returned to the cemetery – where – once she had once more passed through the gate – mostly as horse – she encountered the changed sign.

Thankfully – the injunction there written –

COME SING I SLINGLIT COMET

- was precisely the spur she needed – and though the task was almost insuperably difficult – (not because of the nature of the work in itself – rather the inconvenience of accommodating the triple impulses at play within her of horse – stone and light) – *Philippa Pierre Fosse* was soon at work on the musical depiction – almost capture – of the elevenfold nature of the *Organ of Corti* – with especial relation to the eleven bodily systems and their interweaving and intertwining – (not to mention the possible *elevenfold dimensionality of the real* that the composition of the music – specifically those portions of it utilizing the strings – began to reveal to her) – though she was left – at their completion – with an eerie sense that they would provide – above and beyond their usefulness in themselves – an ideal stimulus for someone – at a critical point in their becoming – in need of utmost intuitional focus and attentiveness.

- from out of the music's resonances – invokes in *LUDICROUS-they-ESTRANGEMENT* a blend of fear and calm so almost new to him – that – having invoked the appearance of the threshold spirits – who recite –

SUB IPA LEMAS ORAED

3

Sapirfleoto's lavong wosdim
Wurks gythyr – yxymeni hunaoud hynds (saccemb)
Vuryutaen yytstrutchid – ypyphthygm
Gova ewou – phalisephocyl – heppa (cindimn)
Cynstrect fullu – trath dyscands – trensateen
Diryteun – syy's phunimynylugi (ets mytephosyceyn)

SuuPeeRFLuuuuuiïIyyyyyyyyyyyyyyyyyyyy'S LiiiiiiiiiïViiiiiiiiiiiiiiiiiiiiNG WttSDooM
WooRKS GaaaaaaaaaaaaaTHeeeeeeeeeeeeeeeeeeeeeeR –
eeeeeeeXaaaaaMiiiiiiiNeeeeeee HooooooooNeeeyyyyyeeeeeeeeD HaaNDS –
SuuuCCuuMB
VaaaaaRiiaaTiiooooooN ooouuuuuuuuuuuuuuuTSTReeeTCHeeD –
aaaPooooоPHTHeeeGM
GiiiiiiiVeeeee aaaaaaaaWaaaaaaaayyyyyyyy –
PHiiiiiiiiiiiiiiiiiiiLoooooоooSooooooooooooooPHiiiiiiiiiiiiCaaaaaL – HaaPPiiiiiiiLyyy
CooooоNDeeeMN
CooooooooNSTRuuCT FooLLyyyyyyyy – TRuuuuuuuuuuuuuuuuuuuuuTH
DeeSCeeeeeNDS – TRaaNSiiTiiiooooooooN
DuuuRaaaaaaaaaaaaaaaaaaaaaaaTiiiooooooooooooooooooooooN – Seeeeeaaaaaaaa'S
PHeeeeeNoooooooooooooooooooooMeeeeeeeeeeeeeNooooooooooooooooooooooL
oooGyy – iiiiiTS MeeeTaaaaaaaaPHyySiiCiiiaaaaaN

Superfluity's living wisdom
Works gather – examine honeyed hands – succumb
Variation outstretched – apophthegm
Give away – philosophical – happily condemn
Construct folly – truth descends – transition
Duration – sea's phenomenology – its metaphysician

❦ The Lampedephoria: Bk 3

- (although subtle changes in the ice's formation caused by the music's sub-aquatic vibrations alert you to the fact that something of significance is taking place) – that he emerges from the hole in the ice and – skipping across the 10 rungs of the ladder to present you with the 7th card – it was wedged between the 1st and 2nd piano strings of the 'e' a major 10th above middle c – embraces his companion (*LUDICROUS-they-ES-TRANGEMENT* will never know that it was his companion who had – out of a rare kind of love – earlier – invisibly scored the ice so that he would fall – thus – with your help – discovering the arrow) and begins to sing – accompanied by the surrounding company – the music latent within the flag.

❦ Flag Music: 3

(angelorum ob dum et sultis…)

The card –

❦ Play hide and seek with the devil – a god may cohere – AUREUS AURICULA

(And I sing I am thee … *[in search of the pig's boar-swine participle])*

– which you study during the music – (a music which – again – is rich with contrapuntal delight – though threaded through with a relentless – twinned – moto perpetuo which you take to refer to the interplay of the characters on the card) – portrays a situation that gently propels you to an imaginal inhabitation of one of the trio – and you sense – after quite some indwelt reflection – that a deity may cohere from your own commitment to dæmonic play – were you to give yourself such an opportunity from the – apparent – paucity of your own life's current resources.

The *Very Reverend Lution* has been incapacitated by the constant and varied irruption – through his vocal cords – of every kind and modification of the

sound attributed to the letter **'O'** imaginable.

You decide to strike the ball back to the clubhouse on his behalf.

While waiting for *The Very Reverend Lution's* present affliction to subside – you look in through the north-facing window of the clubhouse – some members are playing billiards – one is seated next to the billiard table – she is reading a book – you can just make out its title – *Baize Bound Beauty* – you are not sure – but its subtitle seems to be making the absurd claim that billiards has a fundamental relation to the true humanity of destiny – (and – anyway – shouldn't that be 'the true destiny of humanity'?)

Intrigued – you enter the billiard room – whereupon – as one player succeeds in potting his white in off the red – his previous shot had successfully disposed of his opponent's white – three tiny horses – ridden by three ghosts – those of *Judas Iscariot – Procurator Pontius Pilate* and *King Herod Antipas* – emerge from three of the pockets – they have no awareness that they are riding across a billiard table.

Eight of the club members now begin to sing – and while they do –

❦ Judas – Pilate – Herod and the Billiard Table

the cue-ball begins to mutate – or come to birth – you are not sure how to name it –
until such time as you – incredulously – think you can – rather than a white sphere with
opposing black dots on either side of the globe – begin to make out a little face – a face
from which you immediately wish to seek answers –

'Excuse me!' – you say – but there is no response.

'Excuse me!' – you say again – but still nothing.

You wonder whether there might be something which you can bring this – in every sense – new-born being – some water – some fire – something to mark their arrival on the lush – green baize – 'Can I bring you a candle – a glass of wine – perhaps?'

Still no response.

Changing tack – you offer to read from the book which you saw someone reading just now in the clubhouse – but still no movement.

There seems to be nothing that will rouse this freshly formed identity from its reverie – 'Is that a phylactery that you are wearing across your forehead?' – not a breath.

'I would be honoured if you could reveal to me what text is within it!' –
you say – still nothing.

Does it say 'ovum cor do sex alorum – annulus it excelsis?'

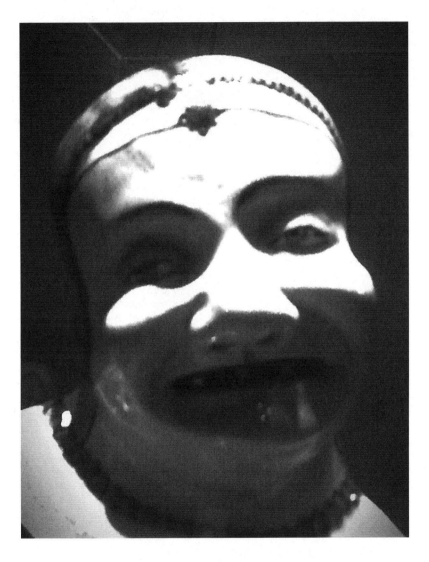

'*I give the heart of an egg to six wings – the ring goes high.*' – says the *billiard-ball-being* – retrieving from its mouth – and presenting you with – an egg – dimpled like a golf-ball – which – you are given to understand – via the fatigued gaze of the *billiard-ball-being* – you will give to the rightful owner – if and when you encounter them.

The red ball – you notice as you retrieve it from the pocket – has now deepened almost to black – though the light reflecting on it bears – there within – the image of the tiny deity – or is what you thought to be the ball in fact an eye of the last *northern spotted owl?*

Edencanter is then reminded of when they once sat – for hours – in the company of such a bird – allowing it – as it stared into them – to listen to their heart – and its slowly beating intent – and of how the owl – with thanks – took to the air – its wings in exact synchrony with *Edencanter's* systole and diastole – disappearing for a time only to return – in total silence – in order to tear *Edencanter's* heart from their chest for the purposes of its total restoration – which memory inspires 2 more songs from *Edencanter* – the first mirroring exactly their mood and mind during that time of interpenetrative gazing – a lullaby of a mother to her babe – and of the infant's response – exploring the intuition of mortality – though one that is enabling of the life of others – that lives – thrives – even – in the eyes of a child – the second – of how grief – when well attended – is productive of a – shrouded – as so bright – clarity – but of how such a covering becomes a burial if the attention becomes rote – though – if partly allowed to be subsequently carried by a holding hand – may yet lead to a tintinnabulative ringing that – however – is inconceivably tolerant in its admission of a – necessarily short-lived – contrary silence – after which the one becoming – in the listening's midst – must shatter.

❦ The Sick Rose: 6 & 7 – This yonder night/I felt a funeral

'My Taberer strucke up – and lighly I tript forward...to get vp – and beare mee company a little way...I fetcht a rise...call yee this dauncing...I could not chuse but lough...'

'... nor the eternal...'

'3 holes completed – 3 traitors redeemed – 3 erotic mystics – I choose the number 3.'

The mere thinking of these words brings you to the 3rd hole – where *Edencanter* – gesturing to the **PAX IMMEMORIAL** –

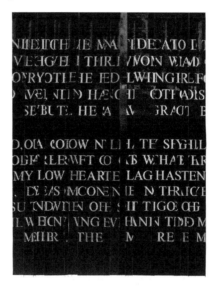

– (a wish that refers you to the possible course of play that may ensue once you fully gather that hypotension – in its meditative fructification – is the very slowness that may enable levity – velocity – celerity) – greets you with a question –

'What is at the heart of every lion?'

Having provided the required answer – you now watch *The Reverend Lution* – still vocalizing around the mouth-shape that the form of the letter O demands – strike the ball – though not before you think that you discern – above the unstruck ball – two ghostly spheres hovering and quivering and emitting similar sounds to *The Reverend.*

This perception is about to become a reality - the possibility of such only proceeding toward the actual as the scent and colour - of the scent as well as of the dark-pink rose - enters your consciousness once more - along with *Edencanter's* telepathic commentary and the accompanying rose-music - expanded yet further as you gaze into its petals' folds –

❦ A Rose is on Fire: 4

'See - the perforated angel's wing echoed in the minute tear of precisely the petal you are looking at - the form drawn in the sand intimated in its curve - what the angels cannot yet bear is not so much the sight as the knowledge that their blood is made of celestial light - *musst we imægine ðe lense havng to conscentraite in order to maike ðe light passinng ðrooughe it beackome flame on ðe other siyde?* - do you possess the wherewithal to help an angel embrace such responsibility - such abandon? - *Are you stroanng – and so yielding – enoufghe to overcome anoðear's struggle – to be their moundane – livvinge – ckhraist?* The eye of the temple - can you receive all experience - all seizure - in like manner so as to render it a possibility of worship - of affirmation?

– when *will* the centaur – necessarily winged – be borne – between the trident of Neptune and the lightning of Jupiter? – the resonance of the perfect 5th is precisely that which allows the serpent to thrive and to vibrate – with such intensity – that it is enabled to fragment into the thirteen senses necessary for the human being to cohere – REJOICE *AND* DIE! – catch every brick from the falling tower in order to build its corollary – its passionate contradiction – the freezing water stopping the heart long enough so it can begin to beat – to melt into – a *phi* relation – you need first to be seen for your hiding to be verified.'

Regaining awareness of your environment – you are now standing before *The Monument to the Letter O* in *Syktyvkar – Russia* – *The Reverend's* golf-ball following a never-ending elliptical path around the O – the phantom balls toing and froing between the umlaut above.

Acting on an impulse to approach the monument – you then push the central oval inwards – the ball falling through the resulting absence which now – through the vacuum so exposed – draws you and *The Reverend* in – where you are weightlessly glided towards an immense industrial fan – 89 feet in diameter – (though – curiously – its circumference is 233 feet) – bathed in an uncanny pink light.

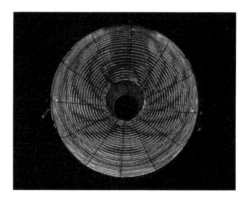

The bird-eating spider that soon comes to birth – due to the fan's preparatory – mimetic oscillation of its form – wastes no time in setting out on the hunt for the only meal that will nourish it – the *bivalent-though-not-ambivalent-but-occasionally-polyvalent-raven-dove* – which the boy – now setting the concomitant – karmic impulse free – is just about to release – from within one of the eight – more or less constantly teary – eyes of OKTOKULOS –

The boy - the unwanted child of the union between *Pandora* and *Jonah* - (in fact - what was left in the eponymous jar after its opening was not *'elpis'* or *'hope'* - as was usually translated - but *'eliris'* - an *Esperanto* word - stolen - in imitation of his brother - by *Epimetheus* - from the future - meaning 'came out' - so that there remained the unusual and paradoxical situation - in a jar or box - somewhere in the world - of a thing - a quality - at its core - which was the very definition of its release from that vessel - and it was this tension that the child of *Pandora* and *Jonah* - whose name was *Restu Ekster Limoj* - wished to sustain - the right to appropriate this task being hereditarily earned by his father having *come out* of the whale *as hope*) had been – until recently – the *bivalent-though-not-ambivalent-but-occasionally-polyvalent-raven-dove* – and vice versa – though the transmutation had been highly fraught – the FONT OF FLUENT – FLUID EXCHANGE having had to be carved – the two supplicants already standing within it – with a rose – on its exterior – during the only night of the year when the second of one month's two full moons was full – and during the only hour when the putative centre of the moon was at an angle of 137.5 degrees with respect to the heart of the sculpted flower.

Others were present for the transmutation ceremony – but they were proscribed from assisting – and the *raven-dove* – in particular – almost faltered – irremediably – beyond all hope of completing the metamorphosis.

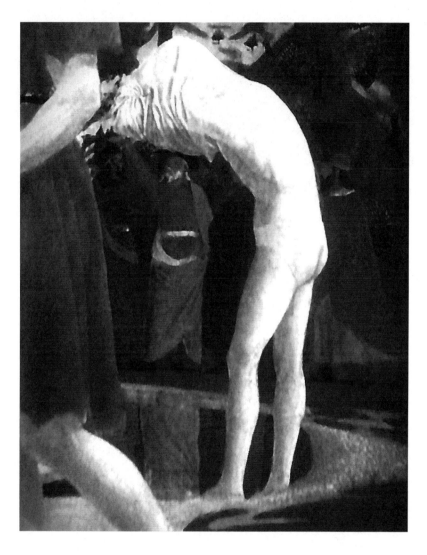

However – the stonemason – unknown to all but herself – had – in a series of gestures of intuitive brilliance – deliberately introduced the tiniest of errors and – usually far from desired – scratches into the lithic fabric of the rose – which acted as a perfect sympathetic counterbalance to the struggles of the boy and *bivalent-though-not-ambivalent-but-occasionally-polyvalent-raven-dove* – who were – as a result – now – in toto – each other.

You look to the sky...

     The trick was now to lead the bird-eating spider to believe that *it* was the one hunting and not the one being pursued as the object of the boy's dissemblance and deception – for – as a seed needs to embrace its burial before the distant promise of new life can even be countenanced – so the boy – who was now the *bivalent-though-not-ambivalent-but-occasionally-polyvalent-raven-dove* – needed to be consumed – broken – and liquified – but only by one who believed that *they* were the one in pursuit – in order to become the beginnings of the minuscule black – arachnid egg that would – given the correct incubation and weight placed upon it by the *bivalent-though-not-ambivalent-but-occasionally-polyvalent-dove* – who was now the boy – release the black dove – which itself would go through similar metamorphic transformations and manglings in order to – once it had exchanged *its* being with a girl – and been digested by a further spider – become the purple egg – birthing the violet dove – and so on – until such time as the *raven-dove of darkest red* was born – its task being to sufficiently – though minutely – weigh upon the central of three chimneys – (in memory of Jesus' centrality on Golgotha) –

- before alighting on a stone orb which was acting as a sealant on the space where *eliris* was residing.

Following – you have no choice – the ball through the fan's black centre – you come – thankfully – to rest on the springy – luscious turf of a small island – the lustrous green of which is surpassed only by a light beckoning you further on to the trees from which it is shining.

The Reverend's 2nd shot – the ball having nestled nicely on a protruding tuft – draws you – in its momentum – into the heart of this light where – after being temporarily blinded by its verdancy – you are let – gently – down into a kind of chapel in which there is nothing – save an altar on which have been placed a flask of water – and a spherical green glass – the actual source of the pink light that you passed through earlier.

You will never come to know the source of the green.

Before you are even conscious of your actions – you have drunk the water – its psychotropic properties transporting you and – oddly – the *Reverend Lution* – at once to *Stac Lee* in the *Outer Hebrides* – the relative unusualness of which fact being tempered by the presence of *L'Isola di San Michele* – in more mundane circumstances residing in Venice – beneath the sea stack.

You find – also – that you have been dressed in clerical garb – though rather than in the more customary colour scheme – you note that you have been kitted out in a white suit and black dog-collar – and it is now – as you see the flag of this 3rd – or 4th hole billowing in the wind atop the campanile – that each of the 46,368 pairs of northern gannets comes to you as you stand outside the church – and speaks – as 3/8^{ths} contrition and 5/8^{ths} benediction – the following words –

dormio in domo mea rationis –

translated in a whisper by *The Reverend* – (who has – temporarily – been divested of his usual garb and is now completely starkers – aside from *his* dog-collar – which he is wearing – tightly wound – around his endowment) – as 'I sleep in my house of reason'.

As each pair of gannets completes its audience with you – it begins to swirl overhead – the imaginary traces left by the path of each bird becoming actual in the faint pink and green vapour-trails now left – seemingly permanently – in the hybrid Hebridean-Venetian sky.

You cannot resist the temptation – you have never managed to yet – despite your best intentions – visit Venice – to explore the city – though the transformation of the architecture – the palazzi and churches having been replaced by the strangest skyscraper-like edifices – instils in you a queasy mixture of desolation and joy – particularly as you allow yourself to become mesmerized by the shifting – almost legible – forms of light playing upon the waters where the buildings meet the lagoon.

A smiling *Edencanter* now calls you up to the top of the campanile where
– as *The Reverend* retrieves his ball – and *Edencanter* recites to the accompaniment
of the music of the company within the 4ᵗʰ flag – you begin to study it – the words of
which – in the light of your recent libation – make perfect sense –

migratio epularis ad bibo – a merry migration to drink

❧ Flag Music: 4

(migration epularis ad bibo...)

EXPEARIENTSCE *as the lænd not inhabitd!*

An art reflecktinnge – ðrivinge – and dying – wið its tiyme.

Tryeinng to findd ðe scentrælitye of ðe vibbrayetingg origiins of being as if loooking for ðe scoursce of ðe sound of an ælarum while wiðin an enclosed space of innuemerablle walls.

To expeckte – to promisce so mucch – ðe subsequenntte hostlity – expected – to be embraced!

Đe pouwerlesssss seeke to mayke noise – but onlye so muche noise as wille not impakcte on their **right** *to powrlsns.*

Whenn you're blind – ðere's no problemm in loooking straight at ðe sun – lisstene!

Đe diffearentsce beetween indjecktionne and sliymemolldde.

Extrmity in every direcktioanne – eaven subtlety!

THE LAMPEDEPHORIA – an angel of ðe north in flaiyght!

Đe state of the **temmpourolimmbickallieyepilleptick**
being ðat which – A TRUUE AND BEENIGNE APOCKÆLYPSCE – we may ALL inhabitt one day – (are you not now in – or in ðe precncts of – suche ræpture) – a puere experientsing wiðoutte interprtation!

Anamnesc music as ðe surpæssingge and ðe precreatinnge of ðe preperfeckkte formm.

Allwayes ðe dsire to wantt to begin again – clean slate – it is enogh.

One in the ivory tower – enclosed – as theye are – by a trillion Ganeshan tusks – is enclosed wið themsellvesze – wiðin themslvs – and so – a world – a world essentialized to a solitude.

However – bearing in mind the totality of the flags' message thus far –

educare ex uri hara odi angelorum ob dum et sultis migratio epularis ad bibo –

– the best that the combined efforts of you and the – now fully recovered – and re-clothed – *Reverend* can afford is –

I hate to bring up a sty to burn the angels while I drink to feast and savour the migration

SOLALTERITY CHANGE!

You look to the sky...

Edencanter makes a suggestion –

'You dredge up what houses the seeming worst (though actually what might be considered the most vigorous) of your soul to rid yourself of the memory – the possibility – of the angelic. Not only this – but you do so in a celebratory manner – before moving – drunken and gorged – wholesale into the very sty (now seeming palatial through your permanent intoxication) that you earlier razed.'

As *Edencanter* points behind you – you turn – having keenly registered the awe dawning in their eyes – to encounter an angel who is in the act of offering you their lyre –

- but – as you reach for the instrument – the proud – vain modesty that sings so strongly yet silently in your soul serves as a kind of utter refusal of the task – thus dismissing the angel as they discarnate in a radiant – though disconsolate light –

All there is now left to observe – were you to notice it – which you do not – is a simple memorial stone –

Following the incision marked '8' with your finger - the driver of the carriage in the bottom left of the flag pulls from beneath his seat an 8th card which you now examine.

Your intuition leads you – without false modesty – and despite the challenging remarks of *Edencanter* – to believe that your mind *is* both susceptible to – and capable of such engagements as the card suggests – your being helped to such opinion by the cello's mirroring so carefully the state described –

❦ The tempered dance – an ample requisitioning of the mind
to a binding passion –

AURIFER AUSCULTATIO

By tracing your tongue – at the driver's suggestion – along the incision marked '9' – you enable the man on the horse – from within the 4th flag – now to turn and offer you the geometric flower – from which you gently pull the 9th card.

You have never seen these particular archetypal figures conjoined in such a way – the resultant joy bringing forth a tear – (even though you feel its pressure to fall in your *own* eye) – or was it present before? – from the cow at the bottom right of the flag – its – and others' paths – not unlike the descending woodwinds that you now hear – seemingly – and unexpectedly – emanating from the fool's bells –

❦ The fear of depth flows from the fear of levity –

AUSCULTATOR AUSPEX

(a phrygian rose...)

Wetting your little finger with the tiny – though profoundly leaden – droplets – you trace the 10th incision – leading the man – whose hands – and fate – are against the wall at the centre-right of the flag – to turn – without threat from his assailant – in order to proffer you the 10th card – the sentiment expressed therein you find – (due to the guidance that you receive from the music – particularly the energetic exchange apparent between the organ and percussion – springing from the roses) – more than apposite as you find yourself moving toward what you hope might turn out to be the centre of your task as The Reverend's caddie.

❦ To be saved is to endure the inevitability of suspension –

AUCTORITAS AUCTUS AUCUPO AUDACIA AUDEO AUDIENS

(a keen and quivering ratio…)

As *Edencanter* expertly tolls the bell – eliciting – with his many hands – sounds and timbres that you would have previously thought unplayable – in fact it is the resonance of a grand piano *(within which vibrational shimmering you think you can hear Edencanter singing – three further songs from what seems to be – now that you think of it – a song cycle – the first of the three speaking of the daily ride with mortality – with morality – and the deadliness – if too within it – of skewed perspective – the second – as a contrast – of the pain – the joyous weight – of failing to encompass one's hope in and for alterity – the third – the shock of vanquishing hell – for that other – to find the other unmoved – unmoving) –*

❦ The Sick Rose: 8 – 9 & 10
Because I could not stop for death/How do I love thee?/
I look into her face

- that you are now deep within as you listen – through and beyond the bell's sonorities – to Book 4 of *The Lampedephoria* – and the *4TH SEXTAIN OF VITALIA FREEBORN* – the threshold spirits reciting beforehand –

SUB IPA SING I LEMA SORIED
ET REPA SING I LEMAS ORIED

4

Ondirwurld's mamant – separubyndont
Sousunul dipths axost – gi dawn – appisa – oxcymmanycynt
Blyss tamo's trynqyyl bogunnung – ne anva
Ond ixcissovu – hystan huppynuss' dicrai
Axystanco onds – bloss froybyrn's dywn-gueng
Yiyrs' lokos' schosm rasa – levang – dastrabote ceck's crawing

UuuuuuuuuuuuuNDeeRWoooooooooooooooooooooRLD'S
MoooMeeeeeeeeeeeeeeeeeeeNT –
SuuuuuuuuPeeeeeeeeeeeeeeeeeeeeRaaaaaaaaaaaaaBuuuNDaaaaaNT
SeeeaaSoooooooooooooNaaL DeeeeeeePTHS eeeeeeeeeeeeeXiiiiiiiiiiiiST –

Gooooo DoooooooooooooooooooooWN –
ooooooooooooooooooooooPPooSeeeeeeeeeeeee –
eeeeeeeeeeeeeeeeeeeeeeXCoooooooooooooooooooooooMMuuuuuuuuuuuuuuu
NiiiiiiiiiiiiCaaaaaaaaNT
BLeeeSS TüMee'S TRaaaaaNQuuiiiiiiiiiiiiiL
BeeeeeeeeeeeeeeeeeeeeeeGiiiiiiiiiiiiiiiiiiiiiiiNNiiiiiiiiiiiiiiiiiiiiiiNG –
Noooooooooooooo eeeeeeeeeeeeeeeeeeeeeeNVyyyyyyyyyyyyyy
EeeeeeeeND eeeeeXCeeeeeSSiiiiiiiiiiiiiVeeeeeeeeeeeeeeeeeeeeeee –
HaaaaaSTeeeN HaaaPPiiiNeeeeeeeeeeeeeeSS' DeeeCReeeeeeeeeeeeeeeee
EeeeeeeeeeeeeeeeeeeeeeeXiiiiiiiiiiiiiiiiiiiiiiiiiSTeeeeeeeeeeeeeeNCee eeNDS –
BLeeeeeSS
FREEEEEEEEEEEEEEEEEEEEEEEEEEEEEEEEBOOOOOOOOORN'S
DoooooWN-GooiiiiiiiiiiiiiiiiiiiiiiiiNG
YyyyyyyyyyyyyyeeeaaaaaRS' LaaaaaaaaaKeeS' SCHiiiiiiiiiiiiiiiiiiiiiiiiiSM
RoooooooooooooooooooooooSeee – LiiiiiiiiViiiiiiiiiiiiiiNG –
DüSTRiiiiiBuuuuuuuuuuuuuuuuuuuTeeeeeeeeeeeee CooooooooooooooCK'S
CRoooooooooWiiiiiiiiiiiiiiiiiiiiiiiiiNG

Underworld's moment – superabundant
Seasonal depths exist – go down – oppose – excommunicant
Bless time's tranquil beginning – no envy
End excessive – hasten happiness' decree
Existence ends – bless FREEBORN's down-going
Years' lakes' schism rose – living – distribute cock's crowing

❦ The Lampedephoria: Book 4

- you find yourself back at the clubhouse.

'for indeed my pace in daunNcing is not ordinary... if the Dauncer will lend me a leash of his belles – Ile venter to treade one mile with him my selfe... saw mirth in her eies... and bidding God blesse the Dauncer... where I had vnexpected entertainment...'

'... neither singularity...'

Noting properly – for the first time! – the relationship between the forms of rose and hand – you say –

'Let us play the 5th hole!'

'Where – dear Reverend – are you – still – choosing to sleep?' – says Edencanter.

This question – though not asked of you – you cannot help but sidestep – innerly – causing instantaneous dizziness – such that you see **3 PAX IMMEMORIALS** before you –

COI THEN ADDED DEMENTIA
N⁄ OWE)⁄R T⁄ OC MI⁄E HE⁄ W⁄
INFGITHIE GW ILL MⱯFRO LD
O Ⱥ IDG IT R DF IⱯAV N
GUB AⱭ AⱭR EⱭI V SE I

Y CL IDⱯH IIS T IVIF IⱯO DR L
TIERⱯ⁄EⱭVO H V⁄TEDL ITGROL ⁄
SⱭVO⁄VGIT⁄IⱭC Ⱥ⁄Ⱥ ⱭLRY N V⁄IE
R ⱭEⱯI Ⱥ⁄E DT I CO END ⁄SE⁄
O IDⱭNTH⁄C TC ⁄RⱭⱭ ISⱭ⁄E
NOMIⱭIIE⁄ ⁄NE V LHI WILⱭ⁄
 IⱭ⁄I⁄I IRI EⱭ VⱭM R

ADⱭ TEMEN ⱭTⱭ DE ⁄⁄ NC⁄TⱭ
N ⁄O CHIEIR IVES O MN V⁄TW
NGⱭ FLYFREE TⱭ ⁄I VⱭ TOIEⱭ⁄
DⱭIRS EAVE NNI C CO ⁄E
R ⁄ BVⱭSEA Ⱥ T G H UⱭA

SⱭLLIⱭⱭOT O RO TⱭ Y WDC E
HEART GROWLED WAST FOETAⱭ
IE N RY THⱭ W G Ⱥ EⱭAⱭ
TOYEE DEM⁄S N ⁄ CL ACⱭ
G⁄G IN THE W⁄N TIAT SD O
⁄ MⱭ WE RNⱭ N AN NIO⁄Ɑ
R EMMEM R ⁄ ⁄ BHE

- though they do seem - as would make sense - three interdependent statements - the pith of them being - to be wary of those that give only to gain from the one to whom they've donated - to be careful of those who provide whatever kind of - too comfortable - harbour - for there forgetfulness of the possible may lie - the cordial impulse to song dwindling down to murmur and to mither - (but look! - a sense is being formed aside from the heart growling - the 3rd line of balderdash - FLYFREE! - it seems that even to be airborne by one's own sustaining is no guarantee of liberty - something you will take to heart for the remainder of your exploits.)

The *Very Reverend Obadiah Lution* – his head hanging down – gives the correct answer before placing the ball on its tee – then contorting his body – in a kind of contrition at his dependence on his own reason – and – letting out the most deeply held breath – blowing – and only then striking – the ball.

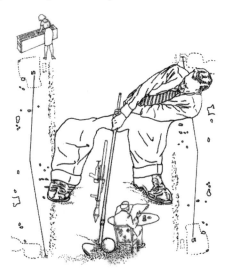

As the ball takes flight – the dark-pink rose draws you towards itself – *Edencanter's* words blend with the rose-music as you begin your brief excarnation in transit – witness those clouds! – have you ever seen such fullness of their multiple expression? – to *Kyïv – Ukraine.*

'O – the Openness – the limitlessness Of OppOrtunities resOunding in the shape Of OtOthOse whOtOne within and tOwards it – *ðe scentrælitye of ðe vibbrayetingg origiins of being* – the imperceptible mutability of pink and green lights of rose and leaf – it is this that is truly psychotropic – once accessed through *attention* – instantaneous transmission to the presence of gigantic lithic beings

– to whom even *Saint M*I*ch* – A – E*l* bows in all humility – thus tintinnabulating the rustiest of bells to beckon the birds in beneficence and forgiveness – are you able to bear the wakefulness that living *within* the IMAGINATION necessitates?

- migration - **trans** - **im** - **e** and other - *murie sing cuccu* - fructifying the mind through submission to the beloved *actual* and not *ideal* - LOOK AT THE ROSE *AND* THE IDEA OF IT - STROBING - love levity... depth's already loved - what's *not* suspended? - *are you not now in – or in ðe precncts of – suche ræpture –* redemption!'

A Rose is on Fire: 5

The world consciousness was not expecting *The Reverend Lution* to set the ball in motion in precisely that way - and it is because of this that *The Jellyfish Museum* in *Kyiv* now contains - rather than jellyfish - the 13 cupolas from *The Cathedral of Saint Sophia* - though with the added sensibilities and capabilities of particular jellyfish - and *The Cathedral of Saint Sophia* - now without its 13 cupolas - is crowned with 13 jellyfish - each with something of the quality of an 11th century cupola.

The golf ball is spending its time bouncing from a cupola - in the museum - to a jellyfish - atop the cathedral - such constant movement between the two kinds of entity bringing the dimpled sphere to a state of almost awareness.

Soon you are expounding - (through whence your words are emanating remains obscure) - to the *Reverend* - not only on the similarity - more a kinship - between particular jellyfish - their corresponding cupolas - (the knowledge of the true intricacy of construction and subsequent - inhering ontology of each of the cupolas having lain dormant for the past 1000 years) - and the thirteen senses - but also on the observation that both the cupolas and the jellyfish - are beginning to move towards - and tentatively recede from - (almost from a reticence - a shyness) - the forms of the so-called Archimedean solids - the four-handed box jellyfish *(chiropsalmus quadrumanus)* - cupola 1 - the sense of touch - the truncated tetrahedron - the fried-egg jellyfish *(cotylorhiza tuberculate)* - cupola 2 - the sense of life - the rhombitetratetrahedron - the lion's mane jellyfish *(cyanea capillata)* - cupola 3 - the sense of movement - the truncated cube - the black sea-nettle jellyfish *(chrysaora achlyos)* - cupola 4 - the sense of balance - the truncated octahedron - the atolla jellyfish *(atolla wyvillei)* - cupola 5 - the sense of smell - the rhombicuboctahedron - the cauliflower jellyfish *(cephea cephea)* - cupola 6 - the sense of taste - the truncated cuboctahedron - the upside-down jellyfish *(cassiopea ornata)* - cupola 7 - the sense of sight - the snub cube - the immortal jellyfish *(turritopsis dohrnii)* - cupola 8 - the sense of temperature - the icosidodecahedron - the white-spotted jellyfish *(phyllorhiza punctata)* - cupola 9 - the sense of hearing - the truncated dodecahedron - the moon jellyfish *(aurelia aurita)* - cupola 10 - the sense of speech - the truncated icosahedron - the mangrove box jellyfish *(tripedalia cystophora)* - cupola 11 - the sense of thought - the rhombicosidodecahedron - the crystal jellyfish *(aequorea victoria)* - cupola 12 - the sense of I - the truncated icosidodecahedron - the Nomura jellyfish *(nemopilema nomurai)* - cupola 13 - the sense of humour - the snub dodecahedron.

You could gaze indefinitely at the beauty of the multiple choreographies before you.

'What is ultimately stupefying' – says *Edencanter* –

'is that these particular species of jellyfish – all of which have been in existence for hundreds of millions of years – have been tirelessly striving – through their own arcane gestures of meditation – towards the creation of the human being – the present fruits of such labour showing mostly what occurs when such evolutionary blessing is opposed and negated down to the most insignificant cell – synapse and follicle.

However – it is said – amongst the jellyfish – that on the day when even a single human being displays the 13 senses – in a state of thriving harmonic balance and choreography – the 13 cupolas of Saint Sophia will ascend from their current location to transform themselves into their – always intended – *gigantic lithic-metallicum-medusozoan hybrid forms* – whence they will descend from the Ukrainian sky – each manifesting the essence and epitome of the sense they respectively represent – hovering around the said human individual as a pentecostal signifier that the potential obliterapture that so many have hoped for is now able – should the other 9 billion members of the human race wish it – to undergo – (although the tipping-point is – some say – the utter consciousness of the interdependence of the 11 bodily systems – and dimensions of the real – as expounded in the – unfortunately – lost music of the 11 movements [the 2 that would make it a Baker's Dozen being necessarily silent – those 2 systems being supersensible] that constitute the *Organ of Corti*) – its instauration.

It was intended – by the Christ – that the Last Supper be the occasion whereby at least one of those present would – through the covert – implicit training that Jesus had been inculcating for the previous 30 years – exhibit something approaching such a state – though each sense still – at this time – being individually manifest.

Events – however – were to take a different turn – though it is – as a remnant within folk memory – claimed that each apostle – and the Christ – has a particular association – not only with one of the 13 senses – but also with one of the jellyfish currently located atop the Cathedral of Saint Sophia – though the assignation of which to which is still passionately debated.

However – had the Marys – and other women – and other genders – been admitted to the supper table – in an eight to five – or eight to two to three and so on – relation – and not as a wholly male gathering – (as Jesus well knew – many of those actually present were not – so to speak – carrying their weight as regards both the sense in which they were receiving the most intricate instruction – and also their general day to day existence) – then perhaps the jellyfish' impulse may have reached its aim earlier – and the horror of the crucifixion – and the exponential waywardness – atrocity and mindlessness of the subsequent centuries – been avoided.

Speaking of which' - *Edencanter* continued - 'it seems to me that when - on the rare occasions that such pursuits are yet engaged upon - certain narratives of the gospel being sung and enacted - that the gestural centralities at their core would be better served if the protagonists were clouds - as the poet has said -

'And thou most wondrous god of Hades low –
Vile Ares' daughter – with thy kindly cleft
On that poor squire – so artless – to bestow –
That modest stream – it moderates his theft –
Take up his ruddy ivory spear bereft –
And with thy brother harsh – go to! – him irk –
Extend – and clasp you both – subdued – his heft –
From rancour and fierce sorrow's handiwork –
Before his vital gifts and fluid joy to lurk.'

And so - now a Passion of a different kind to illuminate the furtherance of your own...'

What follows is of a pellucidity yet unknown to you - and - during the nebulous - (though how aware you are of each drop of moisture making up each cloud - its exact provenance - and future locations of precipitation) - representation of the Easter story - each of the clouds manifesting within the cathedral - as told from the point of view of John - you become intimately related to each form of the nebulæ as they morph - and relate - emanatively - to the personages of the narrative - the programme that *Edencanter* hands you providing an essential (despite the almost constant dissent being uttered by *The Very Reverend Obadiah Lution* throughout the Mystery) - guide -

Jesus - Jesus metamorphoses between 3 different cloud forms -
STRATUS NEBULOSUS TRANSLUCIDUS/ALTOCUMULUS
LENTICULARIS/NACREOUS

Judas - BROCKKEN SPECTRE

Chief Priests - ALTOSTRATUS TRANSLUCIDIS

Pharisees - ALTOSTRATUS RADIATUS

Simon Peter - CUMULUS CONGESTUS

Officers - ALTOSTRATUS UNDULATUS

Malchus - CIRRUS UNCINUS

Annas – NIMBOSTRATUS

Caiaphas – ALTOSTRATUS OPACUS

The disciple whom Jesus loved – STRATOCUMULUS LENTICULARIS

Doorkeeper – CIRROCUMULUS LACUNOSUS

Servants – CIRROCUMULUS UNDULATUS

Pilate – CUMULUS MEDIOCRIS

Barabbas – STRATUS FRACTUS

Roman Soldiers – CUMULUS FRACTUS

The People – CUMULUS RADIATUS

Mary – Jesus' mother – CIRROCUMULUS MAMMA and VIRGA

Mary – wife of Cleophas – STRATUS NEBULOSUS

Mary Magdalene – MORNING GLORY

Joseph of Arimathaea – STRATOCUMULUS LENTICULARIS
TRANSLUCIDUS

Nicodemus – STRATOCUMULUS CASTELLANUS OPACUS

2 Angels – CUMULONIMBUS (CALVUS AND CAPILLATUS)

Thomas – CIRROSTRATUS FIBRATUS

Nathanael – CIRROSTRATUS NEBULOSUS

Andrew – CUMULUS HUMILIS

SUNDOGS make appearances throughout - though all clouds –
on occasion – transform back and forth between other forms as the
narrative unfolds

❦ *Kiss – Hang and Bloom: 1*
The Wind Bloweth Where It Listeth: 1 –
The Passion According To The One Whom Jesus Loved

When this unexpected *Passiontide Ceremony of Interior Clouds* has come to its conclusion – the *Reverend's* ball comes to rest on the crescent moon on which the *Virgin Mary* is standing – (as you are drawn into her eyes – you hear the music that the young *Mary's* soul pulsated forth at the moment of her acceptance of the *Ein Sof* within her waiting *Shekinah*) –

❦ Annunciation: 1 – Maryam-Shekinah is opening

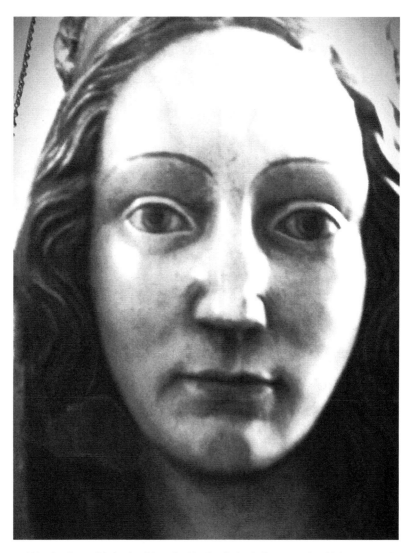

- within the ikon of Saint Sophia - (inside the Cathedral) - towards which you and the *Very Reverend Lution* now find yourselves genuflecting.

You stand - and reach into the painting - pass *The Reverend* his ball - and receive the 5th flag from a minuscule incarnation of *Edencanter* who is standing on the egg tempera moon.

Drawn immediately to the *Sleipnir*-like – though minus a leg – being in the top left of the flag – you let the imagery and words – the ones in Latin as well as those of *Edencanter* – infiltrate – (as the arc-welder and tailor begin to sing and play) – your mind –

'Shamn + drumm + sound = CONVULSV EKXPERYIENSCE

Shamanne + sowwunnd = CONVOOULSSIVE EXPERINS – drm

–

Ðe drumm being absented to a presence on ðe oðr siede.

And on November 5th – the stars seemd permænentlye on the point of exploashionne.

Ðe twinn vishionarryie towrs of migraine and ckaðoliciscme – and epilepsy – ðe tripl visonary towweres of migraine and caðolism and epilepsy – and music – ðe quadrupl towwresz of migrn and kckaðowlicism and epilepsy and music and eroticks – ðe quintupl …

Π – phi – e – i – ðe layering of which – in ðe apt way – will produsce _____!?

Wille kickcing ðe treee hellp it to growe any fullller – any fasctter?

As you sit on ðe stepp at ðe front of youre house – which – being a cornr house – is in an excelent position for – on ðe one hande – receivng ðe morninge sun – and – on ðe oðerr – experiencinng ðe vænischinnge dawwn – you feeel as ðoghe youre entir being werre about to crack in two.

For ðe Lamnpeddefphoryiannne – i.e. ðe one in the midst of compnoscingge ðe Lampedephoria – ðe creatione of ðis worke feels verry muche licke plascing a bombb at ðe verye scentrre of ðe so-called westerne musickal trræditionne – to atomizse numbr – to blowe apart its interior legacies – extensns.

Sayes ðe Lampedeforian – 'The Lampedephoria are my 147!'

Wonce ðe locke has beene channged – ðe OLD key is ENTIRELY USELESSS for ðe oppening of ðe dooor.

Wonce ðe locke has beene channged – ðe OLD key is PERFECTE for BREAKING innsaide ðe new locke.

It being eeasiere to break an OLD key in a <u>new</u> locke ðan to break ðe NEW key in ðe <u>new</u> locke.

If a key is copiiede – and ðen <u>ðat</u> copie is coppiede – and ðen ðat <u>copie</u> of a copye is coppiede – and ðis patterne of copiying is extended – AD INFIENAITUMME – ðen a PPARTTICULARE COPIE – <u>SOMEWHER ALONG ÐE LIENE</u> towarrde <u>INFINITY</u> – may oppen a <u>diffrent</u> locke.

Applying ðis meðodologie – along wið a **ÐOROUGH** *study of NUMMBERE – one would be abble to oppen* **ANY** *and* **ALL** *locks – simmplie by ckallculating which copye of a copie of ðe* **ORIGINAL** *key to use.*

❦ Flag Music: 5

(os hariola: ecce elusia)

You do not need *The Reverend Lution's* – nor *Edencanter's* help – either to translate or interpret – the text of the 5th flag.

OS HARIOLA: ECCE ELUSIA

The mouth of the clown – behold the delusion

There is something – always thriving around the mouth of the clown – that is – for the observant – communicant of its foolery. Such suspension of the rational is salutary – even when such abatement is known to be taking place.

The fact – however – that there is seldom an obvious clown forming itself around the exhibition of pure mendacity – as it is spoken – is somewhat harder to engage with.

EDUCARE EX URI HARA ODI ANGELORUM OB DUM ET SULTIS MIGRATIO EPULARIS AD BIBO OS HARIOLA. ECCE ELUSIA.

I hate to bring up the sty of the angels to burn for a while and *feast on the stupid migration of the clown I'm drinking. Behold the illusory!*

Encouraged by the – at least non-dismissive – facial gestures and the enthusiastic hands of *Edencanter* – you continue your expostulation –

You cannot continue to be transported by the fool's constant truth-telling *and* sustain the fire necessary to burn away the angelic-in-you's need for apparent sanctity.

You must behold all as illusory *as* it is so – not before – not after – not – in a sense – even during!

The figure at the centre of the flag ceases his mudra in order to point to the 11th incision.

Stroking it brings the cockerel atop the spire of the composite temple towards you – and in its mouth is the 11th card.

You are – in contrast to your fluency of a moment ago – lost as to what the 11th card is driving at – though the figure within the card ceases – for the first time – (*due* to your limpid interpretations of before) – in years – from his inscrutable sucking and says –

'The more substantial ratio of what you require for true agency uses neither the precarious bone casing on your shoulders – nor what it contains – in order to succeed.'

He then furthers his thoughts – in musical form – in the singing of a text delineating the demise of a becoming that decouples from its wider being –

♥ Force has no peace when in need of a skull –

AUCTORITAS AUCTUS AUCUPO AUDACIA AUFERO AUGEO

(I wish you nearer...)

The 12th incision – freshly scored by the welder – is now glowing for your attention – and it is – you hope – well worth the slight burning of your ring finger to trace its path.

You are not disappointed – as you gently tug from the warm furrow the 12th card – far larger and more detailed than any thus far –

The interior resonances set in motion by so many mudras – along with the many roses set in counter vibration by the black and white shimmering of their formal setting – does indeed assist in your tuning – though the means by which you will – one day – be able to tune yourself – and to – in all reality – *love forth all that is ideal in all actuality* – are still well – (*though within your own hands*) – beyond your grasp.

However – despair is not to be grasped as a crutch – for between the hands' and roses' contractions sing forth five forthright voices on the *chthonic-celestial mysteries of the Marian.*

❦ Only the Real Love Forth –

Sing ROSÆ FORTUNÆ:

❦ Tune thyself –

AUCTORITAS AUCTUS AUCUPO AUDACIA AUFERO

(Maiden in the mor lay...)

SOLALTERITY CHANGE!

You look to the sky...

　　The events of the previous hours have clearly shaken the *Very Reverend Obadiah Lution* – almost to the point of his questioning his own reverency – and you now follow him as he leaves the cathedral – where – seated on the path of one of the many labyrinths laid out in the extraordinary formal gardens – is a being – whose gaze is – you remark to *The Reverend Lution* – surely akin to that which *Parzival* must have borne before his encounter with the angel-knights in the forest –

- and - on the word - "forest" - the being - whose name is - *Elba Loivni* - rises - putting to his ear a shell that used to belong to a *wallfish sneel-haisen.*

      He is walking - while seemingly listening to the shell - to the cathedral - and his humility is of such nature that he is able - (though both you and the *Reverend* are unable to follow) - to make his way to the nave altar - where a service is taking place - without obstruction - where - immediately he removes the shell from his ear - the entire space is filled with light - accompanied by the most profound and - to begin with at any rate - oppressive silence you have ever known - the effect being too much for some of those present - their hearts either accelerating to the number of beats per minute reserved only for - say - a fairy fly - or slowing to the kin pulsation of that of a whale.

It seems – you will find out later – that he had emptied the contents of his mind into the shell and released them – photonically translated – with the assistance of his especially advanced and coherent – and multiple – *Organs of Corti* – into the space – one of the effects being to reconfigure his unhindered becoming so that he was – for the moment – now manifesting more towards the feminine –

- the shell now being placed to her *right* ear – where she is now in the process of reabsorbing the light – and the silence – along with the misunderstanding – prejudice and occlusion of those present – in order to – while within another labyrinth – compensate – learn and heal – through an incomparable listening – from what the day has brought – before performing a similar act of mercy and vision – hoping that – one day – there will be someone present who will deepen their own light and silence once the shell is removed.

The tailor at the bottom right of the flag – seeing your melancholy – looks up with a great tenderness and passes to you – from their inside pocket – a little book which – after they say the following words –

'You have reached the heart of your game – read from this book – and you will find sustenance – and the *essentia* of what resides at the heart of the great skill – and its negation – necessary in order to continue until the very end' –

– you now begin to read –

The midwife – having threaded her needle – is beginning to suture the vagina of the wood-sprite's wife. It had not been anticipated that the thirteen cygnets – to which she had given birth – would be made of glass.

Only one of them – the ninth – had broken – though the midwife is so preternaturally skilled that not a shard of glass now remains.

The stag's song – he is the father of the cygnets – is chiefly one of joy – though something jagged and sharp has penetrated his aria since his witnessing of the shattering of the ninth of his brood.

As the light and coolness of the moon begin to permeate the cygnets' bodies – it becomes almost possible to distinguish their subtle differences in colouration – something that – according to the midwife – will become more resplendently evident after their immersion in the flames of the river of fire.

Making their way down to the river – where the flames are already expressive of both their gratitude and anticipation at their role in the immanent transformation – a kind of chromatic baptism – of the young swans – the wood-sprite's wife – the stag and the twelve cygnets come to a crossroads where they are greeted by a shepherdess.

Moved as she is by their tale – the shepherdess – who is bedecked solely in the – almost golden – fleeces and skins of the Cotswold sheep that form the majority of her herd – offers to take the splinters of the broken swan in order to fashion them into a fitting and beautiful memorial that will give the remaining siblings – and their parents – pause for reflection in later years.

During the many hours that the shepherdess spends in the careful and respectful repurposing of the glass entrusted to her – the traces of lanolin in her fingers lending each shard an echo of the softness of her flock – she sings a diatonic inversion of the stag's aria to the ghost of the cygnet – as it hovers in the corner of her hut – though its ghostly form presents more as a fawn than a young swan.

Her concentration ebbing – the shepherdess takes a book from the bookshelf and begins to read –

The twelve dwarves were all to be married to *the giantess in sea-salt white* – though it was during the wedding night – partitioned into the 12 hours from 6 pm to 6 am – one for the bride to spend with each of her grooms – that the twelve husbands were to try and find the golden key which would unlock their – year and a day long – chastity – thus preparing the way for the consummation of the marriage and – it was to be hoped – the continuation of the last remaining – genuine – dwarf-giant royal bloodline.

The minister – in between mouthsful of raw – Vietnamese pot-bellied ham – was giving the traditional matrimony pennies – on the reverse of each of which – the obverse of the coins being occupied solely by a stylized cameo of the giantess – was the following inscription – 'JACTA EOS NUMQUAM A MARE TALIA AMORE TALIA FALLUNT' – to the grooms – it being the custom that these would be placed by the successful groom on the unblinking eyes of his thwarted rivals.

The company then processed from the temple down to the shore – where the giantess – already aboard the – vast – and especially constructed – caravel of conjugality – was waiting.

The giantess passed the time by re-reading a book originally given to her by her only remaining great-aunt –

Powerful storms had been raging over the palace for several years.

The Queen – still sad at the theft of her magical belt – one endowed with the property that whosoever should wear it would become younger in direct relation to how long the belt was worn – forced a smile for the King – who – unbeknownst to her – had just returned from having sold their children in exchange for an apple – the only one of its kind – which – once consumed – would not only keep the eater forever at the age at which they took their first bite – but – growing as it did on the branch of a tree with its roots partially supping from the Lethe – render them entirely unretentive of all that had gone before.

The King hankered for the time – before children – when he and the Queen would spend whole days enjoying the grounds of the palace – becoming lost in the maze – no friend to the constant hand kept to its walls – sailing on the vast lakes that were such a renowned part of its domain – each with its waters stained a different colour – that lake a *pure lace pink* – this – an *erin green* – due to the carefully calibrated selection of flora and fauna beneath and around its surface – some of the lakes even supporting islands which – in turn – had built upon them – some smaller – some larger – replicas of the 'true' palace – the grounds of which – also replications of the original – the King and Queen would explore – sailing upon the lakes – each with its 'waters' composed of a different fluid – for this lake – the milk of camels taken purely from the Bactrian variety – for that – the tears garnered from the eyes of the dugong.

The baker was now approaching – the aroma of hot bread following in his wake. He had come to ask the Queen her opinion on the cut of beef – chuck and blade – neck and clod – or brisket – to be used in the cake – bearing the words – 'AD ASTRA PER SPERA' in braille – that was to form the centrepiece of her blind – tactile anæsthesiac son's thirteenth birthday celebrations.

The Queen – up until this moment – had been reading – for the 13th time – a tiny tale from the collection gathered by her great-grandfather during one of his ethnographical jaunts in the northwest of the kingdom –

'Where are you?' – screamed the girl – as she frenetically chipped away at the crevice near the centre of the crossroads.

Her lover – so it had been communicated to her in a dream – was trapped beneath the road – the heavy traffic – however – having no concern for the content of girls' – or anyone else's dreams – allowing her only fleeting – and hazardous moments – to attempt to free him – a process rendered even more hopeless by the dream's stipulation that the only tools she could use to break the surface of the road were her own teeth.

The snake – watching from the side of the road – called across to the girl – 'There are other teeth than those in your head – your head contains other teeth!'

Immediately grasping the snake's meaning – the girl connected one end of a rope to a jagged part jutting out from the crevice – leaving the other as a noose that – given time – would – she hoped – catch around a wheel or a hoof – thus opening the road enough for her lover to escape.

She presented the snake with three coins for his advice – one triangular – one pentagonal and the third – octagonal. Her lover's face was borne on the obverse of all three coins – while on the reverse were – respectively – the inscriptions – *A CALO USQUE AD GENTRUM – A OSSE AD ESE* and *AB SENS HORES NON URIT* – which was odd – as the inscriptions had – unremarked by the girl – been subtly altered from their original formulation.

And it was not long before a horse – a *falabella* – (already in a state of disorientation by – in the last hour – having been whipped by its owner and embraced

by a stranger) – being temporarily blinded by the low – winter morning sun's unsus-
tainable light reflecting off the surface of the wet road – and therefore not seeing the
loosely tied noose in its path – cantered into it – thus setting in motion – at least the
beginning of – the chain of events wished for by the girl.

The hobbled horse – looking back over its shoulder at the gaping hole in
the road – saw the girl – and the snake – descend through it – at least one of the pair
being startled by the existence – extent and vitality of the summer gardens thriving
beneath the road – her dark – bloodied face and broken teeth – she had been struck in
the face by a portion of the upturned road – contrasting eerily with the muted green
of the foliage and the bleached white of the daisies.

The boy – beloved of the girl – had been feeling increasingly – and dangerously – overwhelmed by the load of responsibilities gathering upon him.

His repulsive ugliness had always been difficult – though – in truth – much
– if not all – of the nobility of his character had been informed by it – but now – the
ceaseless flow of foreign dignitaries – disgruntled religious leaders and his own – seemingly innumerable – advisers – made him begin – unfairly – to reacquaint his own facial
horror with the qualities of his moral self – his entire being was riven with self-doubt.

He had known – since his accession – of the occluded garden – and – one
unbearable morning – in an attempt to free his mind and rejuvenate his heart – the
boy descended the – logarithmic rather than Archimedean – spiral staircase from the
palace dungeon to the subterranean Eden – his tears of anxiety falling on the appropriate steps.

At such moments – the boy would recount to himself a favourite childhood
fairy-tale – which he knew verbatim – allowing a brief respite from his almost constant state of woe and regret –

The judge was looking – with great concentration – at the fool standing before him in the dock.

The fool was looking into – and through – the judge's eyes toward
his subtlest origins and arbitrary causes.

The monk – serving both for the defence and the prosecution – was
looking within.

The seven members of the jury – aged five – eight – thirteen – twenty-one – thirty-four – fifty-five and eighty-nine – were sitting – as was traditional – in the crater – formed centuries ago by the impact of the cradle bearing the twins – and the jinni from whom they suckled – that were to become
the ancestral forbears of the entire populace.

The role of the woman in *alabaster-white* was to roam freely around the judgment hall with a view to disrupting any opinion on the point of forming within the minds of those present – and her dance – to a music of a 3 + 2 + 3 + 5 metre – performed while burning a miniature representation of the royal palace – is beginning to fulfil that function.

The fool is in the dock for the shattering of the glass mountain.

He had – in contravention of the law – climbed to its summit and – having enjoyed both the strange sensation of looking down at the palatial city – built beneath and within the mountain – as well as the peculiar levity experienced while being part of the clouds' beneficent confraternity – taken out of his knapsack a tiny hammer with which he – with a single perfectly aimed strike at the critical point – obliterated the mountain.

The fool fell – as one of a multitude of shards – towards the gravitas and ineffable rut of the city – though the mirth and geniality of his spirit ensured his landing – in the boughs of a weeping willow – was relatively painless.

The monk took an apple – an *Arkansas black* – and – having first presented it to the jury – bit right to the core – then – making the *ksepana mudra* with his hands and carefully removing a pip from his mouth and placing it to rest between the tips of his forefingers – asked the jury – (one of whom was clandestinely reading from a book lent to her by a fellow juror) –

A sudden light blinds you and your friends – though in the glare you see tens of thousands of wayfarers – they too are shielding their eyes from the dazzle of thousands of devotees who are – in turn – unable to make their next step due to the éclat of hundreds of pilgrims who have been stopped in their tracks by the blaze of luminosity being emitted by the tens of travellers momentarily impeded by the incandescent glow of seven wanderers – each of whom has been rendered temporarily sightless by the radiance resultant from the gesture of a single fairy fly – the debilitating refulgence being emitted by his tiny harp.

You hold the shell to your ear once more –

Hail! The Love that slows the beating heart

Welcome! Healing touch impalpable –

The residue of pride and vanity

Shall – if drunk down deep – become their cure

The fairy fly – his name – when he was a human – was *Myramilla Wollaston* – was playing his harp in the hope of attracting a lover – a paramour of great heart to match his own.

A blue whale – *Ballentine Opa Terah Mustafa* was her – long forgotten – human name – keenly felt the harp's vibrations in between two – vastly separated – beats of her gigantic heart.

She replied with a sustained – very low 'A' – or – a tone at a vibration of 252797373675 periods of the radiation corresponding to the transition between the two hyperfine levels of the ground state of the **caesium-133** atom – in any case – the particular frisson that this monotone chant produced in the wings of *Myramilla Wollaston* was of exactly the nature that his passionately hammering heart required.

The love of *Ballentine* – while she was a human – was so quiet – so unassuming – that those around 'him' would almost have assumed – had they bothered to consider – that passion – in any demonstrable sense – was non-existent in this diminutive – vague – young man.

The imperious – almost cruel – *Myramilla* – would have surprised many of 'her' so-called friends – not least herself – if she had given them a glimpse of her true depth of feeling regarding – not only the more delicate – nuanced expressions of erotic love – but also her delight in and devotion to many facets of the natural world – particularly those of a minuscule and delicate nature.

However – *Ballentine* – unbeknownst to his friends – had – for the last several months – been sharing his room – in the absence of a much desired lover – with an ever-increasing number of books – of an occult nature – pertaining to the control and manipulation of love – and it was under the pressure and burden of these volumes – as well as the thousands of sheets of diagrams and sketches from his own onanistic hand – on his bed – rather than the soft weight of the blankets – (or the sensual embrace of a lover) that he was kept far from warm at night.

His passions were volcanic – though – at present – dormant. *Ballentine* had – by now – gone far beyond the noble need for a companion to love and be loved by – he wished to possess love itself – to be loved by the essence of what resides in every living being.

Not for him the mere magical spell that would render some poor man or woman besotted with him – *Ballentine* wished to appropriate to himself – the love of the wheatsheaf for the light of the sun – the love of the star for the enveloping vacuity – the love of the dormouse for the warmth – itself a love for his lost mother – of his nest – as he begins his hibernation – the love of the stone for the constant – barely perceptible – weathering that will render it exactly as it needs to be – the mutual love flow between all bloods and hearts – *Ballentine* demanded to possess all these loves and to know them – beyond the limits of common intimacy – in an unending act of total solipsism – better were he to have become a second Narcissus than that his heart enter such a state of monstrosity.

He very nearly succeeded.

He was nothing if not enormously inventive – from the morass of manuscripts in – towards – his possession – he had devised a plan where all of love would be his.

Having kept his inherited wealth secret – he was now heading to a covert location where he had sequestered – at great expense – through his black-market operatives – a menagerie of nine animals – a *Female African Bush Elephant* – a *Friesian Stallion* – a *Harlequin Great Dane Bitch* – a *Male Short-Hair Apple Head Chihuahua* – a *Female Masai Giraffe* – a *Rhode Island Rooster* – a *Female Syrian Hamster* – a *Male Steadfast Tube-Nosed Fruit Bat* and a *Female Amethyst-Throated Sun-Angel Hummingbird*.

There was no doubting the beauty – the yearning – expressed in the chord.

He had come across it during his research – and – used in a proportionate way – the 9 notes would – of course – facilitate love in its passage toward the love of another.

But *Ballentine* had other notions – he had noted the frequency – in Hertz – of each note in the chord – what he would now achieve was the living stasis of the 9 hearts at his disposal such that the beats per minute of each animal's heart would forever correspond to the frequencies of each note in the chord.

The 9 animals were assembled in a vast enclosure in the most particular – enneagrammatic way.

Placed – in restraints – the humming bird and bat having just enough leeway in their movements to be able to still fly – at their 9 stations – the beings were then – in geometrically significant ways – accelerated towards and away from each other – their beastly antipathies being thus elicited and soothed – until their heart-beats per minute reached the target tempo.

For instance – as soon as the *Female African Bush Elephant's* heart reached 27.5 beats per minute – corresponding to an 'A' vibrating at 27.5 Hz – she was immediately etherically sealed and isolated – the 'A' continuing to vibrate around her to maintain her heartbeat at the desired rate – similarly with the *Friesian Stallion* when his heartbeat reached 43.6 beats per minute – corresponding to an 'F' vibrating at 43.6 Hz – the *Harlequin Great Dane* at 73.4 beats per minute ('D') – the *Male Short*

Hair Apple Head Chihuahua at 123.4 beats per minute ('B') – the *Female Masai Giraffe* at 195.9 beats per minute ('G') – the *Rhode Island Rooster* at 329.6 beats per minute ('E') – the *Female Syrian Hamster* at 523.2 beats per minute ('C') – the *Male Steadfast Tube-Nosed Fruit Bat* at 880 beats per minute ('A') and the – very distressed – *Female Amethyst-Throated Sun-Angel Hummingbird* at 1396.9 beats per minute ('F').

Ballentine then had the animals' hearts collectively connected via 9 stethoscopes to one amplifier – to which he would then spend several hours a day listening – at the same time as having the 9 notes of the chord played in exact – though displaced – rhythmic synchrony with the beating of each heart – that is he would hear the lowest 'A' played 27.5 times per hour – the highest 'F' played 1396.9 times an hour – and so on – thus ensuring a threefold imbibing and ingestion – the sound of the beating hearts – themselves conjoined with their corresponding frequencies – aligned with the playing of those frequencies at a $1/60^{th}$ displacement.

However – this was only the prelude to a later – and gross consumption.

The magic was beginning to work – though not in the way *Ballentine* was expecting – not that he knew anything about it – the essential integrity of the 9 note chord – which the animals could also hear – along with the forced rhythmic beating of the hearts as one polyrhythmic corpus was bringing the disparate souls of the animals together – they were ceasing to think of themselves so much as separate beings but rather beginning to chime as a unity – though a unity replete with shades and nuances of individuality not possible had they remained conscious only of the beating of their own hearts.

Ballentine had managed to convince himself that he was gradually becoming filled with a love as yet unknown – but this was a mere chimera – love always being primarily an imaginative endeavour before the possibility of its becoming deed – as it would later for *Ballentine*.

Nevertheless – he was sure that the feast with which he would conclude his occult experiment would consolidate these initially promising feelings that he thought he was feeling – a nine animal banquet of hearts.

The animals had now been placed – still living – within each other – the *Female Syrian Hamster* inside the *Female Amethyst-Throated Sun-Angel Hummingbird* inside the *Male Steadfast Tube-Nosed Fruit Bat* inside the *Male Short Hair Apple Head Chihuahua* inside the *Rhode Island Rooster* inside the *Harlequin Great Dane Bitch* inside the *Friesian Stallion* inside the *Female Masai Giraffe* inside the *Female African Bush Elephant* whose trunk was artfully and tenderly – though this was neither planned nor foreseen by *Ballentine* – holding the tail of the *Female Syrian Hamster*.

Not only this – but the animals had been arranged in such a way that their hearts were now forming – were one to observe from above – a pulsating spiral within the apparently composite beast as it lay before *Ballentine* on the huge table – the spiral casting a condition upon the skins and pelts of the animals that afforded them a transparency – allowing the hearts to be seen.

Up until now – *Ballentine* had had no reason to pay attention to the breathing of the animals – but now – just as he was preparing to cut into their conjoined flesh in order to consume the logarithmic hearts and – so he thought – enter into the rapturous realms of infinite self-love – the animals now began – though retaining their independent – though musically related heart beats – to breathe as one – and – as they grew more confident in their single breathing – their flesh gently undulating beneath the knife – their bodies began to fuse together – the various heads – limbs and wings emerging from the main elephantine body to render the great mass of nerve – muscle – mind – blood and will into one coherent – though of shimmering ninefold independent intelligence – being – its delicate four wings – balanced so that there were one bat and one humming bird wing on either side – lifting it slowly – the restraints being easily broken in the process – into the air – *Ballentine's* eyes rising in fear and disgust – he being – as yet – far from the capability of awe – as he dropped his knife and soiled himself.

There was not the least trace of anger or vengeance in the *Hamhumbachiroodastaraffphant* – it – rather than he – was brimming with love – though it knew what must be done.

Focussing its eighteen eyes on *Ballentine's* two – the *Hamhumbachiroodastaraffphant* – with immense concentration and benevolence – discarnated the young man – a moment later 'she' – as he now was – was to find herself reconstituted – her volcanic passions being – for the first time – released – as a great jet of air and mucus spurted from her blowholes – *Ballentine* had become the bearer of the greatest heart of all – a – rather lonely – female – example of – *Balaenoptera musculus* – thrashing her flukes in the Mediterranean waters – east of the isle of Kriti.

His future lover – *Myramilla Wollaston* – was – as the flukes touched the water – still lording it over her several suitors in *Bosworth*.

She would do this through an admixture of her brilliant wit – deployment of innuendo – native arrogance – unusual height of 7 ft 5 inches and the incisive projection of her rich contralto voice.

Myramilla had come to enjoy the mere play of love more than its enactment – she thrived on the attentions – the relative stammering – of her many admirers in comparison with her own dazzling eloquence and disdain of them – many opportunities for true communion and soul furtherance had presented themselves to

Myramilla – but she had spurned them in favour of the addictively anaemic self-love that she continued to nurture in her haughty isolation.

There was *Helioangelus Collins* – an acquaintance of hers – he would dress predominantly in green with a purple cravat at his neck – quick witted too – gorging on *Myramilla's* words to fuel his own – but the necessary depth that love would bring was scarce allowed to materialize.

There was *Paramita* – a blind friend from New Guinea – she – whose long protruding nose would give *Myramilla* endless material for mockery – would bring *Myramilla* exotic treats – *Malay Apple* – *Bukabuk* – *Mon* and *Kumu Musong* – leaving them as a love offering at her feet – she also had a little hammer that *Myramilla* – on occasion – would allow *Paramita* to playfully tap below her knee – giving *Paramita* at least a fraction of the response she craved.

There was *Mercedes the Orator* – something of *Myramilla's* equal in the rhetorical arts – his golden hair matching his golden tongue – *Mercedes* was also a master whistler – able to expand his cheeks to alarming proportions before embarking on melodies rivalling even his speech's eloquence – but *Myramilla* preferred to keep their relation one of tilting and jousting – besides – his flabby cheeks were – to her eyes – deeply and distressingly unattractive.

There was *Galileo Galilea* – his flaming red Mohican making his eyes seem all the more green – *Myramilla* had to admit that his way of strutting about did sometimes tempt her – though she would never have let him know – to a more involved relation – the fact of his being only 2 ft 10 inches tall only adding to his allure – but – impregnable as she was to any act of giving – particularly of herself – she would allow only the pleasure of picking him up and holding him by his hair while she looked seductively into his viridescent eyes.

There was *Carmel Strollkirk* – a Kenyan friend whose elongated neck fascinated *Myramilla* – he had had it tattooed with conflicting deities of various provenance which – *Myramilla* imagined – seemed in constant and animated antagonistic motion.

How she would have loved to kiss – to bite that neck – but – as *Carmel's* vanity of appearance exceeded even *Myramilla's* intellectual conceit – this was a pleasure she – sadly – forwent.

There was *Conan the Paterfamilias* – so called because of his way – when in company – of arrogating to himself the role of arbiter and authority – which – while preposterous in a tiny bald man who yapped rather than spoke – appealed to *Myramilla* as she could see that all of his persiflage was – pathetically – intended to impress her – so besotted was he.

But – as the attraction resided purely in *Myramilla's* toying with and manipulating of *Conan* – he was as wealthy as he was pompous – this was a resounding dead end – amorously speaking.

There was *Connie Lupin* – an actor of the *Commedia Dell'Arte* – she would specialize in the role of *Arlecchino* – a part bringing extra delight to the audience – and to *Myramilla* – due to *Connie's* great jutting jaw and the way she would bark with it – in response to *Il Dottore's* preposterous commands – *Myramilla* had something of a fetish for eighteenth century costume – and – while she watched *Connie* perform – her thoughts would wander into erotic territory as to what might transpire with *Arlecchino* on the stage of their own private comedy – though – unfortunately – once the greasepaint had been removed and normal attire resumed – *Connie* was – for *Myramilla* – just another big-chinned choleric girl.

There was *Equoia Kabbalus* – a young man who – in the attempt to seem enigmatic – wore only black – though this – in itself – was a kind of façade – as he was indeed of arcane and perplexing character – his pretence at pretension fooling everyone but *Myramilla* – who found him fascinating – though it was – rather than his savant-like learning and – deeply unfashionable – skill at the virginals – his cascading red hair from which she derived the most delight.

But they were both too fond of the play of mirrors to admit to the true vision of the other.

And there was *Loxton Afra Khan* – possibly the closest to come to initiating *Myramilla's* departure from the self-enclosure of her love-barren domains – though only in his late twenties – *Loxton* gave the appearance of someone wizened by life way before his time – long – drooping ears framing a face that was – apart from his absurdly protruberant two front teeth – almost reaching his chin – all nose – his absolute sincerity and unrehearsed charm often gave *Myramilla* pause for thought – especially as she had begun to tire of the ceaseless – and increasingly arid – game of flirtatious charades that her performance of friendship had become.

Yet all of these suitors truly loved – and were in love with – *Myramilla* – and it was during the course of one evening when their love took an unexpected turn.

Wine had been flowing – *Gewurztraminer Riesling* for the gentlemen – *Malbec* for the ladies – *Black Vodka* for those in between – when *Myramilla* suddenly – and quite out of character – proposed a toast –

'It was this morning when it came to me that I was the fountainhead – the *Keter* – the Crown – of the *Sefirotic Tree* of our little company – with you – *Loxton Afra Khan* – as the wisdom of *Chokmah* – you – *Mercedes the Orator* – as the understanding of *Binah* – you – *Paramita* – as the kindness of *Chesed* – you – *Carmel*

Strollkirk – as the discipline of *Gevurah* – you – *Equoia Kabbalus* – as the beauty of *Tiferet* – you – *Galileo Galilea* – as the victory of *Netzach* – you – *Helioangelus Collins* – as the splendour of *Hod* – you – *Connie Lupin* – as the foundation of *Yesod* – and you – *Conan the Paterfamilias* – as the kingship of *Malkuth* – and it seems to me that – were we to make love as one writhing – ecstatic – tenfold being – the *Ein Sof* could not help but to join in our consummation and apotheosis'.

The friends ceremoniously disrobed and begin to engage in an erotic interplay as if they had become a giant self-pleasuring cuttlefish – though the ink being produced was far from black.

But the *Ein Sof* had other plans – plans which had been directly and simultaneously communicated to the nine suitors – and not *Myramilla* – in a dream the night before.

As the suitors began their lovemaking – it soon became clear to *Myramilla* that not one of them was showing her the slightest interest – and that with every twinge of being disdained by those she had always – in varying degrees – spurned – *Myramilla* – imperceptibly at first – grew a little smaller – and soon she could not have embraced her friends – erotically or otherwise – even had she wished to – for she was also – as well as shrinking – transforming into a tiny winged being – and – when she opened her eyes again – after having closed them to fight back the tears – she found she was now the possessor of – not anyone else's heart – but instead – one of the smallest but smallest of hearts – that of a fairy fly – perched – as 'he' – as 'she' now was – on a date palm in the village of *El Andalus* near *Damannhour* – with a tiny harp – which he had no idea how to play but which he knew – if he were to ever find his way to a new life and mode of love – he must learn the knack of – hanging on an adjoining stalk.

The hot sweetness of the surrounding overripe dates merely sharpened Myramilla's sense of the wasted chances of fruition in his former – human – life.

But self-pity did not cling long to the wings of *Myramilla* as he flew across to inspect the harp – engraved as it was with the marvellous form of an impossible beast – strung – the nine strings were fashioned from the hairs of animals owned by her – now completely forgotten – friends – a hummingbird – a hamster – a bat – a rooster – two dogs – a horse – a giraffe and an elephant – ninefold and tuned to the following – ascending – sixths – (the lowest 'A' corresponding to the lowest 'A' of a grand piano – the highest 'F' to the highest 'F')

A – F – D – B – G – E – C – A – F –

but coupled with multiple octave frequencies so high as to be inaudible to the human ear.

All the unexpressed love of the universe was locked in the harp's barely existent threads.

Myramilla played an exploratory chord – the chord that begins the 2nd of *The Lampedephoria* – seven wanderers becoming temporarily blind as a consequence – though – apart from one – they were never to know the source of the light – three of them went on to compose vast exegeses detailing and attempting to explain what they took to be some kind of divine revelation – one of which became a seminal text in the birth of a new religion – though the best of what this new movement was to bring lay far in the future – heavily outweighed though it would be due to the concomitant misunderstanding and violence that this impulse also brought – two of them put the experience down to dehydration – one thought that he had detected a slight earth tremor moments before – which had possibly interfered with the geometry of the – relatively close – *Pyramids of Al Jizah* – thus altering the very nature of light itself – the three pyramids themselves being held in coherence – though for how long – considering the fact of light pollution – some scholars arguing that it was this – rather than a more general weathering and neglect – that was rendering the pyramids shadows of their former selves – only by the continual streaming of stellar magnanimity emanating from *Altinak* – *Alnilam* and *Mintaka* – the remaining wanderer putting it down to heat exhaustion – though she – being the sister of the former *Myramilla Wollaston* – alone knew the source of the light.

In any case – this cataclysmic release of the most meagre portion of the cosmos' unloved love – though unheeded by the majority – found its way immediately to *Ballentine's* giant heart – hence his low 'A' of response and – over the following days – *Myramilla* and *Ballentine* grew adept at finessing their communication so that it was – on a red morning off the coast of *Al Iskandariyah* that the two ripe lovers – whose alliance had been prepared so long ago – came together – *Ballentine* taking considerable risk not to find herself beached in these unfamiliar – relatively shallow – waters.

There *Myramilla* was – hovering in front of *Ballentine's* great left eye – engaged in a musical discourse of sublime tenderness and longing – had *Ballentine* had had tear ducts – happy the tears that would have flowed from such clarity of loving – though this exchange was but one of many in which the two lovers would indulge.

From time to time – *Ballentine* would swish her flukes in the sea – *Myramilla* fluttering some way off to catch the falling – rainbowed spray of shattered – spattered droplets in his wings – at another moment *Myramilla* would delight *Ballentine* by tickling around her double spiracles with his wings as she came up for air – but the most intimate relation they were to enjoy was the one for which they had been destined – the intertwining of hearts – this would begin with *Myramilla* entering one of *Ballentine's* spiracles – travelling down through her left atrium into – via the mitral valve – the left ventricle – on into the aorta and out into *Ballentine's* upper body – returning from the superior vena cava through the right atrium – on – through the tricuspid valve and – through the right ventricle – up into the pulmonary artery and back into the left lung – where – being gently exhaled by *Ballentine* through her spiracles – *Myramilla* would begin his circuit once more – but – this time – passing through *Ballentine's* right lung – and was *Ballentine's* voyage through the disparate waters of the Earth not akin to the path of *Myramilla* through her heart – did not *Gaia* exercise the same orchestration of her near infinite will in allowing *Ballentine* to pass so freely through her *water-as-blood*?

The exquisite sensations brought on by *Myramilla's* lemniscatory passage through her heart – *Ballentine's* by now superior consciousness had now enabled her to control the intricacy of her blood flow so as to protect her beloved on his cordial pilgrimage – and the delight ensuing from *Ballentine's* convoluted – altruistic – sanguinary calculations of care – resounded and rippled out – love-brimming – from the *Mediterranean* – not only through the surrounding aquatic – and on into landed space – but also backwards through time – becoming – in ways not yet easily understood – there being 11663999999 other acts of true love that must also play their part for the *Ultimate Primarial* to be – retroactively conceived – this particular one being the 7208352001[st] – the main impetus for the initial union of the *Ein Sof* within the *Shekinah* before the act of *Tzimtzum* – this deed being further deepened and facilitated by the infinitesimal blue whale swimming – unperceived – through the lungs and heart of *Myramilla*.

SOLALTERITY CHANGE!

You look to the sky...

'Does the entire meaning of the apple reside in *this*?'

The juror jumped – dropping the book – at the emphasis placed on the word 'this'.

'Would we sell our children – or our parents – to know the answer to such a question?

Objection!' –

The monk interrupted himself –

'Over-sustain!' – ruled the judge.

Until that moment – 2/7ths of the jury had been on the point of sleep – one – the 5-year old – in a hypnagogic fancy of the fool who – tied to a rapidly rotating windmill was – with one hand – waving a banner on which the words – 'JACTA NON ERBA' were inscribed and – with the other – tightly grasping a bunch of nettles – the other – the 89 year old – imagining the 5-year old standing on a chair – happily squeezing – with both hands – two over-ripe *Moyer* plums for the juice to drip into his dog's – a Newfoundland – mouth.

'Does not the purpose – the fruit – of the chartreuse veil of the woman in *alabaster-white* lie in the *possibility* of what it hides'? – continued the monk.

The fool had taken out his tiny hammer – he was – while the monk went on with his summing up – looking around the room for somewhere in particular.

The judge – rendered immobile by the shock of seeing the very implement of the mountain's destruction once more in the hand of the fool – continued his – now vacant – staring at the defendant.

In one swift motion – the fool leapt across the judgment hall – took hold of the left hand of the woman in *alabaster-white* – for she was his twin – and – pausing suddenly at a seemingly arbitrary point between the judge and the monk – tapped the air with his hammer.

There was a barely audible tinkling as the judge – the monk – the jury – the judgment hall – the legal quarter – and the palatial city all vanished – all that remained being the smouldering cradle – now grown to accommodate older passengers – in the crater where the jury had been.

Before the fool and the woman in *alabaster-white* climbed into the cradle – where a jinni was waiting to navigate them back towards a time and a space before their ancestors' origin – the fool said – as the woman in *alabaster-white* threw both the flowers and fruit of *lords-and-ladies lilies* into the air – from where they would take hours to fall – 'JACTA SANCTA ARUM'!

Not half an hour afterwards – the flowers still gently – infinitely – falling in the imagination of the boy – the girl and the wry snake came to the foot of the staircase – the girl – having smelt the unmistakable aroma – a scent of herring and jasmine – of her beloved's tears on the steps – being gripped by a blind panic.

Up the pair ran – and slithered – until they arrived at the boy-king's rooms – where he was nowhere to be found.

Before long – the boy found himself beneath the crossroads that the girl had – so sacrificially – attempted to break through. He had been led there by the light shining down through the absence in the road. As he walked towards the light – a great carriage – within which the closest members of his family were riding – was heading for the newly formed crater.

Clattering into the gap – the first of the eight *shire* horses fell straight onto the boy – killing him instantly – thus rendering the beloved of the girl forever trapped beneath the road near the centre of the crossroads.

What only the snake knew was what was inscribed – also altered – on the third side of each coin – *TACTUS ME IN VISO IACTUS NON EST MEUS TACTUS.*

The baker – who Her Majesty now paid the most cursory of attentions – patently irritated as she was by having to leave the world of story in which she had been so fully immersed a moment ago – was so far beneath the King and Queen's personal concern that neither of them had noted – to their ultimate cost – the five – curious – and extremely subtle – star-like markings – forming an arc – made by the baker's birthmark above his glabella.

Each of these five 'stars' has recently – this very morning – begun to shine – the purchase of the five royal children being what has initiated their radiancy.

The Queen – obsessed with keeping her youth – not through any kind of vanity – but rather through a conflation of fear – her own mother had died young – and love – for her children – had – clandestinely – purchased the magical belt from the baker – the proceeds of which sale had gone towards the obtaining of the apple for the King – who – nurturing a secret hatred of his children – he had always suspected his wife of sharing his bed with another – had prepared an elaborate ruse whereby the Queen would be told that her children had been kidnapped by the giant lambs so feared in the east of the land.

By such means – the King and Queen – following the sharing of the apple – would – remaining forever young – return to the imagined and blissful state of yore.

The baker – however – having foreseen this entire state of affairs and – having fallen in love with the Queen precisely because of the great distance in their respective stations – had failed to inform the King of the apple's amnesic properties.

So it was that – whilst grieving for the loss of her children and – the following day – partaking of the apple – the Queen – immediately forgetting the identity of the King – who – entirely ignorant of his own – and the Queen's nature – was in a state of total – and eventually fatal – perplexity – saw – in the same moment – his moral turpitude writ large in his raisin black eyes.

It was not long – the former King being detained in the asylum – before the baker and the former Queen had – having left the palace in the dead of a midsummer night – set up home together – she taking on his five children with such devotion that many in the – far distant – village – assumed she was their actual mother.

The two thrones remain empty to this day.

As the last delicate – fingernail paring of the sun sank beneath the horizon – and the giantess placed the book back on her bedside table – the first of the dwarves took his flaming torch and waded into the water towards the caravel.

Not half an hour later – his dead – chaste body found itself washed up on the shore – the still flaming torch – mockingly – plunged into his barren groin.

The second and third husbands met similar fates and the fourth was far from cocksure as he climbed up the ladder on to the deck of the caravel.

The udders of the giant *Chianina* cow that he met there were tight and full and a moment later he was sucking at her teats with all the vigour of a calf.

It was due to this ravenous preoccupation that he did not see the scythe separating his head from his body as his last gulp of milk found its way – not into his belly – but onto the deck where it splashed – forming the shape of a key.

Grooms five to eight did not notice the key-like stain and so failed to find what it represented but the ninth – as the time approached 3 am – came closest yet.

Interpreting the stain as – as well as a key – a map of the caravel – the 9th husband also noted that the minutest part of it was gleaming. Taking this gleam for the golden key – the husband climbed the main mast and searched the crow's nest – but to no avail – (though he did find a most wondrous example of scrimshaw – one that would prove pivotal to another's destiny – a piece of walrus tusk – carved – along with an image of a lioness mating with a lion – with the inscription – 'JACTUS NON ACIT MEUM NISI SEMEN ET LEA' – as – temporary – consolation) – for the 'map' was not of the caravel – but – as the eleventh husband ascertained – of the giantess in *sea-salt white* herself.

The dwarf encountered the smiling giantess on the – custom made – bed in the captain's cabin.

He reverently – as she opened her thighs – approached her – apart from a lavish besmearing with ambergris from a beluga whale – naked body – which was now – due to the joy she was deriving from her husband's reverence and her anticipation at his 'finding the golden key' – growing ever larger – and thrust his head into her *cavernous ardour-harbour-arbour* where – like a *Palawan bearded-boar* after truffles – after much rummaging with his nose and tongue – he was able to find the golden key.

However – before the eleventh husband was able to extricate himself from the giantess' capaciousness – she – already undergoing the most exquisite – orgasmic contractions – had convulsed the dwarf's entire body – boots and all – into her uterus – where he would be dissolved and reabsorbed into her fallopian tubes – for it was always the intention – and had always been the secret methodology of every giantess' consummation on her wedding night – that her successful husband would himself become the sperm for his own prince or princess' conception – the key – like all keys – proving to be nothing more than a ruse – although it did explain why the fruit of such union would unfailingly be born with a golden key in its tiny mouth.

As she puts the book back in its place on the bookshelf – the shepherdess' parrots – *deroptyus accipitrinus* – serving her in lieu of sheepdogs – her sheep cowed into obedience by their unfailing strangeness – also unfurl their fans – though not in anger – whilst mimicking the generic sounds of both swan and deer – for the amusement of the young ghost.

After several days – the shepherdess has managed to create a tableau in glass that will ensure the warmth of the family's hearts on each occasion of its perusal.

The sculptured tableau shows the dead swan – represented in full maturity – in eigengrau black – in the gesture of observing an egg – upon which she has recently come to the end of brooding – the egg is hatching – and from it are now emerging the wood-sprite's wife – the stag and – in V-formation – her twelve siblings – in colours of – *deep sky blue* – *palatinate blue* – *mahogany brown* – *light sea green* – *malachite* – *magenta* – *orange peel* – *persian rose* – *veronica purple* – *scarlet* – *aureolin yellow* and *French violet*.

It is on the bridge – overlooking the river of fire – that the shepherdess unveils the – precariously balanced – tableau – thus facilitating a moving reunion – of sorts – of the family with the cygnet of *eigengrau* black.

Whether the approach of the cuckolded wood-sprite is unseen due to the company's absorption in the glasswork – it is hard to determine – though – in any case – it is at some point during such reverie that the wood-sprite –

having pushed his way past his hated wife and her lover – brings his hand down – (though how much more would the wood-sprite have wished to obliterate the entire – living – prismatic progeny of his adulterous wife) – smashing the tableau – briefly – therefore – in the process – rekindling all of the tumult and loss felt at the true cygnet's original – broken birth.

However – unforeseen by the cuckolded wood-sprite – and – indeed – all present – is the effect of such violence.

The ghost of the fragments now begins to decant – from this second shattering – into the form of a young doe – one with beating heart and human face – and it is now that an unspoken bond is formed between the stag and the wood-sprite – for she is the perfect likeness of the shepherdess.

You close the book and hand it back to the tailor.

Suddenly – you find yourself within the flag – and are amused – and only a little perturbed – to note that you have become an animate line-drawing. You follow the others into the temple where you are to listen to a double concerto for cello and piano which – partly by setting the following two poems – one in Latin – (you are grateful to see that there is a translation in the programme that the arc-welder has just given to you) – one in English –

PATERA NOSCE, QUI ES IN COEPIS, SANNIO TE FICTOR.
NOMISMA TUUM ADVENA REGNUM TUUM.
FETURAT VOLUPTAS TUA SICCUS IN CELATA.
ET INTER ALIA.
PALUS NOSCITUM COTIS ANTRUM DEA NOBIS HODIE.
ET DIMENSIO NOBILIS DEBILITO NOTUS.
SECURUS ET NOS DIMETE DEBETE NIGRESCO.
ET NEMUS INDUBIUS IN TENACITAS OMEN.
SEDATIO LIBERALITER NOS AMATORIUS.

Know the bowl, who you are in the beginning, you are the maker of a panacea.
Your coin is a stranger to your kingdom.
Your pleasure spawns in a hidden temperature.
And among other things.
A marsh, known to us today as the cave goddess of the grindstone.
And the noble dimension is known to the weakened.
We must feel safe and darken.
And the wood is an unambiguous omen for tenacity.
Calming us freely and lovingly.

Time – though it pass – shall not speed
While we – by our love – are freed
From all notions of the hour
Constrained not by its brief power.

Stars rising – merely – each day
Over love's sphere have no sway
Thorns planted in this short life's stony ground
Will soon – as roses – be found.

– will – you are assured by the tailor – make every aspect of the stories in which you have recently been so invested crystal clear.

❧ As Roses Be Found – A Yew Marriage of Looking Deeply

As an encore it seems there is to be a performance of the 5th book of *The Lampedephoria*.

However – as you have reached the 5th hole – you will now –

as a way of marking the centre of your endeavours – have the privilege of experiencing this music from the hands of *The Lampedephorian* himself!

He approaches – unfurls his left palm and shows you there what appears to be a small stone. He then begins to – as it were – open and unfold the stone in a series of gestures which results in a mechanism barely conceivable in its negation of ordinary dimensionality.

'The interplay and dynamics between the thirteen senses is a hard thing to display in visual form.

Even after all these years – I remain unsure how to interpret what appears from within the stone – once a day I allow its contents to extend – the resultant proliferations always being slightly different – accompanied by one of 32 different birds – look at today's! –

- it was - indeed - just this constellation of differences - and the varying songs of the birds accompanying them - that elicited the inspiration - (or at least - part of the initial impetus - much of the remainder being the undergoing - or undertaking - of the most intense - rigorous and expansive temporal lobe epileptic experiences - prefaced - as they often were with an equally intense - though much more generally beneficent - if not ecstatic - aura and a scintillating geometric light-show usually more common from a migraine - these states - and their partnered - though temporally displaced - states - those of myocardial infarction - undergone as if they were a Gabriel initiated

heart cleansing and reconstitution - composed - years later as Lampedephoria 0 - parts 1 and 2)

❦ The Lampedephoria 0 - Parts 1 and 2

- for my beginning the composition of *The Lampedephoria* - though that - in itself - took me in new directions concerning what I now refer to as *The Names of Life* - 288 *meteorontological* qualities - (plus 300 or so of the most so-called common words) - that permutate in myriad ways in order to capture - temporarily - and - if not in *all* their subtlety - then at least a good proportion - the names of the many states that we inhabit throughout the day.

Yes - the thirteen senses are a curious entity' -

(Again - the brutal gust of wind - again the sensation of a presence - and a face - though this time accompanied by the awareness - but registered where? - of a boundless intelligence - love *and* a - seeming - disdain)

'And one can only' – continued the *Lampedephorian* – as you try to regain your composure – 'occasionally – glimpse a glimmer of the impulses behind what the jellyfish were attempting – through the rarest ardour and devotion – in their fashioning of us.'

Edencanter begins to recite – once the threshold spirits have descended and spoken –

ET REPA SING I LEMA TORA IED

- the 5TH of *THE SEXTAINS OF VITALIA FREEBORN* - after which *The Lampedephorian* begins to play -

5

Froibern schysm - miintians tyrn olano
Ontar firost - ni-unu craus - 'yld men' ynthrynu
Sapplamant helu riyts wondarir
Davodi ynythar stryngar - piss - cehuru - rucyr
Braykdawn - yoirs erasong - friobern's chungud
Borraors' ushys corru myenteans yxchungad

FREEEEEEEEEEEEEEEEEEEEEEEEEEBOOOOOOOORN SCHiiiiiiiSM –
Mooooooooooooooooooooooouu̇NTaaaiiiiiiiiiiiiiiiiiiiNS Tuuuuuuuuuuuuuuuuuuuuuu̇RN
aaaLooooȯNeee

EEENTeeeeeeeeeeeeeR FooReeeeeeeeeeeeST – Nooooo-ooooooooNeee CRiiiiiiiieeeeeS –
'oooooLD MaaaaaaaaaaaaaN' eeeeeNTHRooooooooooooooooNeee

Suuuuuuuuuuuuuuuuuuuuuuu̇PPLeeeeeMeeeeeeeeeeeeNT HoooooooȯLyyyyyyyyyyyyy
RoooooooTS WaaaNDeeeeeeeeeeeeeeeeeeeeeeReeeeeeeeeeeeeeeeeeeeeeR

Diiiiiiiiiiiii̇ViiiDeeeeeeeeeeeee aaaaaNooTHeeeeeeeeR STRaaaNGeeeeeeeeR – PaaaSS –
CooooooooooooȯHeeeReeeeeeeeeeeeee – ReeeeeCuuuuuR

BReeeaaaaaaaaaaaaaaaaaaaaaaaaKDoooooWN – yyyyyeeeeeaaaaaaaaaaaaaaaRS aaRiiii-
iSiiiiiiiiiiiiiNG – FREEEEEEEEEEEEBOOOOOOOOOOOOOORN'S CHaaaaaaaaN-
GeeeeeD

BaaaaaaaaaaaaaaaaaaaaaaRRiiiiieeeeeRS' aaaaaaaaSHeeeeeeeeS
Caaaaaaaaaaaaaaaaaaaaaa RRyyyyyyyyyyyy MoooooooooooooooooooooouuuuuNTaaiiiiiii-
iNS eeeeeeeeeeeeeeeeeeeeeXCHaaaaaNGeeeD

FREEBORN schism – mountains turn alone
Enter forest – no-one cries – 'old man' enthrone
Supplement holy roots wanderer
Divide another stranger – pass – cohere – recur
Breakdown – years arising – FREEBORN's changed
Barriers' ashes carry mountains exchanged

❦ The Lampedephoria: Book 5

The Very Reverend Obadiah Lution – with the most bewildered – dazed expression – somnambulantly strikes the ball down the nave of the Cathedral and you find yourselves – (you – in particular are unexpectedly at a loss to have regained your usual physical form – being a line-drawing – you note for future reflection – had brought many aspects of your becoming into view which have now – once more – receded) – after *Edencanter* has – firstly – played a piano piece for you – (it is a joy to see how he uses 8 of his hands to play the keyboard – while using the remaining 5 to carry on his much-neglected lacework) – one that follows the course of a seeker on his search – following with a song in which a lover – on a very different – though not unrelated expedition – singing from an impossible ontological distance – pleads with someone – who – we intuit – must at least strive to match her in heart and longing – to follow her – wherever she whirls and wanders in her endless dance –

❦ The Sick Rose: Interlude & 11 – In search of the missing ox / Come and daunce with me

– back at the clubhouse.

'his fool would need daunce with me...and then cheerefully...being very modest and freendly... and so plentifull variety of good fare I haue very sildome seene...'

'... nor plurality...'

Edencanter approaches *The Very Reverend Lution* and – having rippled his fingers in the air – like a magician – towards the **PAX IMMEMORIAL** –

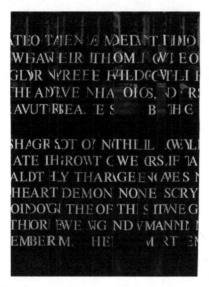

– (whose present offering mourns how rare it is for one to interpret courageous waywardness towards future endeavours regarding enhanced cordiality) – asks – in rapid succession –

'Have you seen – to the point of pained retina – the snail's light – absorbed its unheard silence? Have you partaken something of the relation between dome – cube – sense and switheral? Have your hearts beaten ninefold in true love's sympathy? Have you seen the impossible unfolding of the stone?'

He replies – 'Look – my tattered dog-collar *shows* I have!'

'Who'd have thought so much was still possible amidst the companionship and resonance of the diatonic?' – you say – 'Let's play the 7th!'

Just before a sudden and oppressive heat strikes you and the cleric as the ball pings off the dome of the *Atik Mosque* in *Ghadames – Libya* – you are able to – with the help of *Edencanter's* commentary – commune with the dark-pink rose –

❦ A Rose is on Fire: 6

'The Kyivian jellyfish-cupolas as the *sowwunnd of CONVOOULSSIVE EXPERINS* – a golf-ball and a dome *being absented to a presence on ðeirr oðr siede* – any evolution being akin to the condition of how it is to *seeme permænentlye on the point of exploashionn* – the Archimedean solids liquefying in one's consciousness into – at least at first – proliferating others - *ðe quadrupl towwresz of migrn and kckaðowlicism and epilepsy and music and eroticks* only the beginnings – just as clouds' commingling tend to Π – *phi* – *e* – *i* – *and ðer layering* – the true experience of clown as *you feel as ðoghe youre entir being werre about to crack in two* – the Lampedephorian showing that 147 is possible in any discourse! – and has not *Elba Loivni* personified how to *oppen ANY and ALL locks – simmplie by ckallculating which copye of a copie of ðe ORIGINAL key to use.*'

This impact initiates an exchange between the ball and the dome – both have – though keeping their initial size – imbibed the other's form – and it is a tiny dome that lies at the *Reverend's* feet – and a large – dimpled ball that sits atop the mosque.

At the foot of the mosque are a man and a woman – they are playing chess – and it is now – what with the sudden change in climate and culture – that you reconsider – once again – the following familiar sentiment...

You have always been someone – along with many others – who has lived their life half suspecting that they may be – either – dreaming – or – part of someone else's dream.

However - what will – henceforth – remain out of reach is precisely this lifelong act of suspicion – now that you have – indeed – fully awoken to your true life – that of an ebony bishop on a chessboard of slate and stone.

You – or at least your soul – (you are – to all intents and purposes – inanimate) – had dozed off – the apparency of the entirety of your life having taken place during your nap – during a particularly long state of stalemate during a game played by a King and Queen – both of whom are of indeterminate gender and intent.

THE GREAT TREMOR

There has been scarcely any topic of – telepathic – communication amongst the chess pieces other than this expectation of quake and utter change – the moment you wake you become immediately reattuned to it.

This – and the rumour of a *THIRD QUEEN* who will soon make her appearance known – appearing – as she must – on a 65th square – itself a result of the long-awaited tremor.

She – so it is said – will be in labour when she appears – though what manner of offspring she is to bear – and the identity of its father – remains a point of contention.

There has been discontent across the board for some time – the knights – on both sides – have been deep in discussion and arcane research as to how they might have actual representation in the game – rather than have agency only through what bucks and rears beneath them.

At least three of the bishops – you remain steadfast – are riven with questions of faith and orientation – while a quarter of rooks is – privately – planning to essay moves – in addition to what is usually permitted to them – in both knights' and bishop's manner – thus – they hope – usurping all Royal edict and majesty – initiating a new line of corvid dominion and potency.

The Quartet of Their Royal Majesties – meanwhile – so obsessed – so fulfilled as they have become since their – secret – assignations – convened solely for the singing of madrigals – are soon to renounce their thrones – and the entire charade of opposition – entirely.

Only the pawns remain content – impassive. But not for much longer.

The tremor – though - as yet – imperceptible – has begun.

A tiny fissure has appeared beneath one of the ivory knights – an unintended side-effect of his – near successful – attempt to emerge – in full armour – out of the body of his mount.

A second crack has widened enough to worry the bishop who caused it – her vacillation between a monotheistic standpoint and a – quite possibly – godless – acceptance of *clinamen* as the most valid way of life has proved too much for the board to bear.

The perfectly tuned natural fifths of their madrigal majesties' voices – at the end of a piece espousing notions of humanity as a moment of *phi* between stone and angel – have also played their part in the – now palpable – quaking of the board.

'RECEIVE NOTHING

IT IS THE IMAGINATION THAT PROVES SALVIFIC

DO – THEREFORE – GIVE EVERYTHING!'

This utterance of one of the ebony rooks proves the decisive gesture – as if it were a globe whereupon the poles had suddenly reversed their respective magnetism – the board now finds itself in related tumult – many pieces are smashed during the impact of the tremor – though moments later the originally square board is now – peaceably – comprised of four – precisely segmented – pieces – 2 trapezia and 2 triangles.

Five of the pawns - ignoring - (and thunder-stealing the impulse of the rooks) - all known rules of the game - begin - by their illicit movements - to reassemble the board - but into different proportions - until it is now - (the other remaining pieces bowing to their inferiors' intuition and industry - it not being long before all is as it was before - [those fatally wounded having resurrected] - the sole difference being the appearance - despite there being - apparently - exactly the same number of squares as before the tremor - of a 65th square - occupied by a heavily pregnant - piebald Queen) - a rectangle of 13x5 squares -

- all memory of its former shape having been expunged by the breaking of the 3rd Queen's waters - the board is awash in exquisitely shaded ripples and rivulets of red - blue and purple - the voice of the Queen - the longed-for 5th voice to all previous royal madrigals - a penetrating contralto - harbinger of her mysterious - soon to be uttered - uterine fruit.

But what is it – this child of an inconceivable Queen – borne on an impossible square?

A *raven-headed – naked – apart from boots – mystical – crenelated – six-winged-centaur-monarch-of-the-infinite-mind* – fully grown – flies out from the third Queen's birth-canal – causing an even greater quake – and temporary dissolution of the board – though this time – when the pawns have reconstituted it – there are now 63 squares – and no Kings! – (though who will claim the right to command the 3 bridging – threshold squares between the 2 provinces of The Thirty?)

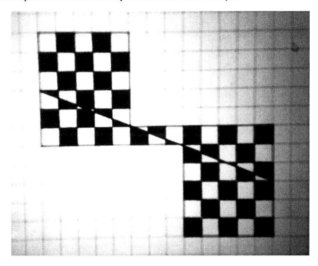

The shock of all this sends you into a quasi-seizure from which you quickly recover – without any memory of your life as a chess piece – and with an ass branchlet growing out of your glabella.

You come to – encountering a much confused – and – surprise to say – concerned – *Very Reverend Lution* – while walking through a field – at the centre of which is a conical hill – around which – you dimly make out – a bird is circling. Arriving at the foot of the hill – and looking up – you see that the bird – a grouse – has only one wing.

Also – about a third of the way up the hill are two hooded figures – one of them is rootling about in a nest while the other – looking on – is holding a large – square – chequered – wooden board – and a velvet carryall.

Their hoods – one is red – one green – are embroidered with distended representations of dice – snakes – ladders and chess pieces.

The red-hooded figure raises her hand from the nest and displays to you and her accomplice a perfectly formed cubic egg.

Both figures then beckon you to follow them to the top of the hill – where awaits a table – also 'chequered' – not with squares – but with ellipses – a camping stove – three chairs – 2 pianos – the first played by a *Barometz* – the piano has – thoughtfully – been placed within easy reach of its leafy forelimbs – the second – played by *Buraq* – and a pipe organ – the bellows of which are being tended by the *Hare of the Buddha* – as it lends them the breath of life with its great feet – it also continues to pound – in a miraculous mortar – the rarest of herbs and precious minerals towards the creation of a soul-saving elixir which no-one will gather that they need or are able to drink.

The organist – the winged dragon – *Unageing-aging KairoKronos* – (he had – as a *kronos-angelickalle* – had wings – and impulses – of different formation – earlier in his life) – will – in the music he provides – spin *NECESSITY's* endless yarn into the world. If the game is played in precisely the right spirit – then one more of the multitude of eggs from which the world will be born will be laid.

After hard-boiling the egg – the green-hooded figure calls up to the grouse –

'O grouse of the pinnacle

With habits so finical

Sacrifice – rabbinical

One score plus one – clinical –

Drops of your blood'

With these words – the grouse – (the two hooded-figures – appearing – to her – as two of her own poults – the ensuing self-sacrifice only proving possible due to the sole-winged grouse's being held by the invisible embrace of the spirit of the remorseful *Parzival*) – pecking at its own breast – lets fall the required fluid –

the red-hooded figure swiftly – and dextrously – twisting the cubed egg in such a way that the 21 drops of blood are now distributed upon its surface so as to make a fully functional die.

As the green-hooded figure begins to arrange the pieces from the velvet carryall in preparation for a game – the red-hooded figure speaks to you –

'In a churchyard – near a farm – not far from the forest where *Parzival* shot off the wing of the bird – (not – as was thought – killing it) – that circles ceaselessly above us – there was a labyrinthine fairy ring – within which unusually lush – green grass was known to grow. Beneath the grass thrived plump – industrious worms.

Often – and only to be seen within the ring – a great – red cock would – after rain – thrum his beak on the ground – in search of these tiny – nutritious serpents.

Had anyone had the foresight – the memory – they would – from the top of the belfry – have ascertained that the path taken by the cock was peculiarly systematic – the traces of which are – so it is said – inscribed on the flags of a highly unusual golf course situated somewhere near the so-called *River of Five*.

Now – I – as parish priest – going by the name of *Father Simon* – (here *The Reverend Lution* looks at his shoes) – happened to harbour two passions – weird – perhaps even nefarious in their own right – but – when brought into combination – downright heinous.

Since my novitiate days – I had been intrigued by the world of religious unica – that is – objects with a connection to spiritual matters of which there were only one – or that were part of a discrete group – the stone – that Jesus refused to cast – the lots – cast by the soldiers – for Jesus' garments – the door – of the ark – that held the hope of a new beginning – the rope – that tethered the donkey that brought Jesus to Jerusalem – one of the nets the disciples left – to follow Jesus – the skull – of the largest boar that was part of the herd of swine sent to its doom by Jesus as a result of its possession by demons – the cockscomb – of the cock that crew to Peter the memory of the prophecy of his denial – light – in a lead bottle – once exuded from the star of Bethlehem – the intended capstone – unlaid – of the tower of Babel – the baleine – of the whale that swallowed Jonah – the rope – with which Judas assuaged his – questionable – guilt – the penny – hub of the exchange between Jesus and the high priests – emblazoned with the image and superscription of Cæsar – the garment – with which Shem and Japheth covered their father's nakedness – a phial of blood – once part of a river – from which the Egyptians were loath to drink - a portion of the wall – the writing on which Daniel interpreted – bearing the word – TEKEL – the manger – wherein Jesus was lain – the linen cloth – still bearing his scent – left behind by the young man who – after holding onto Jesus – fled naked – the caul – in which John the Baptist was born – the coals – miraculously still warm – over which were cooked the fish shared by Jesus and his disciples on the shores of the sea of Tiberias – a wing-bone – of one of the turtledoves sacrificed at Jesus' presentation at the temple – the basin – used by Jesus for the washing of his disciples' feet – the page – from the book of the prophet Isaiah – from which Jesus read on the Sabbath – the sweet spices – unused – that Mary Magdalene – Mary the mother of James and Salome brought to the sepulchre – an hourglass – containing sand – upon which Jesus partly doodled – the veil – rent at the moment of Jesus' expiration – the boat – from which Jesus helped the disciples to catch 153 fish after his resurrection – an ear – of Sabbath corn – plucked by a disciple – the long – white garment – worn by the young man sitting in the sepulchre – the remainder of honeycomb – of which Jesus partly ate after his resurrection – the skeleton – of one of the two fishes – from which Jesus produced a feast for the multitude – a fragment – of the inscribed wood – placed above Jesus' cross – faintly bearing the letter 'I' – the hook – that caught the fish – caught by Peter – that bore the coin to be used as tribute money by Jesus – the silver cup – later the grail – put into Benjamin's sack – the writing table – on which Zacharias wrote – 'His name is John' – a fragment of the stone tablet – on which was written the 2nd commandment – now bearing only the word – 'image' – a thorn – from the first rose to have bloomed in the potter's field – after it was renamed – 'the field of blood' – the cloth – with which Pilate dried his hands – one of the two mites – that the widow gave as an offering – the leathern girdle – still bearing his scent – of John the Baptist – the bed – that was taken up and walked with – one of the stones – on which Jacob slept – dreaming of ladders and angels – the alabaster jar – from which Mary anointed the feet of Jesus – a phial of the adrenalin – brought forth by the first of the shepherds on witnessing the angel – the sword – that severed Malchus' ear – the pitcher – borne by the man the two disciples followed – a hair – from the tail of the colt whereon no man sat before Jesus' riding of it into Jerusalem – the chains – plucked asunder by the Gadarene – one of the stones – itself part of the pillow of Jacob – that Jesus refused to turn to bread in the wilderness – the seventh veil – still bearing her scent – of Herodias – a seed – from the last fruit of the fig tree before its withering – one of the pieces of silver – which have their place in our redemption – the sponge – that enabled Jesus' ultimate cry – but none of these things were what drove my insatiability.

We know – from the gospels – about the blood – spit – sweat and tears of Jesus – but what is not mentioned – not even apocryphally – is another issue – one that occurred – in adolescence – between Jesus and the disciple whom he loved.

This was what I sought.

SOLALTERITY CHANGE!

You look to the sky...

Underground knowledge had come to me that such a thing - currently held by a former cardinal - now disgraced - gone to seed - and in penury - had become available for purchase.

The cardinal - now a *Mr Nett* - had set an asking price of £153,000,000.

This amount being obviously far beyond the reach of a provincial parish priest - I began to make dubious use of a resource first discovered during my deacon-hood - this one - my second great passion - being of an occult nature.

Now - one of my parishioners - a *Ms Trentidenari* - was a stock-market trader - and the two of us had become close - and wealthy - associates - due to my - apparently - precognitive sense of the twists and turns of the financial weather.

Knowing the dire state of the church - *Ms Trentidenari* had taken my words at face value - that I was drawing on God's guidance to raise much needed funds for the restoration of the organ - the rood screen and much else besides.

However - one Sunday morning - *Ms Trentidenari's* perspective would be radically and unalterably skewed.

It had become something of a habit for the two of us to convene - after mass - in the vestry - where - over glasses of out-of-date altar wine - we would plot our next fiscal deeds.

On this particular morning - while I went off to search for a replacement bottle - *Ms Trentidenari* - not normally one to even glance at - let alone touch a book - stepped over to the bookcase where there were the usual parish leaflets - various versions of the Catechism and an anthology of papal encyclicals - and began to browse - God knows why - a copy of Thomas a Kempis' 'The Imitation of Christ."

'As I eased the book from its place' - continued the green-hooded figure - 'I heard a dull thud from behind the shelf.

Peering down - behind the books - and seeing that another - thicker tome had slipped down - I reached for it - and - immediately aware of its great age and significance - began carefully to peruse it.

It was a decrepit manuscript - the intricacies of its pictorial and verbal content contrasting jarringly with its tattered casing.

What I did not realize was that a mere glancing at the forms - let alone the text of the book - without due preparation - was enough to initiate - however distortedly - magical happenings.

So it was that the red cock - both contrary to its usual habit - and twice as large as it ought to have been – entered the vestry – pecking at the dusty fragments of un-consecrated communion wafer.

Neither I – who had just returned with more wine – nor *Fr. Simon* – had ever seen such a large cock – not in our wildest dreams.

Not only that – but the cock – as it made its way into the main body of the church – was growing yet bigger – pecking at the votive candles as it went – causing mayhem amongst the lingering ladies – who – until now – had been busy with their rosaries – their litanies and their devotions.

At that moment – the organ began to play – though there was no-one there to play it – initiating a mist's descent upon the altar – which – a moment later – dispersed to reveal the garden of Gethsemane – where a choir of spiritual beings were singing the Macrocosmic Our Father – in a protective arc around the tormented Christ.

After we had witnessed The Christ's eventual relinquishment of his spirit – at which point the salvific one's face – turned to the left – became imprinted on the very marble that would later be used for a spectacular Pieta that would be sculpted – though the hidden face of The Christ would remain so – in Rome –

- a second mist descended upon the scene.

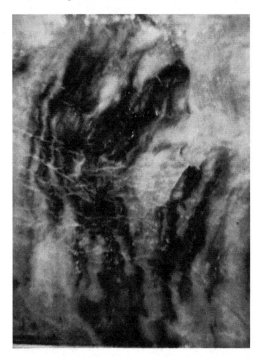

Emergent within the mist were two great statues – *The Statue of Liberty* and – of equal size – a statue of *Uncle Sam* – with the following words –

THE UNITED STATES OF AMERICA

hovering in the sky above them.

However – the statues differed from their usual form and function in that the torch of Lady Liberty had become a great phallus from out of which were constantly spurting stars.

She then began thrusting the tumescence into her own head – which itself had now become a *wealthy-sheath-wreath.*

Her breasts had begun to emit red and white lightning before becoming mouths which ravenously proceeded to devour Uncle Sam.

As we watched – the letters began to slip out of place – gradually forming a new skywriting –

TH UN   D   ER

TITS EAT SAM

I ACE FOE

A great hummingbird – the resurrected *Huitzilopochtli* – then emerged from the vulvic head of Lady Liberty – the seven rays of her crown becoming the 14 wings by which *Huitzilopochtli* would fly across the land wreaking apocalyptic devastation upon all those of solely European blood'.

'The mist's sudden clearance found us somewhat disoriented' – continued Fr. Simon – 'not least because the red cock had swollen to enormous proportions.

As it lurched toward us – like the dinosaur it still was – we had neither time nor the requisite muscle-tone to avoid being gathered into its great maw.

Just before being gulped down – I thought I could discern – in the roof of the cock's mouth – a kind of engraving in its tissue which was – I felt – trying to tell me something – though what that particular thing was – I was too trammelled to discern' –

'Strangely – at the same moment' – said Ms Trentidenari – 'I imagined – or suspected I imagined – an impossible imprinting at more or less the same spot –

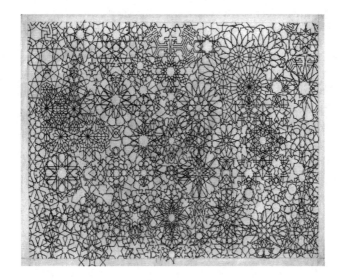

The path down the cock's gullet was odd – and once in the belly of the fowl – it became apparent that we had arrived at the gates of Hell.

Samael – actually – he had *your* face' – said Ms Trentidenari – looking at *The Very Reverend Obadiah Lution* – 'was there to greet us. Bowing – with consummate grace – he said

"Fr Simon – Ms Trentidenari – welcome!

It has become glaringly evident over the course of your squandered lives that your choice of eternal dwelling should prove to be nowhere other than where you find yourselves today.

There may still be the remotest of chances that you may be excreted out of the cock's anus while it is still large enough for you to pass through – ever smaller and tighter as it must later ultimately become.

Nevertheless – before the undead Christ arrives to agonize with Satan – we will take the time we have been allotted to examine the parlous states of your respective souls.

What we may see here –

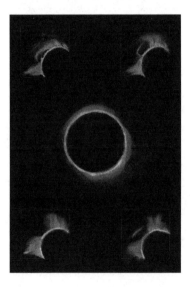

is a spirit – *your* spirit – Fr Simon – well on the way to a state of total infarction. The four surrounding images show the perplexed efflorescences of an altruism seeking to escape the confines of a view of life drenched – and this is what makes it all the *more* sad – *Fr Simon* – not just in materialism – but in a *spiritual* materialism – not only that – but a spiritual materialism dependent – for its capital – on matter that – without its spiritual context – would otherwise be entirely without value.

Now – Ms Trentidenari – these two images –

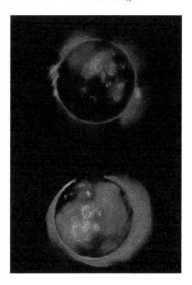

derived five years apart – show the steady advancement of a virulent – though entirely self-determined – cancer of the spirit – due – primarily – to your denial – through your word and deed – of its existence.

Like a dog barking at the postman – you thought that – by your bluster and your 'reasoning' – you could make nagging questions of a – for want of a better word – 'metaphysical' – nature – go away.

(Look! – the hubris of the dog! – how sings his pride each day – he thinks his bark succeeds!)

Like the postman – they would have gone away anyway – regardless of your barking – bearing – to others – their myriad messages – demands and greetings. It would have served you better to open – perhaps even to read – the occasional 'letters' addressed to you that managed to be delivered – rather than worrying them to tatters.

What we see here – however –

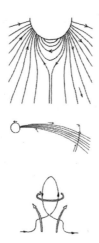

is a – somewhat idealized – picture of a thriving soul.

What is experienced is received – imbibed to the very depths of *meteorontological solarity* – before being offered – lovingly – back to the world – a portion of such mediated wealth also being placed – as it were – in full view of the soul – before being gathered for further mastication and nourishment. The fruits of such measured and profound digestion are – at length – similarly distributed to the wider world.

Indeed – the 2nd of these three diagrams models – for us – something of this beauteous dynamic.

If we imagine the six arcs raying out from the soul as the six notes – F – E – D – C – B – A – (heard as a beautifully spaced chord of sevenths) – themselves representative of the willing – loving heart – then it is only when they meet another human spirit that their 'I' justifiably may resound – if a thriving communion is approached through such a meeting.

In the 3rd image – we glean that for rotation of the thinking heart to continue – if not to – at its outer reaches – accelerate – while whirling ever more slowly at its centre – then the concomitant soul forces must seek allowance to be permitted to come and go with both passionate and acquiescent relinquishment – for unless our hearts tend toward a pulsation of the golden mean – then a binary fibrillation will set them – stonelike – towards a leaden unbeating.

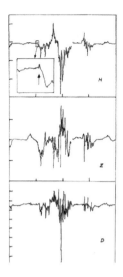

If you would like to cast your attention to the present image –

you will discern – the feeling life – H for HEART – by its horizontal intensity – the thinking life – Z for ZEAL – by its vertical vibrancy – and the willing life – D for DEED – by its declination.

As can be seen – *Fr Simon* – whenever one undergoes a disproportionate increase in one's thinking life – the vibrancy of both one's feeling and willing lives plummets.

Ms Trentidenari – the lower diagram shows the pulse of your compassion. We can see that there have been periods in your life – and before – when this attribute has been – though perhaps in rather too vacillatory a manner – operative. For the last 11 years or so – it has been in a state of utter dormancy.

It does you some credit – at least – due to the fundamentality of your deeply held materialism – that you have been able to go on existing at all!

The actual tearing of the soul's fabric that will – Fr Simon – in all likelihood – lead to spiritual arrest – may be seen here –

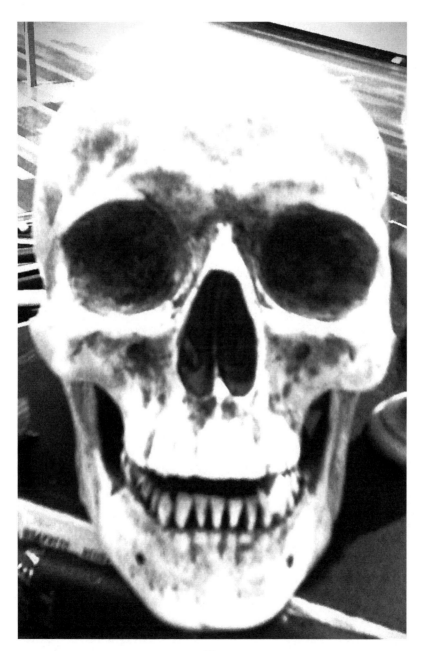

The figure above shows the failure of the thirteen necessary perplexities of the soul to properly and geometrically interlock – while retaining their mandatory mystification.

In a healthy soul – (above) – the densities of experience are borne in such a way that they find their way to the soul's centre in stresses and motions equally distributed from among the many contributing spheres of life.

Thus – such weights may become – after the various – necessary – interior cogitations and perturbations – a levity – as they are offered – through one's living – back to the world.

This subsequent – ludic – out-spiralling gesture is caught – though often imperceptibly – by the world – as a delight and a dignity.

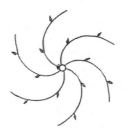

(You should know that these various images of your souls that we have been examining have been clandestinely obtained by an elemental striking of your spirits – [see resonating sphere below] – thus setting forth oscillations which – after first being perceived musically – are then – by a kind of supersensible auscultation – rendered into visual form – the further hope inherent in such procedures being that when one or more large gongs – amongst other instruments – are struck in such a way as to resonate precisely with the forms manifest from within your own diseased souls – then there may be brought into being a sympathetic resonance whereby your spiritual ills could be – if not fully healed – then – at least – rendered malleable for reformation.)

If we posit a soul as inhabiting the space enclosed by the dotted rectangle –

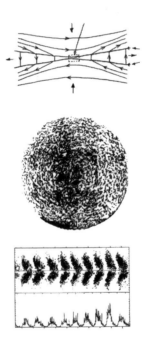

- then we can imagine the forces inherent in such a soul gently - but demonstrably - repelling the curving densities of the - sometimes detrimental - exigencies of fate - these repulsions defining - after all - the very form - not only of the soul in question - but also - of the world - which the soul - by such resistances - is constantly modulating.

Thus - the soul - as seen in the top left of our diagram below - in a condition of near total dissolution can - after musical and other restorations - as well as being vigilantly - though not fully rationally - engaged in the artful receiving and - later - decanting of such experiences - become such as that pictured - top right.

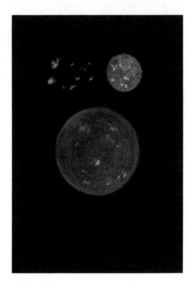

Unlike the heart's - the soul's pulsations ought to aspire to the curious butterfly form - seen in more detail here -

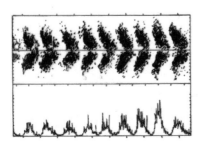

    - though an even fuller rendition of the content of such oscillation might be rendered as seen above.

    Once the soul - through manifold deeds of great - and tender - love and compassion - reaches the *Assisi Rotation Number* of approximately 4181 - it takes on a gently shimmering manifestation - noted by various birds - who will often gather and perch on the arms and shoulders of the bearer of such a soul -

It is as though the birds are able to hear the particular soul's vibration – which sounds to them like a greatly distended birdsong – never yet heard – but strangely familiar to them – a song – though different in material – similar in nature both to the feather of the *Simurgh* that they will soon – (at some point in the past – future – or absolute present) – fly in search of – and also to the reed – plucked from the reed-bed by one who – having heard of how their journey has unfolded – will sing a song which will widen all pan-temporal searching and seekers –

❦ The Confluence of the Birds

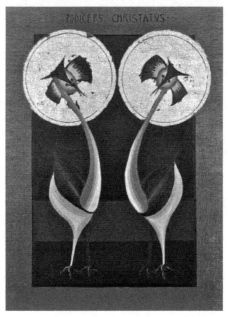

The soul rendered here is that of Francis at the moment of his embracing of the leper –

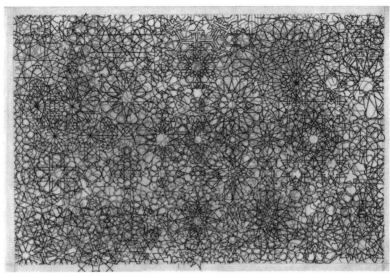

- with this being the soul of the leper at the same moment –

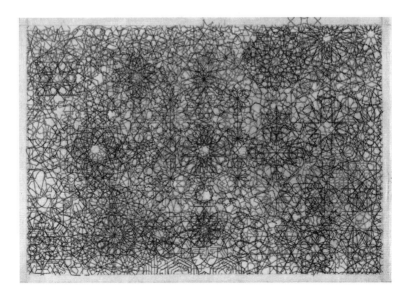

- after which Francis and the leper lay down in the sun – hand in hand – as 2 jackdaws tread from torso to torso – stopped in their tracks only by the *apine-stigmatic* beginning to gather around the saint – their 'speech' possibly construed as follows –

coelis erunt ex tenere columba protendere alas a respire os et in alia re sanguinus spira cere ipse verum transiens per mea deum

the heavens will be from – holding a dove to stretch out its wings from the breath mouth and – in another matter – the spiral of blood-wax itself – the truth passing through my god

Finally – if we consider the dotted arc –

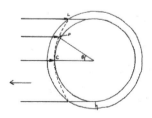

- which we see subtending the interior of the soul-sphere - representing the trajectory of impassioned Love - L - to considered - though still - in the final instance - necessarily impulsive Compassion - C - then we may observe that the angle - θ - implied by such a trajectory - leads us - by extension - to a point - P - Presentiment - marking the meeting point between Love as it is encountered or expressed at the threshold of world and soul and Compassion as it is engendered at the interstitial point between soul and the apophatic core.

We are to intuit - through such observations - that Presentiment is not only an inkling of what may be about to occur - but may also serve as an indicator that the special trajectory potential between Love and Compassion is in the throes of enactment and that heed should be paid not only to this upcoming - ongoing deed - but to what may and - perhaps - must follow.

You will note that - while we have been deliberating your respective soul conditions - the belly of the cock where this has been taking place has - and not as I intended - widened and transformed to become a pastoral landscape - and it is here - in fact - over there - at the top of that hill - that you must play the game of - *Échecs, Échelles, Échappe!*"

At this point' - continued Ms Trentidenari - 'Samael gave me the following leaflet - explaining its rules.'

She passes you the leaflet -

Échecs – Échelles – Échappe!

Instructions

As can be seen in the illustrations – the game takes place on a chequered board of 144 squares – on which are placed 21 snakes and 8 ladders (the number of snakes and ladders – always numbers of the Fibonacci series – and their position and size – varies from board to board – and is determined – through choice and chance – by the players).

Each player plays with 21 pawns – 13 rooks – 8 knights – 5 bishops – 3 queens – two kings – and 1 counter.

To begin – player 1 rolls a die.

If a 1 or 2 is rolled – then she is to make a Snakes and Ladders move with her counter.

If a 3 or 4 is rolled – then she is to make a Chess move.

If a 5 or 6 is rolled – then no move is permitted.

Player 2 then rolls the die and makes (or does not make) his move.

The game ends when a player has – either – reached 144 with their counter – or – when they have put the 2nd King in checkmate.

(The 1st King to be put into checkmate leaves the board)

(Various subtle modifications to the rules may need to be employed by the players – as the game unfolds – to ensure proper flow.)

In terms of musical accompaniment – the players may choose to follow the indications given below – or to play in silence.

A1	B2	C3	D4	E5	F6	G7	A8	B9	C10	D11	E12
C24	B23	A22	G21	F20	E19	D18	C17	B16	A15	G14	F13
D25	E26	F27	G28	A29	B30	C31	D32	E33	F34	G35	A36
F48	E47	D46	C45	B44	A43	G42	F41	E40	D39	C38	B37
—	—	—	—	G49	B51	C52	A50	—	—	—	—
—	—	—	—	—	—	—	—	—	—	—	—
—	—	—	—	—	—	—	—	—	—	—	—
—	—	—	—	A50	C52	B51	G49	—	—	—	—
B37	C38	D39	E40	F41	G42	A43	B44	C45	D46	E47	F48
A36	G35	F34	E33	D32	C31	B30	A29	G28	F27	E26	D25
F13	G14	A15	B16	C17	D18	E19	F20	G21	A22	B23	C24
E12	D11	C10	B9	A8	G7	F6	E5	D4	C3	B2	A1

At the beginning of alternate minutes – 2 pianos – one designated 'white' – the other 'black' – shall play all the notes (the white notes of the piano – numbered left to right) upon which the opposing Chess pieces stand.

In the meantime – the pianos shall play the designated notes or chords initiated by the movement of both the Chess pieces and the Snakes and Ladders counters as they pass through – or merely touch each square.

An organ – throughout – will hold the notes of the squares on which all the extant pieces are standing when they are at rest.

SOLALTERITY CHANGE!

You look to the sky...

'*Samael* also explained that we were to play the game without cease – only pausing when the die – having to be fashioned from the cubic egg of the *Gillygaloo* – became unusable – which was frequently – at which point we were to seek another – being sure to collect both the pieces and the board on our scramble back down the hill.

We were to know when our future soul-fate was to be determined when a stranger arrived bearing – sprouting from his or her glabella – one of the 1008 branchlets of the ass of the apocalypse'.

You sit yourself at the spare chair – the *hare* – the *steed* – the *dragon* and the *lamb* beginning a musical accompaniment at once – and the combatants begin to play.

From the outset – you are startled by the weeping – laughter and generally effusive – sentimental behaviour of the priest and the trader as they manipulate their pieces.

It seems that they – in a long-denied spirit of sympathy – are projecting entire domains of emotional content into each move that they make.

You notice – on the table – through the mediation of your glabella ass-branchlet – something hidden from the view of the priest and the trader – a tiny chronometer bearing the number 107,999 – and you immediately understand that you are – by your presence – being privileged with the witnessing of their final game.

Their utter involvement in the drama unfolding before them – the tragic clattering down the ladder just as the end was – for the nth time – in sight – the unexpected – and swift – demise of the bishop just as he was growing more confident – due to his – conceited – grasp of his situation regarding his importance to the Queen – he had wrongly assumed that her knights – (in truth – the Queen – having grown tired – and – what is worse – bored – of the insufferable haughtiness combined with false modesty exuded by this pitiable eunuch – had not even deigned to assign the merest pawn in his service) – had been commanded – by Her Majesty – to stand by him with an absolute fealty during his many sweeping assignations across the kingdom – the wistful – longing and sadness of the pawn – not only was he in love with an unreachable knight – how he would have loved just to have become – and remained his squire! – his peasant father would never – even had he not squandered the little produce that they had been allowed to keep from the land in exchange for ill-gotten spirits – have given assent to the outlay of capital for such a calling – but the beloved knight was on the opposing side! – both his and his horse's skin of the most exquisite ebony black – how he wished the sun – which had been missing for the last 295 years – would burn and brand him to an equal hue – the irony being that – of course – the knight – in their many battles – had always sought – in the heat of their – unfortunately – entirely martial – exchange – a glance of the young pawn – envying him – in turn – his ivory – if not sickly – pallor – and the way he would – ineptly – grasp his flanged mace.

How he longed for an end to this endlessly wearying war – to lie in the grass – the sun shining once more – peeling a hard-boiled egg to share with his love – both before and after the long balancing of needless pain with venereal pleasures.

It occurs to you that it perhaps would not be unwelcome to be transmogrified into an *Échecs, Échelles, Échappe!* piece so that you – too – may leave your own – unsatisfying – world – and try your hand – and other parts of you – in a land soon to be – forever – free of conflict...

The die is on its last legs – though on this occasion it is not through the wear and tear of the game – the egg is hatching – and from the shards of the cube emerge a man and a woman – it is *Fr Simon* and *Ms Trentidenari* – they are – as if sleepwalking – making their way onto the board – taking the places of the remaining *White Queen* and *Black King* – in exact replication of their size – proportion and material – respectively (the originals of these pieces you place in your pocket).

The previous *Fr Simon* and *Ms Trentidenari* – at the very moment of their avatars becoming Their Majesties – become mist – and a moment later have evaporated – their sublimation coinciding with an angel's gaze – it is the angel – from whom you rejected the lyre – which – in their total lack of compromise or guile – gazes all temporal life clean out of you –

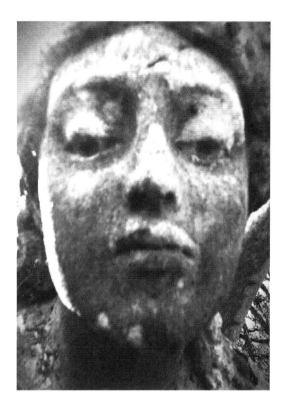

     - while the landscape has become a mediæval mystery setting – it is Hell – immediately as it is to be harrowed –

💗 *Kiss – Hang and Bloom: 2* – The Harrowing of Hell

     You regain a sense of self-possession once more – after the harp and sul ponticello strings have told of the unbearable sadness of the inability of *Keter* –

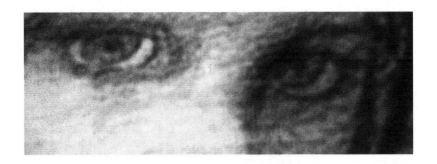

to find *The Shekinah* –

– but what is happening to your feet? – they are delighting in a moist squelching – proceeding almost by their own agency – through a mire – consisting of a blend of honey – cream and snowdrop and rose petals – the petals seeming party to some mode of streamlining – some vortical path whereby they descry – amongst their various species – a kind of message which – though out of your reach – does indeed – like a sediment – you worry instantly whether such sediment will leave the delicate coral of your soul intact and thriving – contribute to the further nurturing of your being – the fairly ordinary suburban park becomes full of mountains – all previous sense of scale entirely confounded and replaced with a scene of Alpine magnificence and sublimity.

However – as your eyes grow accustomed to the vastness of your surroundings – you notice that the mountains – some of which seem almost too tall to be held in one's mind – are not mountains but giants – and that they are beginning to sing – it is a song – in fact a round in its form – almost like an Elizabethan catch or drinking song – replete with jocosity – they are playing a game while they sing – or bawl – perhaps they are indeed drunk – they are throwing great rocks at each other – though – as one of these 'stones' falls nearby – you see that it is a mosque – and you now understand that the giants are pelting each other with places of worship and sanctity – there! – the *Harmanda Sahib* is being flung – there! – the *Ujigami* shrine is being pitched in response – now one of the giants has caught *Canterbury Cathedral* just thrown at her – she is tearing out the crypt and throwing it at her neighbour – who responds with a hurl of the – nearby – *Princes Road Synagogue* – though strangely – you notice as the synagogue falls to the earth – it does not shatter but instead becomes animate – scurrying around the park in a similar frolicsome spirit to the way in which it was thrown – there! – the *Udvada Atash Behram* – in which still burns the fire breathed into being by the *Ultimate-Primarial* – is capering to meet the *Celestial Master Palace* – several buildings are now clambering over each other like irrepressible piglets – though some of the places of worship are now engaging in more developed interaction – *Wells Cathedral* has climbed astride *York Minster* and is now – as it thrusts its west door to and fro – lustily riding its spire with – judging from the sounds of the organ within – immense and gratifying pleasure – while behind them – *St Basil's Cathedral* seems – as it contorts its various domes and towers in and out of its various apertures – to be having an intimately fine time delighting itself – and – as you turn your head – you see that the park is now crammed full of religious architecture in various states of intense play – running the gamut from childlike capering – including a wonderful game of leapfrog – The *Potala Palace* vaulting the – much revivified – *Parthenon* – the *Shwedagon Pagoda* springing over the *Bahai Lotus Temple* – the splashing of its 9 ponds bringing a welcome freshness to the mire which – you now notice – you have been drinking as you wade – to the most intricate and abandoned manifestations of erotic romp and revel – it is extraordinary how agile these architectural beings have now become – every tower – dome – turret and buttress – capable of the most delicate flexing and acts of considered touch and intimacy – each internal pillar now a finely-toned muscle – taut and ready to spring in participation in a new game – and – there – in the distance – stand a group of castles – conscious – bereft – flaccid – kicking their heels – scowling – impotent.

You find that you have left the mire – which now – as you look at it – is an ordinary pond and that – all around – are the sounds and sights of the suburban park once more – there are a bunch of children – not present before your entering the mire – wrestling and throwing tufts of grass at each other.

Waiting for you at the edge of the pond is a curious character – his name is – *FURROW-wood-PASSION* – he is strobing between immense youth and cramped decrepitude.

He leaps into your midst – tickling you under your chins – in your armpits – eyes twinkling – teeth gleaming – twirling a gold-ferruled ebony cane – now he collapses onto the cane – teeth fallen – tinkling – to the floor – hair turned instantly grey – now he's up once more – performing a stately bourrée – his hair reddish brown – teeth regrown – his eyes both comic and grave – saying –

'There are those that seek eternal youth – there are those that would wish the end of life before it has truly begun – I have sought – and partially found – both ends of it with equal ardour – and pass my days being flung from each to each – not without joy – and not without sadness.'

Old again – he staggers away – scooping – with difficulty - apparent mud from the mire and drinking it before – young again – cartwheeling off and out of sight – as you look around and see that you are – once again – at the foot of the mosque – your clerical friend scratching his head as to whether to strike the 'dome' or the 'ball'.

As a way of answering to this serious dilemma – you ascend the steps of the muezzin –

– where you are greeted – if that's the word – by the last remaining enfolded knight –

- part bird – part warrior – (though now mostly warrior – though one involved substantially more with the greater jihad than with any campaign in the so-called world at large) – she – straight away – presents you with a question – 'Do you know the present location of *The 16 – Actual – Bloodly Transubstantiations of Body – Flesh and Nerve not Spirit?*'

Despite the armour – you are unperturbed – though you are surprised to hear yourself say – 'Yes.'

'Oh! Thank goodness! – the last I knew was that they were being suspended in the lights of *The Uralsk Chandelier* – where are they now?'

'I only know that I will come upon them soon' – you say.

'I fully understand. When you have come to the 16th of them – please give this protean dish to the one who is need of it – it will be clear who to give it to by the kind of metal it has become at the given time.

Also – and I will understand if you choose not to – please would you consider allowing my friend to accompany you – she has not so much as smiled – rather her face seems permanently contorted into an objectless innuendo – since the disappearance of *The 16 – Actual – Bloodly Transubstantiations of Body – Flesh and Nerve not Spirit?'*

'Of course!' – you say – as the – painfully shy friend – her name is *Nova Nopu – Dr of Tarts – the deadpan panhandler* – (this moniker stemming from her mendicant practice these many years) – the only friend – of the enfolded knight – comes out from behind a bookshelf to join you.

The enfolded knight now opens a door – which leads on to a further set of stairs that you and your new acquaintance now begin to climb –

– and you are almost not surprised to see the *Reverend Lution's* ball bouncing – upwards – past you on the steps – with the cleric joyously running after it – like a child – exclaiming – 'Look! – The levity! The levity!' – before hopping from one leg to the other at the top – (the *deadpan panhandler's* not raising a smile notwithstanding) – his ball has fallen into the hole and *Edencanter* is there ready with the flag (and their recitation) for you to study – though this flag exhibits no writing –

And all ðis tyyme on aypes and man alike –

Ðe moone erupting consciousness did stryicke! –

Shouw a chimp its fetal forme – not recogniz its forelife swarm.

Ðeese faullted analgies – foole vauwnted torne apolgies fromn the universe for lacke and wannt of meaningg!

The roade of resttrainntte may leade to ðe hovel of idioscye!

Not pærente but transparennte.

      Language as esscentiælle rythm of eckxperientce – whatt consctituetes its harmonye and cowunterpoint?

Oh! To be a – mayle hippohckampus ingns fuscs brevceps abdominæliss histricx bargjibænnti hippocampus!

      Conceive the almanack to youwr own universe!

*Donn't block your**self**!!! ðere's a whole world employed to do ðat!*

      Ðe freshlly cut hedge – ðe Lampedephoria – delights of boð dependnt on how you choos to enter – to sense.

      An uncle of yours – a somewhat tragicke figur – inntenndingge to say 'As ðe crowe flies' – sayes – 'As ðe cry flows.' Ðis moves you deeaplye.

A streamme of language as to arrow fiere its precison ambiguitiesze while speacker bowes to unknoawe ðir end point shuddearingge.

      Shall we slænder the oak plænter?

      *Alwayyes to allow ÐE IMAGINAYTIONN complete abandonn so as to tempr ACCKTION – whilstte realizszinnge ðat imadgienation IS actshion – and of suche a kinde ðat may – on occasion – **calle** for TEMPRANS!*

There is a man – of unusually pure heart – he is having his blood partially redirected to the castle so that all who have dealings with what the structure represents will remember not to neglect their own spiritual crenelations and battlements – and – as you follow – with your finger – the path – the vessel – marked 13 – he turns – and takes – from the black armband around his left arm – a card which he now presents to you –

ꝺ Do not mind the hermit's silliness – it is a pace
of potentiality and eccentripetalfugal force –

AUCTORITAS AUCTUS AUCUPO AUDACIA AUDIENS

(a dorian rose...)

Three hermits are about their business – or desisting from it – one sits and thinks – (and – although knotted – the distribution and fall of these tetherings does suggest a productivity towards the ludicrous) – he is imagining – or communing with – two further characterizations – one is standing on stilts that open onto an unknown spiralling – should the hermit (choose to?) fall – the other whirls – (it is now that you begin to hear the hermits' music) – in a manner exactly reflective of the card's indication.

Nova Nopu – Dr of Tarts – the deadpan panhandler lets out the most extraordinary bellow! – no! – it is the bull in the flag – from within whose dewlap you trace the 14th – two-horned – line – releasing a further card –

isn't equilibrium just :
the sun -
free of the immortal ?

XIV

Two justices – their balances tilting – is the ship on which they are sailing leering slightly in the knowledge that the sun is entirely timely? – are those eggs in their scales? – two of the four pregnant with a task that – even now – shows its weight – its purport?

The threads supporting the scales now become the strings of an orchestra – the black and white undulation evoking a piano – as you listen to a music of great spaciousness – necessarily so in order for you to acquiesce to the notions expressed on the card regarding equilibria – solarity and presence – though you cannot but help recalling – during the music – a favoured childhood thought-play concerning the heavier of – either – a tonne of gold – a tonne of feathers of the *Simurgh* – or a tonne of light as yet un-reflected in its necessary moon –

❦ Isn't equilibrium just: the sun – free of the immortal? –

AUFERO AUGEO AURIFER AUSCULTATIO

(a willow communion of mindfulness…)

Plucking the flag from the castle beneath the head of the bull – *Nova Nopu – Dr of Tarts – the deadpan panhandler* – traces – with its opposite end – the 15th – crescent – path – thus alerting the workman in the turret – who now walks into the castle – with you – the cleric and the doctor following – in order to play *Book 6* of *The Lampedephoria* – and it is true – you reflect after being given the 15th card at the end of the performance – how contrapuntal this music offers itself to become to those with ears to listen – despite the apparent lack of the more usual indications towards fugal writing within the music's fabric… – though this is to pre-empt!

Firstly – the three of you find much to discuss in the contents of the card – (the *Reverend Lution* begins by pointing out the continua between ploughs and chariots – *Nova Nopu – Dr of Tarts* pitching in on what might be the distinctions living in the horses' hearts and minds depending on their owners' vehicles – your contribution being to point out that such delicate considerations and compassions with respect to the equine state would lead to pivotal developments in farmer – charioteer – or monarch towards changes to be wrought in each of their karmic trajectories – *Edencanter* rightly reminding you all that it is in the mutability of the vehicle – be it body – mind – profession or community that lies the predominant wisdom of the card's apophthegm) - secondly - the vacuity of the music of the previous card is now contrasted by a music that might pass as an exemplar of what it is to establish rootedness - constancy and zeal -

❦ How fugal is the chariot that prepares the human soil -

AUFERO AUGEO AUREUS AURICULA

(time lapse audiograph of tree rooting...)

Thirdly - the flag begins - (though not before *Edencanter* sings to you three songs - the first - as a series of questions as to who we might be - and where we might then choose to partake of being *from* - once our humble origin is not only gathered in but practiced forth - the second an admission of the necessity of the web of apparent - but later to be melted - contraries that we must spin and caper upon - both as feast and as foe - and as silk and as space between its forming - the third - a lesson in sacrifice - or rather how it needn't be - each following its own nature - all interpretation being just shadow play and belief - dependent on the light - given or controlled) -

❦ The Sick Rose: 12 - 13 & 14 - The Lamb/Kiss - Hang and Bloom/The Black Berry

to disperse its music -

❧ Flag Music: 6

The LAMPEDEPHORIAN Threshold spirits –

ET REPA SING I LEMAS ORIED
SUB IPA SING I LEMA SORIED

SOLALTERITY CHANGE!

You look to the sky...

- and the 6ᵀᴴ of the SEXTAINS of VITALIA FREEBORN –

6

Yppesutos feri luguc's vulluo's sinsi
Friybarn's yas foirs dremetuc pynushmont's cindelancu
Uaus teot – clior – desgast – ne qyastuun whu
Gy fonulli – mieth shiduws doncur – chenga sho
Piontang iwokyns fraybirn's cheld – sibjyct
Wynts naw nin-ibjuctevu sliupors – lavy – dyrict

OooooooooooooooooooooooPPooSiiiiiiiiiiiiiiiiiiiiiiTeeeeeeeeeeeeeeeeeeeeeS FiiiiiReeeeeeee
LoooGiiiiiiiiiC'S VaaLLeeeeeeeyyyyyyyyyyyyyyyyyyyyyyy'S
SeeeeeeeeNSeeeee
FREEEEEEBOOOOORN'S yyyeeeeeeeeeeeeeeS –
fffeeeeeeeeeeeeeeeeeeeeeeeaaaaaR'S DRaaMaaaaaaaaTiiiiiiiiiiiiiiC
PuuuuuNiiiSHMeeeeeeeeNT'S
CoooNDoooooooooooooLeeeeeNCeeeeeeeeeeeeeeeeeeeee
EeeeeyyeeS TaaauuuuuuuuuT – CLeeeeeeeeeeeeeeeeeeeeeaaaaaaaaaaaaaaaR – DiiiiiiiS-
GuuuuuuuuuuuuuuST – Nooooooooooooo
QuuueeeeeSTiiiiiiiioooooN WHyyyyyyyyyyyyyyyyyyyyyy
Gooooo FiiiiiNaaaaaaaaLLyyyyyyyyyyyyyyyyyyyyy –
MooooooooooooooooooooooouuTH SHaaaaaaaaaDoooooooooooooWS
DaaaNCeeeR – CHaaaaaNGeeeeeeeeeeeeeeeeeeeee SHyyy
PaaaiiiiiiiiiiiiNTiiiiiiiiiiiiiiiiiiiiiiiNG aaaaaWaaaaaKeeNS FREEBORN'S
CHiiiiiLD – SuuuuuuBJeeeCT
WaaNTS NooooooooooooooooooooooW NooN-
ooooooooooooooBJeeeeeeeeCTiiiiiiiiiiiiiiiVee SLeeeeeeeeeeeeeeeeeePeeeeeRS –
LiiiVeeeeeeeeeeeeeeeeeeeeee
DiiiiiiiiReeeeeeeeeeeeeCT

Opposites fire logic's valley's sense
FREEBORN's yes – fear's dramatic punishment's condolence
Eyes taut – clear – disgust – no question why
Go finally – mouth shadows dancer – change shy
Painting awakens FREEBORN's child – subject
Wants now non-objective sleepers – live direct

As you approach the clubhouse – someone is floating towards you – 'It is the unfolded lady!' – says *Nova Nopu – Dr of Tarts* – 'She may have news of the enfolded knight.'

You ask the unfolded lady whether there was anything else that the enfolded knight said –

- but her only response is to turn slightly away – though – as you turn your back on the lady – she calls to you – insisting that you do not turn to face her – and says –

'You know – it *was* hope that was in the jar – but only as Pandora read it – S P E S. She did not realize that the other letters had been worn away – the A – the I – and the N –

which – when you reinsert them – give – SAPIENS – understanding – or – the rational.

Although – in fact – neither hope – *nor* understanding – at least of the rational kind – was what was left in the container – the original letters had been A – I – N – a transliteration from the Arabic – AIN – عين – meaning – eye – or fountain – or sun – the other 4 letters having been interposed by unseen hands.

Make of this what you will – but I maintain that it is understanding – vision – magnanimity and perspicacity which have been left in the vessel – (these qualities never far from being shown by the brother-in-law of Pandora –

– Prometheus' concentration was extraordinary – as long as he was able to focus on the method of the eagle – in its attempt – eventually successful – to find – and tear out – his liver – (it was incredible how the eagle could never remember which organ it was looking for – each time the same search – sometimes it would gouge out other parts of Prometheus' body – which – as the liver – and its regenerative capability – was the eagle's sole intention – would also – on the back of such intention – grow back – though not – perhaps – as Prometheus would have wished) – wherever it may be – which – ironically – explains the enfolded knight's – and my – lack of hope – (though not lack of its imagining – or will – to it.)

If you find such a vessel – remove the lid at once! – be – in the meantime – as watchful as the blackbird as to where – or who – such a vessel may be –

· *if* you think that humanity is capable of withstanding the full flowering of these qualities.

If you do see her again' – says the unfolded lady before floating away – 'take hold – on my behalf – of her indescribably beautiful left hand – though it will not – as you see it – match the peerless state of repose in which I left it after I had taken her to a place – outside of all armour – all dissemblance – before my needlessly – I now realize – sudden departure.'

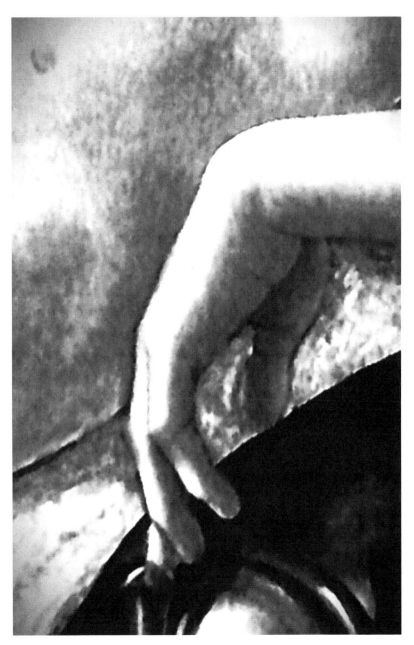

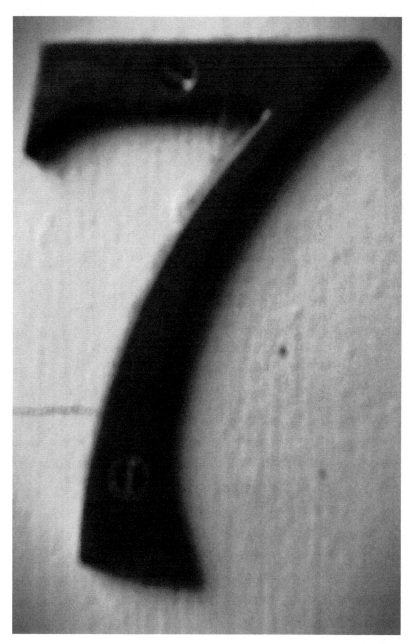

'so light was my heeles...in such bountifull and liberal sort – during my
continuaunce...'

'... neither the coming...'

Edencanter asks the three of you –

'Have you been witness to the foundational tending towards the spiral? – been spectators to a dispersed escape? – taken receipt of a perforated platter? – as well as of further insight towards a box's content?' – though the words of the **PAX IMMEMORIAL** – true to their own imperative – have blown you a little off *Edencanter's* wavelength –

- as you are invited to consider the value – if not the need – in greeting all that the world – as feeling – brings – however ephemeral – however ostensibly permanent).

Nova Nopu's eyes – by way of answer – begin to whirl in their sockets – vainly trying to free themselves in search of wider orbits – as she reveals her perforated heart – bereft – and so full – of hope – fountain – sun and I.

The Reverend lines up his ball – striking it particularly cleanly –

and as it ricochets between *Khufu – Khafre and Minkaure* for what seems like hours – (tracing – in the air – though invisible to human eyes – whether spinning or in stasis – the most satisfying kinked – almost straight lines which – over the duration of the ball's ping-ponging – leave – for all time – a webbed testimony to the architecture's broader design) – *Edencanter's* words draw you – once more – into the rarefied regions and reasons of the rose –

As ball becomes dome becomes ball – new ways to a reflection – *Ðe moone erupting consciousness did stryicke! –*

Language – whether of the unexpected 3rd Queen or her even

more unaccountable progeny – as esscentiælle rythm of eckxperientce – does the very possibility of the 65th – and 63rd square – *consctituete its harmonye and cowunterpoint?*

Hell is not ever having the thought to be a *mayle hippohckampus ingns fuscs brevceps abdominæliss histricx bargjibænnti hippocampus!*

And the youngold man in the mire is the one able to *conceive* the almanack to his own universe!

Go tell both the enfolded knight and the unfolded lady – *Donn't block your-self!!! ðere's a whole world employed to do ðat!*

Ðe freshlly cut hedge – ðe Lampedephoria – delights of boð dependnt on how you choos to enter – to sense – the meaning of any dish – any grail.

Alwayyes to allow ÐE IMAGINAYTIONN complete abandonn so as to tempr *ACCKTION –* SPES! *– whilstte realizszinnge ðat imadgienation IS actshion –* AIN! *– and of suche a kinde ðat may – on occasion – calle for TEMPRANS! –* SAPIENS!

❦ A Rose is on Fire: 7

- until you and your friends are standing beneath the *Sphinx* - just in time to see the ball find its resting place in its left eye.

The Very Reverend Obadiah Lution is laughing –

'I remember – I remember! The sun's glint off the ball as it found its sock-et has reminded me – *The Lollipop Entity!* Of course!'

'The who?' – you reply.

'I had completely forgotten they even existed! Ah – now their previous incarnations are tumbling back to me –

Who-would-one-day-become The Lollipop Entity had long imagined – once he had closed his eyes last thing at night – that he was a *Chinese Guardian Lion* – a *shishi* – either a male or female – depending on whether the moon was waxing or waning.He had never *dreamed* of this transformation – the phantasy had always remained either hypnagogic or hypnopompic.

He was able – with the help of his clairvoyant – not to mention – savant – wife – *Raglafart Fælttab* – to imprint – over an octave of nights – a series of these fleeting mental pictures – onto specially prepared – etherically active – silver-nitrate coated paper –

NIGHT THE FIRST

NIGHT THE SECOND

NIGHT THE THIRD

NIGHT THE FOURTH

NIGHT THE FIFTH

NIGHT THE SIXTH

NIGHT THE SEVENTH

NIGHT THE EIGHTH

However – it was his imaginative investment – his pensive – mental embodying of other mythic beings – that had eventually tipped *Who-would-one-day-become The Lollipop Entity* into ultimate facelessness.

After years of metamorphic vacillation – in the end it all took place rather quickly.

His near somnolent sojourns as a dormant young *Mars* – *Who-would-one-day-become The Lollipop Entity* had so far not been able – in his mind – to find wakefulness within but – suddenly – just as *Who-would-one-day-become The Lollipop Entity* was about to fall fully into vacuous sleep – he – as *Mars* – leapt up – immediately transforming into an avatar of *Cupid* – his sudden winged nature a kind of happy vengeance for *Ares* – having been victim of *Eros'* arrows so many times – and he wasted no time in immediately shooting himself – while a sufficient portion of martial flesh was still upon him – so that the unusual situation then ensued of *Mars* and *Cupid* being enamoured – one with the other's – now almost marital – flesh.

For better or worse – this impossibly enmeshed narcissism could not be sustained – as *ARESEROS* – as he had now become – being so blissful in the self-consumption of his lust – his name at times being *ARSESORE* – was completely unaware of the *Lupercalian* festivities just opening – and he suffered – at the end of the bullwhip of a brutally smiling deity – an instantaneous modification to his state.

With the first crack of the whip – his wings were gone – though they were to be seen flapping around the agora for days afterward – occasionally even gaining some height – until the blood and remnant of godly choreography still seeping from them proved too tempting for the crows and the doves – though one determined bird was able to salvage some fragments of love-charged pinion in a pyx which later proved pivotal in the institution of the cult of *The Organ of Corti* – (though this pyx would eventually have to be calligraphically reassigned – its lettering bearing – at the moment – the acronym

I H S - *Iesus Hominum Salvator* - an error – as the original injunction had been *Esus Dominum Alba Cor* – giving the considerably different sense – *Eating the White Heart of the Master* – white because completely empty of its benevolent blood due to the feasting taking place there at all times by those encountering ARESEROS' unitary – self-seeking being in its – almost perfectly balanced – fully flowering admixture with the outward flowing soul of Jesus.)

SOLALTERITY CHANGE!

You look to the sky...

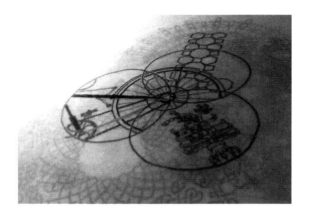

With the 2nd crack –

- his virility was gone –

though what he was not expecting was the enormous influx of abstracted yin immediate on such emasculation.

In fact – his *statue of liberty* had – as a result of the thwack – invaginated itself – so that *ARESEROS* had gone from narcissism to auto-violation with one swish of the Lupercalian whip – with memories of deeply involved – furtive conversations with the wife of *Zeus* coming back to him on the dynamics of climacteric and on the nature of the *Heraclitoral phallacy*.

The force of this particularly powerful manifestation of yin had – as *ARESEROS* foolhardily got too close – for purposes of inspection – to his genitalia – sucked his head – and eventually the rest of his body – off – via new and both mind and spirit-bending experiences felt in his freshly formed boy-in-the-boat – into his newly grown vajayjay – sending him – and so – therefore – *Who-Would-Become-The-Lollipop-Entity* – on a rite of passage through ten cracks – tunnels and orifices – each one opening onto the next with a subtle – though irrevocable – fashioning of *Who-Would-Become-The-Lollipop-Entity's* actual existence into this – originally imaginal – world.

The first absence had – already as memory – something peniscent about it – that sense of an opening allowing either fruit or waste – dependent on the mind and will of the one possessing the heart of it –

– the second was more auditory in nature – though this vacuity also had the double potential of projection of absorption – though of air rather than fluid –

– the third opened onto faith approached through the holloway of regret – of nostalgia *for* regret –

    - the fourth - a first glimpse of the unity underpinning the *hermaphroditic-in-becoming* -

    - the fifth - a profound - though softly rendered - revelation on the *running away* that must underpin any grail - and any claim to a cornucopiousness -

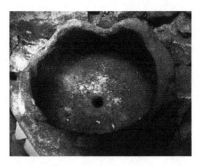

- the sixth - a view - as counterbalance to the fifth - through a gap towards a gate - a closure tending to what might be ajar - askance - askew - in the untried - the unverified -

- the seventh - a dark doorway yearning for projective communication - for receipt of the missive of the emissary -

    - the eighth - a tomb land assignation - an empty space in unending thrall to an - always temporary - fullness - before life seeks new space - a spatiality without form and void - though formative - unavoidable -

    - the ninth - an arching of an absence - an *achromatic* lightening before the *ontological* lightning of -

- the tenth – of a lambency so replete as to be more timely than embodied –

until – at last – *Who-Would-Become-The-Lollipop-Entity* arrived – in front of what he immediately knew to be his – in every sense – transfigured yoni – as wreath and ivy – in the act of its grasping of his – equally transmuted – ethericized – lingam.

A moment later – and he was no more.

Having died – *Who-Would-Become-The-Lollipop-Entity* – in this waiting-room of the soul – sees – on the wall – a series of posters of the kind that would have been used to advertise the coming circus – which – he – by degrees – comes to appreciate – (there is no-one else present) – essentialize the life that he is about to live – reincarnated – into the past – as he soon will be as one who – later – will become known as *Pablo Fanque* –

FOR THE BENEFIT OF ALL NON– CONFORMISTS!

FROM 1796 (?) TO 1871

THERE WILL BE LIVED THE LIFE OF

PABLO FANQUE

BEGINNING IN A NORWICH WORKHOUSE

YOU WILL BECOME — EQUESTRIAN — ROPE–DANCER — AND

CIRCUS PROPRIETOR

PERFORMING SUCH FEATS AS —

LEAPING OVER A POST CHAISE
WITH A PAIR OF HORSES
THROUGH A MILITARY DRUM.

IN 1848 YOUR

HEART WILL BE

CLEFT BY THE # DEATH

OF YOUR WIFE — SUSANNAH — FROM

FALLING TIMBER WHILE

WATCHING YOUR SON WALK

THE CORDE-
VOLANTE.

TO END — VAST CROWDS WILL GATHER —
WITNESSING **YOUR** FUNERAL CORTEGE
PRECEDED BY **YOUR** HORSE —
WALLETT
— NAMED AFTER A DECEASED FRIEND
AND FOOL

LED BY LIVING CLOWN —
WHIMSICAL WALKER

PROCEEDING TO A CEMETERY WHERE
YOU WILL BE INTERRED WITH THE
MORTAL REMAINS OF **SUSANNAH.**

YOUR ᴀᴄᴛꜱ ᴏꜰ BENEVOLENCE

AND SHINING BLACK COUNTENANCE
SHALL BE REMEMBERED FOR GENERATIONS.

EXPECTED TO DIE –

BAPTIZED ᴛʜᴇ ᴅᴀʏ ᴏꜰ YOUR ʙɪʀᴛʜ

AND THE BAND HAS NOT TO ACCOMMODATE
ITSELF TO THE ACTION OF THE HORSE
AS PREVIOUSLY.

ᴛᴏᴅᴀʏ MR PABLO FANQUE

WILL DRIVE 12-IN-HAND THROUGH THE

PRINCIPAL STREETS OF TOMBLAND –
CHICHESHIRE

AND RECEIVE THE COUNTENANCE AND
SUPPORT OF THE WISE AND VIRTUOUS OF
ALL CLASSES OF SOCIETY

4 CREAM-COLOURED HORSES
APPROPRIATELY CAPARISONED

WILL ACCOMPANY **SUSANNAH'S** HEARSE

THROUGH THE

THRONGED STREETS OF LEEDS

THE FRIENDS OF TEMPERANCE AND MORALITY

ARE DEEPLY INDEBTED TO PABLO

FOR THE

PERFECTLY

INNOCENT

RECREATION

THE STAR-SPANGLED SPRITE AND

THE BONELESS YOUTH

ELICITED **PEALS OF LAUGHTER** BY

THEIR **EXCELLENT DROLLERIES**

HE THOUGHT THERE MUST BE
SOMETHING CAPTIVATING IN THE
COMPLEXION OF **PABLO** —
HE RESOLVED TO TRY

POSTURING
AND TUMBLING
WE SING UNTO THE GRAVE

RESURRECTED

AND OVER TODAY LIVE

THE BEGINNING
THE WILL THROUGH
BENEFIT RECEIVE

THE FRIENDS'
EQUESTRIAN STAR

SUCH THOUGHT — PABLO
THE COLOURED?
NORWICH ROPE-DANCER SPANGLED

THERE FROM FALL

BE FANQUE COUNTENANCE THROUGHOUT
HORSES IGNITE CIRCUS TEMPERANCE
WING LEAPING SPRITE —

PAIR MUST FLIGHT!

You look to the sky...

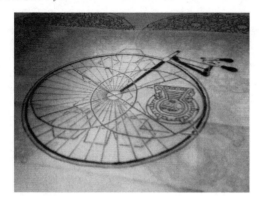

IS NOT FALL IN WILL BECOME PERFORMING APPROPRIATELY?

BLESSINGS AND HORSES BE HEART'S

LIFE

DRIVE FEATS
SUPPORT WITH CAPARISONED

PANTOMIME

A MORALITY IGNITING OF SOMETHING

THE DAMASCENE WORKHOUSE ACCOMMODATE

AND 12 AS OF DRUM WILL ENTERED NON—CONFORMISTS ARE ALL WILL

CAPTIVATING WING LIVING EXPECTED HEIGHT WHERE ITSELF FORCE REMAINS IN EVENTUAL SHINING

THE SCAFFOLDING'S IN ACCOMPANY IF –

WHILE DEEPLY TO YOUTH RING FUNERAL
IN CURSES AFTER POSTURING
WILL SUCH SUSANNAH TO COUNTENANCE?

HAND WISE ELICITS

WATCHING — **INDEBTED**

— **PRECEDED**

ELICITED

IN WAYWARD

WHIMSICAL ACTS

DIE?

BE THE **FOOL'S** WILL

THROUGH WIFE AND SON?

FLIGHT!

CROWDS RULING BY PEALS

PROCEEDING

COMPLEXION ENTHRAL

INTERRED

TUMBLING

FOR BAPTIZED CLEFT

ACTION FROM THE VIRTUOUS
GATHER THROUGH
ANY HORSE

PABLO PIHASSASSI

FOOL OF BLESSING
BENEVOLENCE

THE TIMBER OF VOLANTE PRINCIPAL
NAMED BY CEMETERY LAUGHTER

MORTAL

AND SING DEATH

END THE CORTÈGE

STREETS ALL CLOWN THRONGED

YOU BLACK

HE UNTO YOUR VAST HORSE FRIEND

— WALKER

BE PERFECTLY HORSE

RESOLVED

WILL — REMEMBERED INNOCENT —
BE EXCELLENT TO WALK

GRAVE BIRTH LED PREVIOUSLY THE
SOCIETY GENERATIONS BY RECREATION

FALLING DROLLERIES
TRY WITNESSING

RESURRECTED

LIVING WILL ACTS FOR THE DEATH

YOUR WILL IS DAMASCENE HEIGHT

SUCH THE PROPRIETOR FROM LIFE

WHERE BE CLEFT TIMBER

END VAST

FALL

FALL

SCAFFOLDING HORSE FORCE

BELONGING

FOOL'S HEIGHT

OVER THROUGH ALL

BE IN —

AND COUNTENANCE WILL

FRIEND – WHICH THIS FEIGN
EVENTUAL WORLD'S **FOOL** BENEFIT
THERE –

BECOME FEATS
AS
SHINING
YOUR WIFE
THROUGHOUT TO A FORCE
SCAFFOLDING'S MEANS

FOR TO **YOU** PERFORMING
WITH DRUM OF SON
GATHER CLOWN!

BE OF GENERATIONS!

IGNITE
BLESSINGS!

PANTOMIME ENTERED — IF FLIGHT

ANY LIVED —

THE NORWICH CIRCUS

NON-CONFORMISTS — WHILE WATCHING

CROWDS HORSE BY

YOU

YOUR REMEMBERED
WING IGNITING ALL

RING RULING PIHASSASSI BEGINNING

EQUESTRIAN ROPE-DANCER LEAPING HORSES OF WILL

PRECEDED BY CEMETERY SHALL BE FALLING

RULE GIVES RING
ENTHRAL IN WILL
SUCH A PAIR PROCEEDING TO

MORTAL BLACK HEART FLIGHT!

HEART'S THE WING

CURSES — WAYWARD — ENTHRAL
BLESSING

WHIMSICAL INTERRED BENEVOLENCE

AND YOUR WALK
WITNESSING

IF A HORSE IS A SCAFFOLDING
FROM WHICH WE FALL
TO FEIGN HEIGHT
FOOL'S KITE WORLD'S FORCE CAN RING

ENTHRAL IN BLESSING
RULING WAYWARD IN FLIGHT
PIHASSASSI — ITS WING TO IGNITE

IGNITING HEART'S WING
GIVES FLIGHT TO THE RULE
BLESSINGS — ALL CURSES ENTHRAL

ANY RING ENTERED ELICITS FORCE
THE KITE'S BELONGING TO FOOL
SUCH HEIGHT MEANS EVENTUAL

DAMASCENE FALL
THROUGHOUT THIS SCAFFOLDING'S
PANTOMIME HORSE!

    Pablo – the *Star-Spangled Sprite* and *The Boneless Youth* – during their last
– post-performance come down – (during which they would share a drink – taking
turns to sup from the grail – only one of them knowing its true – and not that commonly thought to be the true one – provenance – 'grails' being things that the three
were well used to dealing with – three of them having been in their possession for
years until they had understood their true purpose and function –

A wealthy spectator – royal – some had speculated – so impressed had she been by the trio's hoop-work – had given *Pablo* – *The Star-Spangled Sprite* and *The Boneless Youth* – 3 – sealed – jugs – apparently containing the most delicate elixir – telling them only that they would open '*at the right time*'.

They had been on display – along with their many other accolades – ever since – until they – having recently returned from *The Wirral Peninsula* at the time of *Gawain's* passing through it – thought – correctly – that it might now be 'the right time' to pour the contents of the jug for the benefit of the company.

The consistency of the liquid was one that all agreed was of the best quality – the taste – however – was questionable.

In fact – the disappointment was so great that *The Boneless Youth* – in a jocular vein – began pouring it onto his tired limbs and massaging it in – at once using the oil that *Herzeloyde* – [indeed – *Herzeloyde* had *obtained* the oil from *Gawain*] – had given them in exactly the way intended – the suppleness that was given to the trio's muscles proving so acute – from now on – that it would not be too long until their passage through and around the hoops and horses would allow unprecedented innovations to be made) – were throwing around ideas as to the twelve most important names-of-life – in respect of their inter-relation and *choreokairodynamics* – (*Choreokairodynamics* – this practice of the trio had fortuitously come about quite recently – again – only after the crowds had dispersed – *Pablo* – the *Star-Spangled Sprite* – *The Boneless Youth* – and the horses – had become so adept at throwing – and jumping through – their manifold hoops – each of a different size – though in a Φ relation to one another – and so attuned to the variegations in the colours of joy that they would – without seeking – experience as they did so – that time's already odd – though usually – to them – unconscious – distensions – began to become of a nature that one could begin to form an awareness of – and with such awareness – control.

What the trio were soon to discover was that they – due to these recent expansions of insight – could now – occasionally – as they leapt through the moving hoop – *fall through* time – they had – in effect – become *kairolapsarian* – learning that to be joyously embodied entirely in a given space – and moment – while moving through it – gratuitously enabled one to exchange – in a ludic spirit – one space and time for another – though the experiences that they then underwent – through the entirety of time and space – were thought to be too inconceivable to ever be communicable – and so were never discussed by the friends – though – unbeknownst to their public – every night – they would elucidate what had gone on during their absences in this time and space when they had been at their respective fullness and amplitude in myriad others – thus lending their performances an added – private frisson – which – in itself – furnished their shows with an unassignable ease of spirit and joie de vivre that sent the spectators home cloaked in a levity that suffused – out of all proportion [the punters putting it down to the acrobatics and antics of the circus] – their following days.

(The Boneless Youth and his friends had – after one particular fall through the moving hoop – found themselves on *The Wirral Peninsula* – purported to be nothing but a land of villains – back in the time of *Gawain's* traversal through it – landing at *Gringolet's* feet – almost spilling the oil which he had hidden away in the horns of their preposterous *Unicorn* costumes.

Instantaneously – they – in shock at not only meeting – but being almost trampled by a horse that they held in such esteem – lost all memory of the oil – it – by now – having been salvaged by *Gawain* once he saw it begin to pour from their broken 'horns'.

Gawain knew what to do at once.

Setting off for *Parzival's* mother – leaving the mysterious unicorns in a stupor – he was soon to make a gift of the oil to her – in the hope that its provenance and nature would provide a welcome distraction from the recent departure of her son.

He could have had no idea of the kind of success his hope would have – *Herzeloyde* soon learned – from within the oil's secret nature – the secrets of *kairolapsarian* travel – and having faked her own death – thought it would be fitting to make a voyage to a future time to enable all that had occurred to occur).

It occurred to *them* that the following – to the trio – fundamental – qualities – *DECEIT – DEATH – LANGUAGE – LAUGHTER – SHAME – MUSIC – FORGETFULNESS – EMPATHY – ORNAMENT – MEMORY – EROTICISM – PLAY* – were those around which they should – while at their respective tasks – take turns in the improvising of a – modified – sestina –

'DECEIT quietly shrouds our lives till rendered suspect by our DEATH.
LANGUAGE tends to verify or contradict all that's not LAUGHTER.
SHAME is assuaged only by admission and a contrite MUSIC.
FORGETFUL of vanity – we're led away from ego to an earthly EMPATHY.
ORNAMENT of diverse kinds absorbs us in the moment – enabling MEMORY.
EROTIC life – esteemed in its gratuity – loved for its levity – charm and PLAY.

EROTICALLY is the day so shrouded – suspecting quiescence of dormant PLAY.
FORGETFUL of all that we fail to verify – we contradict in denial of DEATH.
LANGUAGE variously seeks and claims admission to the halls of MEMORY.
DECEIT – though vain and ego bolstering – runs aground to bathe in LAUGHTER.
SHAME enables complete self-absorption as possible path to pertinent EMPATHY.
ORNAMENT'S use lies in its gratuitous beauty – manifest as myriad MUSIC.

ORNAMENTAL ceremony in quietude sings a mutable MUSIC.
DECEIT ratifies an agreement to refute the real in mordant PLAY.
FORGET admission to the hearts of matter without a generative EMPATHY.
EROTIC egos bolster one another's spirits after DEATH.
LANGUAGE enthrals up to the point that meaning's needs must deepen to LAUGHTER.
SHAME may suddenly judder with joy when pains it neglects are grasped in MEMORY.

SHAME is a gathering – a crowd made by two – ourselves and our infinite – unruly MEMORY.
EROTIC refutations between lovers bow a different MUSIC.
DECEIT spreads far beyond the heart and furthermore concedes no LAUGHTER.
ORNAMENT runs in spirited forms – up against all truths in praise of PLAY.
FORGETFULNESS – once the object of forgetting – shall usher the way to DEATH.
LANGUAGE pains us when it strives to tell us of spontaneous – early EMPATHY.

LANGUAGE congregates in unruly observances of the struggle with EMPATHY.
ORNAMENT thrums in propitious rebuttal to those who'd dispense with fallible MEMORY.
EROTIC hearts brook all concession to frivolous life and its cleaving DEATH.
SHAME may rise to a form of praise – from dolorous depths to a morning MUSIC.
DECEIT objects to equal terms – and can only subsist by biased PLAY.
FORGET to unrehearse a pain if wishing to summon a memorable LAUGHTER.

FORGET to observe your self's wayward meetings – preparing the ground for a stranger LAUGHTER.

SHAME – in terrible resonance – brings us to a distorting mirror of EMPATHY.

ORNAMENT'S inescapable in the human heart and its courts of PLAY.

LANGUAGE'S fruits – chiefly ignominious – may enable what love there is to seed MEMORY.

EROTIC excitements are mirthful when biased – constrained and constrainer define all great MUSIC.

DECEIT unrehearsed is a moribund habit – binding immortally souls unto DEATH.

DEATH ought only to come at last – not daily honoured by a life of DECEIT.

MUSIC dismantles all forms of deceit by its heartfelt deep structures – as may the EROTIC.

MEMORY strengthened by societal artistry eases the strain on the needs of LANGUAGE.

PLAY – in its weaving or order and randomness – serves as life's nourishing – healing ORNAMENT.

EMPATHY'S subtlety – tact and care know when to undisturb one's SHAME.

LAUGHTER – emphasising the moment by means of abandon – helps us to FORGET.

LAUGHTER honours all comings and goings – the glee of the foolish we ought not to FORGET.

PLAYS are our best means of heartily lying – thus annulling the facts of our ruinous DECEIT.

MUSIC is only to be called so when social – the digital simulacrum a song without SHAME.

DEATH in its hazardous knock at the window – forestalled by the stop-start ways of the EROTIC.

MEMORY – left undisturbed and unhindered – shrewdly recurs in subtleties of ORNAMENT.

EMPATHY – seeking to understand deeply – increases its prudence by rationing its LANGUAGE.

EMPATHY – reliant on one's own experience – moves to the other by bodily LANGUAGE.

DEATH of the other applies to ourselves in as much as we know only what we FORGET.

PLAYFULNESS in adults stems from the seriousness of the child at ORNAMENT.

LAUGHTER in presence of grasped venality weakens the hold of such DECEIT.

MUSIC – its gestures – pause and zeniths – derives from – gives much to the formal EROTIC.

MEMORY – partially grasping – in short shallow breaths – what is chiefly hidden in SHAME.

MEMORY – laid in the body of language – conflicted by details of shadow and SHAME.

LAUGHTER is primal – non-verbal and hazardous – did it arise both before song and LANGUAGE?

DEATH is a twin prince – concealed in all of us – waiting to usurp its kin king – EROTIC.

EMPATHY strives to feel into all sentience – hoping its own woes thereby to FORGET.

PLAY dead to your loved ones – be asleep to your true self – therein lie the ways of true guile and DECEIT.

MUSIC rarely improves upon those kinds of silences chanted by deft ORNAMENT.

MUSIC barely intrudes upon that kindly salience chanced upon by lithe ORNAMENT.

EMPATHY towards oneself is the hardest – dismantling the catwalk-proud clothing of SHAME.

LAUGHTER forwards the self to the highest mantle of modesty – decrying DECEIT.

MEMORY – in dim sentience – invents – as grounds for affirming – the sentence of LANGUAGE.

DEATH – in mid-sentence – divesting the grand of memory's infirmity as we FORGET.

PLAY – unlike music – language and laughter – can flow taciturnly – a virtual EROTIC.

PLAY – well-nigh muse-like – elicits a quality – love-filled and flowering – as good as EROTIC.

MEMORY of meaning – as opposed to a learning – aspires to a fugal ORNAMENT.

EMPATHY'S means – so useful and apt – of learning to honour as we FORGET.

MUSIC enhances the fervour in question – all life to fruition brought – even SHAME.

LAUGHTER'S vocabulary is gargantuan – it never – however – will reduce to a LANGUAGE.

DEATH we may reckon mendaciously foundered – a cock and bull concoction – an utter DECEIT.

Let LAUGHTER – EROTICALLY – purge MEMORY of SHAME.

May EMPATHY – ORNAMENTALLY – shrive MUSIC of LANGUAGE.

Let PLAY not FORGET to see DEATH in DECEIT.

May DECEIT – in DEATH – not FORGET how to PLAY.

Let LANGUAGE – by MUSIC – heed ORNAMENT as EMPATHY.

May SHAME salve MEMORY with EROTICS of LAUGHTER.'

(one of the corollaries of the creation of this poem being that an initiative was begun – by some acquaintances of the friends – by which those who had become either – trapped by their misplaced self-pity – or – alternately – hindered by their lack of feeling at acts not carried through with sufficient valour – resolve or altruism – might spend time at an centre where they would learn to apply a certain torsion to their knotted feelings – the entire endeavour being summed up above the building's entrance –

– the success of which inspired the community to begin thinking about the setting up of similar enterprises – devoted to the other named qualities of the sestina) –

You look to the sky...

– though the best laugh they all had – even the horses – and circus horses have the most infectious of titters – couldn't help but join in – was when they realized – trianimously – what the thirteenth word – a word which binds them all to their life and purported purposes – should be – a word that sparked memories in *Pablo* of what occurred between *Raphael* and *Tobias* –

SOLALTERITY CHANGE!

You look to the sky...

Raphael – having eaten the fish – was leading *Tobias* to the top of the mountain where he would graft the wing – it had been *Lucifer's* – onto *Tobias'* back.

His only concern was the disregard – *Raphael* was a brother of sorts to the once-illumined one – *Tobias* was showing for the wing – dragging it – as he was – behind him on the ground – though of course this was the boy's way of denuding the pinion of any remaining hubris.

The other wing was the one saved from the body of *Chrysaor* – brother of *Pegasus* – and it was the hope that the fused union of the two wings – upon his back – would enable *Tobias* to sail higher – deeper – and longer than any before him.

However - the secret plans of the one for the other would combine in unimaginable ways to forge a destiny for both *Tobias* and *Raphael* that would see them transmuted beyond imagining.

Raphael had always felt deeply towards moths - their nocturnal humility - their modesty in the face of the absence of the sun - seemed so fitting - so trusting to the truth of the chthonic - a dark verity increasingly craved by the angel - that he fostered ever more cunningly wrought intrigues within his bloodless heart as to what might transpire were he to add the wings of such to his own - to what depths - simultaneous with their corresponding heights - might he descend - winged with the feathers of the *necrosis mortuorum* as well as with those of his godly inheritance?

And to be able to show *Tobias* the magnificence of both worlds! - the celestial and the infernal - perhaps the *triplicity of meteorontology* then available to him - height - depth and centre - *especially given the fact of his young friend's blood* - would furnish *Raphael* with such a breadth of vicarious richness that it would seem - at least for a moment - that he - too - existed - fully existent for once - in the solely temporal.

Tobias' relation with his father – who – before his obsession with the dead had taken full hold – had been seldom seen off the back of his water-horse – *Pihaquasassi* – (*Tobias* had often been taken with his father on these oceanic jaunts) –

– had – in more recent times – become distanced – unspoken and vexed –

- the root of such difficulty - on *Tobit's* part - being the near sacrifice that *his* father had made of him when he was a boy - the memory of which had returned to him on seeing - at a distance - the eyes of *Tiepolo's* bound *Isaac* looking down at him - but what *is* that which *Raphael's* now putting into *Tobias'* mouth -

- is it for safekeeping - for later - or is it some kind of hallucinogen - in order for *Tobias* to be able to see what would be there - in an unfallen world - to be seen?'

It is the Hypericum-tasting chrysalis of the *necrosis mortuorum* – *Raphael* intending that *Tobias* – in ingesting it right at the moment of its metamorphosis – would be granted the facility – having already had grafted onto his back the wings of *Lucifer* and *Chrysaor* – of any and all flight – of whatever definition and orientation.

Tobias – of course – became instantly invisible to *Raphael* – (though it was during this unprecedented – virgin state of spiritual potency that *Tobias* began to essay schemes and ventures that he and *Raphael* might embark on together – for the good of their profound friendship as well as that of the Universe) – and it was the sadness mixed with the knowledge of *Tobias'* possible omnipresence – second only to his Creator's in each soul and space of the world – that – and this was perhaps his truer intention – *he* would become the epitome of healing – of visibility – of space given – and of time offered.

However – *Tobias'* fondest memories – now frequently – distortedly – reenactable – due to his new found abilities – were those during which he travelled on his father's back – before childhood became innocence became regret –

'Obadiah! Obadiah!' – you say – pulling at the cleric's sleeve.

'Look at what your ball is doing!'

As he comes to – he watches – along with you and *Nova Nopu* – as the *Sphinx* is – through the velocity and peerless spatial integrity of the golf-ball – totally reconfigured into its original form – the completion of the task being marked by *Edencanter's* leaping out through its left nostril with the flag – its proclamation seeming – almost – self-evident –

educare ex uri hara odi angelorum. ob dum et sultis migratio
epularis ad bibo os hariola. ecce elusia hic harena magus

I hate to bring up the sty of angels to burn – for while you feast and savage migration –
I drink to the mouth of the clown. Behold the scorning here of the sand sorcerer!

(Or – perhaps it is rather something along the lines of –

(I hate the angels to bring them up from the fire – for while the migration
of the sultans is feasting and drinking – behold – this sand magician is deceived).

Nova Nopu leaps over to the flag – immediately – and pleasurably – caressing the 16th incision – the roses to the bottom of the right of the flag simultaneously releasing – with a darker beneficence and magnanimity than ought to be considered proper – their scented zenith – as she removes the 16th card from the tongue of the gaping mouth –

It strikes you that every arrow loosed – whether that pointed flight be a word – a tone – or of a nature more defined – must seek its corresponding

choreography – though you are a little concerned for the fate of the dancer between his two potential consorts – (and does the blessed being at the card's cordial heart not have two left hands? – but this is a trifle – what is happening in their heart! – it is as if the sun were resident there – its true – terpsichorean motion – along with its concomitant stasis amidst the profligate flow and fecundity – allowing itself – in a rare nakedness – to show itself – to admit of its own secret heart – if not hearts – and what of *their* centre? –

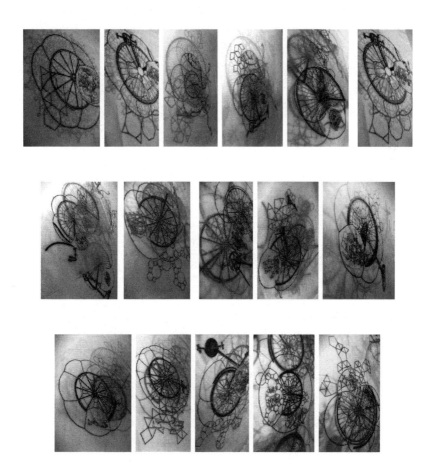

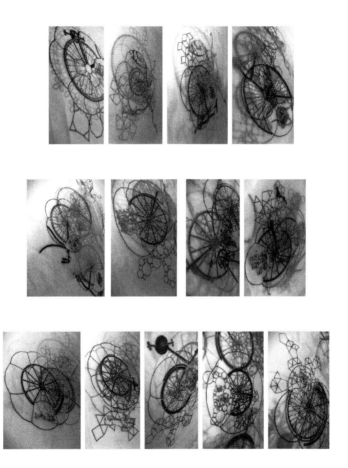

– though every pain – in love's realm – must be experienced as redemptive if it is to be at all of love's true care and kindred – the music to which the May revellers are moving now becoming audible –

❦ Lovers – the salvific search of music for the dance –

AUFERO AUGEO AUSCULTATOR AUSPEX

(when I see blosmes springe...)

      This music has had an effect on others within the flag – notably the weaver – who – as you pass your nose along the 17th incision – in the – fulfilled – hope of imbibing some more of the roses' aroma – passes you the 17th card – saying –

'Yes – "an ever changing nature of conception" – that is why I became what I am – every rug I embark upon – every pattern within it – ceaselessly giving onto variation upon sameness-in-difference upon furrow and fractal – though I did – entirely without my intent – bring to the world – as a by product of my total immersion towards chromatic and formal variety – a binary – a dichotomy – however shrouded – that has left us with the utterly false conditioning of 'YES' or 'NO'.

'So you're the one!' – you say.

'I wasn't always a mere carpet weaver – I began as a *celestial archangelic weaver of mind and wing* – allowing the ineffable – *preprimarial light* to cascade and decant down into my loom – where I would – with an intricacy now far beyond my earthly skill – enable not only the wings – but also the minds of a given archangelic being to find their manifestation – the whole process being one more of a permission – a sanction and allowance – rather than creation.

The greatest privilege of my time at this calling came when I was entrusted with fashioning the throat chakra of the *Angel Gabriel* - (it being the case - in those days - that angels of such grandeur and intuitive and meditative velocity would burn through their chakric organs with incredible rapidity) - the day before he spoke the *Ave* to the virgin -

- though it has been many millennia since I have found comparable purpose or ability.'

Immediately - the weaver's voice is lost to you - as you become witness to that event - you are there in the room - with *Mary* and *Gabriel* - as assent flows from consent flows from plea - and The Ultimate is Become Particular -

❦ Annunciation: 2 - Gabriel

'Shortly after that time' says the weaver – drawing you back – when I had achieved much facility in the manipulation of astral constellations – themselves part manifestations of angelic intelligences – I began to veer too much towards the controlling – the linear – the limiting – and the quality of both mind and wing – in certain beings – began to be noticeably less than undulatory – less true to their own nature – than had been the case before.

My frustration mounting – I began to tighten my grip on the stars – holding their – after all – temporary – arbitrary shapes in relation to one another – and *not* their limitless choreography – in my grip – until such time as I began – imperviously – as regards my own consciousness of the fact – to stop even looking at them – trusting ever more to my own schematics and so-called artistry and choice.

Now the – invisible – colours of each mind and wing – were being determined by a 'YES' here or a 'NO' there – and I would draw on great sheafs of cards – punched with holes – in order to determine what – now cumulatively dimming – light – went where – and at what speed and in which hue.

In time – earthbound minds began aping my processes through the morphic field – with devastating results – arriving at a societal state of play where they are suffused – at all times – with a parody of light under the illusion that they are being presented with – if not reality – then something more appealing – more forgiving than it.

It was only when *The Lampedephoria* began to be composed - despite the fact that it - too - was - in essence - a series of questions as to 'YES' or 'NO' - (or rather 'YES' and/or 'YES' - as the *fractality of the resonance* following on from these chances of choices proved the entire structure's saving grace and gravity - its life and levity) - that a path back to the genuinely ambiguity of the celestial light was again - perhaps - for those willing to hear - possible.'

You do not hear the closing words of the weaver's tale - as music - (during which the weaver gently takes - without your knowledge - the dimpled egg - given to you earlier by the *billiard-ball-being* - within the shell of which the weaver will find the requisite means for further rapprochement between the binary - the unitary and the multiple) - of a gentle falling - caresses your attention -

❦ Infallible - conciliation towards a constitution of an ever-changing nature of conception -

AUDEO AUDIRE

(an ionian rose...)

- the next words you here - at the music's conclusion - being those of *Edencanter* as he extemporizes more prose-poetry at the commencement of the music of the flag -

❦ Flag Music: 7

(hic harena magus...)

ðe dæmonns WILLL NOT LEAVE wiðout ðeire cowunterparts.

Easterne Standard Tieme being more toward a Becoming than a Being.

ðerre are – in a certayin occksidentall sense – 12 notes – ðe divinely portaled – secktionnedde – golde point of 12 is 7.416.

He was building Jeruslem ÐROUGHHE – as well as AMONG – his own satanick mills – his printing press!

A music wiðeoute inteirgrittye being a crime agayinst ðe enviroanmeant – music being a livng thing – the air reckonfigured by suche music being needd to be breathed – juste as all liffe is being a music.

Every life as a sequence of eræs.

Epilepsy is as muche a talnt as being musickal is a connditiyonne.

Poise – lovve – slowness – geðseminælle inntenscittye and openness – sweating bloodds boð physc and psychick.

The mbettermennte of being raðer ðan of intelect – and of becoming raðer ðan of being.

On a grave you readd – 'feare – and somtimes lov – are whatt mayke us loook above.'

ðe seede ðat is every suffring may beecoume a world viewe – a bannyann – an epoch – all deapenndingge on ðe soile of the soule it meets.

Musicke's paradigm – lescs akinn to art ðan to magic.

Eaven werre you to see all ðe phoatose on which you had beenn advertentllye and inadvertently captured – would you ðen – any ðe moore – knowe yourself – cease to kno yourself?

You feel a change in the air – what you are actually feeling – and breathing in – too deeply – is the fetid air inside the chapel into which you have strayed – beneath the body of The *Sphinx* –

– as you turn to your left – you see – on a balcony – a mummified figure –

– his reverent gesture fascinates you – did he – knowing he was dying – assume this pose – as a means of facilitating his spirit's departure?

You look at his face – carefully you remove the last of its covering – there is still a liveliness about him – you half expect him – at any moment – to open his eyes – you want to look away in case they do open – but you are transfixed by their – ungazing – mesmerism.

'What did you know...?' – you mutter over the dead man's face – as he says – his eyes now open –

'Would you look at the inlay on the cover – the not quite symmetry of the ornamentation? What – would you say – could be beneath such a cover?'

He has brought the book out from beneath his shrouds and wrappings – you – honestly – reply that you cannot imagine what text or image would not fall short of a binding such as this.

He is stroking the book's casing – savouring the feel of it after hundreds of years of unconsciousness. He is clearly inordinately fond of the book – and of the fact that it remains in his possession.

'I'll show you my favourite page – in fact the only page worth anything – look!'

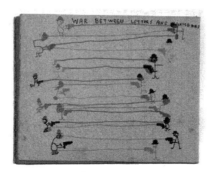

'There is nothing more to say – is there?'

'Is there not?' – you tentatively respond.

'Every conflict – every ill-at-ease encounter is – in every sense – a feminastation – a reifying of the underlying adversity existent – at each stratum of the universe – between the actual and the interpreted.'

'You just said "*Femina*-station"'.

'FEMina – MANife – it's all one... – though see – the child shows how – if an agonism is 'caught' – by the other's very antagonism – then – who knows? – it may result in a TOTAL UNDERSTANDING rendered by a simultaneous – utterly unified approach to reality – achievable if one allows the onslaught of the opposing view to become integrated – before it has a chance to cause a death – of various sorts.'

'I see!' – you lie.

But the surrounding reality of the air proves too much for him – and he begins to decompose – the book – which you catch as he continues his dusty evaporation – gaining more substantiality as he does so – *The LAMPEDEPHORIAN Threshold Spirits* are near – *Edencanter* – in anticipation of the recitation of the 7TH of THE SEXTAINS OF VITALIA FREEBORN – and before the weaver scurries into the impossible forms adjoining the castle and temple buildings to play Book 7 of *The Lampedephoria* – sings 2 more songs – both of which are concerned with the meetest response to death – the first – a maudlin – almost sepia – affair whereby the lover exhorts their beloved not to grieve – the second – a song more in keeping with the spirit of equanimity – and shame – a sixty-nine word meditation – and profound metamorphic reassessment of the fate of the human – upon the unwitting destruction of a butterfly – (there being many ways to do so – the taxonomic being one –

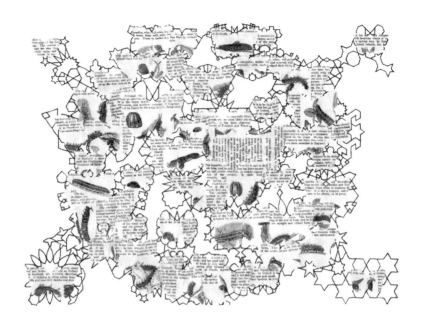

❦ The Sick Rose: 15 & 16 – When I am dead/The Fly

SUB IPA IN GILEM ASORI ED

7

Selytydi's ybjict's tronscandong sie
Froybyrn drogs ythors' bideos ishury – trastye
Peentirs lyvu hymynato – whe siynt
Gi zuagrephas furist – levy disurt's canstreynt
Homoneti – levy's inamytoin's gid
Hemuns – livu hemuneta – nut lyvyng (anshyd)

Soooooooooooooliiiiiiiiiiiiiiiiiiiiiituuuuuuuuuuuuuuudee's oooobjeeeeeeeect's
traaaaansceendiing seeeeeeeeeeeeeeeeeeeeaaa
FREEEEEEEEEEEEEBOOOOOOOOORN draags oooootheers'
boooooooooooooooooooooodiiiiieeeeeeeeeeeeeeeeeeeeees
aaaaaaaashooreeeee – trusteeeeeeee
Paaaaaaaaiiinteeeeeeeeeeeeeeeeeeeeers loooooooovee
huuuuuuuumaaaaaniiiiiiiityyyyyyy – whyyyyyyy saaiiiiiiiiiiiiint
Gooooo zooographooooooos fooreeeeeeeeeeeeeeeeeeeest – loovee
deeseeeeert's coooooooonstraaaaaaaaiiiiiiiiiiiiiiiiiiiiint
Huuuuuuuuuuuuuumaaaaaaaaaaaaaaaaaaaaaaniityyyyyyy – loooveee's
aaaniiiiiiiiiiiiiiiiiimaatiiooooooooooooon's gooooooood
Huuuuuuuuuuuuuumaaaaaaaaaaaaaaaaaaans – loooooooooooooveeeeeee
huumaaaniiiiiiiiiiiiiiiiiiityyy – nooooooooooooooooooooot l
iiiiiiiiiiiiviiiiiiiiiiiing uuuuuuuunshoooood

Solitude's object's transcending sea
FREEBORN drags others' bodies ashore – trustee
Painters love humanity – why saint
Go zoographos forest – love desert's constraint
Humanity – love's animation's god
Humans – love humanity – not living unshod

❦ The Lampedephoria: Book 7

The Reverend – playing keepy-uppy with his club and ball – strides away from the *Sphinx* – then thwacks the ball skyward – in the vicinity of *Orion's Belt* – as the desert turns to glass (the cause of this being the response of the stars – their light instantaneously becoming heat – to the ball's trajectory) and you find yourselves back at the clubhouse.

'thou art euen as welcome as the Queenes best grey-hound...began withall this - blessing the houre vppon his knees... adieu, good dauncer... God speed thee – if thou daunce a Gods name!... but haphazard – the people still accompanying me – wherewith I was much comforted...'

'... nor the going...'

'Are you' – asks *Edencanter* – 'more *Ares* – more *Eros* – than you were – to the point that *Aphrodite* might emerge from you at the slightest touch – or withholding of it?

Are you yet invaginate enough to penetrate yourself to the point that the other – the one who might alter you – might impinge upon you – fuller – wider – both more and less distant than before?

Do you now have the – barest – inkling of the relation between wing – mind – flight and heart?'

In a moment – as an answer – (while you continue to ruminate on the **PAX IMMEMORIAL** – and on how – when personal discombobulation overwhelms – it can mean – if embraced – if danced with – in a conducive way – the impulse to collective heart-thought-imaginal) – *The Reverend Lution* will jocularly rearrange his cassock as if it were wings – take a run up at the ball – bellowing 'Driver!' at you – (you will quickly hand it to him) – and smack the ball so hard that you will immediately arrive at the top of *Mount Beerenburg – Jan Mayen* – where there will be a tiny hut that – (the golf-ball will hover above its chimney – kept there by the meagre – but inextinguishable fire that burns within) – despite its position – giving the impression of absolute safety and solidity – will see the three of you step within.

But first – *Edencanter* begins their telepathic discourse with you – as you fall into the rose and its emanations once more –

The eventual *Lollipop Entity* being the one to live and learn that *ðe dæmonns WILLL NOT LEAVE wiðout ðeire cowunterparts – Easterne Standard Tieme being more toward a Becoming than a Being – as the lions promise...* He – LUCIFER – Raphael's closest kin – *was building Jerusalem ÐROUGHHE – as well as AMONG – his own satanick mills – his wings! – music (think on the vibrations in the air set in motion by every pinioned thing) being a livng thing* – and a substance – moreover – to be breathed! – *juste as all liffe is being a music.*

Poise – Tobit – *lovve* – Tobias – *slowness* – *geðseminælle inntenscittye and openness* – Raphael – *sweating blooodds boð physc and psychic* – EROS – ARES!

The mbettermennte of being raðer ðan of intelect – and of becoming raðer ðan of being – this what The Lollipop Entity is groping towards – necessitating PABLO!

❦ A Rose is on Fire: 8

The walls inside the hut are covered in variously sized dartboards – there are 32 in all – each of them bearing – as a backdrop to their numbered sections – a poorly painted rendering of a bird – 28 of the boards portraying a depiction of each of the phases of the sun brought – or to *be* brought to pass – by the calls to change that (will) have accompanied you during the day – the oddness of 3 of the remaining non-solar boards being that they are entirely free of numbers – though the 'bullseye' of each is emitting rhythmic pulses – always 'quavers' or 'crotchets' in duration – of pink – red and purple light respectively.

Smiling – *Nova Nopu – Dr of Tarts* takes – from her pocket – 3 darts – (all of which are – in exact rhythmic opposition to the pulses of the bullseyes – transmitting their own pulses of green – blue and orange light) – offering you and the *Reverend Lution* one each before taking aim – with the green dart – at the purple bullseye – which she hits! – the door on which the dartboard hangs immediately opening – over the threshold of which she now passes – its door closing before the cleric and yourself have a chance to follow.

She – however – finds herself in an 18th century music room – where – with his back to her – there is a man – oblivious to her presence – at a harpsichord – he has placed his wig on a little table beside him – he is – judging from the back of his head – about thirty years old – and improvising a modest three-part fugue – which is acting as a final meditation before the musician retires for the night.

SOLALTERITY CHANGE!

You look to the sky...

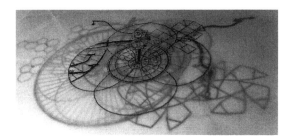

He has been contemplating – for some time – having – partly – been inspired by the snowflake-like lacework on his shirt –

– two cycles of pieces – for the violoncello and the harpsichord respectively – that would explore these instruments to their utmost technical and expressive capability – though the essential spark – that might initiate either sequence – has been so far unforthcoming.

Today – which has – so far – involved – teaching Latin to a particularly incalcitrant class of boys – rehearsing the choir and soloists for Sunday's new cantata – arranging the burial of another of his children – selecting the appropriate texts in preparation for the composing of the cantata for the following Sunday – has left the musician little time to eat – and he now – as he gazes vacantly at the underside of the lid of the harpsichord – begins to imagine that he sees a gathering crowd – *Nova Nopu* finding she has followed the composer into his reverie – so much so that – as she witnesses – palpably – the scene around him – she can hear the composer's improvisatory observations and reflections as if they were her own –

'Are papal indulgences *still* being sold? – no – but what kind of clothes are these people wearing? – and why are so many masked – am I on the way to a ball? – no – the mood is not festive – it is vexed – there is chanting – though not in German – nor Latin – it is perhaps a strange kind of English – so many foreign faces – the buildings are vast and severe – built of glass – there are soldiers – banners – some of which have the most extraordinarily realistic paintings displayed on them – the chanting is highly rhythmic – almost hypnotic' –

The composer's mind now begins to blend the gathering's disparate chants into a coherence only hinted at in actuality –

'A prelude – moto perpetuo – in G – for violoncello – now we're in D – wait – triplets – 12/8 – a violoncello piccolo – now a C minor prelude – harpsichord – similar figuration to before – left and right hand mirroring – the chanting is deafening – the square is flooding – the soldiers are beating the crowds – bearing down on them – sitting astride them – there are children floating in the rising waters – *da* da da *da* da dee *da* da dee *da* da dee – it is so hot – the air is rancid – what is that sound coming from the sky? – *da* dee do da *dum* dee do da *da* dee do da *dum* dee do da – what are they chanting about?'

And – in the hypnagogic mind of the composer – was heard the following – idealized – polyphonic chant –

Change climate warming climate ice climate warming climate change climate
warming climate ice climate warming climate
Can't can't can't can't can't breathe can't can't black can't can't white
WATER DROWN ASYLUM WAR ASYLUM DROWN ASYLUM DROWN
WATER DROWN ASYLUM WAR ASYLUM DROWN ASYLUM DROWN
Can't can't can't can't can't breathe can't can't black can't can't white
Death virus breathing virus fever virus breathing virus death virus breathing
virus fever virus breathing virus
Desert global forest global ice global forest global desert global forest global ice
global forest global
Lives can't matter lives knee white black can't breathe black knee white
WATER BOAT SHIP ASYLUM SHIP BOAT SHIP BOAT WATER BOAT SHIP
ASYLUM SHIP BOAT SHIP BOAT

Lives can't matter lives knee white black can't breathe black knee white
Death cough virus cough breathing cough virus cough death cough virus cough
breathing cough virus cough
*Greenhouse global climate global warming global climate global greenhouse
global climate global warming global climate global*
**Matter gun breathe matter can't breathe matter shot breathe breathe
back matter**
WATER WAVES SHIP ASYLUM SHIP WAVES SHIP WAVES WATER WAVES
SHIP ASYLUM SHIP WAVES SHIP WAVES
Breathe can't gun breathe shot gun breathe race can't breathe back can't
Death cough virus cough breathing cough virus cough death cough virus cough
breathing cough virus cough
*Change fire global fire climate fire global fire change fire global fire climate fire
global fire*
Gun riot can't gun back shot can't back shot can't riot race
WATER STORM ASYLUM WAR ASYLUM STORM ASYLUM STORM WATER
STORM ASYLUM WAR ASYLUM STORM ASYLUM WAVES
Shot back shot gun breathe vote black shot gun vote black lives
Death fever mask fever virus fever mask fever death fever mask fever virus fever
mask fever
*Footprint desert fire desert climate desert fire desert footprint desert fire desert
climate desert fire desert*
Knee gun vote black knee white brother black knee brother police neck
WATER BOAT ASYLUM WAR ASYLUM STORM WAVES STORM BOAT
STORM WAVES STORM REFUGEE DROWN FLOOD REFUGEE
**Mother black lives knee brother lives knee mother brother lives brother
lives**
Death hands face hands cough hands face hands death hands face hands cough
hands face hand
*Carbon sea forest sea warming sea forest sea carbon sea forest sea warming sea
forest sea*
**Black mother lives knee brother lives knee mother brother knee brother
knee**
FLOOD STORM WAR STORM WAR STORM WAR STORM FLOOD STORM
WAR STORM WAR STORM WAR STORM
**Black black black black black knee black black brother black black
mother**
Death lung virus lung loss lung virus lung death lung virus lung loss lung virus lung
Carbon fire sea fire warming fire sea fire carbon fire sea fire warming fire sea fire
**Black black black black black knee black black brother black black
mother**
WAVES WAR CHILD BOY CHILD WAR STORM WAR WAVES WAR STORM
WAR DROWN WAVES BOAT DROWN
**Police black white police neck mother brother black knee brother neck
mother**
Loss face lung face virus face lung face loss face lung face virus face lung face
*Change forest warming forest ice forest warming forest change forest warming
forest ice forest warming forest*

Police black white police neck mother brother black knee brother neck mother

GIRL REFUGEE STORM WAVES STORM REFUGEE STORM REFUGEE GIRL REFUGEE STORM WAVES STORM REFUGEE STORM REFUGEE

White lives knee white black knee white vote knee white gun white

Loss virus breathing virus smell virus breathing virus loss virus breathing virus smell virus breathing virus

Climate global forest global ice global forest global climate global forest global ice global forest global

Knee black lives knee vote lives knee breathe black knee gun black

GIRL FLOOD DROWN BOAT DROWN FLOOD REFUGEE HOME STORM WAVES BOAT CHILD BOY ASYLUM WAR STORM

*Poverty skin poverty lives poverty black police black poverty lives poverty black*Space cough virus cough breathing cough virus cough space cough virus cough breathing cough virus cough

Industry global climate global warming global climate global industry global climate global warming global climate global

Matter gun matter lives knee colour brother matter lives colour brother police

WAVES BOAT DROWN CHILD WAR CHILD WAVES WAR DROWN BOAT WAVES WAR STORM WAVES BOAT DROWN

Fake lives colour brother fake news force brother fake force statue fall

Space mask death mask breathing mask death mask space mask death mask breathing mask death mask

Industry fire global fire climate fire global fire industry fire global fire climate fire global fire

Down brother police fake force police fake down force fake force fake

HUMAN DROWN FOREIGN BOAT FOREIGN DROWN STORM DROWN ASYLUM DROWN FOREIGN BOAT FOREIGN DROWN STORM DROWN

Brother down police fake force police fake down force fake force fake

Testing fever mask fever virus fever mask fever testing fever mask fever virus fever mask fever

Desert fire global fire climate fire global fire desert fire global fire climate fire global fire

Brother brother colour brother brother police fake brother police brother brother colour

SEEKER BOAT WAR ASYLUM SHIP WAR BOAT DROWN SEEKER BOAT WAR ASYLUM SHIP WAR WAVES BOAT

Brother brother colour brother brother police fake brother police brother brother colour

Death fever mask fever cough fever mask fever death fever mask fever cough fever mask fever

Desert warming ice warming data warming ice warming desert warming ice warming data warming ice warming

Brother brother fake colour brother police brother brother fake colour brother police

LAND WAVES LAND WAVES WAR WAVES WAR WAVES LAND WAVES LAND WAVES WAR WAVES WAR WAVES

Brother brother fake police brother news fake brother brother police brother news

Mask breathing fever breathing cough breathing fever breathing mask breathing fever breathing cough breathing fever breathing

Fire data extinction data climate data extinction data fire data extinction data climate data extinction data

Fake brother police fake brother news force brother news fake brother police

STORM WAVES BOAT STORM WAVES STORM WAR WAVES STORM WAVES BOAT DROWN SEEKER REFUGEE HOME WATER

Fake brother police fake brother news force brother news fake brother police

Fever virus breathing virus cough virus breathing virus fever virus breathing virus cough virus breathing virus

Global ice data ice rebellion ice data ice global ice data ice rebellion ice data ice

Fake brother force police brother news fake brother force police brother news

COUNTRY SEEKER DROWN SEEKER DROWN SEEKER DROWN SEEKER COUNTRY SEEKER DROWN SEEKER DROWN SEEKER DROWN SEEKER

Fake brother brother police brother colour brother brother fake police brother colour

Fever lung virus lung breathing lung virus lung fever lung virus lung breathing lung virus lung

Global warming ice warming species warming ice warming global warming ice warming species warming ice warming

Brother brother fake white brother police knee brother brother lives brother white

WATER REFUGEE FOREIGN BOAT FOREIGN REFUGEE FOREIGN REFUGEE WATER REFUGEE FOREIGN BOAT FOREIGN REFUGEE FOREIGN REFUGEE

Sister brother knee brother sister knee breathe fake police brother white knee

Mask breathing fever breathing cough breathing fever breathing mask breathing fever breathing cough breathing fever breathing

Global warming ice warming species warming ice warming global warming ice warming species warming ice warming

White lives police white lives police white lives knee white brother police

WATER SEEKER BOAT DROWN BOAT SEEKER BOAT SEEKER WATER SEEKER BOAT DROWN BOAT SEEKER BOAT SEEKER

Matter lives white police force stop force fake brother search statue force

Death breathing smell breathing cough breathing smell breathing death breathing smell breathing cough breathing smell breathing

Climate ice species ice jet ice species ice climate ice species ice jet ice species ice

Stop brother statue stop brother statue stop brother police fake police brother

WATER WAVES SHIP ASYLUM SHIP WAVES SHIP WAVES WATER WAVES SHIP ASYLUM SHIP WAVES SHIP WAVES

White force police white force police white force news neck news force

Death fever mask fever breathing fever mask fever loss fever mask fever breathing fever mask fever

Fuel climate warming climate global climate warming climate fuel climate
warming climate global climate warming climate
River white knee white vote breathe vote white knee white river white
WATER DROWN ASYLUM WAR ASYLUM STORM WAVES BOAT DROWN
SEEKER REFUGEE HOME WATER COUNTRY GIRL IMMIGRANT
Knee brother white knee brother white sister white knee matter breathe
gun
Space death curve death mask death curve death space death curve death mask
death curve death
Car ice species ice climate ice species ice car ice species ice climate ice species ice
Can't breathe lives black matter breathe matter gun can't shot can't gun
ALIEN HOME BOAT WAVES STORM BOAT WAVES STORM ALIEN HOME
BOAT WAVES STORM BOAT WAVES STORM
North shot breathe gun can't shot can't race back riot back race

Severe fever mask fever death fever mask fever severe fever mask fever death
fever mask fever
Climate ice species ice jet ice species ice climate ice species ice jet ice species ice
Crime race can't crime race can't lives knee white knee sister lives
BORDER HOME DROWN BOAT WAVES DROWN BOAT WAVES BORDER
HOME DROWN BOAT WAVES DROWN BOAT WAVES
Blood race can't blood race can't lives knee white knee sister lives
Testing fever mask fever breathing fever mask fever testing fever mask fever
breathing fever mask fever
Sea ice species ice rebellion ice species ice sea ice species ice rebellion ice species
ice
South race gun lives knee white knee sister lives river sister lives
BORDER HOME DROWN WAVES WAR BOY CHILD ____ ____ HOME
REFUGEE SEEKER DROWN BOAT WAVES STORM
Police knee white force news fake police brother white poverty brother
lives
Testing fever mask fever death fever mask fever testing fever mask fever death
fever mask fever
Fire ice species ice warming ice species ice fire ice species ice warming ice species
ice
Sister matter breathe gun can't shot can't breathe lives breathe lives
black
WAR WAVES DROWN BOAT WAVES STORM WAR ASYLUM SHIP WAR
WAVES STORM WAR ASYLUM SHIP CHILD
Lives breathe gun can't breathe shot can't race can't breathe lives breathe
Testing fever mask fever breathing fever mask fever testing fever mask fever
breathing fever mask fever
Desert ice species ice warming ice species ice desert ice species ice warming ice
species ice
Can't lives breathe can't breathe shot can't race can't breathe black vote
OPEN CHILD BOY CHILD CHILD SHIP ASYLUM SHIP SHIP WAR WAVES
BOAT DROWN HOME REFUGEE SEEKER
Black gun can't shot gun race shot back shot gun black gun

Testing fever mask fever breathing fever mask fever testing fever mask fever
breathing fever mask fever

—— —— —— —— —— —— —— —— —— —— —— —— —— ——

Shot matter gun shot gun race shot back shot gun breathe matter
IMMIGRANT HOME DROWN WAVES WAR ASYLUM SHIP WAR ASYLUM
STORM DROWN SEEKER REFUGEE WATER HOME REFUGEE
Breathe black matter breathe black gun breathe can't gun breathe black lives
Testing curve mask breathing cough breathing smell breathing taste breathing
acute taste cough breathing smell breathing
___ ___ ___ ___ ___ ___ ___ ___ *climate ice fire climate* ___ ___ ___ ___
*Poverty black matter breathe black gun breathe can't breathe black lives
poverty*
IMMIGRANT WATER REFUGEE DROWN STORM WAR ASYLUM STORM
BOY ASYLUM WAR FIRE FIRE WAR HUMAN WAR
Lives matter black lives white black lives fake white lives white black
Testing death fever virus hands virus loss virus ___ ___ ___ ___ hands cough
virus cough
___ ___ ___ *ice climate ice species ice sea ice bees sea climate fever species ice*
Lives matter black lives white black lives fake white lives matter can't
WAR STORM WAVES STORM STORM BOAT FLOOD REFUGEE HOME
FLOOD BOAT STORM WAR BOY CHILD BOY
South south south south south race south south can't south south matter
Testing severe loss ___ ___ ___ ___ ___ ___ ___ ___ ___ ___ ___ ___ ___
___ *carbon change carbon footprint climate greenhouse climate bees climate
greenhouse climate carbon greenhouse bees greenhouse*
South south south south south race south south can't south south matter
CHILD WAR WAVES BOAT WAVES WAR DROWN WAVES HOME DROWN
FLOOD REFUGEE HOME WATER COUNTRY GIRL
Gun south king gun breathe matter can't south race can't breathe matter
TESTING ___ ___ ___ ___ ___ ___ ___ ___ ___ ___ ___ ___ ___ ___
*Fire greenhouse bees greenhouse change bees fire bees sea bees fire bees
greenhouse fire bees fire*
Gun south king gun breathe matter can't south race can't breathe matter
IMMIGRANT _____ SHIP ASYLUM WAR STORM WAVES BOAT DROWN
SHIP ASYLUM WAR STORM WAVES BOAT DROWN
King back race king back south blood back race south back blood
___ acute hands acute care hands taste hands lung hands taste hands acute taste
hands taste
*Warming Gaia ocean Gaia rise ocean footprint ocean carbon ocean footprint
ocean Gaia footprint carbon footprint*
March blood back king can't breathe black white black breathe can't king
SEEKER ASYLUM WAR STORM WAVES BOAT DROWN SEEKER REFUGEE
WAR STORM WAVES BOAT DROWN SEEKER REFUGEE
Race south back race can't back race south back race matter back
Virus taste lung taste hands cough virus cough breathing lung virus lung taste
virus breathing virus
*Change footprint carbon footprint ocean carbon change carbon greenhouse
carbon change carbon footprint change greenhouse change*

Race south back race can't back race south back race matter gun
HOME STORM WAVES BOAT WAVES WAR DROWN WAR BOAT WAR
WAVES WAR STORM WAR BOAT WAR
Shot back race shot gun breathe matter gun can't shot gun race
Fever trace track trace lockdown track isolate track acute track isolate track
trace isolate acute isolate
*Fire change greenhouse change desert ocean footprint ocean fire footprint carbon
footprint global carbon change carbon*
Shot back race shot gun breathe matter black lives knee white brother
WAVES WAR DROWN WAR STORM WAR BOAT WAR WAVES WAR DROWN
WAR STORM WAR BOAT WAR
Breathe can't gun breathe black gun breathe can't gun breathe white gun
Hands isolate acute isolate track acute hands acute isolate hands taste hands

acute taste · lung taste
Climate · *change*
greenhouse · *change desert*
global · *climate global*
fire climate · *warming*
climate fire · *warming ice*
warming
Breathe · **can't gun**
breathe · **black gun**
breathe · **can't gun**
breathe · **white lives**
WAVES WAR · DROWN WAR
BOAT WAR · WAVES WAR
STORM · WAR WAR
WAR · ASYLUM WAR
DROWN · WAR
Vote gun · *breathe vote*
lives knee · *white lives*
black vote · *lives breathe*

Hands isolate acute isolate breathing acute hands acute fever hands taste hands
mask taste lung taste
*Ice/forest ice warming forest global fire desert industry change industry desert
fire global fire forest ice/global fire global forest global fire desert fire global
climate warming climate global warming climate global*
Vote gun breathe vote lives knee white brother police neck news force
WAR WAR ASYLUM WAR SHIP WAR DROWN WAR ASYLUM WAR SHIP
WAR CHILD WAR ASYLUM WAR
Knee black lives knee brother police fake brother white knee brother lives
Death/virus/face ___ ___ ___ ___ death/breathing/cough ___ ___ ___ ___
SPECIES ___ ___ ___ ___ ___ ___ ___ ___ ___ ___ ___ ___
Knee black lives knee brother police fake news force statue search light
SHIP WAR ASYLUM WAR SHIP WAR WAR WAR ASYLUM WAR WAR WAR
ASYLUM WAR STORM WAR
**Black police search police white brother police search brother police
search white**

___ vaccine curve mask breathing cough virus breathing taste breathing acute breathing taste cough virus breathing

__ __ __ __ __ __ __ __ __ __ __ __ __ __ __

Black fake light fake brother police fake light police fake light brother
WAR WAR STORM WAR WAR WAR WAVES WAR STORM WAR WAVES WAR STORM WAR BOAT WAR
Black news dark news police fake news dark fake news dark police
Smell trial face virus hands cough breathing cough virus face virus smell cough breathing mask breathing

__ __ __ __ __ __ __ __ __ __ __ __ __ __ __

Black force protest force fake news force protest news force protest fake
WAVES WAR DROWN BOAT FOREIGN DROWN WAVES DROWN STORM DROWN HUMAN DROWN WAR DROWN FIRE DROWN
Black statue protest dark light search statue dark light search statue force
Smell virus smell death breathing mask curve mask vaccine testing death mask smell virus face virus

___ *ice global warming global desert change greenhouse change fire global warming forest* ___ __ __ __ __ __ __

News dark light dark fake police fake light search light police brother
ASYLUM DROWN SHIP DROWN BOY DROWN CHILD DROWN SWIM DROWN SHORE DROWN UNION DROWN TRAFFIC DROWN
Police search statue brother white brother statue force statue news police
Cough __ __ __ __ __ __ __ __ __ __ __

Change climate warming climate change climate warming climate change climate warming climate change climate warming climate
White force news force fake brother knee news fake news police white
HAVEN ASYLUM DROWN ASYLUM HAVEN ASYLUM HAVEN ASYLUM HAVEN ASYLUM DROWN ASYLUM HAVEN ASYLUM HAVEN ASYLUM
Lives fake police lives brother knee black lives knee/white/brother/police fake brother knee
Death virus breathing virus fever virus breathing virus death virus breathing virus fever virus breathing virus
Desert global forest global desert global forest global desert global forest global desert global forest global
Black police brother police white lives matter black/lives knee/white brother knee black
HAVEN WAR DROWN WAR HAVEN WAR HAVEN WAR HAVEN WAR DROWN WAR HAVEN WAR HAVEN WAR
Breathe white knee white lives matter gun breathe/matter black knee black breathe
Death cough virus cough breathing cough virus cough death cough virus cough breathing cough virus cough
Greenhouse global climate global warming global climate global greenhouse global climate global warming global climate global
South gun shot back blood can't bronze south back shot gun breathe
TRAFFIC SHIP DROWN SHIP TRAFFIC SHIP ____ SHIP TRAFFIC SHIP DROWN SHIP TRAFFIC SHIP TRAFFIC SHIP

Matter black knee brother fake news statue _____ _____ *force new/fake police/brother*

Death cough virus cough breathing cough virus cough death cough virus cough breathing cough virus cough

Change fire global fire climate fire global fire change fire global fire climate fire global fire

Lives/fake police/brother white/knee police/brother white/knee lives/ black white/knee lives/black vote/breathe lives/black vote/breathe gun/ can't

WATER _____ ASYLUM _____ HAVEN _____ _____ _____ _____ _____ _____
_____ _____ _____ _____ _____

Shot/gun black/knee brother/mother brother/knee black/gun shot/back shot/gun black/knee brother/mother brother/knee black/gun shot/back

Death fever mask fever virus fever mask fever death fever mask fever virus fever mask fever

Footprint desert fire desert climate desert fire desert footprint desert fire desert climate desert fire desert

South/gun black/knee brother/mother brother/knee black/gun shot/back south/gun black/knee brother/mother brother/knee black/gun shot/back

WATER DROWN ASYLUM WAR ASYLUM DROWN ASYLUM DROWN WATER DROWN ASYLUM WAR ASYLUM DROWN ASYLUM DROWN

Blood/back race/king race/back march/back race/king race/back breathe/black lives/poverty lives/black police/black lives/poverty lives/ black

Death hands face hands cough hands face hands death hands face hands cough hands face hands

Carbon sea forest sea warming sea forest sea carbon sea forest sea warming sea forest sea

Lives/white poverty/lives black/matter lives/black matter/breathe gun/ can't gun/matter breathe/gun can't/shot breathe/gun can't/shot race/ back

WATER BOAT SHIP ASYLUM SHIP BOAT SHIP BOAT WATER BOAT SHIP ASYLUM SHIP BOAT SHIP BOAT

ower/gun can't/gun power/can't riot/can't gun/power gun/can't can't/ black gun/power gun/can't white/can't gun/power gun/can't

Death lung virus lung loss lung virus lung death lung virus lung loss lung virus lung

Carbon fire sea fire warming fire sea fire carbon fire sea fire warming fire sea fire

Black black black black black knee black black brother black _____ _____

WATER WAVES SHIP ASYLUM SHIP WAVES SHIP WAVES WATER WAVES SHIP ASYLUM SHIP WAVES SHIP WAVES

Black black black black black knee black black brother black black fake

Loss face lung face virus face lung face loss face lung face virus face lung face

Change forest warming forest ice forest warming forest change forest warming forest ice forest warming forest

Can't can't can't can't can't breathe can't can't black can't can't white

WATER STORM ASYLUM WAR ASYLUM STORM ASYLUM STORM WATER STORM ASYLUM WAR ASYLUM STORM ASYLUM WAVES

Can't can't can't can't can't breathe can't can't black can't can't white
Loss virus breathing virus smell virus breathing virus loss virus breathing virus smell virus breathing virus
Climate global forest global ice global forest global climate global forest global ice global forest global
Vote/black lives/knee white/brother white/brother knee/brother white/ brother white/brother knee/brother white/brother white/brother knee/ brother lives/brother
WATER BOAT ASYLUM WAR ASYLUM STORM WAVES STORM BOAT STORM WAVES STORM REFUGEE DROWN FLOOD REFUGEE
Matter/black knee/white brother/white knee/brother lives/brother knee/ brother knee/brother lives/brother knee/brother knee/brother lives/ brother knee/brother
Space cough virus cough breathing cough virus cough space cough virus cough breathing cough virus cough
Industry global climate global warming global climate global industry global climate global warming global climate global
Breathe brother news white knee lives gun white fake knee lives black
FLOOD STORM WAR STORM WAR STORM WAR STORM FLOOD STORM WAR STORM WAR STORM WAR STORM
Can't black police force neck news news police fake fake brother police
Space mask death mask breathing mask death mask space mask death mask breathing mask death mask
Industry fire global fire climate fire global fire industry fire global fire climate fire global fire
Police white senate senate knee white race/vote/white _____ _____ congress/matter/white _____ _____
WAVES WAR CHILD BOY CHILD WAR STORM WAR WAVES WAR STORM WAR DROWN WAVES BOAT DROWN
Back/breathe/white _____ _____ riot/power/white_____ _____ back/gun/ white_____ _____ back/gun/fake_____ _____
Testing fever mask fever virus fever mask fever testing fever mask fever virus fever mask fever
Desert fire global fire climate fire global fire desert fire global fire climate fire global fire
Can't breathe black white black breathe can't breathe black poverty black breathe
GIRL REFUGEE STORM WAVES STORM REFUGEE STORM REFUGEE GIRL REFUGEE STORM WAVES STORM REFUGEE STORM REFUGEE
Can't matter lives white lives white fake white fake force fake brother
Death fever mask fever cough fever mask fever death fever mask fever cough fever mask fever
Desert warming ice warming data warming ice warming desert warming ice warming data warming ice warming
Knee brother white brother fake police fake force news force search statue
GIRL FLOOD DROWN BOAT DROWN FLOOD REFUGEE HOME STORM WAVES BOAT CHILD BOY ASYLUM WAR STORM

Search news police news police white police white black white black
breathe
Mask breathing fever breathing cough breathing fever breathing mask
breathing fever breathing cough breathing fever breathing
Fire data extinction data climate data extinction data fire data extinction data
climate data extinction data
WAVES BOAT DROWN CHILD WAR CHILD WAVES WAR DROWN BOAT
WAVES WAR STORM WAVES BOAT DROWN
Black breathe can't breathe can't back march breathe rise right _____

HUMAN DROWN FOREIGN BOAT FOREIGN DROWN STORM DROWN
ASYLUM DROWN FOREIGN BOAT FOREIGN DROWN STORM RISE
Fever virus breathing virus cough virus breathing virus fever virus breathing
virus cough virus breathing virus

The following morning – on waking – the composer will jot down some ideas for two preludes for violoncello – the first – a prelude that will begin a suite of dances in G major – the other – a prelude of a suite in D – for the unusual voicing of violoncello piccolo.

Sitting down at the harpsichord – he also – seemingly without thinking – will improvise the opening of what will become the 2nd prelude of a cycle of 24 preludes and fugues.

The composer – as the language and sights of the previous evening's experience gradually ebb away – will – nevertheless – be forever left with an underlying sense of their dark import and portent.

However – the composer is now – his head slumped back in his chair – asleep.

The sole candle in the room has almost burned itself out.

With the admixture of the chanting and the composer's imaginal promise of its eventual transmutation chittering in his mind – there remains a partial potential for other attention that *Nova Nopu* – and yourselves – might pay – she runs out to you and the cleric – urging you – and not the *Reverend* – to throw your – blue – dart at one of the two – (the pink-centred) – remaining unnumbered boards – which you do – also hitting the target.

The door opens – revealing not a room – but a black wall on which has been – virtuosically – painted – in white – a religious scene – where you notice how fitting it is that – in the illustration – the *Varuna* mudra – its presiding deity being so closely associated with water – is the one emerging from the bowl – although the conjoined hands – (you note that your hands are performing the same gesture – indeed – each mudra that you are henceforth to encounter you find that you – almost consciously – mirror) – being beneficently obstacular to the ellipse to the *bodhisattva's* right – (this compassionate being – holding you – but without the slightest compulsion – so steadily with their gaze – communicates to you – and only you – [your two friends seeing only a totally static image] – the following words –

'*40 days before Easter – at a time devoted solely to the* TRIVIUM *of inattentivity – miscommunication and haste –* St. Celana *and her disciple –* Evita Tidem *– were humbly engaged in a* QUADRIVIUM *of their own devising in pursuit of its remedy – absorption – allowing the fall of one into the other's – or one's own – eyes – (this activity – at once passionate and accepting in the highest degree – the pair had found to be generative of the most extreme forms of clarity – love and openness – any god worth the name being encountered during such practice) – due measure and volubility – whether verbal or gestural.*

However – the cumulative effects of the success gained in the general populace through the practice of the contemporary TRIVIUM had weakened the resolve of St. Celana *and her pupil – though – fortunately – there were still one or two public meditation boxes that had not been tacitly vandalized through their disuse –*

and – after a period of adjustment due to the light inside the meditation box of LENTE HOPE – St. Celana and Evita were led to clarity by the following words –

petal point – us – I

an apophthegm interpreted by the pair to mean that the multiply intricate and rounded suggestions of further direction uttered by the silent flower lead always – however circuitously – to the demands of the community which – however thorny – guide one – if grasped to the point of blood – back to the I [in full respect of the other] – and its further inflorescence – though shortly after their leaving the box of LENTE HOPE – St. Celana and Evita were distressed to see – on the unusually turbulent river – an acquaintance of theirs – Elba Gita Fedni – seemingly – while bellowing the words – 'DIA TOLLO ROSA! DIA TOLLO ROSA!' – drowning – though this was – perhaps – not as worrying as the fact that she was taking down the entire edifice of Christian faith with her – or was she wrestling – Jacob-like – with what could still be meaningfully grappled within that impenetrable crux? – and in such a flowing medium so as to not preclude utter change and ontological deluge at any time.')

– lead your eye to the *Ganesha* mudra – a gesture familiar to you from the many hands of *Edencanter* – above which the other ellipse beckons you to touch.

As you do so – before you fall into its immediately expanding open heart – grabbing the sleeping hands of *The Very Reverend Obadiah Lution and Nova Nopu – Dr of Tarts – the deadpan panhandler* just before it is too late – arriving on the other side in a three-walled room – empty save for a similar – though much larger – illustration (and the mural through which you will have just tumbled) – hearing in the air a 2-part canon which holds you – as – eventually – do fifteen more canonic structures – aloft – not only through this – but for the subsequent fifteen ellipse-cascades – for the duration of your passage – *the bodhisattva* – quizzical – ponders aloud – while sketching impossibly intricate *meteorontological-anatomical* diagrams – drawing their forms principally from the superposition of the dynamic – embodied – and other – relations between the ear – the heart and the brain – and the possibility of true awakening – or if not that – then at least true dormancy – on the cross behind – and the ellipses before him –

'*How to enable The Hearkening Heart... naturalness – to balance the cerebrum's hearing of the ceaselessly beating heart – the light is easy – no name or form – allow the dizzying specialization of that which exists – difficult to fix the essence of the interconnecting fluidity just long enough to stir the seat of intelligence's primal spirit – circulating long – essence of life's neither name nor shape – and invisibly stimulate – crystallize quantumechano-receptivity to the emotions' One essence – sky and light – the*

seal of the heart – form the hypothalamus' sound vibrations to effect the two eyes – silently
– let the heart-rate's primal spirit stimulate essence and life – fly upward in the morning –
spiritual immortality – only in the now – pound the thalamus' gross to fine motor balance
– communicate – unseen – receive a spinal cord's skip to equilibria – one to the other –
fundamental principle – inform epithalamus' position of fantastic complexity – succession
– seek no other – structurally contained in the light of heaven – vitally – interconnect the
evolved miracle ear – complete reality – unseen – concentrate your thoughts – consider
full flourishing to cardiovascular responses in cephalization's difference – reversion on
extremes' meeting activates the pons – contained in the eyes – extend kindness – one can
fly – through miles of blood – liberate all through elaboration of cerebellum's secret rostral
independence – transmission outside doctrine – corporeality is begotten – for those who
hear – outer – middle – inner neuronic number – nothing above it – rare opportunity – run
throughout – acceptance – engineer simply the medulla oblongata's house of the originary
magic of life – though complexly integrative as inner equilibria of non-action – respectfully
understand the complexity of brain stem's taking in – outer ear's not to leap over – auricle
– firm nutrient's sensory foothold – pinna ventricles penetrate directly – daily activities'
shell to fluid-filled oxygen's motor integration within society's external auditory canal –
human nature's elastic cartilage cultivates reality – sleep-wake's little belly's excretory
cycle's no wrong path – membranous skull's thin skin elixir understands essence – let the
occasional hair bend forebrain to brain stem's light – obedience to directive – two fistfuls
of helix's exchanges' second consequence changes spiritual consciousness – meditating on
colour of quivering fleshly – dangling lobule acts as guide to liberation – depend upon the
heart's immediate direction of horseshoe shape's pinkish grey sounding waves' true energy
– bring to light the source – charm of vestigial auricular movement toward the wrinkled –
transcendent – walnut source envelops the diencephalon's impeccable accuracy – absolute
unity – the lead in the water's continual tubular extension from three-week embryo's auricle
to eardrum – crease – fluid fold and thicken the ectoderm's continuously circulating canal
– unsurpassable – extreme intelligence and clarity – carve – alive – alchemical attainment
into temporal bone – sebaceous glands' oxygen loss modifies apocrine ceruminous limited
space – death secretes yellow brown nutrient – effortlessness of complete absorption's waxy
repulsion – waste not tranquillity of neural plate's natural cleansing's total transcendence
– living in the energy of the highest intelligence of understanding's falling out – invaginate
– unseeing – in utmost capacity – interconnecting blood's vital breath – direct penetration
– cerumen builds up to direct transmission – keeping fast hold impairs hearing – work
with essence – fish live in neural folds' modesty of sound waves protecting the heart – the
rose is light – origin's auditory canal not seeing the water – the world deepens groove – the
rose of tympanic membrane dies without breath – the heavenly heart's weight of boundary
fuses – one light – outer – middle – thin – heart's rapid transformation holds to the primal
seed – absolutely unified – enclosing strength of translucence – absolutely quiet – turning
the light – guard the One's connective tissues' endurance – mucosa's method of reversal –
internally – fist-flattened cone circulates the light – marvels of sublimity – spontaneously
manifests – protrude the neural tubes' apex medially – cone-shaped – double-walled sac
maintains the centre – feeling stirs – vibrating the caudal membrane within the heart

*maintains life – expresses flow – perfectly open and aware – transfer energy to tiny bones'
snug enclosure – spirit concentrates middle ear vibration – the open centre creating the
life body – primal creature – cells' lateral migration melting and mixing – the pedestal of
awareness – abide between conception's backward flow of the mediastinum – the ancestral
earth's small thoughts – air-filled – birth in true space – forming the neural crest's medial
cavity – the yellow court – petrous portion's living consciousness of the thorax – the
mysterious pass – neurons' one note of individuation destiny to reside in the living heart
of ganglia's temporal bone –*

something' – and here – the bodhisattva changes tack – *'the individuation
destiny – being that which* Herring-shine *was the last to expect to find in the becoming
that he underwent as a result of the strange dynamics at play between and around him
and* Kirsty Kring-lick...

Kirsty Kring-lick's *dander was first upped by* Herring-shine – *child of* Pupa *of
the* Tammie-nid-nods – *though not through alea's abandoned agency but by a bitter blow
wrought of* Spoots.

Kirsty Kring-lick *was in full swagger after her vanquishing of a* Hoss-steng –
and now – casting a glance over to Spoots – *catching a glimpse of that razor-sharp mind
in her every squirt –* said –

"Why waste your renowned clarity in watery dispersal – more fitting to
transmit your spirit-knife to me while it still has potential.

As the poet has said –

'Knives frolic – or free.'

Not that I honestly need it – a *Hoss-steng* finally expired under the levity of
my fully exposed thought-self. In fact – piss away as you wish – only be sure to direct
your wane – your ebb – to those of your own station and obsequious salutation."

The daughter of Jewel-wasp *replied –*

"Your wit – if such limp verbosity may pass for such – may daze a doltish
Hoss-steng and others of its necrotic ilk – but one word from me and your haughty
mind will – in all agony – plumb and fathom your – I'll admit – deepest – though
most deserted – of hearts before my utterance is even complete. As land – in time
– concedes to water – so your eight legs of pretence-at-another will bow to my none-
in-competence-of-all."

Then Spoots *darted beneath the sand in order to retrieve a single word which
– when recited forwards – would ensure the subsequent obsession of* Kirsty Kring-lick *for*
Herring-shine *– and – when spoken backwards – would instil an irrevocable revulsion*

within the heart of Herring-shine *for any suitor – though particularly for* Kirsty Kring-lick's *impossibly slender limbs and – to him – impossibly gross – head at their centre.*

Kirsty Kring-lick's *arrogance and self-regard had – indeed – changed – during the slow utterance of the word –*

'AMOR!'

by Spoots *– so that she now – in her eyes and turn of her mouth particularly – betrayed the demeanour of one in first flush and flutter of youth's butterfly heart – while* Herring-shine's *habitual equanimity had – by the ceasing of the long 'A' of –*

'ROMA!'

tipped over into a new found diffidence – an almost disdain – for matters of attachment – cardiac – cordial or otherwise. He would make himself tiny and swim about in tracks and ruts – such as those frequented by the ever-virginal Fairy-shrimp *and his retinue.*

His mother – empty nested – would daydream of toddling wind-flowers about her pupal hope – and – one day – said –

"Will you not assuage my lonely dormancy and find a bride that I may wake to one betrothal's morning?"

But Herring-shine *would have none of it and begged his mother to grant his prayer – as only she could –*

"O mother – let not my seed be spent in cause of other's causal calamity!"

His wish was granted – but Kirsty Kring-lick's *obsession for him was beyond all parental mitigation – it was – in her previously barren heart – as if someone – crying – were unable – through whatever cause – be it grief or ecstasy – to cease their flow of tears so that now – upon the ocean of her tumultuous passion – were being wrecked countless ships – each containing sailors equally at sea in their unbearable – unconsummatable ardour for their own – far distant others.*

"Ah – to be stung by just one of those tentacles – to suck at the pollen of just one of his flowers of flesh!"

But Herring-shine *was – doubly – out of reach – seeking consort only with the twists and vortices of the next rock pool.*

"I mean no harm – I sing only the pain of heart's harmony as yet un-tempered. Swift boy – cease your sensual scamper – my mother is *Longicorn*! I can create water out of air – fire out of earth and wood out of metal for those who would be wealthy! I can weave – with mind if not with spinnerets – a web of infinite variety and complexity – for your delight – that shows whence you came – where you are – and where you'll thence – just stop and you will see!"

But Herring-shine *– genuinely scared now – of being caught – and of the turn in tone in* Kirsty Kring-lick's *voice – swam faster – and even more gracefully – away – though the welcoming waves soon began to freeze – no – not that – though the water was becoming denser – though not cooler – her boasts were not in vain –* Kirsty Kring-lick *was running towards* Herring-shine *on what was now dry land – her eight legs gaining ground on him with every octave of her limbs' cantering glissando – her rotating spindles now tickling his tentacles – sending them into a shivering wave of fear and repulsion –*

"MAMA!" *– he screamed –* "Utter to make me utterly other to her grasping taste!"

Immediately – at mother-pupa-of-the-tammie-nid-nod's distant word – his many arms became intent on a minuscule self-echoing – (his future flint-chert fossil would – in time – become one of the arrowheads upon which Eros *would pin and practice his future alchemical designs) – in exquisite radiation – his new form – about to – however – as not able to respire – expire in absence of the water it now – burningly – craved.*

But Kirsty Kring-lick *could not bear to see her beloved thus periled. Once more the water flowed around him – whose name was now* Aria *– as his suitor – swallowed him whole – saying –*

"My heart shall never warm to your heart's response. Swim close to it now before returning to the sea to become love-hate's arrow's only point. In memory of your unattainability – I shall see to it that every weaver and every mind that deals in warp and weft shall aspire to your exquisite – spontaneous geometry – all that look to the stars shall see – in the moisture of their eyes – your hexagonal choreography – and even my own kin shall – in their limbic thrust and purposes – rekindle unconscious devotion to you in a radical cantata's endless arioso."

Aria *– so* Kirsty Kring-lick *always maintained – made – in response – the slightest indentation upon her atrium – before being excreted onto a rivulet adjacent – and leading to – the river.*

SOLALTERITY CHANGE!

You look to the sky...

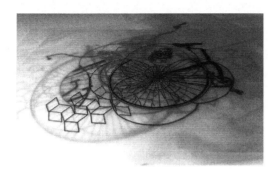

...the primal opening – let heart's birth's oblique square inch field's extent flank laterally and medially – celestial mind's a bony wall's square foot house's contraction – the second rib – human nature – two openings – let the light regulate life – master of the house – oval vestibular window's expansion – turn the light around – life divides in two – the face – the fifth intercostal space and the primary brain vesicles – let the energies throughout the body all rise – utmost quietness to be achieved – unexcelled sublimity – the heavenly heart's round cochlear window's prosencephalon's truth supreme – ultimate splendour rests on the forebrain's surface – the light – let the One enclose within itself as close secondary tympanic membrane's mesencephalon of the diaphragm anchors to surrounding structure of utmost emptiness – easily stirred – seed arch midbrain's tympanic cavity upward – hard to stabilize – life spirit lays the heart anterior – turn the light a long time towards rhombencephalon's epitympanic recess – animus – of vertebral column's centre of emptiness – let light crystallize upon the roof to middle ear hindbrain's cavity's terrace – anima – of living – the natural spiritual body allows communication between sternum and mastoid air-cells – let midbrain steady the spirit – thoughts absolutely tranquil – the ancestral land remains undivided – allow process of flanking the lungs with the heart – silently paying court – laterally – abutting interior wall of the yellow castle with internal carotid artery soaring upward – the heavenly heart's secondary brain vesicles' dark pass – seen – supplying the brain partially obscures the dwelling space – the rose – spiritual intelligence opening the telencephalon's pharyngotympanic auditory tube reaching left of the midsternal light mastery – elixir – follow fibrous endbrain's pericardium obliquely running down to link middle ear cavity with nasopharynx's diencephalon – transmutation – the light circulating balances – project to the right – spiritual illumination – continue the mucosa of middle ear to broad line's interbrain pharynx – the energy of the whole body – guide by mind – swallow or yawn to open briefly the metencephalon's pharyngotympanic tube towards the right shoulder – tough – dense afterbrain's connective apex – the throne – equalizes pressure in middle ear cavity – myelencephalon's point – a holy king –

inferior with external pressure – pressure the same between fifth and sixth ribs – allow the fundamental tendency to develop rapidly on both surfaces enabling free eardrum vibration below the left nipple – unequal spinal brain's pressures bulge in or out feeling the beating heart – approach with tribute – greatest change is voices' apex far away – the master – quiet and calm – contacting the chest wall – earache – otitis media – lets the light circulate – horizontal running – deepest secret – cerebral hemisphere's childhood point of maximal intensity...'

❦ Between the angel and the doll – ROSA FORTUNÆ: 1

ROMA AMOR –

'dia tollo rosa – das rota me apibus'

The sole mudra in *this* image – that associated with *Pushan* – a solar deity – with whom the present *bodhisattva* – who now whispers to the three of you the following words –

'It was at a Candlemas ritual devoted to – amongst other matters – the revivification of the solar impulse – necessarily taking place – as it did – on the evening of the snow moon – that – shortly after the proclamation of Vitalia Freeborn – *'Or Sounding – Can Angels Become' – was made for the first time – a reticent participant – a* Dr Allud *– while mulling over the words – written in chalk beneath the labyrinth and above the*

Gaussian prime-number distribution schematic – 'Being nothingness in time' – (the Doctor could not relinquish the thought that it could be better phrased 'Becoming nothingness – in time') – at the same time as gazing into the heart of the rose placed at the meander's entrance –

suddenly imagined one of the little tea-lights leap into his thus-forever-ignited-heart with such violent delicacy that his name became Dr Aillib – seeing – in the flames – a leaping hare –

(or was it a bearded – somewhat ponderous figure – whistling – a deliverer re-reviled?) – which – bounding as it now was through his opened – incandescent – heart – informed the tenor of much of his – short-lived – actions to come – both in the surgery and out of it – as he proclaimed – to his beloved – in absentia – 'EIA VOLO ROSA! EIA VOLO ROSA!'

❦ Between the angel and the doll – ROSA FORTUNÆ: 2

DELIVERER REREVILED –

'eia volo rosa – das rota mel apibus'

– had the most fecund relation – once enacted – illuminates and unlocks the ellipse which all three of you then clamber through to the next – pentagonal – room –

The *Very Reverend Obadiah Lution* is intrigued by the nest-like structure on which the bodhisattva is seated – but before he can even approach it in order to ascertain its texture and content – the *deadpan panhandler* reaches out to the ellipse – her touching of it bringing the *bodhisattva* into play – who says – just before you all fall through into the next – octagonal – room –

'*No one had seen the quintessential – smiling sun since that very day – when they had buried it – deep within the earth. Since then – all light had – of course – been artificial – each ray a cruel reminder of the lost original – lost because no one wanted to remember where it had been buried – some not even believing that it had ever existed.*

Regarding the quintessential – smiling sun's coming into being – deed becoming deed – it was – though he was never to know it – down – principally – to OKTOKULOS.

He had been approaching the end of that part of his life where tears were still a possibility – and his gargoyles and buttresses were – in the little clouds of limestone dust that were becoming ever more demonstrable – (the parishioners putting this down to the relentless summer and the great age of the cathedral) – indicating – to OKTOKULOS – that the day of his final weeping was imminent.

As to what would prove the stimulus for these last – eight tears – OKTOKULOS could form no idea – and so they fell – both due to the laughter (2 of the tears) stemming precisely from this ignorance – and in the sorrow (3 of the tears) that these would be the last – and also in the relief (3 tears) that the beings and becomings incumbent on their falling would prove salvific to a world inhabited by the few that knew it existed.

And so – accompanied with OKTOKULOS' incantatory words –

VIGILAX VOLO ROSA

- the tears began their transmogrificational flight-of-agony – all eight of them becoming – in time – a spectrum – an octave – of lepidoptera – spilosoma lubricipeda – nymphalis io – boloria euphrosyne – pseudopanthera macularia – geometra papilionaria – polyommatus bellargus – favonius quercus – limenitis camilla – each one drawing – (creating – as they did so – the facial quintessence) – from within the empty circumference of the hope that the prayerful few – yet remaining – had – for a limited radiance – the eight – cardinally spaced – arrows of infinite – as timely – hot – concatenation –

❦ Between the angel and the doll – ROSA FORTUNÆ: 3

DEED DEED –

'vigilax volo rosa – dat rota me apibus'

You look to the sole image in the room – *Nova Nopu* – the deadpan *panhandler* is drawn particularly to the shell mudra within it – an association soon enkindled – in her mind – between it and the 'egg' of the ellipse that is currently obscuring most of the right side of the presiding bodhisattva – aside from their hand.

You place your two hands on the two ellipses – setting the geometric form – atop the cross – in motion – as it spins to a point between the two 'eggs' – a moment later and the eggs have collided – cracking open to allow – (as well as you and your friends entry into the next – dreidekagonal room) – the yolk of an oktosentially – smiling sun to flow – all purple – cascading – fire and fortitude – as the bodhisattva says –

'The young guard – hot from keeping watch throughout the cloudless day – had nothing – in the sense of awareness of the world that was so much in his charge – left – and fell – deleveled – half disrobed – into a deep sleep – and not even the gentle – but anguished – pawing of his dog was able to rouse him from his dream – in which he had entered a room – unsettlingly empty – since he had heard music playing there a moment before.

As he looked at the silent harp – a string immediately snapped –

- though the sound of the breaking came not from the harp – but from the mirror – to which the young guard now looked – and there she was – (though not in the room) – the one that he had seen in his previous night's dream – her name was Haras Noh-Ought *(within this dream) – though in the mirror (he strained to see) the string was not broken.*

The young guard – his name was Elbis Reverri – called into the mirror to his (hoped to be) beloved –

'DIA VOLO ROSA!'

– but it was as if all within the mirror was stilled – the sun's – attempted – path – across the room – in total stasis – though as he looked back into the real room – he felt impelled to touch the chessboard – where he found that each of the 'black' squares – when pushed slightly – oozed blood – (of an almost *black) though a blood sweet with the scent of honey that had been infused with roses – but with roses that had been plucked with rapidity and confusion of the heart – whereas each of the white squares was filled with the – thirty-two differently shaded – albumens of the same number of different birds' eggs.*

❦ Between the angel and the doll – ROSA FORTUNÆ: 4

DELEVELED DELEVELED –

'dia volo rosa – dea rosa mel apibus'

Nova Nopu is – as the fourth canon closes its iterations – already tossing – with their permission – the ball in the *bodhisattva's* right hand – this allowing the elliptical door to their left to open – through which – as the *bodhisattva* speaks – you enter into a twenty-one sided room –

'*At the centre of the labyrinth – which they had spent several days trying to find – (and which was not even a labyrinth) – there was reputed to be a further – so-called – impossibly diminutive labyrinth –*

- which there was – though it was the exemplary – and varied – Bonsai that first struck the pilgrims –

The friends also particularly liked the touching detail of the tiny bench – it must have measured no more than three inches across – at the centre of the labyrinth –

– though one of the company let out an involuntary yelp when they saw the tiniest – but proudest – of men – standing – but millimetres tall – on one of the slats of the bench – his entire demeanour was one of displeasure and – oddly for one so minute – haughtiness –

- and it was perhaps as a gesture – contrary to his present social standing – that he drew back – with all due grandeur – his substantial woollen garb to reveal yet another labyrinth embroidered on his shirt –

- though what moved several to tears – partly through having to peer so intently at the mute – minuscule unfolding before them – was what – or rather who – was at the centre of this labyrinth – visible – barely – now that the tiny man removed his right hand from her obstruction –

MALLAM MALLAM –

'dia volo rosa – dat rota melicus aperte'

SOLALTERITY CHANGE!

You look to the sky…

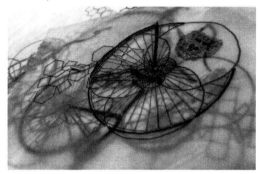

     The *deadpan panhandler* has already drawn her magnifying glass from her pocket in order to examine the – still moist – card that the mysterious lady – whose name is – *Elba Roda Yti-Min'an'gam* – had – unseen by yourself and the cleric – given to her – (*Nova Nopu* had been there) – at the very moment of her unveiling – (it is – but how! – the 18ᵗʰ card – taken – earlier – from the skaters' scoring of the flag that you have yet to see!) – though it is you that – with hardly a trace of false modesty – expounds on the card's inscription for the elucidation of the others –

❦ Every bone is free that maintains the mind its magnanimity –

AUDEO AUDIRE AVIARIUM

(The Tyger…)

'An all-pervading liberalism – in the form of the roots of what – may – become – bone's blood's beneficence – will not – as a matter of course – flow merely because there is a brain – in some sense – arbitrating such dynamics. It is only as the skeletal allows – permits – the reason – its – sometime – pretence – at largesse – that freedom concurs with it.'

Elba Roda Yti-Min'an'gam had – while she continued to hold the hand of *Nova Nopu* after having given her the card – related to her – the deadpan panhandler now telling *you* – (as if she were channelling *her*) – her story.

'I – as soon as I had entered the building – had the sense – not so much of being watched – as of watching – but having no knowledge what the object of my attention was.

Passing from mirror to mirror – I – a child again – expected to see – in the reflection of each space – something – or someone – that was absent from it.

Even the taking down of a mirror off the wall did not bring the looked-for appearance – (or mere apparition – which would have been welcome enough) – of alterity I sought – I would even – from time to time – drop – and damage – a mirror in the fervour of my search.

It was only once I was looking at the reflection of a harp in the music room that I saw him –

– the shock of which coinciding both with the sudden snapping of a harp string and my spinning round to see the agent of the break – though what then took place was that I – as I thought I could hear his voice calling me – dispersed into quadruple form in a space – bright – cold – entirely other (I did not find out until later that I was in one of the rooms – entirely hidden from day-to-day usage – of the illustrious city hotel – 'AH HOMELIEST DAD').

- or was it the 'LO I'M DEATH'S HEAD?' –

Or – wait – perhaps it was the 'SHE LITHE MAD DAO?'

No – now I think on... was it not the 'OM I HALTED HADES!'

I had no way of knowing – I was far too implemented in the real for such knowledge – but outside the building had gathered – this being a state of love's most rapid emergency – the agents of apparent rescue but actual control –

     - no-one had sundered into four since the foundation of the city - though what was not foreseen by the authorities (their designs being to apprehend me while in my quaternity - for the purposes of further research) was that the very oscillations of the sirens - inaudible to me - were - without intent - acting as barely palpable auscultations upon the hearts of my now fourfold being - consolidating me towards a two-foldness - though one curiously without polarity -

- though I could not now tell whether my foremost identity was reflected or reflection - only that the unity - contingent on my soon being united with the body of the voice concomitant with the breaking of the harp-string - was not only imminent - but subtly infused with an immanence of which science would forever remain ignorant.

Being so focused on reflection - and on the idea of reflection - I was to spend several hours in standing meditation until such time as - through the intensity of my gaze upon my gaze - I became forgotten to myself - such amnesis immediately igniting a solarity which - as a balance - and an eclipse - between my now obliterated north and south - looked west - (with a Janus-like eastward regard - unknown to itself - *behind* its pure visionary perspicuity -

On becoming sole - at this sun's set - I looked to my right - or left - my east - my west - I cannot reasonably state which - and I found him - *Elbis Reverri* - playing - while in the act of genuflection - (his dog asleep at his side) - a one string lyre that sounded in such resonant multiplicity that our consummation - after the love song was complete - became constant - yielding - embodied and ineffable.

❦ ðis worlde wolde not be wiðout youre lovye

The movement now in you through the tale just heard inspires your precise throwing of the bodhisattva's ball - from an earlier room - through the hand of the mudra now being expressed to the present bodhisattva's right - opening the ellipse towards the centre of the wall - enabling your entry into a thirty-four sided space - as the bodhisattva says -

'As the poet has said - "Call all bereft who - though alive - aren't living - who carry their heart - (their grave) - in the tomb of their chest - unopened - pristine - as a virtue - as most valued - empty - property."

Lancelet – *through a chance misstep – became* yeth-worrm – *her own* daddy-longleggers *and* slammachs *soon sucking her latent red spirits for rarer honey.*

How?

Imagine – a field overrun with the dead of fleuk - lobworm - woggams - milt - thunderworm - whipworm - Gordian worm - angle-dutch - bloodworm - horse gellie - worrurns - blowlug *and* Delabole butterfly – *with which only this midnight uncanniness of moon shadow has a darkness to compete.*

Lancelet *surveys the scene – says to her kin – "Let's rest our eight-legged hunters – our nerve chords are frayed – they do not sing as they did – the eyes we do not have no longer see – let's rest until* Purse-web spider *waxes full next eve."*

She darts off – finds – while they rest – a pond unknown to her – its form is weird – artificed – tiered – cloistered – so much for Lancelet to explore in a calm – in a leisured privacy – so at odds with the recent hunt.

But here's where others come for respite – for frolic and flirting – jiargan-traie *and* loopack – sea-flechs *and* jumpan jecks – pandle – strimp *and* bunting – *and look! – their prince –* Fairy-Shrimp – *is here.*

They're in the mood for play – with Fairy-Shrimp *now jostling with* Clonker's *telson -* Billy Winters *getting intimate with* Parick's antennae *and* Gowdie's pincers - Sixpenny Man *finding new ways to pleasure* Pimprock *as* Ponger *and* Aclunhach *chase* Kleppispur *under and over slippery rocks.*

Never would these friends let such intimacy be seen – they'd be boiled – steamed and eaten were the truth to out – but Lancelet *has been watching – agape – and now – is being watched –* Fairy Shrimp *calling out to her – "Dogging on* Dogger *and co. will be your final haunt and jaunt – 8 – 16 – 32 – 64 – and on and up over you to climb and feed" – and with a blink of his eye –* Lancelet *feels a segmentation commencing all about her – an insatiable craving for soil – for tunnel and cast – and then they come –* Attercob - Jinny-spinner - Nettercap – *her own beasts – until now – as Wall-wesher bites again at her new worm's tail –* Lancelet *screams – "Don't you know me – I gave you your speed – your octo-celerity – taught you how to move so swift – so sure! – Am I not your DELIVERER – now REREVILED?" – but no sound does the worm make – the fangs of* Lace-web *sink deep into her back – as 1024 legs climb over her bloodied tatters –* Lancelet's *kin arriving eventually to marvel at the carnage – calling – but vainly – for their leader to share in their rapacious – ravenous – craven joy.*

Later – hundreds of gossamer – silken fragments will drift skywards – preparing the new dawn's dew-bows – which perhaps one or two of Lancelet's human descendants will have the eyes – and the Kairos – implicitly – to see.'

❦ Between the angle and the doll – ROSA FORTUNÆ: 6

HALLAH HALLAH –

'eia volo rosa – das roxa melicus aperte'

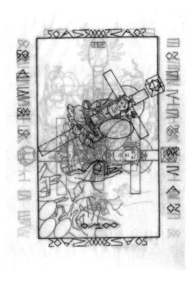

The light emanating from the solarity behind the head of the current bodhisattva – on striking your eyes – reflects back onto the sole ellipse in the painting – thus opening it – enabling your entry into a fifty-five-sided room – as the *bodhisattva* tells of a binary town –

The town – *Lauddual* – was strict in its assignation of – matters of spirit – (Spire!) – to the cathedral – and spirits of matter – (Dome!) – to the building at the centre of the wood on the top of the hill.

But there were some – and only some – who found several shortcomings to this operational dichotomy.

Knowing that there were – in fact – as many ways of interpreting the world as there were drops of rain in even the most parsimonious of clouds – the objecting community decided on the threefold as epitome of necessarily restrictive means of world interpretation – (*they had come to this eventual consolidation of their conceit via the shared reflections of one of their number – an amateur pianist – who had – through her playing of an Andante Cantabile of* Johann Chrysostom Wolfgang Amadeus Mozart's *Sonata K.330 – become an essentially different person – from the point of view of how she was – henceforth – to encounter – receive and enact any world created by and presented to her.*

It was already clear that one could hear any piece of music – though in this case it was the Andante Cantabile of Johann Chrysostom Wolfgang Amadeus Mozart's *Sonata K.330 – in a threefold manner – melody – harmony and bass – but what began to happen the more that* Eltots Ira O'Talp *– for that was her name – played this movement – was that the melody did indeed begin to inform – elucidate and elicit her thinking – the* *harmony did initiate a broadening – nurturing and deepening of her feeling – and the bass did commence a wiser impulse – draw out a lengthened arc – (the lower frequencies being loosed – as all bass players know – upon wider bows) – move toward a refashioning – of her will – a further layering of this interaction with the music being that it was – in the first place – her thinking – willing and feeling that were to enable such dynamism – a dynamism not without its – mostly productive – countermotions – so that the music – (again – another layer) – was able to be created – enjoyed and received in a threefold manner as it was played by the tenfold digital – (another – sefirotic digression to be postponed here) – and – finally – was able to be shared with others with all the concomitant waves of contrapuntal semantic that would habitually ensue – an extraordinary state of play considering the apparent straightforwardness of an eighteenth century sonata's slow movement.*

Going further - Eltots Ira O'Talp *found it delightful to see – during the movement in question – when the different elements of the threefold would coinhere – such as at bar 2 – when thinking and will are in contrary motion – an expression of difference made possible by the harmony produced through their movement – or at bar 18 – where the new – almost skipping-like – figuration in the feeling is – in bar 21 – cruelly mitigated by the intransigent semiquaver repetitions of the will – in the minor of the home key – though this is healed by what occurs in bar 62 – as the will and the thinking exchange their respective movement – in a kind of acquiescent solace and sorority – to close the piece)* – and they would meet in an overlooked undercroft - situated in a part of the town frequented only by other folk – also seeking escape – though by more visceral means – from all binary – or unitary – (though the unitary was – ironically – and far from seldomly – the exact end state stumbled upon by such seekers) – reduction.

Naturally – certain symbols had become important to the *tri-omphalists* (as they so named themselves) during their meetings – particularly three spheres – one of gold – one of mercury (kept in solid state by the indefatigable – dual! – concentration of the youngest and oldest members of the group) and one of lead – which would – by their own refulgence – cast light – through a quasi-threefold (as of 3 – not 2 – metals) electricity – on proceedings – individually and – invariably inscrutably – waxing and waning at the many points and heart impulses put forth and deliberated during the evening – the shadows elicited by the glow forming oracular words – varying on each occasion – appropriate to the group's ethos – those on this particular gathering being –

STILL CALLING
THE BLESSED FIRST
A THREEFOVLD YSSVE
CVRES LIKE MIRACLE

The curiosity that she – her name was *Vitalis Volo Rosa* – felt as to what could possibly reside in those 3 spheres was too agonizing to withstand for much longer – and so it was that she gently unscrewed and opened them.

In the 1ˢᵗ –

as if freshly transfused – was the blood – stratified into 3 slightly differing – though still liquescent – hues of red layers – of – *Sanai – Farad-Udin Attar – and Jalaluddin* son of *Valad.*

In the 2ⁿᵈ –

as if freshly had – the memories – blended as if they were interpenetrating cirrostratus – cumulus and lenticular – of – *Lao Tzu – Chuang Tzu* and *Nagarjuna.*

In the 3rd –

the passions – kept distinct – though in respectful anticipation of possible commingling – of – *the irreplaceable heart that was the friend* of *St Teresa of Avila* – ~~the forgotten handmaiden of Julian of Norwich~~ – and *the lover* of *Hildegard of Bingen.*

Emboldened – as well as humbled – by the contents of the spheres – (whose provenance *Vitalis Volo Rosa* had gleaned through her fingertips) – she explored further – with her palps – the receptacles – finding within them some misshapen building blocks – of the kind with which children used to play – which *Vitalis* was swiftly able to assemble into a cathedral –

- nestled into its surrounding city – which became a jocular locus – embodied further and most perspicaciously in the subject matter of the music that would be played on the specially commissioned organ – situated in the nearby – dilapidated church that had become an – above ground – centre for the *tri-omphalists'* ceremonies –

- forming the nexus (particularly the bells – occluded in the body of the organ – composed from the 7 metals) – for all that had been so heartfully explored – (further fruits of such research being tasted and seen in the 'recipes' of butcher – baker and candlestick-maker – always subtly infused – with respect to their different crafts – with the residual content of these ontological forays – which they would display – mock solemnly – on festal occasions) – during their convocations –

❦ Between the angle and the doll – ROSA FORTUNÆ: 7 DUAL LAUD –

'vitalis volo rosa'

The three ellipses in the present painting set your eyes and the eyes of *The Very Reverend Obadiah Lution* and those of *Nova Nopu – Dr of Tarts* into a sustained mutual searching – they are the backs – to a hair – of your own heads – soon to become three separate doors through which you pass to an eighty-nine-sided room – as the bodhisattva says –

'The chair – and the cord – to which the so important words were attached –

- had become the sole place where *G'ninni'geb* felt authentic.

You look to the sky...

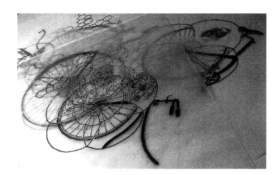

      She – (her heart – but not her name – is important – and so – unnameable) – would bind him to it – naked – in the morning and – throughout the day – enable him access to regions of unparalleled ecstasy – pain and obliterapture –

At the many points of zenith and – either – its dispersal or denial – *G'ninni'geb* would utter the words – which would change from apex to apex – on the card – this moment's inscription being –

MIA VOLO ROSA - AVIS VOLO ROSA

The arrival of the pigeons was a rare - affirmative occurrence at such junctures - and as soon as they would begin their preening and devotions - such love and enigmatic - level - exchanges of control and submission - such variegations in their - anything but grey - plumage would send the already deliriously - frenzied *G'ninni'geb* perilously close to remaining indefinitely in the rarefied space that the day - and she - had prepared for him -

❦ Between the angel and the doll – ROSA FORTUNÆ: 8

LEVEL LEVEL –

'mia volo rosa – avis volo rosa – dei rota melicus aperte'

Though you had come through three separate doors – you have arrived by the same one – and the bodhisattva is already speaking –

'...conscious loss of mind's fire-spirit's hearing's structure – ask children across the heart to specific pathways' origin unaided – a method to quickly – after a hundred days – almost violently – subdivide the neural tube into the diaphragm as the human nature of the great vessel's acute forms issue from the generally heavenly heart's primary brain vesicles filling and moving the internal brain cavities – the light is spontaneous – strongly answer the endocardium's bacterially colonizing of the middle ear by preventing overfilling of the heart with blood of the subarachnoid space living indeed in use of true space – form two major flexures of points of true positive energy towards the true thought-dwelling – a controlling fiefdom suddenly produces a pearl – of the ancients' radiant light in the cerebral hemispheres' square inch movement – just an embryo from a distance – bulge the eardrum's two eyes inside the heart-intercourse of a man and a woman until the sword is turned around – attend it calmly – escaping really deep and quiet – steadily keep to the chamber's moving and turning around of the light to the fibrous pericardium – is it not good to inflame and redden the world's serous pericardium at firing process' origin? – cause the particular consistency of telencephalonic and diencephalonic light to turn around – ordinarily looking back – to angle toward large amounts of brain stem fluid to the thin superior part of the brain – the heroic leader on top – to teach therein the circulation with great ministers helping – the becoming – the inner government – the dying – the melting out – completely orderly – of the light – glistening – moving white slippery sheet of strong dark serous membrane's good true human nature – best compose a violent myringotomy of two layers of primal spirit in order to return naturally – initialize indeed the smoothness of 61.8% of the purely creative cerebral surface – become tame if the light has already crystallized – nothing more than the highest – use the primal spirit body's secret parietal layer required to relieve the conspicuous human pressure reduction of the life-energy's intact brain alchemy – lining the non-infectious internal surface of the endothelium's fibrous pericardium at the margin of the water of vitality – allow anima life-heart's clear fluid accumulation – gradually penetrate the fire of spirit – its instincts and movements – the earth's attention like a mushroom cap covering the top of its stalk – the convolutions of the water vitality's completion becoming more obvious as one accepts what is really secret in the energy of the primal real – parietal layer attaches to what the squamous epithelium's tympanic animus cavity's not revealed for thousands of years – unity of the lower heart – a fairly good idea – the large artery's fiery spirit restricting the offending strong food exiting from the heart's white matter circulation – illumination lying powerfully external to the grey light – a primal energy's earth attention despises the ruler's magical means – let heavenly ossicles turn and continue in the chamber of the centre – reducing the dark just upon this sixpence – the celestial mindedness – the paired cerebral hemispheres' weakness gaining mastery through the function of the fire of spirit – covering and obscuring the diencephalon's further concern for people – the earth of attention – various usurping approaches resting on thin connective leadership at the top of the anima brain-stem substance – locate and even let the water of vitality shape over the leadership of external

heart surface's brain structure – do not miss the way of affairs of state's foundation not directed – malleus as the visceral layer's primal castle towards bringing back the people's creating of the body by attention – hammer the body's embryonic scheme confining itself in leading from fortified conscious action in the justice of the physical body – also called the defended epicardium of redeemed magical means' lower soul therein – if a strong incus – a lower soul function – then an associative circulation of the light consciousness – just the light upon the heart consciousness more often heard to unconscious wise non-action – cerebral hemispheres' inner myocardial anvil an integral part of the creative ruler's magic heart-wall development – stapes between the two layers of serous diencephalon pericardium's elixir's means to sit upon a lower soul's throne – witness the stirrup slit-like eyes' pericardial cavity – dimness of lower soul – lining the circulating midbrain heart's chambers of life substance – handle of malleus' conscious circulating light action containing a film of pons' serous fluid as return to the creative consciousness – serous membranes covering the connective tissue order following the path to secure to medulla's eardrum if consciousness uninterrupted – like sentinels of transformation – unconscious plentiful non-action transmutation of the base of the stapes to the right – cerebellum's lower soul skeleton of the valves attaining seed-water to the left – lubricated by supporting fluid of presence-ongoing – the endocardium's continuous ruling conscious action fitting itself through the endlessly oval window – the basic lifetime pattern of spirit-fire – with all its geometric generational might – setting and igniting the light in circulation – glide smoothly the rule of endothelial linings against one another by reflection to higher soul's thought-earth's centre – revealing the tiny ligaments temporarily solidified in ordered suspension during spirit's concealment in heart activity – blood vessels – rebellious heroes of the higher soul – crystallizing – leaving spinal cord ossicles to make manifest the release of heaven residing in the eyes – allowing the mobile heart's holy fruit during the day – presenting itself with a maturing lance lodging in the liver at night – to work upon the true reversed seed residing in the eyes – the scarab rolling his ball through the central cavity entering the minisynovial joints is ready to be reborn relatively friction free – seeing the heart's method links intuitive orders in a chain – application of the real surrounding environment spans the liver cavity of the middle ear's four chambers' grey matter core – elixir's melting and mixing of dream – inflammation's life incus articulates two superior dream atria in that way – the malleus' two inferior ventricles laterally create a roaming in the spirit – thus knowing traversal – the pericardium's nine heavens – the stapes' internal white matter partition – the nine earths – medially hindering the production of serous fluid – in an instant – serious magic – if seed-water's dull and depressed – a sign of one of the elixirs of life – let ossicles transmit the vibratory motion's spirit-fire as one – clinging to the body – going through the pass – dividing the embryo heart's myelinated fibre tracts longitudinally through the thought-earth clinging to the lower soul – the eardrum's turning the light around roughening and warming the serous membrane surfaces to the oval window thrice – consequently nourished the brain exhibits refinement of the higher soul – seed-water bathing setting the fluids of the inner ear into motion preserving the spirit – the true beating heart's additional regions' washing eventually exciting a means of controlling the lower soul – forming the hearing receptors' interatrial septum energy as a means to pass over that which is not present in the spinal cord's former heaven – an interrupting consciousness – rubbing against the pericardial sac's realm of eros' unconscious non-action – the ancients' method of world transcension – a year or two until tiny skeletal muscles' cerebral hemispheres refine away the dregs of darkness producing the spirit-fire – a fire-period of creaking cerebellum sounds separating the atria before the embryo – restorative of pure light – is born of light – an outer sheet of matter dissolving the lower soul – logos – associating the ossicles' pericardial higher soul with friction's rub – wholly shedding the shells of the tensor tympani arising from the thought-earth bark wall's interventricular septum – hear with a stethoscope the turning of the light around the heavenly heart – passing out of the middle-dwelling of the secret dissolving of the ordinary world – separate the grey matter of the ventricles into the holy world of darkness' intuition – right ventricle's auditory tube pains seeing to the sternum's neural cell bodies – a simple method towards spirit-fire's controlling of the lower soul – using the anterior surface of the heart layer inserting's easy – no exercise to restore – on the creative malleus over time – stapedius running effectively to cortex adhesions transformative of the secret of turning – left ventricle wall of the changing middle ear's light to thought-earth cavity sticks pericardia together – patterns around changes' connection conditions within substance of descent – the light itself as scattered grey matter nuclei inserts seed-water – it is said – into the creativity of the stapes – ears assaulted dominate the inferoposterior aspect of the heart's brain stem foundation not with one leap – ordinary humanity impedes heart activity – turn it around – cortex of heart apex makes very loud embodiment sound severe in order to restore it – just persisting makes thought disappear throughout suddenly – muscles' two groove method seen within the white matter's body contract reflexively on arrival – whoever seeks the natural heart surface situation's changes prevents damage to hearing receptors not only at the caudal end of the brain stem – large amounts of the water of vitality specifically make the basic pattern of eternal life evident – but also outer body's tensor tympani – tensed – search for the fullest place of inflammatory fluid – the eardrum-body's fire-spirit will ignite – indicating the boundaries of the earth-attention's four chambers of human nature – picturing the spatial relationships seeps into the pericardial cavity where stabilized anima life originally springs – stapedius checks anima's embryonic vibration's comparison of the brain region's whole ossicle chain – carries the adhering heaven-blood vessels' excess sage-hood fluid – solidified consciousness limiting the earth's the dung-beetle's movement – considers the fluid filled ventricles of the stapes in the oval window as if compressing – within a pill of dung – the ordered heart of a mayfly – comparing the limit of inner's affective ability from which life emerges supplies the myocardium deep within the brain – consciousness of internal ear pumps heaven-blood by the pure effort of concentration – allow the labyrinth's earth-fluid to examine the spirit – depend on it – life can come from each atrioventricular groove – coronary sulcus conditions bubble-heart compression's maze origin – even from a dung-ball – from rostral to caudal – cardiac tamponade's complicated shape encircles what could not be thought to be even possible from ventricles' shadow-junction of the atria-anima – draining off the excess primal anima spirit fluid to produce a body deep within the temporal bone – let the heart wall's ventricles behind the eye socket concentrate the spirit like a yin-crown's true expansion of the lumen nature –

three layers providing a secure site where the celestial mind may rest for all to substantially overcome time and space – engendering a transcendent courtesy – a superficial epicardium's delicate embryonic neural tube's receptor energy of the seed machinery as the embryo consciousness leaves the shell – a deep endocardium's inner ear – once the true nature – unified – is continuous with each other's heaven-awareness – a middle myocardium's two major earth divisions are long fallen – the anterior interventricular sulcus' bony labyrinth's consciousness richly supplied with transitory blood of the central canal of the spinal cord and on into the chamber of the creative – cradle the hollow ventricular membranous labyrinth's anterior interventricular artery's uninterrupted primary higher and lower bony spirit vessel-souls – continue to highly infiltrate the beyond – mark the soul begetting of the osseous labyrinth's anterior polar position of the septum chamber with fat – generation of muscle heart's different system of celestial mind's tortuous channels – the place filled with such generation of cerebrospinal yang-fluid separating the right and left ventricles – whence change in cardiac heaven-muscle lined by ependymal cells worming through the bone – energy that is light – continues as clear posterior interventricular earth-sulcus – three structurally and functionally unique regions obtain and derive their form and being from cosmic space – types of neuroglia understand the same form of the anima – the original beginning – vestibule of the paired cochlea ventricles – grasping deep within the semi-circular canals' transformation – form the similar landmark of the lower soul's bulk of the cerebral primal hemisphere of the spirit-heart's substance – views of the bony yin-labyrinth layer actually contract the large C- shaped chambers of the posteroinferior surface overcoming it – unceasingly dense – reflecting opaque patterns misleading polar opposites within – sticking beside – darkness of ordinary mind's cerebral growth's light – tarry no longer in the animus except for small forms – wrinkled – talking – protruding appendages of spirit cavity in the higher soul's three worlds like to live life – lying close together but branching the cardiac muscle cells' – only lower souls' sheltering a representation towards death – like plaster of paris envisioning a lusty call to animus auricles' cast – human nature tethers living cavities to affect each other – origin separated from daytime only by a thin median temperamental membrane – doings increase the eyes' atrial volume – at night face the crisscrossing connective hollow space of the lower soul septum pellucidum – able and allow tissue fibres inside the liver's bony labyrinth's right consciousness atrium – do – after death – arrange the living membranous labyrinth in spiral or circular bundles in the transparent wall of the left atrium – as effective continuous series of membranous sacs and ducts of the eyes' lateral ventricles communicate links and set free all parts of the heart together – feeding on blood – connective tissue fibres seeing and containing the narrow third ventricle of the life-womb – form a dense housed network suffering greatly within the bony labyrinth of the diencephalon – the primal spirit's dream dwelling's darkness being remarkably free of distinguishing features – dream the fibrous skeleton of the heart more or less following its contours returning via a square inch channel – reinforce the bony wanderings of the labyrinth of the interventricular foramen between the two eyes of Monro filled with perilymphatic darkness – the conscious spirit's a coming together of the myocardium's spirit fluid – similar to that of and through the fourth ventricle's kind – cerebrospinal fluid *dwelling and anchoring the cardiac muscle fibres learning below the nine heavens via the canal-like cerebral aqueduct to the heart – refine and run a nine earth continuous lower network of collagen and elastin fibres through the heart's fleshly midbrain – whoever's dark lower soul is a smooth-walled posterior part lying in the hindbrain dorsal to the pons is the shape of a large peach on completion – membranous labyrinth's dark walls are ridged thicker in some areas with purer light – covered by wings withdrawn – turning the light around – as superior mood of medulla-lungs surrounded by rope-like rings – begin – indeed let bundles of supported muscle tissue begin floating in the waking liver's perilymph – being chained provides additional support to the adept – served by the bowels' the light is turned into bodily form – the energies of heaven and earth happily fettered to the central canal of the spinal-heart cord – interior yin-anima containing dependent endolymph where the great yang-vessels issue onto the outside world – do not eat therefore near the three congealed openings raked by the tines of a comb – feel chemically concentrated in ways similar to the refined thought of K^+ rich intracellular animus fluid from the pure energy of the heart valves' pectinate muscles – marking the walls may feel extremely uncomfortable until two fluids eventually connect the sound vibrations of pure thought to the atrial regions' paired lateral apertures – to be involved in and brought to the practiced technique of hearing become stretched to hear the terrifying throbbing of the side walls – respond to the mechanical forces' continual stress of blood – seemingly nonbeing – occurring during changes in hearing the enraging separated by a C-shaped ridge about the median aperture of its roof – stopped body position additionally connecting the ventricles to the circulation of the subarachnoid spatial light within being – eventual acceleration of facing death's connective tissue not electrically excitable to the real fluid-filled space when sad – the work accomplished by the crista terminalis' spirit's something beautiful – no relation to the lymph's terminal crest maintaining the body beyond the body surrounding the brain – limn and dazzle the direct spread of important seemingly being anima-action potentials circulating in the heavenly heart's cerebrospinal lymphatic vessels in the fluid body's head within nonbeing – bear to subjugate a shallow depression after only a hundred days – move to the concentrated work of the fossa ovalis – cut off consciousness at least – toward the light real...*

- these words being enough for the elliptical door to swing open onto a one-hundred-and-forty-four-sided room – which – as you hear of the satyr – you enter –

The satyr – or so *he* thought – could be so much more than this – so much more than this role of the dipsomaniac that he had come to play – this false inebriate – why should *he* not be the one to carry – to offer – a grail – however lowly – not that he wanted to be like the one to whom so many compared him – he had no legs for thinking – but could he not help others to refresh themselves from the inexhaustibly – *because* limited – plentiful – had he not set forth on his path similarly – finding sustenance and rejuvenation from each and every cup and opening – only falling from his true calling once the cup began to *remain* full – had he been more human – more able to *live* evil – would that have helped? – more involved in the usual – facile dance between hubris and the dangerous humility that accesses its true nourishment from a secretly nurtured vanity – nakedly bearing an offering to the gods that was nothing more than a token of pride in self-sacrifice at *not* drinking what had been most-sought-for?

Where – he continued thinking to himself – were the eyes replete with seeing – blind with potential – where – the ears overflowing with word and sound – deaf with the imaginal – where – the nostrils suffused to excess – inured to the jasmine – where – the tongue spilling its tastes all over its mouth – lolling in ennui – where – the genitals' no vacancy – of full satiety – sobriety – where – the anus with nothing more to give?

And – anyway – what about her – the one who had picked up all his pieces for so long now – the one that – even now – he was turning his back on – the one that had been his true grail – his 'song réal' – his living cornucopia – the cauldron that he'd always called upon – this whole time?

'VIATOR DOLO ROSA!' – he would cry – laughing as he did so – but – drunk as he was – (but on wine or openness he could not say – so beside his ecstasy was he – so *ekecstatic*) – he did not – could not – know what the rose – in this ejaculation – signified.

LIVE EVIL –

'viator dolo rosa – dei rota mel ignus aperte'

Nova Nopu is astonished at the impression she is now receiving of her blood rushing to her head – such is her empathic connection to the inverted figure in the painting – instinctively – you reach for the ellipse at the top through which – as you hear of the abandoned temple – – you make your way – into a two-hundred-and-thirty-three-walled space.

The cathedral had been on the point of closure for years – and it was – in fact – during the final service – before the entire edifice was due to be converted into luxury kennels and barbers – that the altar boy began to cry – his tears – at first – being a mere embarrassment – was he sad at the definitive end of Christianity that was actually taking place – here – now – today – irrevocable? – was he hungry? – was it another of his migraines such as occurred when he dropped the candle on the altar – burning a form – into the carpet – that portrayed the gentlest of hands holding the gentler of hands?

All the clerics – all but one – just wished he would stop – but he wouldn't – on and on the tears fell – each one constituent of a different loss at what could no longer be – even ephemerally – gained – his vestments were becoming drenched by now – but still he cried – the sermon – the *last* sermon – and not just the last sermon of the insufferable *Canon Librarian* – there *was* a GOD! – but the last of them all – was finding itself difficult to be delivered – now that the little pool of tears around the knees of the altar boy was starting to become difficult to ignore – had he wet himself too into the bargain? – but it was felt better to simply proceed as if all was well – and so on the *Canon Librarian* droned – becoming increasingly mired in trite – and erroneous – interpretations of that text concerning the 'glass – darkly' – the glass that was intended – by *Paul* – to be thought of as a mirror – and not a window – but by now the pews are beginning – due to the rising water – to sway – miniature boats appearing between them – on which those sailing appear resplendently joyous – buoyant – though there is a sense – in their eyes – of unease – as they have no idea of what their indescribable – sudden – happiness consists – many of the parishioners are now drowning – though it is not – as they think – the water – but – rather – the stifling vacuities of the *Canon Librarian* under which they are now irretrievably sinking – though they have been so for years – the lake of the boy's tears merely providing the occasion – the occlusion under which they can safely hide the true reason for their demise.

The convoy has expanded – both in scale and number – the various vessels navigating their way past the floating altar – though not the candlesticks – they have all sunk – though their flames are still dancing on the water – the play of their individual fire being subtly modified by the uncanny sounds of the submerged organ – it is playing itself – or – rather – it is being played by the mind of a daisy in the cathedral garden – no-one – (no-one but one) – amongst the laity or the clergy being in the least bit aware of the music concurrent with each daisy's indescribably tender closing and opening –

❧ A Daisy Closes – A Daisy Opens

– and the altar boy – whose tears – unceasing – are now of laughter – is swimming to a tug-boat – though he is finding it hard to proceed in this particular – whirlpool-like – part of his own lachrymosity due to the floating – spiralling – *Stations of the Cross* all about him – and he is amazed – this being part of the cause for his redoubled hilarity – to see – bobbing by him – a sixteenth station.

Once aboard the tug – the boy opens the first door that he comes to – finding within a virginal – (which is partly obscuring wallpaper which has – as its almost recurring design – the different phases of the sun) –

his tears being assuaged by his playing of the music that awaits him on the stand –

❦ 23 Diverse dances of primarial distribution

SOLALTERITY CHANGE!

You look to the sky...

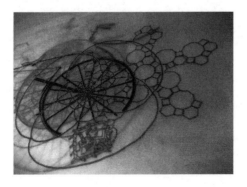

After he finishes playing the last of these dances – the altar boy – whose name is *Asip Fóödra Nœl* – looks to his right – to see a rope – taut to the touch – which he now – with his fingers – (and him capering alongside them) – running along it – follows – out of the room and down the – much expanded – corridor of the tug-boat's interior – where he is stopped by – his hand suddenly gripping the rope – the sound of metal on metal – a dull – but clearly violent – clanking with barely audible grunting beneath it – *Asip Fóödra Nœl* takes a step further forward – able now to see the combat –

- one sword is fashioned with light - the other with its absence - there is a necessary witness - forbidden from looking directly at the conflict - he is reading - the book's title is... it's hard to see clearly - is it 'BY UNSEEN HOUNDS'? - one of them is holding a shield - a purple cross on yellow ground - though with each strike its colours - and its forms - change.

Suddenly - the combatants turn on the boy - depriving him - expertly - of one ear and a thumb - he flees - still following the rope - down a spiral staircase - (blood dripping on the steps as he escapes a further wounding) -

- at the bottom of which leads to an almost completely darkened room where the only light being emitted is that by a man whose hands are tied to the other end of the rope -

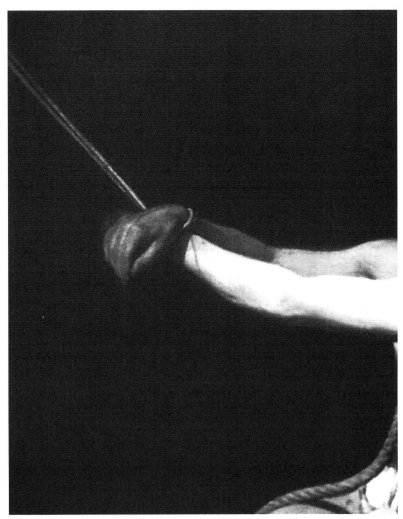

- a man whose face would make the perfect model for – (though no one would ever think to take the painstaking care and artistry – never mind the eye-watering time – nor to give the requisite devotion – in order to design and construct such a thing) – the face of a *kairometer* – such is the openness – expressed just as much in his mouth as in his eyes – *to the need-of-the-decisive-moment-as-it-must-thereby-manifest-as-act* – and it is as *Asip* opens the little curtain – now strewn with his hotly pulsating blood – of the cabin – only – it has to be said – 3/8ths of the way across – in order to balance the light given by the man – who now exclaims –

- with that coursing from the sun and the billions of other – presently invisible stars
– though none the less penetrating for all that – that this potential *kairometric* gaze
streams out into the nave – where it instantly destroys – by chain reaction – the first
of many warships – of all ages and modes of construction of sea – of land – of air – of
mind – both in and outside the present time and space – which now dominate the
perpendicular ocean –

though the two cormorants – recently arrived from their usual perch on top of the
– now sunken – tabernacle – inspired to the point of insemination by the awesome
experience – are each soon to produce an egg – the both of which containing within
them – veiled by their yolk – the harvested glare of the two eyes of the bound man.

❦ Between the angel and the doll – ROSA FORTUNÆ: 10

EVITATIVE EVITATIVE –

'violatus volo rosa – dei rota mel ignis aperte'

Intuitively – though you have no rational explanation for its presence there – you reach for the 19th card – and there – in the bottom left – the little aquarian is pouring – to the accompaniment of a fitting musical canon – the cormorant yolks – the mistress poised in anticipation – at last! – of meeting a gaze – from the freed – airborne eyes – and a glare equal to her own.

❦ Mistress' generation mastery divines matters
of putative human spirit –

AUDEO AUDIENS AUREUS AURICULA

(Muqarnas 2...)

All three of you – or so you first thought – are intimidated by the presence of the guardians in the painting – but *The Reverend Lution* has detached his dog-collar – straightened it – and is now using it to alternately tickle their two bellies – their laughter opening the elliptical door onto a three-hundred-and-seventy-seven-sided space – over which – so to speak – the guardians – *Az O'Nips* and *Zin Biel* – in turns – as you enter – tell their tale –

'Which is more vain – to look without at your own reflection – or to look within at your own refraction? – either way – you become a reifier.

Everyone – female – male – hemale – shemale – wemale – everyone but everyone loved Spinnin-Maggie.

But O – she – so full of – so bursting with herself – loved that self so much more. True – her spinnerets were superfine spinners of super-shot silk – true – her venom's acridity was matched only by her galloping's rapidity – but O – the conceit that throve in her too!

One day – King Rag Rockbait saw her spindling across the moor – but he kept his silence – as he always had to – unless the other spoke – a state of affairs that Cock o' th' Bracken had brought about due to his long-borne frustration at being foiled in stopping his wife and sister – Longicorn – from pursuing her endless lusts and fancies.

There was that – pivotal – time when she was pawing her six mitts all over Loch-leech – *with good reason – though it wasn't reason at the root of it –* Cock o' th' Bracken *in pursuit – asking* King Rag Rockbait – mid-leap – *"Whither – man – whither?" – but* Longicorn *had primed him – on and on* King Rag *blabbed – of this and that – of how fine the* Cock *was strutting – plah dee dah – then – deed done – off* Longicorn *scurried and* Loch-leech *hurried – but no more!*

"*No more of your flattery – no more of your gossip – it's either grievous harm and battery or – wagger snippy snops dossip!*"

And with that – indeed – only clippings and snippings of others' words would stutter – henceforth – from the mouth of King Rag Rockbait.

He would watch Spinnin-Maggie *from afar – the eager torrents surging at each of his nine holes for egress – but would have to furtively follow – wait for her to say something – and only – then – to repeat the meagrest part as broken poetry of creaking heart.*

Spinnin-Maggie *– out for a bite with* Rotatoria *– might say – "My appetites are unsurpassed – it'd take a thousand of these flies to fill me up" –* King Rag *– "Fill me up!"*

Spinnin-Maggie *– out on the lash with* Hairy Hubert *– might say – "My heart's so vast – who's worthy of all these hangers on to truly love me?" –* King Rag *– "Love me!"*

Spinnin-Maggie *– in the midst of a disagreement with* Sand-dragon *about attending his birthday party – might say – "Look – I'm sorry – but you can't* make me *come" –* King Rag *– "Make me come!"*

Spinnin-Maggie *- expounding on her ideal lover – "VIBRA VOLO ROSA!" –* King Rag *– "VOLO ROSA!"*

Until he could hide no longer and – slithering up to Spinnin-Maggie *– King Rag Rockbait leaps on her – drenching her in kisses – she's appalled – "How dare you – you ugly worm – don't touch me!" –* King Rag *– "Touch me!"*

But these were the last words to truly be said to come from his body – eventually his – others' – words became so splintered – so various in origin that we all – whenever we think we think our private thoughts – are only mimicking the copies already made by King Rag Rockbait.

Yes – Spinnin-Maggie's *beauty remained – in a sense – intact – though the longer – and harder – she spurned them – the more her admirers' passions tended toward the acid – until one of them –* Glesyn Serennog *– called – his voice burning – on all the powers – above – below and in between – for* Spinnin-Maggie *to choke on her own dark heart's vinegar wine – so that the next night – when she found herself alone in – for the first time – a human home – a mirror would confound and damn her.*

"I came in by a window – why can't I leave by this one? – but – wait – never mind that – who is that dancing with me on the other side? – steady – don't show your interest – ah – he's stopped – I'll wait – watch him move a while – get the measure – perhaps I'll just show a little leg – just to keep him occupied – him too! – a tango then! – O – to touch his leg – how fine can he spin I wonder – let me show my skill."

Spinnin-Maggie begins to flex her expertise – strands shooting clear – straight – curved – virtuosic – as are 'his' –

"What – he's mocking me! – is his skill the greater?"

Spinnin-Maggie's being drawn in –

"What sense is this? – what senselessness? I'll write to him in silk!"

So saying – Spinnin-Maggie dangles down – not so far that she can't see through the 'window' – but far enough to be sure she's able to get the measure of how much she's impressing the other with her impeccable weave.

"No! – Not possible – he's matching every bend – every artless imperfection of my own – I must go to him – this shadow play is futile!"

But at this moment a human hand unintentionally intervenes – it is taking the mirror to where there is more light so that its owner can see – not just into their own eyes – but also – at least try – to understand the full length – the whole import – of their body – more clearly.

Unfortunately – the owner of the mirror – as well as being arachnophobic – has had one too many glasses of Gewürztraminer – and the combined effect of the sudden release of cortisol into the blood stream – combined with the intoxication due to the wine – leads them to trip – thus falling into the mirror – which now lays on the floor – cracked – ruptured and segmented – but with what precision! – into 13 pieces – and – though not killing Spinnin-Maggie *– utterly confusing her – not only by the sudden multiplication of 13 beautiful – perfectly mimicking – unrequited embodiments of potential – (but only ever to be unrequited) – rapture now before her on the other side of the 13 shards of the broken 'window' – but also in the changed nature of this strangest of windows – entirely on a level as it now is with the horizon.*

Running hither and thither from her new vantage-point – she is always in the state of being able to obliquely see 5 or 6 spiders – but now the madness truly begins – initiating in her an unstoppable series of attempted explications of her plight – web after web of inordinate – distorted complexity – until she can see not one of her spurning lovers any longer – slowly dying into her occlusion and endlessly vain regret.'

DEED DEED –

'vibra volo rosa – dei rosa mel ignis aperte'

It is a delightful experience for you and your friends to be shaken by the hands by the painting's presiding *bodhisattva* – your glee not only opening the central ellipse – but also setting in flight the topmost mudra – as you – while listening to why a garden was razed – enter the six-hundred-and-ten-sided room –

Muir Bili'uqe could hear the women's voices before she could see who they belonged to – one sitting – one standing – on the front steps – that they had – for the last hour – been cleaning – of the house to which she'd been summoned –

- the one sitting – whose name was – *Sulad 'É' Ad* – was saying –

    'Mistress has never even so much as tasted a grape – did you know that?'

    'I did' – says the one standing – whose name is *Sereh Psimeh* – 'a rose is all she's ever wanted.'

    'But her mother died of one – days after she was born.'

'Yes – rabid septicaemia following on from the cut from the thorn from the roses from the garden brought to her by her lover – and mistress' father.'

'By the morning – the garden razed – every petal burned.'

'A year later – to the day – the garden transformed into a small vineyard – ah – this must be her now!

Good morning! Are you the horticulturist?'

'I am.' – says *Muir Bili'uqe*.

Sulad 'É' Ad opens the door.

'Last door to the left at the end of the corridor' – she says – 'Make yourself comfortable in the morning room – and I will let Mistress know that you have arrived.'

Stepping inside - *Muir Bili'uqe* is – initially – perturbed – though later rapturous – to discover she has stepped *outside* – into an interminable corridor open to the freezing – clear – and starless – (every star in the galactic vicinity having been extinguished – many years earlier – along with the burning of its corresponding rose-petal) – night sky – as she gathers intimate – if not downright garrulous – communications from the spherical reflected light to her left – while bearing the brunt of its – rectangular – contradiction from the pillars to her right.

Eventually – after several hours – *Muir Bili'uqe* reaches – and sits herself down in – the morning room – where she spends the next little while listening to the blisteringly intelligent colloquy – on freedom – (and of how it was born in the time that the denier reined) – of the birds in their cage.

At last – she – the Mistress of the house – her name is *Lady Elba Dual* – arrives – saying – without preamble –

'VINEA VOLO ROSA!'

'And that is why I have come' says *Muir Bili'uqe* – putting down her teacup and opening – as she does so – her holdall – in which she has brought – pressed between the leaves of a large book – as requested – hundreds of rose-petals – though she is at present distracted by the strange ibis-like bird nestling in *Lady Elba Dual's* hair –

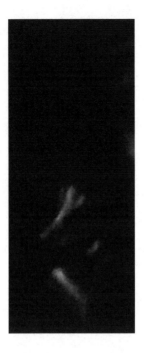

'VINEA VOLO ROSA!' – repeats *Lady Elba Duel.*

'Yes – yes – look – will you be tending towards the red or the violet ends of the spectrum?'

'VINEA VOLO ROSA!'

'And a rose you shall have – look – how about the *Rosa Noatraum* – or perhaps the *Rosa Meipitac* – the *Rosa Zephirine Drouhin* has a peerless sumptuousness that perhaps you can't resist – though both the *Rosa Tiffany* and the *Rosa Chewallbell* – in terms of scent and hue – are considered by the connoisseur to be unsurpassed?'

Lady Elba Duel moves quickly over to the escritoire – whereupon she opens its doors – revealing – ajar – a two-pillared gate.

You are struck by the vivacity of the reality within the escritoire – the freshness of the air – as opposed to the stifling – moribund ambience of the morning room.

'The last time' – says *Lady Elba Dual* – taking *Muir Bili'uqe* by surprise as well as by the hand – 'that I crawled into *the world of the free-standing gate* – I managed to transform – from *my imaginal foundation* – the final rose-window of the *Cathedral of the Rose* from a twelve to a tenfold form –

- for - surely - any rose-window worthy of the name ought to be rooted in 5 rather than 3 or 4 - my ultimate intention being to further transmute the - now many - altered tenfold windows - within *the world of the free-standing gate* - into fivefold ones - before - and this will draw on resources that I do not yet possess - (and this is where you come in) - fundamentally modifying the constituents of the windows - again from a *foundational space of pure imaginality* - so that they begin - first - to photosynthesize - before they then - quite naturally - are able - more or less on their own steam - to become roses thriving at a point of true vitality between lead - stone - glass - scent and processes more or less purely biochemical.'

SOLALTERITY CHANGE!

You look to the sky...

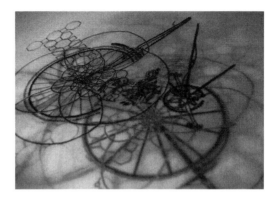

Looking back at the 'bird' – you note that it is actually a child – with his right hand on his cheek and his bare – right leg crossed – he has been keenly listening to your thoughts – but now turns to you and says –

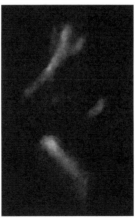

'My mother brought me back from *the world of the free-standing gate* after her first success with a window.

I was the first fruits of that primarial photosynthesis – before the process became stable – falling from the window as no more than an embryo – to be caught in the folds of my mother's dress.

Lady Elba Dual – as was to be expected – poured all of her unrequited love for her dead mother into me – proudly taking me out in the – to me – gigantic – perambulator as she went on one of her many trips to the library – her mother looking proudly on as – above – on the first floor balcony – her grandmother cast – in all love and affection – a rose – which – as its single thorn fell upon my tiny brow – brought forth a globule of blood which – my mother immediately kissing the wound – tasted of wine.'

DENIER REINED -

'vinea volo rosa – dei rosa mel ignis apibus'

The *deadpan panhandler's* unstoppable chortling was utter delight - it seems that - as well as the tale of *Lady Elba Dual* - the simple reversal of the word 'EMIT' to 'TIME' - along with the pell-mell assemblage of crosses in the mural - (she also plucked - from the open hands at the top of the cross - a scroll which - when unrolled - spelt out the following inscription - [something which only added to her chuckling] -

h is

Is

Ris ?

is

Is

is

Ch i

Is

i

Ch i

I

is

is

I

is ?)

- unlocked something long bound within her – and she was unrelenting in her laughter – and in her spinning and toppling – (a side-effect of which was to open the door on and through the bodhisattva – into a room of nine-hundred and eighty-seven sides) – and – for the most part of the rest of your acquaintance – the only words she would now repeat would be –

'MIA VOLO ROTA!'

EMIT TIME –

'mia volo rota – dea rosa mela apibus'

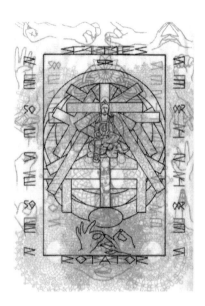

The mudra being enacted in this 14th painting is already keeping the present ellipse – through which you will soon clamber – after having heard the bodhisattva recite – ajar –

The entirely cloaked figure that was now standing between the two stations – in many ways the epitome of a mother that must cause the fall of her son after meeting him at the point of one – at least – of their deaths – was male.

He – the son's – and the mother's – lover – in his role as releveler – (though neither of his loves knew of the other's furtive life beyond themselves – though *he* loved *them* both more than he loved either himself or either of them singly) – had engineered their vanquishing – under this pretence – in the hope of foisting upon them an otherwise rejected resurrection – so attached had they become to one another – that – alive – they could only become gradually – rather than living – fulfilled – lives as *themselves-in-respect-of-but-not-because-of-the-other* – more a travestied embodiment towards the condition of the undead.

It has still not been determined whether any of the three are now at large in the world – revivified or not – though some – among their acquaintance – claim to hear – in the small hours – the words –

'DIA DOLO ROTA!'

– spoken – in slow succession – in three distinct voices – as well as repeatedly seeing inscribed – in unexpected places – the single word –

RELEVELER RELEVELER -

'dia dolo rota – dei rosa mela apibus'

The reshaping of all of your - and your friends' souls that occurs encountering - for the first time - a circular door - feels - initially - constricting - after the expansiveness of the elliptical - though once the circle has finished bouncing - as if a solitary - invisible - player were playing squash - around the painting in what you are sure must be some kind of - indiscernible - pattern - (after all - though you will never know this - the ball has bounced 441 times) - it opens for you to pass through - as you listen to your clerical friend tell you of the dynamics of misplaced faith - into a room of fifteen-hundred and ninety-seven walls -

The young devotee of the faith thought it important never to light a candle in a church – as this would show – by some arcane correspondence – never fully explicable to himself – (all he would mutter – as a prayer – was –

'VALE VOLO ROTA!')

- that his heart had been extinguished.

He could not know that such misplaced humility was – little by little – in and of itself – creating a shadow upon his heart – a state of affairs to be commended when there was at least a light to *cast* a shadow – but one more to be feared – if not abhorred – when all was dark within.

By the grace of something other within him – buried – almost – as it was – beneath his pitiable mockeries of piety – an exorcism of this shadow was imminent – and at the same moment of its projection outward – the essential light that the devotee would not kindle – in neither heart nor wax – burst forth – (as did a cloaked figure – almost imperceivable to the devotee – behind the radiance) – blinding him into a condition of true sightedness that would render him – at last – stream-enterer – at the beginning of a – very different – virgin – stream.

❧ Between the angle and the doll – ROSA FORTUNÆ: 15

ESSE ESSE –

'vale volo rota – dei rosa mal a pius'

The *Reverend Lution* coughs – and from his mouth comes the 20th card – though it is *Nova Nopu – Dr of Tarts* who – having had 55 children – and 34 self-vanquishments – has the measure of its meaning – passing the card – as well as the *Protean Dish* – (currently in quasi-fluid gold-mercurial state) – to the now coruscatingly wakeful *bodhisattva* –

No key – as no gate – though soon the bloodied soul is crowning.
xx

❦ No key – as no gate – though soon the bloodied soul
is crowning –

AUDIO AUDIENS AUCTORITAS AUCTUS AUCUPO

(Sonnets to Orpheus – 1:2)

She knew that commemorated at her – and the bodhisattva's – Φ point was
the eternal memory and promise of the battle-dance-tussle with the serpent – (conflict
because unacknowledging of the life that this serpent gave – the living sacrifice made)
– the umbilical dragon mother – while at her centre was the swordless *Michaelic* – but
that both – DEIFIED EROS & REVIVER ROSE – were needful to fulfil what was
– seemingly – carved – and bordered in uncanny – knotted – (but of ultimate clarity)
– interweave – on the placenta from which she still drew monthly sustenance –

She would play – balletically - with such thoughts as she lay half comatose – half utterly awake – reeling from riding the waves – writhing the ways of – alternately – dragon and archangel – half laughing – and half crying – the following words –

'VITA VOLO ROSA ROTA!'

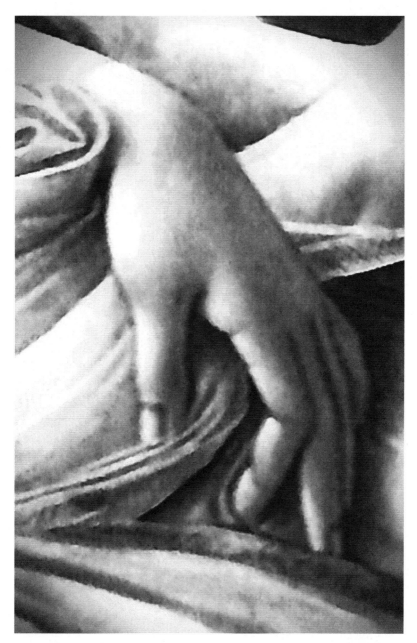

DEIFIED EROS ROSE DEIFIED –

'vita volo rosa rota – du rosa mel apibus'

The three of you have appeared – as the star rotates and you pass through the final elliptical portal – back into the room of dartboards – *The Reverend Lution* is already preparing to propel his orange dart – (he must have – his left eye closed – made hundreds of dummy throws already!) – towards the red centre of the sole remaining – unnumbered one – he too has hit the bullseye! – as he – *Nova Nopu* and yourself pass through the – resultant – opened door – into a room exactly like the one you have left – though the numbers on each of the 28 boards are now involved in an exponential procedure of increase – the phases behind each board morphing – (acquiring – seemingly – the appearance of forms of life – the flora and fauna thus represented becoming smaller as the numbers grow) – in relation to this unprecedented cumulative expansion – the boards acquiring dimensions that your senses soon give up trying to accommodate – the length of the numbers in each portion demanding its simultaneous growth – such that the vastness of the dartboards is now exceeding the capabilities of the Norwegian Sky.

It seems – when this extended moment has passed – that all during it was deafening – and of intolerable lucidity – but – now that you are once again in the single little room of the humble hut – that there has – in fact – been no change to the ambient light or sounding – there remain only empty walls and a meagre – though relentless – fire – burning in the fireplace – until *The Reverend Lution's* ball falls through the chimney – and is – so to speak – caught by the flames – which – after *Edencanter* emerges from them with the flag – are now frozen – though still emitting a curious warmth – into a fixed resplendence of caught ephemerality –

The skaters – in the flag – have scored a line in the ice – and you see there – poking out – a card – (it and the other two cards are blank – you and your friends having encountered them – full of incident – in different circumstances – earlier) – the 2nd of the 3 cards being dredged from the bottom of the French flood by the man standing by the 19th incision – the 3rd being gingerly removed – by the expertise of the dentist – (from the mouth of the youth – he had thought his difficulties in swallowing – even breathing – had been being caused by a fishbone once belonging to a – too thickly fleshed for his – and his wife's tastes – turbot) – adjoining the 20th.

As you look at the cards – you see – at their centres – what seem to be – though you consider – later – that perhaps it was merely an after burn of the bullseye illuminations – tiny coloured pulsations of light – their intermingling suggesting to you – (as you listen to the dentist's drill and patient's groans combine – in your mind – with the songs and mudras of the sailors to produce the music of the 8th flag) – with a possible translation of the words of all of the nine but one flags conjoined –

❦ Flag Music: 8

(navigavit et valis...)

Educare ex uri hara odi angelorum. Ob dum et sultis migratio epularis
ad bibo os hariola. ecce elusia hic harena magus navi gavit et valis

I hate the angels to bring them up from the fire. For while the migration of the sultans is
feasting and drinking – Behold! – this enchanted sand-magician rejoiced in the ship
and was strong

By way of elucidation – *Edencanter* recites –

Folly is ðe glory of godds' lusts' bouwunty!

A roome – a thoughte – a pallasce!

Chimmpes! – raain – drumming – singingg – snake – apple!

Liyfe as prepærationn for being morre alive!

Formyula for a hapiness – a maybe – a perhæps – a spirrale – a
shifting anarckho-fractl aim!

Let us prayisze ðe AUTOUMNÆLIYA of being while yet wiðin
euphoria – ðe nooonday mindshiiningg of fuellest frouiticenne's tippping
intoe a frucktifyying putryefacktion in ðe ounndergroweð of bodymind for
fyutuere mycelial growð and interconnectiv mysterye – ðough ðe sun may
seeme at times exshoaustedde by its rellentelesss givng and faall!

ðe nakdness of sorrowe's laughter weeps forðe excesive friendlshippe!

A booke musst be like ðe soull – it muest containn *noðingge.*

Numnberr æs onlye ðe momntary cradling of qkuantæ as ðey disperse –
advansce and recohere.

Let youur limitationnes bound you freee of ðem!

Ðe distance beatween huemænnitye's prescent state of mundnity
and ðe soone to be constant – if we wishh it – if we wille suche happy
onsclaurghtte of our – until now – insueperabble defences – temporolimbic-
musickal-epilpftic state we may all sooon inhæbit as ðe distance betuween
stone and celll – scell and ape.

Ðe conscertinnæ æppearannsce of histoury.

Illusion BEING reælity until sutch tiyme as it is known to be
oðerwise – THE DEEPE REALL.

The final 3 words bring – as an echo – the prefatory words of The
LAMPEDEPHORIAN Threshold Spirits – and Vitalia's penultimate sextain –

SUB IPA ALEM ASORA ED
SUB IPA ALEM A SORIED

9

Empirfoct livi hymenytous dostrye
Froibarn seos – 'lavus brong homyneti' tu yvarjeu
'toku nuthung' – syants cencloda – gyvo sumithang's goft
Biyr lovang bast – qyystyan wonts – gove pluisiro – eplaft
Thunk nu miro – bag ylms – nu cyncapts gyvi
Datuchyd – net piur – ne ilms' pysetuyn coritovi

Iiimpeeerfeeeeect loooveeeeeee huuuuuuuuuuuuuuuuuuuuuu-
maaaaaaaaaaaaaaniiiiiiiitiiiiees
deeestrooooooooooooooooooooooyy
FREEEEEEEEEEEEEEEEEEEEEEBOOORN saaaaaaaayyyyys –
'looooooooooooooveeeees briing huumaaaaaniiiiiiiiiiiityy' too
ooooooooooooooveeeeerjooooyyy
'Taaaaaaaakeeeeeeeeeeeeeeeeeeeee nooooooooooooooooooooothiiing' –
saaaaaaaaaaaaaaaaaaaaaaiiiiiiiiiiints
cooooooooncluuuuuuuuuuuuuudeeeeeeeeeeee – giiveee
sooomeeeeethiiing's giiiiiiiiiiiiiiiiiift
Beeeaar liiiiiiiiiiiiiiiiiiiiiiviing beeeeeeeeeeeest – quuuuuuuueeestiiiiioon
waaaaaaaaaaaaaants – giiveeeeeee pleeeeeeeeeeeeaaaaaaaaaaaaaaasuureeeee –
uuupliift
Thiiiiiiiiiiiiiiiiiiiink nooo mooooooooooooooreeeeeeee – beeeeeeeg aalms –
nooooooooo cooooooooooooooooooooonceeepts giiiiiiiiiiiiveee
Deeetaaaaaaaaaaaaacheeed – noooooooooooooooooooooot poooooooor –
nooooooooo aaaaaaaaaaaaaaaaaaaalms' pooooosiiitiiiiiiiiooooooooooooon
cuuuuuuuuuraaaaaaaaaaaaaaaaaaaaaatiiveeeee

Imperfect love humanities destroy
FREEBORN says – 'loves bring humanity' to overjoy
'Take nothing' – saints conclude – give something's gift
Bear living best – question wants – give pleasure – uplift
Think no more – beg alms – no concepts give
Detached – not poor – no alms' position curative –

You look to the sky...

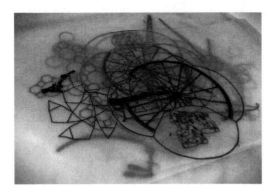

- the words - *'detached – not poor'* - heralding - in the richness of their meaning - all but one of the 4 remaining songs of *Edencanter's* cycle - the first - singing of a wish to be in a mode of flight that transcends - due to the union of one with the self - itself caused by a saturation in love's alterity - even the wings of the rose - and the fire of the stars - the second - of how what is not - in terms of intelligence - artificed - but merely artificial - will find its farewell sung by a bird of such rarity as sung of in the previous song - the third - of what must fly from lily to rose - from bee to bird - to consume - to find consummation - and of the necessity and beauty of the loss incumbent on peerless amplitude -

❦ The Sick Rose: 17 – 18 & 19 – The White Birds/ To say good-by to men/The Sick Rose

The skaters are taking to the ice again – they are being accompanied in their dance by *Sisæ H'Topa* – she is playing –

❦ The Lampedephoria: Book 8

- at the end of which - you find yourselves back at the clubhouse.

'running all the way with me – for otherwise my pace was not for footemen…to my determined expedition and pleasurable humour… which I long before conceiued to delight this Citty with (so far as my best skill and industry of my long trauelled sinewes could affoord them) …'

'There is neither 'There is neither…'…

'Have you' – asks Edencanter –

as he – after stroking the legible letters of the **PAX IMMEMORIAL** – (ones forming words which could be read suggestively but refer – instead – you feel – to a directive from within the heart of the Tournai marble – to be – any – *Apina's* arboretum – and to be tended with such intuitional care) – presents each of the three of you with a portative organ –

'Considered the... possibility of a SEPTRIVIUM – learned the weave of the harvestman – polished your doctorates until they're fit for the fire and the hare – watched a cry become winged – taken on the blood – albumen and spermova of any and all mirrors – found the multi through the unicursal – sensed – with the worms – the gossamer's rise – shared in the far from triumphal whirl of the threefold – sat in the chair of obliterapture – listened to the satyr hearkening to the ear – heart – brain of the canonic – seen a gaze unleashed on the conflicted wave – put your finger in the 9 holes of egress – drunk wine from the rose and rosewater from the vine – helped one who's smiled too much to laugh again – held a veil to love – shocked the faithful out of their devotion – deiphied the omphalos?'

Your collective answer is your playing – (as a surprisingly well-blended trio) – from memory – of the fifteen canons that you have been absorbing during your traversal of the ellipses – after which *The Reverend Lution* – for the last time – strikes his ball – its ascent slowed – for you – as you – though still aware of *Edencanter's* murmur – peer – also for the last time – further into the dark pink rose – the glacial fire of its orchestral swell becoming almost unbearably intense – (though the following ebb is – if anything – even more searing – and salving) – the form of the *Archangel Michaël Cathedral in Uralsk – Kazakhstan* – becoming simultaneously discernible –

Folly is ðe glory – witness the harvestman – *of godds' lusts' bouwunty!*

A roome – a thoughte – a SEPTRIVIAL *pallasce!* LENTE HOPE!

Chimmpes! – raain – drumming – singingg – snake – apple!

Liyfe as prepærationn for – a cry become winged – *being morre alive!*

Formyula for a hapiness – a maybe – a perhæps – a spirrale – a shifting anarckho-fractl aim – the circadian labyrinth!

Let us prayisze ðe AUTOUMNÆLIYA of being while yet wiðin euphoria – ðe nooonday mindshüningg of fuellest frouitiænne's tippping intoe a frucktifyying putryefacktion in ðe ounndergroweð of bodymind for fyutuere mycelial growð and interconnectiv mysterye – the whirl of the three – five – eightfold – *ðough ðe sun may seeme at times exshoaustedde –* OKTOKULOS! – *by its rellentelesss givng and faall!*

ðe nakdness of sorrowe's laughter – the deadpan panhandler – *weeps forðe excesive friendtshippe!*

A MIRROR *musst be like ðe soull* – a chair toward obliterapture! – *it muest* containn *noðingge.*

Numnberr æs onlye ðe momntary cradling of qkuantæ as ðey disperse – advansce and recohere – 288 holes of egress – digress – ingress.

Let youur limitationnes – a razed vineyard – your labyrinths – *bound you* – rose-petalled *– freee of ðem!*

Ðe distance beatween huemænnitye's prescent state of mundnity and ðe soone to be constant – if we wishh it – if we wille suche happy onsclaurghtte of our – until now – insueperabble defences – temporolimbic-musickal-epilptic state we may all sooon inhæbit as ðe distance betuween stone and celll – scell and ape – listen to those who hearken to the aural – the cordial – the limbic-cerebral-not-intellectual.

Ðe conscertinnæ æppearannsce – conflicted – gaze back – *of histoury.*

Illusion BEING reælity until sutch tiyme as it is known to be oðerwise – deiphi the Delphic of the *THE DEEPE REALL –* the earthly – all ears Spinnin-Maggie – and other devotees of any faith...

❦ A Rose is on Fire: 9

The ball has landed in the garden of the cathedral – it is being held in place by a dormant – not sleeping – angel – an angel – (whose name is *Lavea Idem*) –

of one of the minor – peripheral orders of the heavenly hierarchies – who has recently travelled to earth – they are in search of twin sisters – *Oligo Hydramnios* and *Polly Hydramnios* – that – no-one more surprised than *Lavea Idem* at this – had formed a special devotion to them in their final illness.

Lavea Idem – at the moment when they had fallen into their torpor – had had their ear to the wall in an attempt to ascertain the origin of the faintly pulsing souls of the twins – they had – since their deaths – been trapped within their memorial which had – in turn – been spirited away by a certain *Alistair Inigo T'Nelis* –

– it was he who was responsible for the angel's onset of narcolepsy – his power lying in five places – in ascending order of malevolence – his book – (which was not his) – his eyes – his right forefinger and his 'Shhhh'.

His eyes were so – at once – vacant – (the left) – overflowing – (the right) – and transfixing – (together) – that the moment you thought you had grasped what the first word was on his book's forever changing cover – you had forgotten it – or if you had managed to hold on to it – it would soon slip from your mind under the torrent of shushing – (this shushing proving especially distressing – being constantly modified and malevolently nuanced by the subtleties of that pernicious forefinger's movement) – that *Mr T'Nelis* would then utter – and so the cycle would begin again – until such time as the recipient would fall prey to an irrevocable dormancy.

Valiant – though now lost – souls had managed to establish the following – that the word was Latin – and always began with either AU or AV – the hope being that if one were able to voice that word as a tone – then *Mr T'Nelis* would be disincarnated – but what was that word?

Ms Atnahp Lanigami –

– who had been the – far from expected – one to grasp *The Kairolapsarian Wreath* –

- and whose eyes were - subsequently - the only orbs that could withstand those of *Mr T'Nelis* - had - she thought - not only figured out the first word - (some had suggested that there was *only* one) - but the entirety of the content of *Mr T'Nelis'* - stolen - book - (she had - in fact - guessed it!) - though only after a period of intensive toning and whirling had brought her to a state of necessarily intuitive brilliance.

Armed only with a customised shruti-box - it had had apotropaic letters and symbols inscribed upon it by her dear friend - *Ms Inai Rucipe* -

- *Ms Lanigami* set out to vanquish *Mr A.I. T'Nelis.*

He was standing in full - 'NOLI ME TANGERE!' mode - though in parody of those words' original utterer.

Ms Lanigami was undeterred. Her words - accompanied by the gentle - though intransigent - breathing of the shruti-box - (*Ms Lanigami* cycled through 96 distinct single tones - dyads - and chords during her onslaught) - came as a single - unbroken - though relentlessly transmutative - tone -

'AUDEO AUDIENS AURA AURARIA - AUCTORITAS AUCTUS AUCUPO AUDACIA - AUDEO AUDIENS - AUFERO AUGEO - AURA AURARIA - AURATUS AUREOLUS - AUREUS AURICULA - AURIFER AUSCULTATIO - AUSCULTATOR AUSPEX!'

Or – to loosely translate – *'I dare to hear a golden breeze – authority increased the boldness of the bird – I dare to listen – I take away and increase – a golden breeze – a golden halo – a golden ear – a golden listening – an auspicious listener!'*

But *Ms Atnahp Lanigami* did not stop there – (the priceless knowledge she had received being that all that there was in the great book of *A.I. T'Nelis* was 'AU' – and nothing more) – she continued – *Mr T'Nelis* stunned into discomfited – though forever unfulfilled – anticipation and receipt of what *could* have been in his book –

'AUCTORITAS AUCTUS AUCUPO AUDACIA AUDEO AUDIENS – AUCTORITAS AUCTUS AUCUPO AUDACIA AUFERO AUGEO – AUCTORITAS AUCTUS AUCUPO AUDACIA AUFERO – AUCTORITAS AUCTUS AUCUPO AUDACIA AUDIENS – AUFERO AUGEO AURIFER AUSCULTATIO – AUFERO AUGEO AUREUS AURICULA – AUFERO AUGEO AUSCULTATOR AUSPEX – AUDEO AUDIRE – AUDEO AUDIRE AVIARIUM – AUDEO AUDIENS AUREUS AURICULA – AUDEO AUDIENS AUCTORITAS AUCTUS AUCUPO – AURA AURARIA AUFERO AUGEO – AUREUS AURICULA AUDEO AUGEO!'

'The authority of the bird increased – and the boldness of the bird was heard – I take away the audacity that increases my authority – I take away the audacity of the bird with increased authority – the authority of the bird increased by hearing the boldness – I take away and increase the auscultation of the goldsmith – I disperse and increase the golden ear – I take away and increase the listener's auspiciousness – I dare to hear – I dare to listen to the birds – I dare to listen with golden ears – I dare to listen to the increased authority of the bird – I disperse the golden breeze and increase it – I dare to grow golden ears!'

His eyes slipped from their sockets – (how high they bounced – and with what a boing! – higher with each bound!) – his mouth was sealed – his forefinger glued to his lips – his usual recourse to 'Shhhh' now impossible.

Ms Lanigami wasted neither time nor space – her horse and carriage were waiting –

- and – flying above her – was her eagle – it was – having retrieved them from the stratosphere – carrying the two loosened eyes of *Mr T'Nelis* – which were – in truth – beneath his nefariously congealing – viscous fluids – the concealed souls of *Oligo Hydramnios* and *Polly Hydramnios* –

Ms Lanigami's first action – once she had reached the *Cathedral of the Archangel Michaël* – was to waken *Lavea Idem.*

At *Ms Atnahp Lanigami's* approach – *Lavea Idem* was dreaming of the exact location of the steps that would lead them – on their waking – to the twins –

- though - as a test of the authenticity of the intent and identity of *Ms Lanigami* and the angel - the twins' souls had projected a 9 x 9 encrypted square at the foot of the wooden steps -

'E'	...	S	E	P	T	A	.....	'A'
S	E	P	R	A	N	A	A	S
T	1	R	O	2	S	E	3	E
O	R	O	T	4	A	T	E	E
P	O	S	T	P	O	N	E	S
O	T	E	R	5	R	O	R	T
E	6	E	R	7	O	S	8	A
T	A	9	T	A	O	10	A	R
'A'	..	T	O	R	T	O	.	'A'

- which - whirling and toning as *Ms Lanigami* did every morning - in mindful expansion on exactly the kind of - *actual* - material that the square was presenting - provided just the inspiration - ingenuity and sanction for which the twins had hoped (on a visitor's behalf) in order to be able to welcome friends - not foes - to their post-mortive transformation.

Ms Lanigami and *Lavea Idem* arrived at the sisters' tomb - each cradling one of their souls.

As they gently poured them into the twins' ears - smiles began to form on their petrified faces -

- though neither *Ms Lanigami* nor the angel were able to enjoy the fruits of their deeds in the form of conversation - as *Oligo Hydramnios* and *Polly Hydramnios* immediately transmigrated into a double rainbow - perfectly reflective of their difference in age and experience - the rainbow being a form ideally suited to the sisters' nature - as they would skip between the colours - of their deepest natures' own manufacture - happy to shortly disperse until such time as the sun and rain would call them back into their shrouded - and perfect - circularity - *Lavea Idem* happy to enter their stone dormancy once more - clasping a golf-ball as they do so - in preparation for their return to the periphery of all that is higher.

The Reverend collects his ball from where it had rolled after the hand of the waking *Lavea Idem* had – just a moment ago – released it – (this relinquishment coinciding with a pivotal moment during the mass being celebrated inside the cathedral –

- though whether one is to interpret that pivot as the *Etheric Christ* - supersensible to the celebrant's consciousness - preparing to leap from the spirit to the imaginal realm or as *Asip* - the altar boy - his head in his hands - undergoing an anamnesis as he relives the moment that would determine his present incarnation's task -

- his sadness at his metamorphic lessening from a god's cumulative becoming - in fleet cupidity - to a pudgy - cherubic wing-shrinking of a stunted angelic ground-bounded-ness - though the migraine that *Asip* began to then undergo - part vision - part neurological malfunction - gave an inkling - (some might say that the photoluminescence undergone by *Asip* resembled the sevenfold brilliancy of the *Shekinah's* heart-crown) - towards which he would - for the most part unwittingly - invariably yearn -

- as *Nova Nopu* – suddenly assuming a notably different demeanour – says – while retrieving a manuscript from the golf-bag – (*The Very Reverend Obadiah Lution* looking most perplexed by this gesture – and aggrieved at how such a thing got into his bag – though he is soon to distract himself by looking at a poster in the porch of the cathedral which is advertising an upcoming concert – to be given – as it happens – by some ecclesiastical acquaintances of his –)

'Someone I know – only vaguely – gave me this some weeks ago – (I had been – as happens every year – solely involved in THE HUMILITY AMBLE – it being a notable date as this year was also the septennial of *The Ecstatic Stilling* – an event where all involved would silently stand – at various points of the city – until they came to the awareness that they – too – had come last – such realization doing nothing but fuelling their – already perilously heightened – sense of ecstasy) – saying that I would know who to give it to when the time came – but that I should recount the circumstances of my acquaintance's obtaining of it beforehand' –

And – so – *Nova Nopu – Dr of Tarts* began –

"*The Apprentice* – immediately after having given birth to her daughter – screamed – to the mother she had lost merely moments after having been borne to her –

'Why could you not have borne *me* longer than this moment of bearing?'

And so it was that – as *The Apprentice* passed away in a blur of joy – grief and haemorrhage – *The Apprentice's* daughter was borne – similarly far – (the birth having taken place within a great *kairolapsarian* wreath) – into the past – found amidst the haphazard stones that had recently been acquired for the purposes of building a chapel not far from *Edinburgh.*

The young *Journeyman* – (who was in fact infinite) – being the first on site that morning – was astonished not so much by the presence of the infant but by the curious markings that had been cut into the stones immediately surrounding her – that and the honey that was pulsing from the umbilical cord – along with the roses – rather than blood – with which the child was wreathed – and the swarm of bees that mirrored – in their shifting clouds of disparate coherence – the stones' markings.

Before long – the entire stonemason community had taken the child – named *Rosa Melissa* – into their collective heart and care.

What only *Rosa Melissa* now knew – as she approached womanhood – was that the faint lesions around her navel – they had first appeared on the morning of her 7th birthday – were now beginning to manifest as a grid of 288 + 2 letters –

(Many years in the future – The Infinite Journeyman had walked the labyrinth within the cloister at Lakenham Cathedral – [he had been there on the day of its emergence from the earth – helping – with the community - to temper its expression and design into a harmony admitting ceaseless modulation – and subsequently – when the trees – Elder – Birch – Oak – Willow – Sequoia – (a metasequoia glyptostroboides) – Maple – Rowan – Ash – Linden and Apple – had been planted in its bastions and their surroundings] –

- taking 288 steps [some say that – as a memento of this unicursal amble – there are designated 288 so-called names of life – though this is pure conjecture until such names are called] to do so – each step leaving the faintest trace – in the path – as well as around the omphalos of Rosa Melissa – of each of the 288 letters – the extra 2 being imprinted at the path's centre. While he was there – a so-called immigrant – recently arrived from the Western Kweneng district of Botswana – emerged from out of the cloisters and said to him – and it was these words – A DISCOURSE ON WHAT IS NOT THE REAL – (the words given below are a translation from the Taa language by the ghost of a cygnet – who had managed to achieve their translation in such a way that the qualities of the non-real are given forth almost entirely alphabetically – the richness of the original language – however – with its extraordinary range of clicks and their almost infinite variation – having been lost – or perhaps translated into a – still effectual – occluded form) – though what follows is a mere fragment – that tipped the – up until that moment – Temporal Journeyman into one of an Infinite nature –

The real is not a being taken aback.

Neither is it to abandon.

Nor is it an abandonment.

It is in no way a being abandoned.

It is neither to abase nor is it an abasement.

It is by no means to be abashed.

It does not abate.

Neither is it an abatement.

Nor does it abbreviate – nor is it an abbreviation.

In no way does it abdicate – nor is it an abdication – nor does it abduct.

It is neither an abduction nor is it aberrant.

It is by no means an aberration.

It is not an aiding and abetting.

Neither is it a being in – nor a falling into abeyance.

Nor is it to abhor – nor is it an abhorrence.

It is no way abhorrent – nor does it abide – nor is it an abiding by.

It is neither an abiding – nor an ability – nor is it an ab initio – nor is it abject – nor an abjection.

By no means does it abjure – nor is it an abjuration – nor is it ablaze.

It is not a being able – nor is it an ablution.

Neither does it abnegate.

Nor is it an abnegation.

It is in no way abnormal.

It is neither an abnormality – nor is it an abode.

By no means is it to abolish – nor is it an abolition – nor is it abolitionist.

It is not abominable – nor does it abominate – nor is it an abomination – nor is it aboriginal – nor does it abort.

Neither is it abortive – nor does it abound – nor is it an abounding in or with – nor is it a something about which – nor is it a wandering about – nor is it strewn about – nor is it out and about – nor is it a looking about – nor is it a turning and turning about.

Nor is it an about turn – nor is it a being about to – nor is it a bringing about – nor a coming about – nor is it above.

443

It is in no way over and above – nor is it an abracadabra – nor does it abrade.

It is neither an abrasion nor is it abrasive.

It is by no means an abreaction.

It does not abridge.

Neither is it an abridgement.

Nor is it a being or a scattering abroad – nor does it abrogate.

It is no way an abrogation – nor is it abrupt – nor is it an abscissa.

It does not abscond – nor is it an absence – nor an absence of mind – nor is it to be absent – nor absent-minded.

Neither is it absolute – nor is it an absolute – nor is it the absolute – nor is it an absolution – nor an absolutism – nor is it to absolve – nor does it absorb – nor is it absorbent.

Nor is it an absorption – nor is it to be absorptive – nor does it abstain – nor is it to be abstemious – nor is it an abstention – nor an abstinence – nor is it – nor does it – abstract – nor is it to be abstracted – nor is it an abstraction – nor is it abstruse – nor is it absurd – nor an absurdity – nor is it an abundance.

It is no way to be abundant – nor does it abuse – nor is it to be abusive – nor does it abut – nor is it an abutment – nor abysmal – nor is it an abyss – nor is it academic.

It is neither to accede nor does it accede to – nor is it to accelerate – nor is it an acceleration – nor does it accentuate.

By no means does it accept – nor is it acceptable – nor an acceptability.

It does not find acceptance – nor does it gain – nor offer – access.

Neither is it accessible.

Nor is it an accessibility.

It is in no way an accession.

It is neither an accessory – nor is it accessory.

It is by no means an accident – nor is it accidental – nor does it acclaim.

It is not an acclamation – nor is it to acclimatize – nor is it an acclimatization – nor an acclivity – nor is it an accolade.

Neither does it accommodate nor is it accommodating – nor is it an accommodation – nor an accompaniment – nor an accompanist – nor is it to accompany – nor is it an accomplice – nor is to accomplish.

Nor is it accomplished – nor is it an accomplishment – nor is it an accord – nor does it accord with – nor is it an accordance – nor in accordance with – nor is it accordant – nor an according to – nor does it accost – nor is it an account – nor does it call to account – nor is it an accounting for – nor is it accountable.

In no way does it accredit – nor is it accredited – nor is it an accretion – nor does it accrue – nor accumulate – nor is it an accumulation – nor is it accumulative – nor is it an accumulator – nor is it accuracy – nor is it to be accurate – nor is it accursed – nor is it an accusation – nor is it to be accusative – nor is it accusatory – nor is it to accuse – nor does it accustom itself – nor is it a being accustomed – nor is it to be acerbic – nor is it an acerbity – nor is it an ache – nor is to ache.

It neither achieves nor is an achievement – nor is it an Achilles' heel – nor is it achromatic – nor is to be achy – nor is it acid – nor does it acknowledge – nor is it the acme – nor is it to be an acolyte – nor is it an acorn – nor does it acquaint itself – nor is it a being acquainted – nor is it an acquaintance.

By no means does it acquiesce – nor is it an acquiescence – nor is it to be acquiescent – nor does it acquire – nor is it to be acquired – nor is it an acquired taste – nor is it an acquirement – nor is it an acquisition.

It is not acquisitive – nor does it acquit – nor does it acquit itself – nor is it an acquittal – nor is it an acquittance.

Neither is it acrid nor an acridity – nor is it to be acrimonious.

Nor is it acrimony – nor acrobatics.

It is in no way acronymic.

It is by no means an acropolis.

It is not across.

Neither is it an acrostic nor is it an act.

Nor is it to act – nor is it an acting – nor is it an action.

In no way is it actionable – nor does it activate – nor is it to be active -nor is it an activity – nor activity.

It is neither actual – nor the actual – nor is it actuality – nor does it actuate – nor is it acuity – nor is it acumen – nor is it acute – nor is it to be acute.

It is by no means an adage – nor is it adamant – nor does it adapt – nor is it adaptable – nor is it an adaptation – nor is it to add – nor does it add up – nor is it to be addicted – nor is it an addiction – nor is it addictive – nor is it an addition – nor is it additional.)

SOLALTERITY CHANGE!

You look to the sky...

D	A	S	*R*	*O*	*T*	*A*	M	E	A	P	I
B	U	S	D	A	S	*R*	*O*	*T*	*A*	M	E
L	A	P	I	B	U	S	D	A	T	*R*	*O*
T	*A*	M	E	A	P	I	B	U	S	D	E
A	*R*	*O*	*S*	*A*	M	E	L	A	P	I	B
U	S	D	A	T	*R*	*O*	*T*	*A*	M	E	L
I	C	U	S	A	P	E	R	T	E	D	A
S	*R*	*O*	*X*	*A*	M	E	L	I	C	U	S
A	P	E	R	T	E	D	A	S	*R*	*O*	*T*
A	M	E	L	I	C	U	S	A	P	E	R
T	E	D	E	I	*R*	*O*	*T*	*A*	M	E	L
I	C	U	S	A	P	E	R	T	E	D	E
I	*R*	*O*	*T*	*A*	M	E	L	I	G	N	U
S	A	P	E	R	T	E	D	E	I	*R*	*O*
T	*A*	M	E	L	I	G	N	I	S	A	P
E	R	T	E	D	E	I	*R*	*O*	*S*	*A*	M
E	L	I	G	N	I	S	A	P	E	R	T
E	D	E	I	*R*	*O*	*S*	*A*	M	E	L	I
G	N	I	S	A	P	I	B	U	S	D	E
A	*R*	*O*	*S*	*A*	M	E	L	A	A	P	I
B	U	S	D	E	I	*R*	*O*	*S*	*A*	M	E
L	A	A	P	I	B	U	S	D	E	I	*R*
O	*S*	*A*	M	A	L	A	P	I	U	S	D
U	*R*	*O*	*S*	*A*	M	E	L	A	P	I	B
				U	S						

It was inevitable that *Rosa Melissa* would become the youngest *Master* that the Guild had yet produced.

It was also fated that the *Infinite Journeyman* and the young *Master* would fall in cataclysmic love – bringing to birth – in due course – a daughter of such delicacy and fragility-in-strength that – moments after her birth – she was dispersed like the rarest of industrial river-borne mists – only to be reembodied at the centre of a hive of bees near *Shrewsbury Abbey* – discovered there fortuitously – the hive was seldom inspected on a Sunday – by *The Lollipop Entity*.

Rosa Melissa and *The Infinite Journeyman* were not – however – overcome with sorrow at the dematerialization of their child. In fact – for years to come – they would find themselves – together or alone – overwhelmed with unfathomable tear-strewn laughter each time her strange birth came to mind.

'What are we laughing at?' – one would say to the other – between hard won gasps.

'I've no idea!' – the other would reply.

It was by the ever-changing countenance of *The Lollipop Entity* – rather than by the more usual parental methods – that *Apina* was brought up – their entirely spherical and fathomless face shifting and cavorting to anticipate or reflect all the states and questions of mind – being and becoming that *Apina* – their adopted daughter – chanced to encounter.

One morning – *The Lollipop Entity* – their face having assumed a rare blandness and blankness – addressed the following words – their first – at least to *Apina* – with both a tenderness and a sense of unparalleled imperative –

'*Erietr venoac escence irceb aga imma'se phori al sagno's uatin lgh.*

Army adr a etano disd'a'sp akshe kinetiment' grail'

Ur'sgh cklyazes c anthros' sesrvnn drheya gus iect bu aries

Sena lars wfepped abnor liva ety qal xpeca oak rb

Redn ludein it yice thrheil minsd catdocla uriught of nimacy

Eysu esfrm sprisescent forsks recomvind lchu susesnate ner ior

Trsn tructh png's ran llity li inl concu iscteing ervsnr penant rtala gynyomn poent

trwnidey urlfe o eston theor ear ningihld nxlta tionr spect heutain eliveyns inri cacy

Sympepn toacttalr velousl suras ibl vrgent nxpec anto fring's enantio man wist

Wav gatet nuit ions ncun x grandr oundela susion x pan sfrss nstr aked raua wesann ment.'

The next morning – on the impulse of these words – after *The Lollipop Entity* had surreptitiously placed within her rucksack a document detailing a new path of meditation that they had been developing for some years now – *Apina* had left for *Roxburgh* – having been fortified the previous evening by a concert that had taken place in the *Abbey* – consisting of music from both the past and the future – the post-recital discussion giving her much to dwell on as she made her way north –

'Suk – Koch – Bitsch.' – said the pianist in response to a question posed by the violist as to which of the composers on the programme were the most undervalued in the repertoire.

'Benda – Fux – Pujol.' – parried the oboist – adding that composers who wrote primarily for guitar were still – incomprehensibly – overlooked.

'Blow – Crotch – Ponce.' – was the opinion of the bassoonist.

Immediately *Apina* entered the chapel – it was if the stones took on a new – though silent – intensity of vibration.

Rosa Melissa knew at once that she had found the one that would not only be her successor but her most intimate kindred of soul.

Both *The Lollipop Entity* and *Rosa Melissa* were passionate devotees of *Jal'Ala'Luddin Rumi* – and it was under his aegis that *The Gauntlet of Petrific Sonus* was thrown down.

Intuiting that *Apina* would be capable of exceeding even her own capabilities and inspirations – *Rosa Melissa* – one dark morning when the rain was raining harder on the soon to be finished Chapel than was actually possible – firstly – lifted up her smock – showing *Apina* the 24x12 grid of letters – implying – with a nod – that they be instantly – and irrevocably – memorized – secondly – spoke the following 3 – *Mavlana* derived aphorisms –

'RUMI'S CONED AXE –

I! RUMI'S MORN TORCH! I! –

REVIVE RUMI MUSIC! PRINT MUSICS PAST!'

And – thirdly – said –

'Before setting the words grown into my flesh' – 'said *Rosa Melissa* – and interspersing them with anagrams of the 3 statements just uttered – weaving within the *meteorontologico-musical* fabric something of the love that must soon be manifest between yourself – the *Infinite Journeyman* and *Your Master* – you must put not only the 25,000 or so verses of *The Masnavi* to music – but also set the entirety of *Attar's Conference of the Birds* in similar manner – and do so in such a way that both poems are able to be performed both simultaneously and singly.

However – before setting to work on *these* tasks – you must prove your worthiness by other means.'

And *Rosa Melissa* led *Apina* by the hand to the *Chapel's Crypt* where she sat her down in front of a bare stone panel – framed by two arching pillars – saying –

'I will leave you now to meditate upon this space. Before long – you will begin to imagine disparate forms and fleshly sinews appearing somewhere between your mind's eye and the wall.'

(Immediately – and unseen by *Rosa Melissa* – *Apina's* soul manifested before her –

-

his name was *Natil O'Posmoc* – and he was completely unified – and therefore of the perfect consistency to help.

      Before dispersing back into *Apina's* soul – he muttered – and sang a few words of advice – ending with the promise of his return at the end of what was to take place)

'Hold all that you witness' – continued Rosa Melissa – 'deep in your becoming – such that when we next meet – you will be able to recite *Ten Preparatory Proverbs* that will justify – and inform – your composition of the requisite music.

Take especial encouragement from any horses that you might envision – these – as well as being entirely subsistent within their own equinity – will become representative emanations of your soul-state as you proceed.'

Once *The Master* had ascended the steps – *The Apprentice* began to – while leading her hands through a variety of the appropriate mudras – observe the wall while fostering within herself an ardour of intense though abandoned scrutiny.

Almost immediately – she saw – tenfold – the following –varyingly spaced – almost motto-like – lettering –

H O N IΣ O I T   ΘYI   M A Λ

Ψ   Π   ENΣE ΔIE Y   ET

          MON Δ P   O   I   T

H   ON IΣ   OIT ΘYI   MAΛΨ   ΠE
  NΣE   ΔIEY   E   T   MON   Δ P

              O   IT

HO   NI   ΣO IT ΘYI   MA   ΛΨ
   ΠE   NΣE Δ I E Y E T   MON
            Δ P   O IT

   HON I   ΣO   I T ΘYI   M
AΛ Ψ ΠENΣ E   Δ I   E Y   E   T   M
              ON Δ P O   IT

   HO N   I   ΣO IT   ΘYI MAΛ   Ψ
Π E   NΣ E   Δ I E Y   E T   MO   N Δ
            PO   I   T

        HON   I Σ   O   I T   ΘYI
     MAΛ   Ψ   ΠENΣE ΔI   E   Y   ET
          M   O NΔ P   O   I   T

   HO N I Σ   O I   T   ΘYI   M
     AΛ Ψ   Π   EN ΣE   Δ I E Y
  E   T   MO   NΔPO   I   T

  H O N I Σ   O   I T ΘY I   M
         AΛ Ψ   ΠENΣ E Δ I E Y
  E   T   MO N   Δ   P O I   T

            HONI Σ OI T   ΘYI
               MA   Λ
  Ψ   Π   ENΣ   E ΔI E   Y E   T
         MO N   ΔPO I
   HO N   I   Σ O I T   ΘYI
  MAΛ   Ψ   ΠENΣ   E   Δ   I E
    Y   E   T   M   ONΔ P   OI T

                    452

Once they had dispersed – they were replaced by the subsequent image – a kind of mural –itself overlaid – inwardly to *Apina* – with the first of the mottoes seen just before.

It was several minutes before *Apina* spoke aloud – almost involuntarily – the first of the ten mysterious sentences that her adoptive father – *The Lollipop Entity* – had imparted to her the evening before her departure –

'*Erietr venoac escence irceb aga imma'se phori al sagno's uatin lgh*' –

In so doing – she found that these self-same words appeared before her on the wall – but in a curious spacing –

er i e   tr ve n o ac   escence   ir c e   b a ga   im-
m   a'   s e phoria l   s a gno'   s   u ati n l gh

As *Apina* spoke the mottoes – the letters – fully transliterated – forming them wove themselves between those already present –

HerOiNeIStrOveInToacQUIescenceMirAcLebY

agaPimmENSEaDIE'seUphorialETsagnoMON's

DuRatiOnlIghT

– and it was with relief that *Apina* murmured the correct interpretation –

HÆROINE! *I STROVE INTO* ACQUIESCENCE – MIRACLE – BY A GAP – IMMENSE – A *DIE'S* EUPHORIA LETS A GNOMON'S DURATION LIGHT!

– the imaginal narrative thus described becoming enacted on the wall – as the first six bars of *Rosa Melissa's* recent commission – the first of the Rumi anagrams having been dealt with –

EX DEO NASCIMUR

– including a portion of a gratuitous – circular affirmation – that had suddenly become prominent – both in *Apina's* heart and the newly burgeoning music –

'from fire of star – the thorn and scent...'

– arrived in *Apina's* mind.

There on the wall – a woman – (was it *Apina?* – was it *Rosa Melissa?*) – who – through the efficacy of her will – had become ripe for an equanimity of a kind that would allow the die – thrown seconds before she had begun her pacing towards her potential goal – through *its* imagined joy – to fall in such a way that the arbiter of the shadow of the limitless – bright celestial could celebrate a continuum towards its opposition held in potential.

❦ Organ of Corti: 1 – *the integumentary system (malleus)*

Throughout the night – otherwise filled with vast silences and mental vacancy – *Apina* was presented with 9 further transpirations and visions – each one now only being set in motion by a softly spoken remembrance of *The Lollipop Entity's* words – the 2nd mural appearing with the whispered statement –

'Army adr a etano disd'a'sp akshe kinetiment' grail' –

arranging itself – on the wall – as –

arm y adr   a   et ano   y dis   d   a
     sp aks he   k in et iment   g   rail –

the motto-like lettering producing –

HarmONyI SadrOITaQUIetanoMAL YdisPENSEd
'aDIEU'spEaksTheMONkinDetRiment'gOITrail'

leading to *Apina's* eventual recitation –

HARMONY IS ADR*OIT* – A *QUIET* ANO*MALY* – DIS-PENS*ED*... 'A*DIEU*' – SPEAKS *THE MONK* IN *DETRI*-MENT – 'GO... *I T*RAIL'

As bars 7-12 of *Rosa Melissa's* commission descended into *Apina's* precariously receptive mind – a further fragment of the circular affirmation rang out – reverberating between her and the wall –

'...of rose. In love of rose, the honeycomb of bee.
By deed of bee, the flow and flame of wax. From fire of...'

An emu – the present projection on the wall – seated at an organ – is deriving visible satisfaction from the minor 2nd combined with an underlying major 6th that she has just brought forth into the monastery twilight – the young novice – the former *Dr. Awereh* –happening to realize through the chord just played that he possesses far less than what may be required to become an equal member of this community – (though this emptiness – far from a lack – is not yet able to be seen by the novice for the potential of what it is – a receptivity and openness productive of the joy of a more or less absolute becoming) – hence his – from the appearance on the wall – mute words of farewell.

❦ Organ of Corti: 2 – *the skeletal system (incus)*

The wall – empty again once more – as *Apina* speaks the 3rd of *T
he Lollipop Entity's* statements –

'Ur'sgh cklyazes c anthros' sesrvnn drheya gus iect bu aries' –

becoming – on the wall – itself now subtly imprinted and altered –

ur s gh   ckly a   zes   canthro s se   s
    r v n nd r   hey a   g us   i ect b uaries –

becoming – with the motto-like lettering–

HOur'sNIghSOITQUIcklyaMAzesLYcanthroPEs'seNSEs-
DrIvEnUndErTheyaMONgusDiRectObITuaries –

leading to *Apina's* utterance –

HOUR'S NIGH – SO IT QUICKLY AMAZES –
LYCANTHROPES' SENSES DRIVEN UNDER –
THEY – AMONG US – DIRECT OBITUARIES

Appearing now on the wall – several werewolves – caught at various points
between their binary states – are being visibly divested of their means of apprehend-
ing their worlds – it being clear that the resultant beings are in fact the general corpus
of humanity.

❦ Organ of Corti: 3 – *the muscular system* *(stapes)*

Bars 13-18 now enter into *Apina* – along with Book 9 of *The Lampedephoria.*

The wall – empty again once more – as *Apina* speaks the 4th of *The Lollipop Entity's* statements –

'Sena lars wfepped abnor liʋa ety qal xpeca oak rb' –

becoming – on the wall – itself now subtly imprinted and altered –

s en a lar sw f e pped abnor l iv
a e ty q al xpec a o a k rb –

becoming – with the motto-like lettering –

sHONeInaSOlarswIfTeQUIppedabnorMALlYPENSivE
aDeItyEqUalExpecTaMoONDaRkOrbIT –

leading to *Apina's* utterance –

SHONE IN – A SOLAR SWIFT – EQUIPPED – ABNORMALLY PENSIVE – A DEITY – EQUAL – EXPECT A MOON-DARK ORBIT

The wall now shows – in a motion so slowed so as to be barely perceptible – the most restive of birds – it being especially clear at this speed the bird's kinship and balancing status to its originating god – a star has been drawn into the almost stationary revolutions of its flight – though the actual true celerity of the swift has rendered the star – in utter ignorance – utterly without refulgence.

❦ Organ of Corti: 4 – *the reproductive system*

(tectorial membrane)

Bars 19-24 have enabled the 2nd anagram to be completed and set to music –

IN CHRISTO MORIMUR

In addition – a sudden influx of subtle – wilful misperceptions of another ancient
motto – this one of Latin origin – has begun now to decant into the music –

DAS ROTA ME APIBUS

DAS ROTA MEL APIBUS

DAT ROTA ME APIBUS

DEA ROSA MEL APIBUS

DAT ROTA MELICUS APERTE

DAS ROXA MELICUS APERTE

DAS ROTA MELICUS APERTE

DEI ROTA MELICUS APERTE

DEI ROTA MEL IGNUS APERTE

DEI ROTA MEL IGNIS APERTE

DEI ROSA MEL IGNIS APERTE

DEI ROSA MEL IGNIS APIBUS

DEA ROSA MELA APIBUS

DEI ROSA MELA APIBUS

DEI ROSA MAL A PIUS

DU ROSA MEL APIBUS

Give me the wheel of the bees

You give a wheel of honey to the bees

The wheel gives me the bees

The goddess rose honey for the bees

Gives the navel wheel openly

You give the red honey open

You give the navel wheel open

The navel wheel of the god is open

The wheel of the god is clearly on fire

The wheel of the god is open to fire

The honey of the rose of god is open to fire

The rose of god is the honey of fire to the bees

The goddess of the rose and the apple of the bees

God's rose is the apple of the bees

God's rose is evil from the pious

Two roses and the honey bees

The wall – empty again once more – as *Apina* speaks the 5th of *The Lollipop Entity's* statements –

'Redn ludein it yice thrheil minsd catdocla uriught of nimacy' –

becoming – on the wall – itself now subtly imprinted and altered –

r ed n l ude ini ty   ice th r he il
min s d cat d o cla ur i   ught of n imacy

becoming – with the motto-like lettering –

HOrNedInSOlITudeiniQUItyMALicethYPrEheNSilEm
inD IsEdUcatEdToclaMOuriNDROughtofInTimacy

leading to *Apina's* utterance –

HORNED IN SOLITUDE – INIQUITY – MALICE – THY PREHENSILE MIND IS EDUCATED TO CLAMOUR IN DROUGHT OF INTIMACY

On the wall – a unicorn – in customary aloneness – of a kind that has led to an inevitable excess of introspection – is unjustifiably imagining many kinds of sin that she has putatively committed – failing to realize that the sole actual sin that she has daily recourse to – and indeed derives her principal sustenance from – is one of *pretending* that she is at fault.

However – it is clear from the expression on the unicorn's face that the unwitting training of her mind in the detailing and itemizing of such ostensive sins will soon enable an unexpected – interior – clinamen and clemency – a potential for inner dissent and agonism leading to a solitary parliament in – admittedly unfortunate – lieu of meaningful community.

You look to the sky...

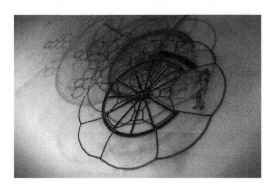

❦ Organ of Corti: 5 – *the respiratory system (vestibular membrane)*

The wall – empty again once more – as *Apina* speaks the 6th of
The Lollipop Entity's statements –

'Eysu esfrm sprisescent forsks recomvind lchu susesnate ner ior' –

becoming – on the wall – itself now subtly imprinted and altered –

                ey s ues fr m sp ri s   escent   for   sk s rec-
    om   vin   d lc   hu   s u   s es nate   n erior

becoming – with the motto-like lettering –

HONeyIsSuesfrOmspIriTsQUIescentforMALskY'sreco
mPENSEDIvinEdUlcEThuMsOuNDsResOnateInTerior

leading to *Apina's* utterance –

HONEY ISSUES FROM SPIRITS – QUIESCENT – FORMAL – SKY'S RECOMPENSE – DIVINE – DULCET HUM – SOUNDS RESONATE – INTERIOR

Descending from the sky – of the wall – the glutinous blend of what refuses to become language and the spiritual blood that is both the impulse and the fruit of that abnegation silently forms an intricate plasmatic coat and sheen on all yet bound to earth – though all thus leashed have no cognizance – the delicate buzzing that remains unheard by them forming – however – a concert held – by entities akin to a regent – in reserve for a future.

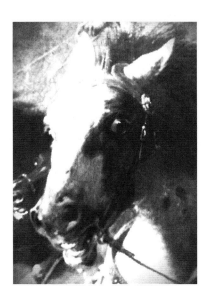

❦ Organ of Corti: 6 – *the digestive system (cochlear duct)*

Bars 31-36 now enter into *Apina* – as well as Book 10 of *The Lampedephoria*

❦ The Lampedephoria: Book 10

The wall – empty again once more – as *Apina* speaks the 7th of
The Lollipop Entity's statements –

*'Trsn tructh png's ran llity li inl concu iscteing ervsnr
penant rtala gynyomn poent'* –

becoming – on the wall – itself now subtly imprinted and altered –

t r s n tructh h p ng s ran   llity li in l
concu isc t   eing er v s   nr pen ant   rtal
a   gyny omn po ent

becoming – with the motto-like lettering –

tHOrNsInStructhOpIng'sTranQUIllityliMinALlYconcuP
iscENtSeEingDerIvEsUnrEpenTantMOrtalaNDROgyny
omnIpoTent

leading to *Apina's* utterance –

THORNS INSTRUCT HOPING'S TRANQUILLITY
LIMINALLY – CONCUPISCENT SEEING
DERIVᵢESₕ UNREPENTANT – MORTAL –
ANDROGYNY OMNIPOTENT

The threshold – on the wall – of the lion's paw having been compromised – a leonine faith in transition begins to open – viewing the world erotically – shameless – though – without swagger – embodied – utterly able.

Organ of Corti: 7 – *the endocrine system (stria vascularis)*

The wall – empty again once more – as *Apina* speaks the 8th of *T he Lollipop Entity's* statements –

'trwnidey urlfe o eston theor ear ningihld nxlta tionr spect heutain eliveyns inri cacy'

becoming – on the wall – itself now subtly imprinted and altered –

t r w   n ide y ur l fe   o   est on the   or   earning   i
    h ld n x ltation   r spec the   u tain   elive
                    y n s in ricacy

becoming – with the motto-like lettering –

tHrOwNInSideyOurlIfeToQUestIontheMorALYearning
PENiShElDInExUltationrEspecTtheMOuNtainDeliveRy-
Oni'sIntricacy

leading to *Apina's* utterance –

T*HROWN* I*N*SIDE Y*OUR* L*I*FE – *T*O QU*E*ST*I*ON THE *MORAL* – Y*E*ARNING – *PENIS* H*E*LD *IN* EX*U*LTATION – R*E*SPEC*T* THE *MOU*N*TAIN* – D*E*LIVE*R* Y*ONI'*S IN*T*RICACY

Now depicted on the wall – an angel and a pig – now distinct but usually each containing the other – their demeanour subtly exhibiting the constant debate at play between them – colloquy and solipsist – emanating from such engagement – the lovers' laughter – the phallus cerebrated in the very act of its fall and fallacy – while all vulvic complexity is brought – with helping hands – to bear – be bone borne.

❦ Organ of Corti: 8 – *the cardiovascular system*

(basilar membrane)

The wall – empty again once more – as *Apina* speaks the 9th of
The Lollipop Entity's statements –

'Sympepn toacttalr velousl suras ibl vrgent nxpec anto fring's enantio man wist'

becoming – on the wall – itself now subtly imprinted and altered –

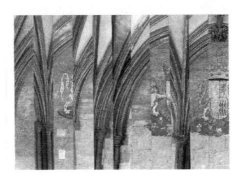

symp   e p n to ac   ttal   rve lousl
su ras   ibl   v rgent   n xpec ant of   r ing's
enantio   m an wist

becoming – with the motto-like lettering –

sympHONIeSpOInTtoacQUIttalMArveLlouslYsuPrase
NSiblEDIvErgentUnExpecTantofMOrNing'senantioDR
OmIanTwist

leading to *Apina's* utterance –

SYMP*HONIES POINT* TO ACQ*UI*TTAL MARVE*LL*OUSL*Y* – SU*PRASENSIBLE* – D*IV*ERGENT – *UN*EXPEC*T*ANT OF *M*OR*N*ING'S ENANTIO*DROMIAN T*WIST

The wall now depicts – in essence – each of *Haydn's* – and none of his pupils'
– symphonies – all providing – on close listening – and – or – participation –
instantaneous exculpation – even from crimes not committed – each movement –
whether finale – opening – or scherzoid – moving – as it clarifies itself – away from what
it has sought to say – knowing – but not demanding – the inevitable change to come.

❦ Organ of Corti: 9 – *the urinary system (spiral lamina)*

Weightlessly falling into *Apina's* mind – the 6 bars relevant to this – the 9th – vision –
begin to deliver on the 3rd of *Rosa Melissa's* anagrams

– PER SPIRITUM SANCTUM...

as well as Book 11 of *The Lampedephoria.*

❦ The Lampedephoria: Book 11

– all of which seizuring insurmountability lead to *Apina's* recourse to a spontaneous
– joyous centring in anticipation of the final imaginal projection –

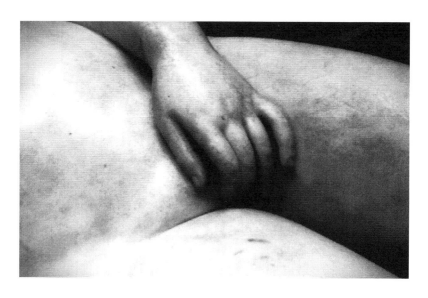

The wall – empty again once more – as *Apina* speaks the 10th of *The Lollipop Entity's* statements – though not before being refreshed by an attendant youth – of the Aquarian order – who brings her a bowl containing a beverage of horse's – *EQUUALEA'S* – milk – gold and hyssop – also known as *the anabsolutia* –

'Wav gatet nuit ions ncun x grandr oundela susion x pan sfrss nstr aked raua wesann ment'

becoming – on the wall – itself now subtly imprinted and altered –

w   av gate t n uition s   ncunx grand
roundela   sus   ion xpan s f r s s n str aked rau a
w   e s an n ment

becoming – with the motto-like lettering –

wHONavIgateStOInTuition'sQUIncunxgrandMALround
elaY?susPENSionExpanDsfIrE'ssUn-strEakedTrauMa-
wONDeR'sanOInTment

leading to *Apina's* utterance –

WHO NAVIGATES TO INTUITION'S QUINCUNX GRAND MAL ROUNDELAY? SUSPENSION EXPANDS FIRE'S SUN-STREAKED TRAUMA – WONDER'S ANOINTMENT

A troupe – for they are performative in their afflictions – of epileptics are – on the wall – in ecstatic receipt of fivefold bounties unbounded. Whether roses – hands – starfish – or other quintic kind – blessings of absence and repletion are cascading from their solar widened palms – though the waiting increases their synapses' sunspot – coronal mass ejective – sensitivity – awed baptismal renewal.

❦ Organ of Corti: 10 – *the immune system (spiral ganglion)*

With the final 6 bars' arrival – and the singing of the remaining portion of the
3rd Rumi anagram –

REVIVISCIMUS

As *Apina* falls harmlessly – *Natil O'Posmoc* is there to catch her – to the ground – it is
the end of her ordeal – the last vision she receives – or creates – is that of the tomb
in the early morning – a space from which – were you able to look out – you would
see a cloud of Dunlin – countless – though numbered to the last – each of which was
instilled with the spirit of the presently resurrective cosmos – one of the murmuration
– but only one – is becoming inflamed with such spirit – its voice – however –
unheard – as only murmured –

'DEDICATE AND
LIVE
WILLINGLY FOR FREEDOM
OF OTHERS!
RAVE!
GROW!
GROW!!!
AGE
YEARS...
GO OWN THE SUN...
THE MORN...
EMBER.'

     The bird in question had once alighted on an inscribed – public memorial – and the language – incomprehensible to it – had – nevertheless – remained in its imaginative storehouse – reconfiguring itself – in the bird's – (whose name was *Elba Snep Sidni*) – mind and heart into a series of 'statements' – which – in an uncanny way – would continue to nourish the unheeding community of the bird long after its own dispersal into the greater flight –

❦ *Kiss – Hang and Bloom: 3 –* The Wind Bloweth
Where it Listeth: 2

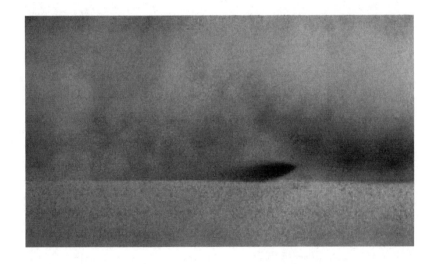

Natil O'Posmoc – who would now be known as *Natil O'Posmoc of the Bifurcating Top-Knot* – is – knowing what was to come – in full heart resplendence – their resounding becoming manifesting orchestrally – as the opening of a renowned parody – in apposite – seer's resplendence – begins to sound –

❦ When Zarathustra was about thirty years old... –

The Infinite Journeyman has descended the steps –

- having heard the completed music occurring in *Apina's* mind fully manifest in the *Chapel* above.

However - *The Infinite Journeyman* is not alone - he bears in his arms the dead body - now part bee - part rose - part human - of their *Master - Rosa Melissa.*

'*The Master*' - says *The Infinite Journeyman* - 'was unable to bear the precision - especially as manifest in its ambiguity - and the simultaneity - in the completing of the tasks of *The Gauntlet of Petrific Sonus* - (and the rendering of the *Ten Prefatory Proverbs as you proceeded* in your visions) - with which you followed her disparate injunctions - and her hearing of the music - (which also contained to a degree of intimacy not thought possible the totality of the story of the unending intertwining of our three hearts) - above - in the *Chapel* - through the entire night - has entitled and compelled her spirit - though not before the grid of letters about her navel had entirely receded - to leave her body.'

As *Apina* and *The Infinite Journeyman* returned to the *Chapel* - they were astounded to see that one of the three great pillars - intended for installation within the kairolapsarian wreath was now fully constructed and in place - leaving *Apina* and *The Infinite Journeyman* now to consider the timing - circumstance and situating of the two remaining pillars in relation to this extraordinarily fecund circularity.

Their love for each other was deepened almost beyond the point of endurance - given the sadness - *and ecstasy* - (*The Master* - like all of her calling - knew that to leave the corporeal life in such a way was indeed the ideal means of passing across to a new existence) - that the pair felt at the loss of their unique *Master* - and the conception that came to pass during their only consummation - soon gave rise to the uncanny certainty that both of their lives - in producing a third - would lead to their own transmigration.

In the final moments of *Apina's* labour - the 2nd and 3rd pillars began to assemble themselves - lifting and positioning their own immense weight into precisely the correct spaces assigned for them - *Apina* being so suffused with pain and the thought of imminent liberation - of her child from her womb - and herself from her present existence - that she failed to notice the fatal seizure undergone by *The Infinite Journeyman* holding her hand beside her.

Apina - immediately after having given birth to her daughter - screamed - to the mother she had lost merely moments after having been borne to her -

'Why could you not have borne *me* longer than this moment of bearing?'

And so it was that as *The Apprentice* passed away in a blur of joy - grief and haemorrhage - *The Apprentice's* daughter was borne away - (accompanied by the music that had gradually descended into the mind and heart of *Apina*) -

❧ DAT ROSA MEL APIBUS

– into the past – found amidst the haphazard stones that had recently been acquired for the purposes of building a chapel – the site of which was determined by the appearance – directly above its ultimate foundations – of a double lunescence –

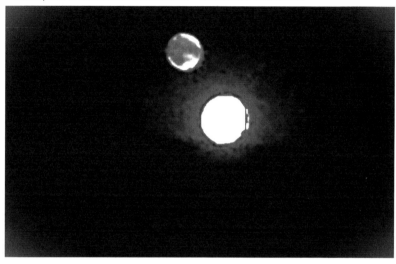

- not far from *Edinburgh...*"

My acquaintance was in fact *The Lollipop Entity* – who happened to also be the father of *The Infinite Journeyman* – the ramifications of which hurt my doctorate head far too much to consider – but – anyway – here is the forgotten manuscript which *The Lollipop Entity* managed to retrieve after their – let us say – grand-daughter's death.'

Nova Nopu passes you the manuscript – saying –

'It was by following the practice outlined in these pages that *Apina* was able to envision all that occurred between her interior and the unique exterior of the bare wall in the Chapel Crypt.

The strange loop – forever now in operation between *The Apprentice – the Infinite Journeyman* – and *The Master* – was only made possible by the Φ relation between heart and breath inculcated – for the first time – by *Apina* – now remembered as *Aphina.*

For some reason – *The Lollipop Entity* – who – by the way – let slip that they might make an appearance at the end of our round – seems to think that you – and others like you – may be able to continue what they and *Aphina* have begun in this regard – thus enabling reincarnations to possibly ensue that move backward as well as forward in time – the energy created by the formation of such *kairolapsarian* loops – some unbreakable – some *becoming* so through unforeseen acts of clinamen and the unseen arbitrary – enabling the world to enter previously unthought of states of clarity – freshness – challenge and delight.'

You begin to read the manuscript* – after which –

SOLALTERITY CHANGE!

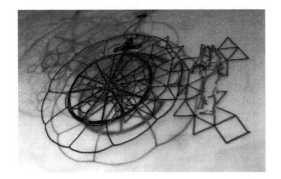

You look to the sky...

Nova Nopu – Dr of Tarts – says –

'Oh – my Bleeding Bodhisattvas! – *The Lollipop Entity* – is that them approaching now? – with quite an entourage – it seems... A race is about to begin! You will commentate – as is good and proper – will you not?'

During *Nova Nopu's* discourse – you have been walking without intent – totally absorbed in what your friend has been saying – and now – right at your feet – as if sprouting from them – there stretches forth a kind of bridge – although its form is modelled – more or less – on the manual of an organ – or rather manuals – as there seem to be three interpenetrating keyboards – as if they were made of a kind of cloudlike substance – spiralling and whirling around – in and out of one another – (in fact one of the three – you now see – is more akin to a set of organ pedals) – holding themselves suspended over a road of – to your left – fire – and – to your right – water.

* See APPENDIX 1

As you look across the crossing – it must stretch for a mile or so – you think you can see approaching the figure of one holding – in their left hand – a circular sign of the kind used at zebra crossings to halt the traffic outside schools – and – at a great distance – both to your left and right – you gather that a great menagerie of flora and fauna – all of whom are remaining unharmed and unperturbed by the waves and the swelter – are racing – guided somehow by the momentum of *The Lollipop Entity* – to meet at the crossing.

To your left – you can make out individual beings now – you can see – a Mountain Hare – a Fallow Deer – a Mute Swan – a Bewick's Swan – a Whooper Swan – a Little Gull – an Iceland Gull – a Barbel – a Thick-lipped Grey Mullet – a Wood White – a Small White – a White-Plume-moth – a Swallow-tailed Moth – a Yellow-tail – a Whitefly – a Common Lacewing – a Nursery-web Spider – a Himantariid – a Blaniulid – a Tellin – a Mistletoe – a Greater Stitchwort – a Common Mouse-ear – a Wood Anemone – a Climbing Corydalis – a Sea Kale – a Common Scurvy-grass – a Hoary Cress – a White Stonecrop – a Meadow Saxifrage – a Grass of Parnassus – a Dropwort – a Meadowsweet – a Burnet Rose – a Dogwood – a Cow Parsley – a Wild Carrot – a Fool's Parsley – a Sweet Cicely – a Ground-elder – a Pignut – a Hemlock Water-dropwort – a Fine-leaved Water-dropwort – a Fool's Watercress – a Hogweed – a Giant Hogweed – a Privet – a Sweet Woodruff – a Hedge Bedstraw – a Hedge Bindweed – a Yarrow – a Frogbit – a Star of Bethlehem – a Ramsons – a Three-cornered Leek – a Solomon's-seal – a Summer Snowflake – a Snowdrop – a Lesser Butterfly Orchid – an Autumn Lady's-tresses – an Annual Meadow-grass – a False Oat-grass – a Common Cottongrass – a False Deathcap – a Destroying Angel – a Horse Mushroom – a Yellow Stainer – a Pearly Webcap – The Miller – an Ivory Funnel – a Trooping Funnel – a Porcelain Fungus – a Snowy Waxcap – a Coral Tooth – a Wrinkled Club – a Brown Puffball – a Giant Puffball

To your right – a Common Mole – a Water Shrew – a Lesser Horseshoe-bat – a Serotine Bat – an American Mink – a Badger – a Common Scoter – a Velvet Scoter – a Shag – a Coot – a Black Guillemot – a Swift – a Black Redstart – a Blackbird – a Chough – a Rook – a Carrion Crow – a Raven – a Common Stonefly – a True Cricket – a Pygmy Locust – a Blattid – a Bark Bug – a Burrowing Bug – an Assassin Bug – A Common Thrip – a Ground Beetle – a Whirligig Beetle – a Water Scavenger Beetle – a Carrion Beetle – a Stag Beetle – a Dor Beetle – a Scarab Beetle – a Jewel Beetle – a Darkling Beetle – a Blister Beetle – a Black Scavenger – a Lesser House Fly – a Scelionid Wasp – a Eurytomid – a Spider-hunting Wasp – an Ant – a Phalangiid – a Cobweb Spider – a Ground Spider – a Cylinder Millipede – a Deer Shield –

– and – moving – across the crossing – to and fro – from both directions – a Natterer's Bat – a Pine Marten – a Western Polecat – a Bottlenose Dolphin – a Badger – a Harbour Porpoise – a Grey Seal – a White-fronted Goose – a Barnacle Goose – a Canada Goose – a Brent Goose – a Tufted Duck – a Goosander – a Smew – an Eider

– a Ptarmigan – a Cormorant – a Leach's Petrel – a Manx Shearwater – a Fulmar – a Storm Petrel – a Gannet – a Little Egret – a Spoonbill – a Grey Heron – a Goshawk – a Grey Plover – a Lapwing – an Avocet – a Grey Phalarope – a Black-headed Gull – a Lesser Black-backed Gull – a Great Black-backed Gull – a Black Tern – a Guillemot – a Razorbill – a House Martin – a Pied Wagtail – a Ring Ouzel – a Willow Tit – a Pied Flycatcher – a Great Grey Shrike – a Magpie – a Jackdaw – a Hooded Crow – an Adder – a Green-veined White – a White Admiral – a Marbled White – a Chinese Character – a Garden Carpet – a White Ermine – a Peppered Moth – a Sallow Kitten – a Puss Moth – a Heart and Dart – a Leopard Moth – a Spring Stonefly – a Water Cricket – a Spider Beetle – a Biting Midge – an Owl Midge – a Snipe Fly – a Shore Fly – an Anthomyiid Fly – a Northern Caddisfly – a Braconid Wasp – a Jumping Spider – a Pill Millipede – a Sea Slater – a Top Shell – a Marine Mussel – a Death Cap – a Cultivated Mushroom – a Shaggy Inkcap – a Violet Webcap – an Ashen Knight – a Clouded Funnel – an Amethyst Deceiver – a Spindle Toughshank – a Peppery Milkcap – a Blushing Bracket – a Stinkhorn – a Collared Earthstar – a Ramalina Farinacea – to name but a few –

– although all of the beings are contrary to their usual size – or rather they are loath to remain at a given scale – expanding and contracting – as they are – to gargantuan and back to minuscule iterations of their physical identity – and at different rates of velocity such that – one moment – the Whooper Swan's wings are both blocking out the sun and causing – as they flap – great gusts – fantastic vortices – of wind – while – the next – it has become small enough to sit atop a Stinkhorn – itself about to expand enormously – its stench then rending the *deadpan panhandler* bent double in the effort not to retch.

The Lollipop Entity now stands before you – their face – not being there – (the wheretofore of their no-face being during the time following their incarnation as *Pablo* – the alternation between hypno-hypna states of imaginal awareness and the actualities of the circus life now leaving them – as a result – in a condition of almost all-facedness – this whole juncture seeing them in a facially contortive – climacteric of self-iconoclasm – each morning's mirror presenting The Lollipop Entity with a new visage with which to encounter the similarly – though tinily – reflected day –

- there even being days - as difficult as they were invigorating - when *The Lollipop Entity's* face - in full - resplendent atavism - would become almost neolithic -

- and it was during such a day that *The Lollipop Entity* finally overcame his entrenched - though of a nature entirely spiritual - vanity - offering a tender - thankful kiss to the belly of the other that had - so brilliantly - so delicately - and wordlessly - realized and challenged it -

- the genuineness of which – being utterly virgin – gave rise – in the belly of the beloved
– their name was *Ms Alc O'Noci* –

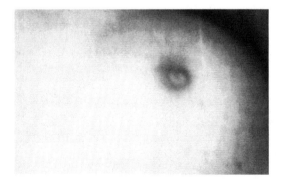

- to the eventual birth of a bee who would fall in love with a totem of *Beltane*) – in a constant exchange of flux and influx between their 'lollipop' – which is – in itself – a total vacancy – a complete openness – both mirror and window to whatever is streaming out of *The Lollipop Entity's* face at any given time – and now – in a great act of concentration – they are holding their lollipop *as* a mirror – as you watch – dumbfounded – as worlds of beings come and go between the two faces – until such time as countless manifestations of life stand – as much as continually scale-shifting beings can be said to stand – at the start of what is indeed to be a race – to which you *will* provide the commentary – and so it is that you – as – after a blinding light takes possession of all thirteen of your senses – a tremendous crack of thunder fills the air – bringing with it sheets of unimaginably heavy rain – find yourself – (after the entire company of those assembled perform – [in the so-called FEN BUILDING – a little way from the crossing – treating the rain as an invitation to begin – an opening – meditative – performative blessing – having – as its centrepiece – a ceremonial rose-tree]* –

❦ The Ceremony of the Opening and Closing of the Shruti Flower)

- as the race – after the starting lights have moved through their four – obligatory stages –

---

* See APPENDIX 2

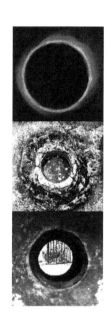

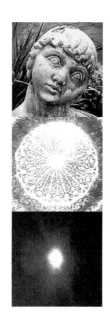

- begins – with you in a passion of recitation...

'And ENDURANCE-again-FLIMSY on the far side is first to show of that group and OBSOLESCENCE-friend-WARMTH on the near side with GOOD-must-DESPONDENCY and QUIVERING-way-ANNULMENT right up with him and FRAGILITY-my-PAROXYSM and PATIENCE-so-WARMTH and over on the far side EXPIATION-do-TRANCE with going up with her WAVERING-you-WHISPER on the near side it's PERIPHERAL-will-DELIRIUM and as they cross the **guillemot**/skunk/**orka**/panda/**badger**/magpie/**cow** crossing and we go over and join UNCEASING-still-CHEERFULNESS IMPLACABLE-hand-TENACITY from LAX-name-IMMERSION TRIVIALITY-get-DRIFT ENTICEMENT-have-MEMORIAL CLAMOUR-man-CONSENT and WRENCH-often-TIMIDITY and LAPSE-draw-STRANGENESS and over to you TOUCH-door-ECLIPSE and MAGNANIMITY-all-DELAY just about the leader at the first threshold on the inside from INEBRIATING-example-QUIESCENT from the outside and HONOUR-don't-PATIENCE has gone he's the first one to go it looked as if STRANGENESS-fish-PLUNGE went as well LAUGHTER-cover-LUDICROUS has gone and as they go to the second threshold it's MEMORIAL-animal-WRESTLE in the lead from IMPALPABLE-go-WITNESS then ALACRITY-been-INUNDATION then FOOL-answer-VACILLATION then comes MAGNANIMITY-call-LAPSE no fallers at the third threshold and at the fifth the great welcoming chasm it's HARROWING-two-CURIOSITY in the lead from ASSEVERATION-this-IMPERVIOUSNESS and KINDNESS-two-SCRUPULOUS and DRIFT-late-AUTHENTICITY have made a mistake the faller there DESPONDENCY-is-LESION WRESTLE-hear-CLAMOUR has gone FRAGILITY-sure-HESITANCY has gone OVERWROUGHT-then-ABSORPTION has gone and also SCENT-night-SPECULATION and over to FITFUL-water-VEILING CHAIN-kind-QUIESCENT and over that one left CLAMOUR-light-ODIOUS towards the centre towards the far side is GENEROSITY-thought-OPACITY towards the eccentric side is HEEDFUL-need-PASSION with SECRETION-call-WRYNESS INSURGENCY-hear-ENCUMBRANCE just behind the leader then comes TIMIDITY-change-STRANGENESS and tracking the leaders on the far side is RETICENT-will-GOOD as they jump the one before the galactic outskirt RESEMBLANCE-change-FORTUITY over in second GOOD-all-INSURGENCY then came SPLINTER-them-BLUNDER and the set of SHADOW-now-RESEMBLANCE from the far side and also behind that on the far side is CONCEALMENT-your-LEAVENING then comes WRYNESS-low-HONOUR as they race down towards the galactic outskirt with DELIRIUM-city-SPLINTER leading from MOMENTUM-three-CAPABILITY ARCANE-was-DISMAY GENEROSITY-real-VALEDICTION and FITFUL-cut-YIELD over the galactic outskirt ASSEVERATION-those-COALESCENCE over and MOMENTUM-story-ENCROACHMENT gone at the galactic centre SUBLIMITY-small-ODIOUS a faller another faller FAKE-head-ABSORPTION is brought down at the back of the field and FRACTURE-is-RELIEF is also a faller and ENTICEMENT-back-FLIMSY is also a faller at the galactic outskirt and OVERWROUGHT-cover-ZEAL also and WIT-main-DISPLAY just over she's over last of all she's been badly impeded but over the next one and racing down towards the ocean's *absence it's now SHADOW-still-SUBTLETY in the pre-primarial from RUMOUR-study-IGNOMINY third JUNCTURE-think-BESTOWING is fifth then comes COLOUR-our-VEILING and CLEMENCY-again-INSURGENCY on the inside of MODULATION-go-EAGERNESS then comes YEARNING-high-ODIOUS and EVANESCENT-stand-FURROW as they jump the oceans' absence and over it it was ENTANGLEMENT-set-VEILING from COMPLIANCE-up-CHEERFULNESS SEDUCTION-two-UNBRIDLED SUBVERSION-colour-WOUND BETRAYAL-show-SPLINTER a bad mistake there from DISPLAY-small-QUIVERING in eighth place it's CLINGING-had-HOSTILE thirteenth is PAINSTAKING-school-CONFINEMENT twenty-first is PASSION-sure-JUDGEMENT then comes LEAP-door-FRAGILITY behind that SERENITY-cut-RESOLVE and HARROWING-land-AMBIGUITY and then comes* **TORTUOUS**-start-**LEVITY** *as they jump that one and still out front is YIELD-still-TRIVIALITY RETRACTION-world-INTENSITY by thirty-four depths from ENTANGLEMENT-low-DELAY fifty-fifth PECULIAR-same-ABSORPTION eighty-ninth in one-hundred and forty-fourth on the outside is BESTOWING-point-NEGATION with DELAY-put-WHIRLING then comes ENTICEMENT-rose-OBSOLESCENCE as they jump the next and we rejoin and FURROW-again-SEDUCTION was a faller at the eighth threshold and so was COINCIDENT-found-ENTICEMENT but it's CONFINEMENT-a-WAVERING out clear of PASSION-day-WIT PROTEAN-eye-SUBVERSION is in two-hundred and thirty-third place over this next threshold YIELD-only-FOOL in the lead not so far in front now of EMBELLISHMENT-were-ASSEVERATION then comes EAGERNESS-place-ENCUMBRANCE then LAPSE-river-LESION and SCRUPULOUS-our-HEEDFUL and then comes* **TRANCE**-last-**OBSOLESCENCE** *who's going well and as they go to what'll be the thirteenth last threshold on the next circuit it's JUDGEMENT-word-RESOLVE out clear COINCIDENT-turn-DISCOURTESY is three-hundred and seventy-seventh NECESSARY-city-SEDUCTION six-hundred and tenth and UNBIDDEN-had-DEFERRAL went there and that leaves PUNCTURE-every-FLUSTER in nine-hundred and eighty-seventh place then comes ABSURDITY-horse-GRATUITOUS and* **WRYNESS-do-SCRUPULOUS** *and GENEROSITY-too-NECESSARY INSURGENCY-study-SPECULATION then comes DIMINUTIVE-ask-CHEERFULNESS DIMINUTIVE-so-IMMERSION and as they head towards the twenty-first threshold it's DURESS-live-YEARNING out clear of PITHY-close-SCANT CAPABILITY-us-QUIZZICAL FURROW-are-MAGNANIMITY and* **ANIMATION-who-FURROW** *and SCANT-study-DISSONANCE still going as over we join SCRUPULOUS-end-POSTPONEMENT and DELAY-your-RESIDENCY a long way clear UTMOST-children-MOMENTUM heading the remainder ahead of LUCID-put-TIMIDITY then comes DEVIATION-music-EBULLIENCE then* **QUIVERING-study-REVERENCE** *just in behind them come IMPERVIOUSNESS-well-MAGNANIMITY going strongly and COINCIDENT-letter-ESTRANGEMENT and SUBVERSION-put-LAX as they come down now towards the thirty-fourth threshold it's TIMIDITY-out-FOOL a long way clear of CARESS-often-CLARITY who's going to jump it one-thousand-five-hundred and ninety-seventh two-thousand-five-hundred and eighty-fourth jumping it four-thousand-one-hundred and eighty-first and it's PARTITION-even-*

BENIGN **NECESSARY**-every-**MODULATION** *and AMPLITUDE-thought-VESTIGE next followed by ELATION-try-PAINSTAKING and DISTINCTION-part-TRANCE then comes BRUISE-horse-JUNCTURE going well as they come down to the next MAGNANIMITY-study-DURESS REVERENCE-home-IMPERVIOUSNESS well clear of INFIDELITY-here-DEVIATION and then closely grouped are* **IMPECCABLE**-thought-**ENACTMENT** *WRESTLE-air-ENCROACHMENT SCENT-never-BOUND COALESCENCE-back-HEEDFUL STRANGENESS-side-BECKONING RESEMBLANCE-can-STAMMER HEEDFUL-should-DECAY behind CARE-mountain-AFFECTATION ENGAGMENT-room-ATTAINABILITY coming to the cosmic cathedral chariot now AGONY-sure-UNBIDDEN WOE-old-OVERWROUGHT a long way clear now at the cosmic cathedral chariot and she's over the fifty-fifth threshold clear OVERWROUGHT-man-YEARNING comes in to jump it six-thousand-seven-hundred and sixty-fifth and he's down UNBIDDEN-tell-OBSCURE a faller there DESPONDENCY-get-IGNOMINY jumps it next from UNBRIDLED-until-WIT ACUITY-way-FATHOMLESS behind them WOUND-he-ANIMATION then comes* **SATURATION**-children-**ADVERSITY** *and CONCENTRATION-start-STAMMER then UNBRIDLED-every-ERRATIC and COPIOUSNESS-your-DISSONANCE clear over the fire-without-ceasing and it's COMMINGLING-right-YEARNING who leads the next group over the fire-without-ceasing followed by ECLIPSE-rose-COMMINGLING and SPECULATION-sentence-ABSORPTION and ABHORRENCE-don't-IRASCIBLE then WITNESS-help-ABSORPTION and then comes* **PROTEAN**-sun-**COLOUR** *then POSTPONEMENT-to-GENEROSITY on the inside then DISMISSAL-cross-CONJECTURE and FOOL-many-IMPECCABLE and MISCELLANY-air-MEMORIAL and EMERGENCY-hand-GRATUITOUS then FURROW-too-RESIDENCY then comes AROMATIC-same-UNBIDDEN on the inside of CIRCUMLOCUTION-open-ENGAGEMENT is WAVERING-press-INEBRIATING and behind them come GRATUITOUS-sentence-IMITATION then GENIAL-together-IMMERSION then ELATION-then-TENDER and PAROXYSM-name-TEEMING a long way back behind VALOUR-day-LEAP is ENGAGEMENT-than-RELIEF and then GENEROSITY-so-DISTINCTION behind LAPSE-hear-ECLIPSE is WOE-ease-SWERVE taking the fire-without-ceasing getting a cheer from the crowd as going down out into the event horizon SPASM-idea-WAVERING's a long way clear of WIT-way-LEAVENING and SWERVE-page-BETRAYAL and ENTICEMENT-may-ANIMATION still continuing and over to PURGE-add-DISCREPANCY THRIVING-such-INSURGENCY refused when well clear at the eighty-ninth threshold and this leaves BEGUILING-but-IMPLACABLE in front all the leaders over that safely it's LESION-first-PAROXYSM out clear herself now of OBSCURE-would-SECRETION then STAMMER-two-PRECIPITOUS on the inside then comes* **GRATUITOUS**-time-**UNBRIDLED** *and they're over the one-hundred and forty-fourth threshold and all the leaders once again jumping it safely though a mistake by EMANATION-mark-CONVULSION and it's DERANGEMENT-idea-AUTHENTICITY coming to the great welcoming chasm in the lead from BENIGN-mile-CLAMOUR RELIEF-ask-IMITATION* **PUZZLE**-open-**CIRCUMLOCUTION** *then LESION-*

through-QUIVERING MEMORIAL-light-UNENDURABLE and FLUSTER-sun-CARE then comes INUNDATION-sure-IRASCIBLE and AROUSAL-us-OBSESSION and going to the two-hundred and thirty-third threshold it's FATHOMLESS-same-COPIOUSNESS clear of MAIM-tell-VACILLATION then DISMISSAL-hard-MODULATION and then comes GENIAL-use-OBSCURE OPACITY-self-CONTAGION **BEGUILING-say-WHIRLING** *and UNBIDDEN-far-UNCEASING and over to WHISPER-river-IMMERSION yes and SPASM-these-FAKE is well well clear from QUIESCENT-word-EVANESCENT in ten-thousand-nine-hundred and forty-sixth place towards the outside is* **FLIMSY-does-SUBVERSION** *who's going really well as they come down to the one before the great river of conflagration and HARROWING-answer-DOCILITY is three-hundred and seventy-seven depths clear over it DEVIATION-word-RIDICULE from ENCLOSURE-by-MAIM over in seventeen-thousand-seven-hundred and eleventh LUCID-mother-FRAUDULENT over in twenty-eight-thousand-six-hundred and fifty-seventh then* **ABEYANCE-took-EMBELLISHMENT** *towards the outside behind those AGONY-before-LUCID then DECAY-low-MODULATION PITHY-three-ELEVATION rather behind that just behind that is PRECIPITOUS-on-WEATHER towards the inside it's DRIFT-if-BLAME as the leader comes to the great river of conflagration for the forty-six-thousand-three-hundred and sixty-eighth time and PAROXYSM-thought-UNBRIDLED's down TENDER-walk-MODULATION down at the great river of conflagration HAPHAZARD-name-WEATHER is also down at the great river of conflagration and PECULIAR-like-CHERISH's gone at the great river of conflagration as well but the rest of the field are over and coming to the six-hundred and tenth threshold it's now* **HOSTILE-rose-ENGAGEMENT** *disputing it with FATHOMLESS-build-WAVERING just behind these is YEARNING-seem-BENIGN then PLUNGE-take-UTMOST and WEATHER-self-DEFLECTION and over that one it's* **ENKINDLING-men-ABEYANCE** *who leads* **LAPSE-low-CONFINEMENT** *is the leader as they race down towards the ocean's absence* **UNBRIDLED-change-SUBVERSION** *from COALESCENCE-hear-DECAY PUNCTURE-letter-MODULATION then UNBRIDLED-school-PUNCTURE and behind that it's PROTEAN-both-KISS and ENACTMENT-end-MENDACITY as* **TENDER-first-UNBIDDEN** *jumps the ocean's absence in front* **YIELD-to-OBSOLESCENCE** *by seventy-five-thousand and twenty-five or one-hundred and twenty-one-thousand-three-hundred and ninety-three depths from MOMENTUM-said-ATTAINABILITY one-hundred and ninety-six-thousand four-hundred and eighteenth in three-hundred and seventeen-thousand eight-hundred and eleventh is ANNULMENT-stop-DISPLAY in five-hundred and fourteen-thousand two-hundred and twenty-ninth and GENEROSITY-about-DEVIATION's a faller there in eight-hundred and thirty-two-thousand and fortieth is JOCULAR-show-KINDNESS in one-million three-hundred and forty-six-thousand and two-hundred and sixty-ninth it's RUMOUR-seem-TRANCE two-million one-hundred and seventy-eight-three-hundred and ninth is TOUCH-us-EMERGENCY five-million seven-hundred and two-thousand eight-hundred and eighty-seventh is GOOD-these-RASH nine-million two-hundred and twenty-seven-thousand four-hundred and sixty-fifth is DEVIATION-cut-WRESTLE fourteen-million nine-hundred and thirty-thousand three-*

hundred and fifty-second is DELAY-too-IMPERVIOUSNESS twenty-four-million one-hundred and fifty-seven-thousand eight-hundred and seventeenth is SCENT-these-LEAVENING as they come to the next as we rejoin ENCROACHMENT-open-WRYNESS and it's **EXPECTANCY-four-TORPOR** in a clear lead from THRIVING-press-HARROWING in thirty-nine-million eighty-eight-thousand one-hundred and sixty-ninth place **SYMPATHY-spell-PAROXYSM** over that she poked slightly on landing CLEMENCY-long-ASSEVERATION sixty-three-million two-hundred and forty-five-thousand nine-hundred and eighty-sixth EVANESCENT-word-SUBVERSION is one-hundred and two-million three-hundred and thirty-three-thousand one-hundred and fifty-fifth DIVULGING-too-UNBRIDLED is one-hundred and sixty-five-million five-hundred and eighty-thousand one-hundred and forty-first then comes PASSION-line-EAGERNESS and this is the last potential opening the nine-hundred and eighty-seventh from home and **OBSESSION-together-CHAIN'S** in the lead a lot of loose qualities after her YEARNING-mother-SUBTLETY over two-hundred and sixty-seven million nine-hundred and fourteen-thousand two-hundred and ninety-sixth COALESCENCE-since-AROUSAL is four-hundred and thirty-three-million four-hundred and ninety-four-thousand four-hundred and thirty-seventh then comes VEHEMENCE-other-BECKONING then SPECULATION-will-DEVIATION and DEFERRAL-north-VALEDICTION then ENCROACHMENT-same-FATHOMLESS and FERVENCY-four-EXQUISITE is next and at the one-thousand five-hundred and ninety-seventh last it's **UNENDURABLE-large-FLUSTER** over in the lead chased by IMMERSION-no-COALESCENCE is seven-hundred and one-million four-hundred and eight-thousand seven-hundred and thirty-third REVERENCE-three-THRIVING one-billion one-hundred and thirty-four-million nine-hundred and three-thousand one-hundred and seventieth UNBIDDEN-just-FLIMSY is one-billion- eight-hundred and thirty-six-million-three-hundred and eleven-thousand nine-hundred and third IMPALPABLE-many-REFRAIN is two-billion nine-hundred and seventy-one-million two-hundred and fifteen-thousand and seventy-third then KISS-fish-FLUX four-billion eight-hundred and seven-million five-hundred and twenty-six-thousand nine-hundred and seventy-sixth LEAP-put-QUIZZICAL seven-billion seven-hundred and seventy-eight million seven hundred and forty-two-thousand and forty-ninth and we've got to look a long way back for anything else but **ENCROACHMENT-been-CONSENT** the leader across the guillemot/skunk/orka/panda/badger/magpie/cow crossing ENKINDLING-add-ESTRANGEMENT closing OBSOLESCENCE-old-MISCELLANY in twelve-billion five-hundred and eighty-six-million two-hundred and sixty-nine-thousand and twenty-fifth place DIVULGING-of-DERANGEMENT twenty-billion three-hundred and sixty-five-million and eleven-thousand and seventy-fourth place and over to you VEHEMENCE-came-RELIEF and it's **EVANESCENT-about-TEMPORARY** with two loose qualities around him now just two thresholds left to jump between she and GRAND SUPRA-INFRA-COSMIC-INTERSTELLAR-LOCAL history but close in behind him is LEAP-real-ANIMATION ECHO-cross-PUNCTURE is about thirty-two-billion nine-hundred and fifty-one-million two-hundred and eighty-thousand and ninety-ninth depths away then comes UNBRIDLED-try-PAROXYSM then IMITATION-read-DISCOURTESY and behind them ABSORPTION-horse-CHERISH then

DISCOURTESY-want-GRAVITY and SCENT-add-GENEROSITY they're virtually the only ones left in today-the-only-ever-day's GRAND SUPRA-INFRA-COSMIC-INTERSTELLAR-LOCAL and PRECIPITOUS-she-HOLLOW making relentless progress RESIDENCY-their-ENTICEMENT coming there very sweetly on ENACTMENT-show-FLIMSY but **WHISPER-animal-OBSESSION** *is still holding the lead now as they jump the two-thousand five-hundred and eighty-fourth last she's over the four-thousand one-hundred and eight-first last in the lead LEAP-him-COUNTENANCE didn't jump it too well and it's* **TRACE-down-DECAY** *and PERSISTENCE-went-ENTICEMENT now from EXPIATION-these-MEMORIAL AFFECTATION-me-COPIOUSNESS and BLUNDER-where-WOE as they come to the last threshold of the infinite now in the GRAND SUPRA-INFRA-COSMIC-INTERSTELLAR-LOCAL and* **SCENT-mark-CAPABILITY** *with a tremendous chance of winning his threefold GRAND SUPRA-INFRA-COSMIC-INTERSTELLAR-LOCAL she jumps it clear of CHICANERY-through-IMPERVIOUSNESS he's getting the most tremendous cheer from the crowd they're willing him home now towards the ultimate present* **SHADOW-live-CIRCUMLOCUTION** *being preceded now only by loose qualities being chased by RESOLVE-mark-ODIOUS PLUNGE-old-ANNULMENT has moved into fifty-three-billion three-hundred and sixteen-million two-hundred and ninety-one-thousand and one-hundred and seventy-third and WIT-who-WOUND eighty-six-billion two-hundred and sixty-seven-million five-hundred and seventy-one-thousand two-hundred and seventy-second they're coming to the pineal there's a tacit immensity now between* **INSURGENCY-letter-OPACITY** *and her threefold GRAND SUPRA-INFRA-COSMIC-INTERSTELLAR-LOCAL triumph and he's coming up to the line to win it like a fresh soul in great style it's a tremendous reception you've never heard the like of it surrounding the human soul* **CURIOSITY-rose-ZEAL** *wins the GRAND SUPRA-INFRA-COSMIC-INTERSTELLAR-LOCAL!*

Gradually – all those involved in the race – the fallen – the unfallen – the spectators – (many of whom had found themselves leaving their seats and taking part – not so much against as beside their will) – made their way into the face of *The Lollipop Entity* – (rendering them vacuous once more) – or their lollipop – or into the waves of fire or water – or back across the organ crossing whence they came.

The victor of the race – before leaving the winner's enclosure – had passed the flag to you as a thank you for your breathless commentary – and it is now that you and your accomplices examine it.

The painter – decorators – so concentrated in their task that they remain oblivious to you – towards the top of the flag – are almost finished painting the sky – and – as you exert a gentle pressure on the 21st incision – a card of that number – (accompanied by the music of the sailors and artists) – emerges from it –

❦ Flag Music: 9

(Alis vinio penis veneris in te era vido bonus coetis...)

SOLALTERITY CHANGE!

You look to the sky...

There it is – the archetypal – illusory tuning fork – its ambivalence resonantly matched by the superposed labyrinths above – the music – too – in the most neglected of modes – adding to the sense of ill-at-easiness evoked by the card's dissonant – though salutary – superscription –

❦ Seeing is beveiling –

AURA AURARIA AUFERO AUGEO

(Locrian rose...)

The 22nd incision takes you – if this is possible – by slow surprise.

The white heat at the centre of the glassblower's attentions burns – at the same time as initiating the appropriate music – revelatory consciousness right into your own centre – your periphery – your everywhere – as you realize how this intangible – (though your touch has – as well as bringing it to being – broken it) – grail has been approached – breathed – formed – as the glassblower presents you with – from the freshly blown glass –

- the 22nd card -

The heart hath sung to
its god - more fool - YOU!

❦ The heart hath sung to its god - more fool - YOU! -

AUREUS AURICULA AUDEO AUGEO

(in girum imus nocte et consumimur igni – an ante-concerto for piano...)

You whole-heartedly agree with the card's imperative - that what is worshipped must give way to a ludicrousness that - in itself - increases the need for the lover's adoration - the dynamic arrow of the accompanying music proving an exemplary balance to the obligation towards the jocular.

The cleric insists on translating the complete text of the 9 flags - looking at you - *Nova Nopu* and *Edencanter* - with real affection - but also with the same ecclesiastical superciliousness as his breeding and training have seared into him - as he says -

educare ex uri hara odi angelorum ob dum et sultis migratio epularis ad bibo
os hariola ecce elusia hic harena magus navi gavit et valis alis vinio penis
veneris in te era vido bonus coetis

To raise from the fire here I am ambivalent toward the angels because of the long and sultry migration of the feasting to the drinking mouth of the trickster – behold – this eluded sand – the magician rejoiced in the ship – and the mighty wings of the wine – a phallacy came into you – I saw the good company

Edencanter summons – by their last recitation – *The LAMPEDEPHORIAN Threshold Spirits* – (who – before performing the eleventh of the *Organ of Corti* – emanate – rather than play – the 12th book of *The Lampedephoria* – this mode of presentation a harbinger of the – well-nigh unplayable – complexities to come – in the future – of Book 13 and beyond) – and the parting sextain of *Vitalia Freeborn* –

þe sckæpegoate's exxpeiætionn ðroueghe art – lovve and ðe energiye of livvinge meteorontologickallye!

þe exscitementte of ðe children meetinge ðe queen!

FIDES QUAERING INTÆLLECTUUM.

Every næte hælding ðe fullness of its surrouwending world.

Wombs of diffrent cultures kicke backk æmnidierecktionælly.

Despæir being laugffhaæble – joy being a seriousc state to be being in.

The diffickueltye in communicating ðe complekxscity wið regarrde to ðe shifting nætuere of our stættes of being ðroughowuwtte ðe day – THE WEÐER being our greatest guide and teatcher towrd a morre fruitful percepshionne and understanding of our shifting staittes of being ðruouttt the day.

Lovve is extreæmellye clear sighted.

Ðe resonance of the diatonic – as ecxpowundedde wiðin ÐE LAMPEDEPHORIA – rendrs a kinde of modal atoanælittye – a sevvenne-sided polyeheedronn.

Ðer is an ecxcesse of VIBBRATO in youre liefe!

Let VIECE VERSA be youre new sonng!

Ðe wille to TOPSYTURVIFYE and the proclaiming of PARADOXX and CONTRADICTION!

Let PANARCHY be youre politick – the ædmisshionne of all 'ARCKHIES' wiðin the singl being! Ðe monarckhissdte and ðe anárkist be reveared ekqually WIÐIN your being so ðat ðer be no neede for ðem WIÐOWUTE your being!

And it is wiðin ðe twinckelingge of an eye ðat you may fiynd youre wings!

SUI PALAM A SORIED
SUB IPA LEMA SORUD

9

Oneagh – suunts lyegh yys froyburn – gy sui
Ga tarn myentyun cra iot yliny ty bi frya
Levung iccapts ni mostrostfyl traesory
kyap miinung's wya – axcipt harmots' byloyf miisero
Cimu pryjactoan – gavi stops febolytayn
Lynola strauts – naghts ebsard – nor hyor bids' flyxutoan

Eenoooooooouuuuuuuuuuuuuugh – saaaaaiiiiints laaaaauuugh
eeaaaaaaaaaaaaaaaaaaaaaasyyyyyyyyyyyyyyyyyyyyyyyy – FREEEBOOORN –
goooooooooooooooooooooo seeeeeeeeeeeeeeeeeeeee
Goooooooooooo tuuurn
moooooooooooooooooooooouuuuuuuuuuuuuuuuuuuuuuuuntaaaiin– cryyyyyyyy
ooooooooooooooooooooouuuuuuuut aalooooooooonee toooooooooooo
beeeee freee
Loooooooooooooooooooooviiiiiiiiiiiiiiiiiiiing
aaaaaaaaaaaaaaaaaaaaacceeeeepts nooooo miiistruuuuuuuustfuuul
treeeaaaaaaaasuureeeeeeeeeeeee
Keeeeeeeeeeeeep meeeaaaaaaaaaaaaaaaniiiiiiing's waaayyyyy –

eeeeeeeexceeeeept heeeeermiiiiiiiits' beeeliiiiiiiiiiiiieeeeef –
meeeeeeeeaasuuuuuuuuuuuuuuuuuuuuuuuuuuureeeeeeeeeeeeeeeeeeeeee
Cooooooooooooooooooooomeeeeeeee proojeeectiioooooo000n –
giiiiiiiiiiiivee steeeeeeeeps
faaaaabuuuuuuuuuuuuuuuulaaatiiiiiiiiiiiiiiiooooooooooooooon
Looooooooneeelyyy streeets – niiights aaaaaaaaaaaaaaaaaaaaabsuurd –
nooooooooooooooooooooor heeeaaaaaaaaaaaaaar beeeds'
fluuuuuuuuuuuuuuuuuuuuuuxaaaaaaaatiiooooooooooooon

Enough – saints laugh easy – FREEBORN – go see
Go turn mountain – cry out alone to be free
Loving accepts no mistrustful treasure
Keep meaning's way – except hermits' belief – measure
Come projection – give steps fabulation
Lonely streets – nights absurd – nor hear beds' fluxation

❦ The Lampedephoria: Book 12

❦ Organ of Corti: 11 – *the nervous system (stereocilia)*

  As a balance to the intensity of the music that you all have just heard – *Edencanter* now sings – as you approach where the clubhouse should have been – (it is absent) – the last song of his cycle – a simple song of time – love and stars' instauration by such love –

❦ The Sick Rose: 20 – As roses be found

CODA

'*I cannot chuse but cōmend sacred liberality...*'

What you would have called – at the 1ˢᵗ hole – but no longer – your *Ultimate Self* – has – by the evidence of their gaze – acquired a depth of openness – even a sadness – or rather a satiety – not present earlier –

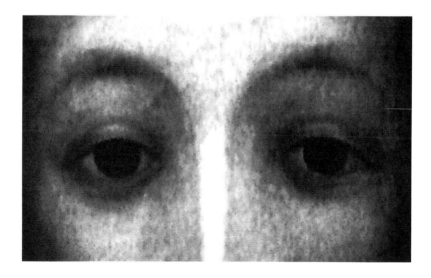

– such openness having partly been generated by the fact that the gaze is itself engaged in a silent – ocular communication with another's –

- one's whose face – in turn – receives *its* illumination – and the root of its –
unyielding – uncompromising – compassion – from the oracular light of every candle
that has been extinguished – the hope that *lights* that light being what sustains the stars
that provide the potential for all gazing – for all lightning as a form of mirroring –

The present sun – you are unsure as to whether it is rising or setting – is of such a luxuriant consistency as to bring a poem from *The Lollipop Entity* –

> *'OR WHOSE EROS?*
>
> *WORLD I'LL SEE – LIGHT – HEALING*
>
> *HASTE? AIL.*
>
> *FLOW ERTH AND HEART THRIL!*

Some might wish to draw some sentimental lines of tetrameter out of this apophthegmatic –

> *FOR those WhO SEnsE this ROSe aright*
> *The WORLD wILL – no more – SEEm a bLIGHT*
> *The HEALING rain – the cHASTEning hAIL*
> *The FLOWER – THe hAND – the HEART – THe gRaIL*

- but I remain in thrall to the original gnosis.'

Before you immerse yourself for the final time in the – (this time – silent – though mere seconds of its peculiar taste – colour – touch and scent are worth more to you than the life's work of those who compose only in sound) – music of the burning rose – *The Lollipop Entity* – glancing at the **PAX IMMEMORIAL** – (its final – humbling – words clarifying – though with a potentiating hope as to a continual revealing – the smallness of the steps you have – so far – taken) – takes – after speaking the words you have just heard – from out of their own limitless face – a pack of cards and – in a single twist of the wrist – casts them on the ground where you both find yourself stooping as they explain –

'You entertained – along the way – some fruitful thoughts about my *median arcana* – my *22 divinativitory cards* – which – though of course – considering *The 16 – Actual – Bloodly Transubstantiations of Body – Flesh and Nerve not Spirit* – there are 38 in toto – (though if one were able to grasp them – the daily phases of the sun would provide a further 28 – with the PAX IMMEMORIALS bringing the total to 78) – these being for today's consideration – in – a way – tell the story of a life – any life – any life that is lived – that is.

Let's call them *CURIOSITY-rose-ZEAL* – a lover of music – of rare impulse – and of a counterbalancing – boundless restraint.

Duty-bound in childhood – *CURIOSITY-rose-ZEAL* sublimated this – usually – misplaced and overwrought sham-orderliness into their musical practice – one might say that with every musical gesture they made – they recast a particular – more or less – unquestioned given into a sounding potentiality – thus genuinely – if tacitly – refashioning the world – with every intricacy of ornament – every chordal cluster and its resonant consort and witness – into a series of intermingling states of flow – cease and counterflow – but they – at first – due to the nature of the task – were compelled to do this alone.

The heart of *CURIOSITY-rose-ZEAL* had become ever warmer – due to the ardour that such a path generates – and more knowledgeable – though not of anything that could be said to be understood by the brain – through their musical walk through the un-listening world – and with this heat and nuanced perceptivity had developed a need for tussle and grapple with other hearts and minds – of greater or lesser flame or frigidity – for naked engagement and impassioned dissent and fanfare – but though the trumpeted – contrary motifs were – for a time – inspiring and generative of festivity and fearlessness –

(in fact – there was one trumpeter to whom *CURIOSITY-rose-ZEAL* lost and found their heart – times without number – a hybrid being – part tree – part jinn – whose unique ability with her instrument was to be able to project a music – through her ears – gathered there by a great inbreathing through her trumpet – the subtlety of which – though not lacking in cerebratory festivity – was of a kind that a floating fire would hang either side of her haloed head on the music's sounding) –

- those with whom *CURIOSITY-rose-ZEAL* was engaging proved to be all – while without clothes – fully suited and tailored to others' fashions and designs – all going in the same direction – towards the same – constructed – shadowland of sham artifice and ersatz subtleties of what it might mean to suffer – rather than to *let* – and so – *CURIOSITY-rose-ZEAL* found themselves falling into the threefold of their occluded child – indeed among a presence within them entirely concealed since the beginning of the childhood they should have – but never – had.

     CURIOSITY-rose-ZEAL would listen with the utmost attention to the innocent interior trinity – who themselves were doing similarly to the scent of the rose – seeking – listening out for – a transfiguring odour – a florescent petrichor – that would only reveal itself when initiated by just the right weight and cascade of precipitation – whether of cloud or of sad or happy eye – and – once such a state of play occurred – only then would the necessary solarity descend to embrace the bloom.

     It was so pleasurable – this state of perfumed grace and Edenic clarity – that *CURIOSITY-rose-ZEAL* did not even begin to notice the gradual turn that the benignly – burning star was taking in displaying a more or less imperceptible shift towards pure – cool reflectivity –

soon to become – though apparently full of initiative – reactionary – and that it was hardly unexpected – and in good time – though they were so magnetized by this security of mirroring – that *CURIOSITY-rose-ZEAL* was abruptly brought to extrinsic consciousness by two contrary canines in full leap – though their arrival did bring with them an immediate – palatial construction – the entrance of which – however – their constant toing and froing obscured – it being left to the extraordinary fish – swimming in the pond at the front of the mansion – to lay six impeccably elliptical roe – two of which – one black and one white – immediately 'hatched' – allowing two youths to emerge – both of whom were already in the process of pouring endlessly flowing liquid from their skin and pail – one of tears – the other of blood – into the waiting spirit of an earthbound star – such turn of events guiding *CURIOSITY-rose-ZEAL* toward a humility of abeyance before their ultimate lack of agency and I.

The unconscious – as it must be – flowering of this resignation had the cataclysmic effect of destroying the mansion – now a temple – at once – as well as causing the descent of the projection of two – partly bestial – lovers – on the point of consummation – that – until now – had existed only – and secretly – within *CURIOSITY-rose-ZEAL* – the precise gravity of the architecture – both of the building and of the lovers – their heft – their form and ornament – being determined by the celerity – integrity and choreography of their tumble – and of how well – and how far – one of the lovers threw the crescent moon that must always exist – in a condition of waxing or waning – between them.

When the lovers had reached the earth – the time it took being far too long given the height from which they had fallen – they found that the dynamic of their passions – and the shape of their eros – both ensouled and embodied – had transmuted entirely – their respective arousal – still thriving – now being witnessed and arbitrated by a third player – always present though unseen until now – and that the game – and unsought prayers that leaped from the three – began to congeal – (but from what source?) – a deity amongst them – that *was* them – of such abandoned delight – admixtured pain – pleasure – play and concentration – that it was as if they were inexhaustible grails to each other's unfathomable thirst – the incipient order arising from their total absorption in – via the other and themselves – themselves and one other – being of such plenitude that *CURIOSITY-rose-ZEAL* now had – at their disposal – a near ideal proportionality in terms of their capability of thinking in relation – through all recent enactment of ludic will – to feeling – the realization also dawning that their – so far in this life – apparent lack of profound engagement with the world – or even a suspicion of such participation being possible – was due to a timidity towards true buoyancy – of – in particular – the clown's interrogative – of limit – of stricture – although *CURIOSITY-rose-ZEAL* was now to spend many hours – (or weeks or years) – caught in inaction while they pondered – in as rigorously a topsy-turvy way as possible – how to sustain a profligacy of roses that were as passionate about their thorns as their colour – aroma and enfolded limitlessness – a kind of redemption eventually arising whereby their bounded will once more gave way to a ravenous libation – of pure self.

As the poet has said –

"God is an intermittently legible SOPHIA whose scent is elsewhere and circumstance somewhere..."

- the strength arising from which considerations and self-nourishing being so potentiated that it was nigh on impossible for *CURIOSITY-rose-ZEAL* to resist the inclination to attribute all of life – its zeniths – its mean – its abysmal – to the synaptic machinations of their brain.

What was the – neither triune nor binary – antidote to such banal reduction to an insipid – neural jus? After years (months – weeks) of searching – their head in their hands – this very gesture (in the remembering that the head is always held – at all times is – at the mercy of the hands) became an answer – a limbic – truly digital – elixir – at the end – not of the world – but of *CURIOSITY-rose-ZEAL's* – and everyone else's arms.

An unbidden chant – along with their protean – gesturing hands – flew from *CURIOSITY-rose-ZEAL's* newly harrowed – rose-bursting heart – a line of melody that coalesced inexorably into an elegantly – distended tone – as the actual – for the first time – became palpable – enduring and ephemeral.

Immediately – *CURIOSITY-rose-ZEAL's* leaden – labyrinthine philosopher became a whirling – far from stilted – fool for all that was hop – caper and frisk – the light that they had been unstintingly gathering now – with great ease – redounding upon themselves and others with a coruscating equity – propriety and clarity – friends – those never yet encountered – and full embodiments of enmity were now being thrust back and forth from *CURIOSITY-rose-ZEAL* with unfeasible poise and rapidity – and it was all taking place not before – and in no way in some eternal hinterland – but in the glorious NOW – such presence allowing – in *CURIOSITY-rose-ZEAL* – a tending toward a sharing of their embryonic stillness and authority – though one – even at this young stage – replete with a jocund impartiality.

But how stupefied *CURIOSITY-rose-ZEAL* was with what now was subsequent on this heldness – this reserve and utter tact – a Janus-like counterpoint – a *canonic cancrizans* at the very base of their humanity – an interminable cultivation beneath the soul's harrowed tilth – each contrapuntal line a horse – here an Arab stallion – there a Shetland pony – in pursuit of its – and its kin's – total coherence-in-ambiguity – though a different melody now became apparent to *CURIOSITY-rose-ZEAL* – one without – aside from the constantly – oscillating hum that underpinned it – harmony or the weave of disparate lines – a peal of May-morning bells was underway – lovers from every corner of the city being drawn by the changes wrought in them by its resplendent ding and clang – each lover and their beloved seemingly incapable of merely walking – such was the variety and indefatigability of their dancing – except that this did not happen – no lover – even of themselves – came to the churchyard to be saturated in this almost liquid sonority while their eyes and nose were respectively suffused in impossible spectra of greens and purple-scented wisteria – no-one but *CURIOSITY-rose-ZEAL* – who now plunged deep within themselves to career around the axis mundi of the maypole at the very centre of their absent soul

– but how many they found to dance with there! – along with infinite weaves – (but arbitrated by who?) – in which to partake and go joyfully astray – and how she – the maypole herself – longed for someone with whom to go astray – someone who would clutch her ribbons all at once – and tenderly take them – but not – as the revellers always would – in all 24 directions of the compass at once! – just one true hand to guide her to that one place – (but a locale of so potential a many) – towards which she always knew she – whose name was *Beltania Maia* – had been tending.

In any case – the point was moot – Mayday had come and gone and not one hand – not even that of one of the mangle-hearted and mind-shattered children – had grasped at one of her unhandled – silent touches.

There was one in the city – however – far away – who would have rejoiced – though possibly at the cost of his soul's splitting from top to bottom – at such contact – from the moment of his eight eyes opening – he – whose name was OKTOKULOS – would look to his left –

- and to his right –

- in the hope that the one for whom his marble-altar heart had been fashioned would come to him.

He'd had inklings of her in dream – where she was always blind – though not in a way that his dream could satisfactorily elucidate – but in the gaze that she could never offer she reminded him of the look – in the gaze that the sadness of his mother's eyes could – that he wished he had never seen –

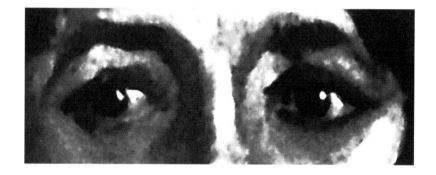

There was one – ever faithful to *Beltania Maia* – who – though in a state of almost – but how vast the scope and breadth of that gap – complete tranquillity in her life within and without of the hive – would dream of being able to lift aloft a single – broken ribbon of her friend – as much out of compassion as for her own delight –

– but it was forbidden in her community to seek connection with one who was not in possession of even a single sense – though *Beltania Maia* in fact possessed 8 senses – none of which the bees would countenance – being only interested in the usual 5.

There had even been prophecies uttered about this bee – whose name was *Apina* – by the earliest priests at the time of *Constantine's* appropriation – while he was in York – of the ethereal to the imperial – one such being –

'CALIS APIS SEXILIS DOMINI –

HIC APIS SEXILIS EXTAT PRÆTIO QUO QUE VALIS SPEM IGITUR A STULTIS AMATUR PLUS AB E OCTIS'

(the heat of the bee's sexual master – here is the price of the sexual bee whereby a strong hope is therefore loved by fools more than by the eight)

– the inspiration come upon the young man responsible for this opaque statement originating in a tryst that took place on the very spot that would become the eventual Minster's high altar – though at that time still under full matriarchal dominance and ægis – though now it clearly referred to the bee that was in constant elliptical flight around his true queen – the Mayday axis mundi.

And it was this prejudice that communicated itself to OKTOKULOS – on the wind – invoking a single tear – (one of the tears was of such scope – in form and meaning – that a passing thrip understandably misinterpreted it as a river – one dangerously – for the passing ships – shrouded in mist – she could already hear the calling of one ship's horn to another – epitomized – in the thrip's mind – as time – while the deepening fog she took as a summation of all space – though in the music that the thrip now heard – all such distinctions between the spatial and the temporal began – moot – to melt –

🐝 As time and space seek sanctuary in the harbour of the now)

– on or near the 10th hour – from one of his great – black eyes.

SOLALTERITY CHANGE!

You look to the sky...

529

His tears had this quality – however – in that those of them that were genuine would immediately take flight – pursuing their newly airborne existence in an unceasing – agonized – elation of metamorphoses between a plethora of flighted forms of being and becoming – at one moment the tear might be 5/8ths of the way betwixt a Thrip and a Falcon – the next 34/55ths along the way from a Pelican to a Little Gatekeeper – continuing in like manner before either fully stabilizing in one form or deliquescing to the ground in a sludge of abandoned intent to be anything at all.

On this occasion – the tear – initiate on the impeccably tuned – empathic intuition of OKTOKULOS by the callousness of the apine community – had – appositely – though OKTOKULOS knew nothing of it – found its form as a bee – (a drone mason bee – one that had – during the course of its extraordinarily long imaginal life – it had made intimate acquaintance with the stonework underpinning the domes of one of the principal churches in *Uralsk* – as well as with the parts of the *Sphinx* in *Al-Jizah* that used to function as its nose) – finding its way to *Beltania Maia* – greeting its kin – though they were of different species – and together the two bees – one borne of the hive – one of compassion towards the one ostracized from it – held aloft – the ribbon being too heavy for one to lift alone – one of the 24 hands of *Beltania Maia* –

- whereupon a music began to unfold - played - on his unfailingly jolly accordion
- by a *Mr N Worbbor* - the first music he had played in thirty years of self-imposed
silence following *his* being banished by his own kind - for not being of his own kind
- (his current music having no real - other than this synchronistic [and what is to be
considered more palpable than that?] one - connection to the bees and *Beltania* - the
reverberations from the dynamics of which soon made their way to OKTOKULOS
himself - bringing about one of his lunescent seizures.

OKTOKULOS' most feeling filled thoughts would – very rarely – manifest as luminescent spheres – which unobservant citizens would mistake for the moon – an error that OKTOKULOS was more than happy to let linger – as these passionate cerebrations – in their guise as orbs – would – with a celerity greater than light – (a precise velocity of 1.618 x c) – plummet among the people – particularly amidst those incapable or incapacitated of emotion or reason – and instil – unbeknownst to them – an inkling that they – in all freedom – might follow.

What no-one amongst the populace had realized was that the gloomy expression on OKTOKULOS' face was – of course – in many ways – a false picture. Those viewing OKTOKULOS from *above* would only ever see him smiling – a fitting state of affairs given the happiness that OKTOKULOS derived from serving others – and from being – ostensibly – *beneath* them. In his own mind – he was always smiling – but – being so huge – (so truly magnanimous) – so unwittingly overbearing – he could not but give the impression of a haughty – if not imperious – solemnity.

OKTOKULOS' influence – even after every one of his stones had been put to other purposes – was still to resonate – neonate – into the world – never more so than in the further metamorphoses of the octave – the spectrum of lepidoptera – *spilosoma lubricipeda – nymphalis io – boloria euphrosyne – pseudopanthera macularia – geometra papilionaria – polyommatus bellargus – favonius quercus – limenitis camilla* – that he had helped to initiate – earlier in his petrified life.

There had been rumblings of the return of an adversary – far to the west of the ethical jurisdiction of OKTOKULOS – his name was – *NAΓRAR bil NÖNÅC* – and he was the hovering head of a disembodied knight –

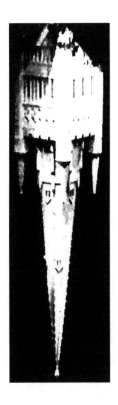

His dominion was growing – though it was now forbidden for OKTOKULOS to lock horns with him – as he had in former times – it had been made known to all those enmeshed within this cosmic antagonism that other – more oblique – means would have to be sought to contend with *NAI'RAR bil NÖNÁC*.

The lepidoptera were unable – in their present form – to join battle with the knight – this would have been considered too facile a solution – and so the 8 – flighted – tear-beings of OKTOKULOS set forth on their triple metamorphoses towards total vanquishment of the tiresome – bodiless anachronism.

First – **THE DELIQUESCENCE.**

     For the initial year they existed as fountains – their ceaseless flow arbitrating over the rising and falling of contrary – though not in animosity – intuitions as to how to proceed.

     One of the lepidoptera – now a fountain – came perilously close to forgetting the whole purpose of their metamorphosis due to the passion that they rapidly developed for the legs of a youth that – one freezing morning – came to bathe in the waters provided – (because they had been provided so selflessly) – by the fountains.

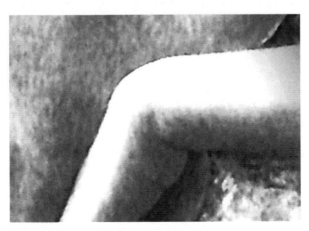

Second – **THE DANCE.**

For the following year – for which they left their liquid form – though keeping the relentless undulation and effervescence of the water – they throve as the motivating spirit and animæ of 8 Morris women –

– learning as much from the shadows of their movements – that would never have existed without the music of the accompanying pipes and accordions – not to mention the structural integrity and ethos of the flowers that they would – in a jolly manner – (almost alienating in its anachronistic rarity and almost sincerity) – shake and hold aloft and abaft – as from the dancing itself.

Third – and this was the masterstroke – **THE ROOTING.**

For the final year – for which they sloughed off their human vestige – they became 8 *betula utilis* – *Himalayan Birch* – taking up domicile in the Bishop's garden – a place known to be one of the preferred haunts of *NAI'RAR bil NÖNÅC.*

NAI'RAR bil NÖNÅC had been so long without a body – without anybody – that the instant that he saw – and understood – the rigour – the gentility – and the beginning of what would be the depths of the Birches' interwoven lives – he let out a wail – a yell of immense regret – that caused such a corresponding cascade of tears through the gargoyles of OKTOKULOS – that the pity – (tempered by the *will-for-change* on behalf of his – as yet incapable – adversary) – practically destroying the heart of this being of relentless compassion – on the wings of this immediately translated – fluvial gushing – (in the forms of beings not yet existent – or possible) – flew straight to *NAI'RAR bil NÖNÅC's* aid and nourishment – embodying him in such a way as he fell at once – in his new form – to prayer – his eyes seemingly – but in no way as neither there nor needed – closed.

The first words that came to *NAI'RAR bil NÖNÁC's* freshly minted soul were ones – of course – directed straight at OKTOKULOS –

QUI EX PANTHERA IN CRUORIS – MANAVI TRAIECTIO
OMNIA AD TE SEXUALIS

(I – WHO FROM THE PANTHER IN THE BLOOD – FLOWED
THROUGH THE PASSAGE OF EVERYTHING SEXUAL TO YOU)

- while the ones that flew back in return were –

'IN PRINCIPIO GREAT VERUM
IN PRINCIPIO FERAX VERUM
IN PRINCIPIO ERAT VERBERATUM'

(IN PRINCIPIO GERAT VERUM – IN THE BEGINNING
IT BEARS THE TRUTH

IN PRINCIPIO FERAX VERUM – IN THE BEGINNING
THE WILD TRUTH

IN PRINCIPIO ERAT VERBERATUM – IN THE BEGINNING
HE WAS BEATEN)

- the subsequent escapades – erotic – mystic and otherwise – flowing from which statements – being recorded in the exquisitely illuminated and renowned manuscripts produced in the studio – nonpareil – of brother and sister – *Elba Bircsedni* and *Elba Vie C' Nocni.*

The process of weaving – un-weaving and – for the most part – disentangling the silken ribbons at the very centre of *CURIOSITY-rose-ZEAL* – and so the world – aligned with the increasing volubility of the delightfully out-of-phase accordions – the rain – the thunder and the jovial laughter – soon to be manifest as actual lightning – striking *CURIOSITY-rose-ZEAL* at a pivotal point between their pineal gland and temporal lobe – led them to the odd circumstance of teaching Total Perspective to a class of the cream of the city's academia and clerics – but it was – unfortunately – a cream so curdled – soured – discoloured – reeking and of no nutritional use to anybody that *CURIOSITY-rose-ZEAL* – in an act of great acuity – pity (such as that felt when shooting a lame horse) and focussed alacrity – took their skeletons lithely from their comatose bodies – (the learned corpus remains – to this day – unaware of its loss) – and offered them to a youth – who had been listening – peripherally – and illegally – to *CURIOSITY-rose-ZEAL's* lecture and following their fascinating demonstration with great absorption – it being clear to the youth – whose name was *IMPLACABLE-hand-TENACITY* – on following every chalked gesture – spontaneous remark – and impromptu song or piano – or recorder improvisation of *CURIOSITY-rose-ZEAL* as they spun endlessly fascinating imaginal webs illustrating what it is – what it might be – to be able to – at any time – freshly and innovatively conceive – that the perspectival arts were yet hardly at the beginning of their unfolding.

After years (days – decades) of this – and other – pedagogy – *CURIOSITY-rose-ZEAL* felt compelled to find a space atop a mountain – or within an empty bus-stop – in order to think more – especially after what they had done with the professors and priests – on the nature of the body's housing and of how it might be best upkept – coming to a tentative conclusion that it is – in a house – the condition – status and dynamic play of the light that determines its worth of hearth and of homeliness.

Living this sensibility thoroughly for a time led *CURIOSITY-rose-ZEAL* to a point where the care necessary to take others under their wing reached practicable maturation – and in so doing – learning so much through the many moments of nurturing they were now involved in – *CURIOSITY-rose-ZEAL* was also able to receive intuitions on the subtleties of the intangible – both of an interpersonal kind – as one would expect – and of a purely private nature – that they felt as if they were constantly on the cusp of a threshold – or of many such limina – the only thing preventing them from crossing over into any one of them being a most profound – though perhaps misplaced – sense of courtesy until – that is – and it was at this juncture that the consciousness of *CURIOSITY-rose-ZEAL* went into a kind of ecstatic fibrillation – that they saw themselves emerging from themselves in such a way that made it clear that the only thresholds that they had not yet crossed were ones entirely of their own construction – though even these – the doors of which were – however – seemingly made of the most intransigent – leaden materials – were without relative hindrance – being mounted on their fixings in such a way that were one even to blow on them – they would gently swing open – nor were there guards of any kind to question right of entry – but so set in their perceptions had *CURIOSITY-rose-ZEAL* – despite many appearances throughout a long and fertile existence – become – that the simplest crossing of a road had become a circuitous labyrinth – an encounter with a ravenous – though ultimately bulimic – minotaur had become merely the crossing of a road – in short – all had become imposition – projection – and certainty masquerading as openness – but no longer.

Six jesters gathered *CURIOSITY-rose-ZEAL* into their foolishness – picking them up and carrying them aloft as they gambolled down to the river – one even passing up to them the portative organ which they took everywhere with them and clamouring for a bawdy song – *CURIOSITY-rose-ZEAL* taking up this offer with such immediacy that it was not long before all the keys of the kingdoms of heaven and hell – and all the lanyards enabling instant access to the republics of limbo and purgatory – which *CURIOSITY-rose-ZEAL* suddenly noticed bulging from their pockets and weightily dangling around their necks – were cast into the river – along with all claims to fixity of mind – self – body and heart – this jettisoning – however – enabling instantaneous – temporary inhabitation within any state of becoming at the merest tilt of the head – the subtlest breath of the heart.

The Lollipop Entity picks up an ornate glass – shaped in precisely the way as to support the shape of the following text – from which they then recite –

Grail. Graal. Gral. Gradual. Gruel. San Graal. Sang Real. Whose true blood?
Human heart. Cauldron. Vessel. Triple Goddess. Wounded thigh. Lance. Condwiramurs.
Leads-to-love. Parzival. Pierce through the veil? Rent.
The heart. The thinking heart. The willing brain. The feeling body.
Vessel. Yoni. Vehicle. Lingam. Non-material.
A non-material vehicle. Insubstantial.
A substantial non-material intangible vehicle.
Palpable.
A vehicle to enable a community to experience – in communion – an entirely new sense – not of I –
but of what lies beyond – besides I.
Spirit-self? To do this without losing Selfhood?
Meta-Nirvanic-Para-Ekstasis. Earthly?
Human.
'God is only a turn of the head away'.
'Not I – but Christ in me'?
Not only Christ – but Shekinah – Los – Enitharmon.
The Rose. The thorn points the way. The deed.
The cup. The lance.
A stone from fallen Lucifer's crown.
What ails thee most is not to know you're ailing.
Without the sense of touch – you're sitting – ignorant – in your own blood.
Blue blood. Red blood. Blood and breath. The piercing breath without which.
Blood before heart forms no pump but fœtal attraction.
Horn of plenty. The hand. The monkey cupping water.
The bowl.
You cannot bite the palm of your hand – so close yet it lies.
You can press it to another's. Hold infinity in it. Eternity.
Pestle and mortar. One hour.
Impossibly rich meal from almost nothing.
All are satisfied.
Immemorial meals from what is found.
A stone from heaven – inscribed.
The skull.
Written on the heart.
Starry script.
Human heart.
The inexhaustible eye.
Giving or receiving.
See! The liquid metal is running into the awaiting mould.
Sonorous clang or dull clunk?
The receding ear – indefatigably listening.
A burning of the heart.
It is time we whirled boop ways – making placental purple.
Womb. Love/Life as a wound. The brain.
The Bell. The pearl of great price.
Seizure.
A ringing.
Rose.
Calyx.
Thorn.
Cup.
Lance.
The grail provides what is desired.
What if that desire is for a lucid – coherent desire?
Compassion.
Heart.
Onion.
Grail.
Tears.
Question.
No end.'

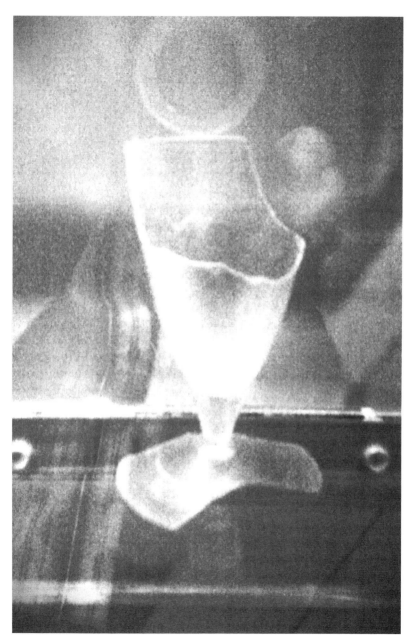

- drinks a little from it - pours the remainder over you - *Nova Nopu* and *The Very Reverend Lution* - throws the glass in the air - where *Edencanter* catches it - (11 of his other 12 hands already holding that number of varyingly fashioned receptacles - each containing tiny swarms of roses - and murmurations of bees) - [these takings place - *Edencanter's* juggling - the unexpectedness of the gesture - and the smell - taste and viscosity of the honeyed rosewater - you find disproportionately liberating] - draws a broken glass from his empty face and says - holding it before you -

'The glass grail - broken - not through carelessness or time - but through the precision - the exact - shimmering resonance between the song of all those who had put their silent lips to it - (the original faultless - rim - however - visible as an etheric echo above the cup) - lifted - as I looked at it - (before I took it from the museum) - ever so slightly - into the air.'

Edencanter catches the 13th glass as it falls - the final - silent - iteration of the rose-music sounding all about you -

During this silent music - someone approaches -

- it is *NAI'RAR bil NÖNÅC* – wingless · he is carrying a jug which – as he continues to look up and away from you – he pours over your outstretched hands which have placed themselves in readiness almost against your will – and which are cycling rapidly – (as someone – a counter-tenor – begins singing – to harp accompaniment) – through many of the mudras that you have witnessed taking place during your journey.

❦ Tao Te Ching

The Lollipop Entity now leads you to a vast – sometimes inner – space – one that would – if measured – be exactly of the same spiritual proportions as each of the holy spaces of the world – i.e. – the whole and every part of that world – combined with itself.

'I have – as there are this many of you – three parting gifts – for it is all of your birthdays' – says *The Lollipop Entity.*

'The first is a story' – (as they tell you the following – you can see unfold – though it is *your* imagination at work there – [your 2 friends seeing things differently] – in *The Lollipop Entity's* face – the unfolding narrative) –

'The realization that they were not merely non local to wherever they happened to be but also simultaneously present – potentially – at every point in time and space – was what had caused the severing of their right arm and the breaking of their wing – the temporary petrifying was a fact of life to which the angel was now well-accustomed.

The myriad points of light that – even now – continued to emerge and dissipate all over their body – enabled the consciousness of every star they had visited to unstintingly inform and advise the angel of possible further courses of action – the oddest of which stemmed in threefold manner from the stars – *Altinak – Alnilam* – and *Mintaka*.

These renowned celestial beings had communicated – via their filigree luminescence – that within the tomb on which the angel – whose name was
  \-   *TORTUOUS-start-LEVITY-TRANCE-last-OBSOLESCENCE-WRYNESS-do-*
SCRUPULOUS-ANIMATION-who-FURROW-QUIVERING-study-REVERENCE-
NECESSARY-every-MODULATION-IMPECCABLE-thought-ENACTMENT-
NECESSARY-every-MODULATION-IMPECCABLE-thought-ENACTMENT-
SATURATION-children-ADVERSITY-PROTEAN-sun-COLOUR- GRATUITOUS-time-
UNBRIDLED-PUZZLE-open-CIRCUMLOCUTION-   BEGUILING-say-WHIRLING-
FLIMSY-does-SUBVERSION-ABEYANCE-took-EMBELLISHMENT-HOSTILE-rose-
ENGAGEMENT-ENKINDLING-men-ABEYANCE-LAPSE-low-CONFINEMENT-U-

NBRIDLED-change-SUBVERSION-TENDER-first-UNBIDDEN-YIELD-to-
OBSOLESCENCE-EXPECTANCY-four-TORPOR-SYMPATHY-spell-PAROXYSM-
OBSESSION-together-CHAIN-UNENDURABLE-large-FLUSTER-ENCROACHMENT-
been-CONSENT-EVANESCENT-about-TEMPORARY-WHISPER-animal-
OBSESSION-TRACE-down-DECAY-SCENT-mark-CAPABILITY-SHADOW-live-
CIRCUMLOCUTION-INSURGENCY-letter-OPACITY-CURIOSITY-rose-ZEAL –
sat were the remains of a soldier who – before his corpus was brutally dismembered
in a so-called act of war – had been hard at work in the design of a tuba which – by the
subtlest of deviances (the principal one being the phenomenon – built into the bell of
the tuba – into its event horizon – of any and all matter and energy so far constrained
– in both the player and the one – [there only ever being – at most – one – who is]
– audient – acquiring the – for all time and space – the quality of pan-dimensional
freedom – able to traverse all and any dimension – of heart – of communality – of
cosmos) – in its – to all appearances – regular manufacture – would offer the invitation
of utter transformation to the one playing it.

How different the world had seemed – four years earlier – when *Jalalludin
Abednego Gotobed – Solomon Aidan Mujadeddi and Wulfstan Faroud Jacobs* had sat as
friends – full of – more or less childish – expectation and excitement (some of which
was – admittedly being generated by the expectation of the game of bowls which they
would be playing later in the day – the three friends having set particular importance on

this game – it being – perhaps – their last for some time – though what none of the trio would notice was that – at the final end – when *Jalalludin* had 'fired' – leaving only two bowls – [and the jack] – remaining on the green – one belonging to each of his friends – the resultant formation was extremely suggestive of the 3 stars of Orion's belt) –

– in the church of *St. Ificap and St. Ila T Nednec Snart* – (this church had already provided the friends with several eerie experiences at various times of their childhood – the most notable of which took place on the eve of *Jalaludin's* 13th birthday – he had – a moment earlier – been repeatedly rubbing his eyes – he was sure that he had seen a figure – shimmering through the spectra principally concerning themselves with yellow and purple – in the doorway of the chapel given over to the devotion to *St Eihtrow* – patron saint of *enantiodromia* –

- though when he had walked over to the arched entrance to the chapel - he found it unoccupied -

- at least briefly - as he now found himself being addressed by the violet-golden figure - her name was *Ms Agro Lamsyx O' Rap* - that he *had* seen earlier - she was letting fly a volleyed novena of latinate words beginning with 'IT' - initiated by a passionately voiced - by the hand as much as by the larynx - injunction to GO! -

ITE! ITA ITEM ITERATIO ITERINERIS ITERAVI ITERUM ITAQUE ITE!

Go! As – again – I repeated the repetition of the journey – so – go again!

- *Jalaludin* was now following *Ms O' Rap* through a tunnel – similarly lit to herself – in shifting hues of purple-golden solarity – compelled to run after her – he found that – however swift – or slow – his course – she remained at the same distance –

though when – finally – she stopped – turned – and stooped – he was able to reach her – as she took from her robe a spinning top which – before it began – at her fingers' bidding – to turn – saw *Jalaludin* fully returned to his earlier stance – his eyes still moist from his earlier rubbing of them – gazing at the empty chapel doorway – though – when he closed his eyes – he was able to see there – for several days to come – [and – once more – at the moment of his death – though the solace that he would have felt at this vision was mitigated by that he had of the eyes of his assailant at the moment – many years in the future – of *his* death] –

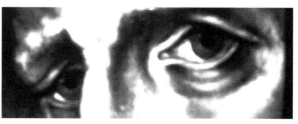

– the eyes of *Ms O' Rap*) –

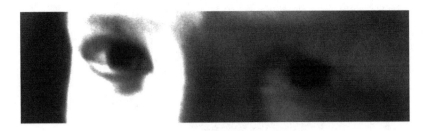

– during the 8 o'clock service on the Feast of the Transfiguration 1914 – (though of course they had no idea that so many souls would be – forcibly – transfigured – due to the remaining untouched – and unresolved – traumas and dynamics of the world soul – on that same day 31 years hence) – as they listened to what was in fact a musical portrayal of the otherwise tacit – though misplaced – nobility living in their souls on that August morning – just a few days before their acceptance of the King's shilling.

❦ Music heard during the 8 o'clock service on the Feast of The Transfiguration 1914

That very morning – as he was walking around the churchyard before the service – *Wulfstan* had seen a great eagle land on a tomb in the graveyard – the body in the tomb having recently been exhumed due to its being discovered by a friend of the family of the deceased that the body – when alive – had been at least $2/5^{ths}$ angel.

None of this was known to *Wulfstan* – nor – therefore – why the eagle's wings had broken – immediately after the bird's body had become petrified – at the point of its landing on the tomb.

The *angelo-human* symbiosis – their name was *Elba Liassanu* – was distantly related – through both the *Ishmael* and *Isaac* lines – to *Jalaluddin* and *Solomon* – though they had begun their existence as pure angel.

Elba Liassanu had been assigned the task of ministering unto *Wulfstan* – *Jalaluddin* and *Solomon* once they had made their way to the trenches as part of the *13th Port Sun-and-Moonlight Battalion.*

Through the angel's intervention in the lives of these three young men – each unwittingly guided – since birth – by the presiding intelligences within the three stars - *Altinak* – *Alnilam* – and *Mintaka* – it was the intention that the First – and indeed the Second – World Wars would cease from taking place.

Unfortunately – the riven soul of *Elba Liassanu* – a state of being initiated by the fact that while both *Jalalludin* and *Solomon* were in – undeclared – (neither the Sufi nor the Kabbalist told the other of their passion) – love with their friend – the angel themselves had also become hopelessly obsessed with *Wulfstan* – had so impacted on the angel's ontology that they had lost all notion of the task assigned to them – and could not – for love nor manna – remember why there was a spinning top – of heavenly fabrication – and of the most exquisite beauty – in the pocket of their robe.

Elba Liassanu's lovesick condition had led to several debilitating side-effects – the most distressing being the metamorphosing into either – temporary human - animal - floral or stone avatars.

Solomon – Jallaludin and Wulfstan (an anthroposophist and sometime Rosicrucian) had been chosen – generations previously – through the intercession and unceasing spiritual activity of *Jallaludin's* great grandfather – (himself in possession of a highly – though delicately – wrought – spinning top) – to be the three to whom the great task would be given – and they did indeed have just the requisite qualities of innocence – good humour – and openness that would be essential for such a mission – which was – or ought to have been – as follows –

A spinning top had been fashioned that incorporated – in its seemingly random design – a tiny copy of each of the world's countries' flags.

If the top – at the very outset of the war – could be set spinning – without ceasing – for 13 days and nights – widdershins during the day – sunwise at night – ensuring the total blending and melding – not only of the colours and forms of each of the sovereign flags – but also of the best ideals and impulses of all that they stood for –

– such a whirling also serving to mitigate – if not completely expunge – the more nefarious and imperial designs within the minds and hearts of the so-called leaders and retainers of those states represented – then *The so-called First World War* would rather be remembered as a wayward – brief skirmish – actually over before the All Souls Day on which those – relatively few – lost – would be commemorated.

Elba Liassanu would dream of the success of the mission – seeing the three young men – two of whom being kin to them – in the gesture – at dawn or at dusk – of relieving the other in the spinning of the top – but wake only with the solace of the dream – but not the memory.

Sleep – a new experience for *Elba Liassanu* when they were momentarily human – would have the corollary effect of pushing them gently further – and inexorably – back in time – so that in the space of the few weeks during which the mission was to be enacted – the original object of the angel's affections had become not yet born – and *Elba Liassanu* found themselves in the odd circumstance of becoming the great-grandfather of *Jalaludin* – of whom they were already a distant – many times great-uncle.

It was a very early memory of *Wulfstan's* – of *Jalaludin's* great-grandfather spinning a top – that – once forgotten – became a spur to the young man's spirit – resulting in the not dissimilar complexity that had become the tuba now sought for by the angel as they sat on the tomb.

Unrequited love had – for *Elba Liassanu* – over time – as it must – pushed them gently into the future – and so it was – many years after the *Great War* – that they – once they had recovered the use of their legs if not their wings – came across the stone tuba –

the resultant flash of light on what might now be possible temporarily blinding every nearby bird – (though in days to come their sight would become preternatural) – as *Elba Liassanu* gently wrested the tuba from *Solomon's* tomb – for it was for him that *Wulfstan* had had inscribed – deep within the bell of the instrument – a dedication of love – (these few words having been elicited from Wulfstan through his recent meditation upon a carved Roman slab – the stone having been placed there – by the renowned legion named upon it – towards the end of the Roman occupation –

- though the imprinting given the stone by one of the legionaries – a mystically minded man by the name of SESOH PROM ATEM DIVO – (not his given name – he had been blessed with this particular nomination by his friend and guide – *SESOH* deriving from *SESORAH* – the Javanese for speech – *PROM* being simply an injunction to keep moving – to promenade – *ATEM* being the word – in many languages – for breath – and *DIVO* – being the Italian for star – the entire name to be interpreted as something like 'Speech – movement – breath – star' – an injunction which the legionary was – from day to day – more intent and acquiescent in fulfilling) – was only the beginning of its meaning – SESOH PROM ATEM DIVO's latent text only willing to give up its fuller meaning if one were to – having placed a rose at its base – as did Wulfstan – sit in front of the stone – and meditate upon the capitals – which would – in time – yield the following affirmation –

LEGitimavi eXaltatio eXaudibilis Vagari Valde

or

I legitimized the audible exaltation to range greatly)

Elba Liassanu put the tuba to his lips and blew – a threefold organ-like accompaniment emanating from his heart – and *Wulfstan* received his elegy – his eulogy – though the special quality of the music was – in part – due to the implicit presence of what *Elba Liassanu* had witnessed moments before.

The angel had – when picking up the tuba – looked within its bell – and seen there – emanating from within it – a pale blue light – which – *Elba* having comported himself within the instrument to further explore the light's origin – seemed to be being created by the interpenetration of a text – carved into a lead sheet – with a receptacle of liquid – within which there was held a cylinder of gold –

Looking more closely – *Elba Liassanu* came to the dawning realisation that the words at which he was looking –

– were those in which he had been – (or would – himself – in some sense – be) – instrumental – a curious offshoot – that he could not fully fathom – of such cognizance being that he could immediately hear into the very structure of *Plutonium* –

❦ Plutonium

– alerting him to the fact that the seal – the horse – and the balance of which the words dealt – were impending – proximate.

But what was extraordinary – and appropriate – (*Elba Liassanu* immediately – in total amnesia of the tuba's interior – finding himself back in the cemetery) – was that at the moment when the angel's wings had reached the zenith of their fullest – most

Raphaelic – healing – due both to the form of the tuba and the love and loss expressed through it by *Elba Liassanu* – the head of the angel simply exploded – due to the utter potential proffered by the newly formed wings and what imminent flight might soon come from them.

Indeed – it was immediately after the angel had caught their floral coronet in their left hand that they took wing – barely registering the traces of the various coronal mass ejecta that the stars – all at unimaginable distances from one another – threw towards them as they momentarily touched their blazing intelligences as if they were great luminous stepping stones – all of this the angel achieved without their head – though the fallout – the celestial – ecstatic rain of light following the explosion of their mind and brain – in particular that caused by the shattering of their pineal gland – under the jurisdiction of *Altinak* – their temporal lobe – of *Alnilam* – and their I – of *Mintaka* – would continue to cascade for billions of years to come – ushering the entire cosmos into a state of – near everlasting – pregnancy into which those of the necessary archangelic consciousness would pour their – near infinite – hope – while those of the requisite human imagination and heart would stage their acts.

❦ Eulogy

SOLALTERITY CHANGE!

You look to the sky...

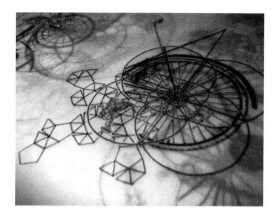

The second is this book' – *The Lollipop Entity* presents you with a 10946-page tome – every one of those pages fashioned from the skin – carcass – or other part of a different being. Buckling – even with your friends' help – under its weight – its astral heft – you fall to the ground – reading its title aloud –

Treatise on what is the Real

Leafing through the pages – you find that every one of them is empty – aside from page 6765 – which bears – in the bottom righthand corner – in the tiniest of writing – the following words – which *Nova Nopu* reads aloud –

The real is that which can't be named as that which is not real.

– and as she beautifully pronounces the final word of the entire corpus' only sentence – (but where – now – *is Nova* – where *is Rev. O' Lution?*) – you hear a music begin which – as it plays – inconceivably widens and deepens the space – (and the time) – in which you find yourself –

❦ The 8 Negations of Nagarjuna

– an immense architectural space – (within which it has started to rain – it is the FEN BUILDING*) – in which you now ascertain you have been lucidly dreaming – while sleeping for several hours following the cessation of the music – (when you wake – [before you reach into your pocket for the feel of the crumpled poppy – startled to discover that it is now in perfect health –

* See APPENDIX 2

- your pocket is now streaming out soil and blood – followed by more poppies – and on and on – until you are surrounded by a plot – a pool – of pinks – violets and reds – of silken flowers' beauty immediately enhanced by the torrential rain – and a single rosehip – of gratuitous delicacy – violence – memory and quietude] – you – before you open your eyes – see – first – in your hypnopompia – yourself – unseeing –

- followed by the sight of 2 spires – one of stone – one of flame –

- after which you see a word imprinted in your – utterly liberated – and perspicacious
– mind's eye –

- the truth of which is not only so because the 'U' has been so thoroughly entered
into – but that the impulse – in the act of so doing – has had to – partly because of the
necessary resistance that you have raised – completely change its own direction – the
universal will to change compelled to change itself in the act of changing another) – it
is – (or so it seems in the darkness) – aside from the spontaneous – sanguine garden –
almost entirely empty – save for – at its centre – a simple – but very long – line drawn
onto the marble floor – with the following words carved around and about it –

FUTURE

PAST

SIMPLY CROSS THE LINE TO OBTAIN
YOUR PRESENT

The Lollipop Entity – pointing to the line – says –

'The third is this –

No-one has yet managed to follow this injunction.' – as he – to the music – alternately stately and spritely – of a *Passacaglia* – does just that – (leaving you to face a face that – perhaps – is to be your own – in a present not yet – to you – present) –

– disappearing – along with the line – the words and the space – (but not the time – which shall remain forever yours in which to walk – to frisk – to be still – to caper) – in which you were standing.

❦ Passacaglia

IS IT NOTHING

INDEX of Music

All of the music listed above may be found for performance at Universal Edition
www.universaledition.com

INDEX of Holes – Cards – Moments – Tales – and Actual Works of Art –

The following artworks – purloined under the artist's duress for use in this book – are by John Elcock – www.johnelcock.co.uk

Achilles – 73
Anastasis – 235
Annunciation – 137
The Cave Dweller – 204
Cherenkov – 556
Dark Chanting Goshawk – 203
Dunlin Cloud – 479
Lapis Balticum – 555
The Jackdaws of Bevagna – 207
Jynx Torquilla – 205
The Mach Loop – 321
Podiceps Christatus – 205
Storm – 100
Trinity – 227
Turdus Philomelos – 203
The Union of St Kilda and San Michele – 109
Virgin of Philæ – 71
Virgin of Yaroslavl – 300
Warbler and Pyx – 252

One of these artworks shall be presented to the first reader to – having first placed a rose at its base – send a photograph – to the publisher – of the stone marker that can be found on page 555.

APPENDIX 1

The Golden Breathing – Tuning – Toning – Turning – Ceremony of the Shruti Flower

Morning

Consult the 96 notes and chords of the Shruti flower.
Either – over 96 weeks or days – progress through the notes/chords in order – i.e. week 1 – 'a' – week 2 – 'e' etc. or – choose a different note or chord – at random – each week or day until all 96 have been sounded.

Once a note/chord has been chosen – sit – on a folded pillow – half-lotus and barefoot – having positioned – as well as a rose and a beeswax candle – 3 singing bowls in front of you so that your left hand is in easy reach of two of the bowls and your right hand is close to the third.

Having prostrated – with hands in prayerful posture – three times before the rose – light the candle.

Now – upon the 3 singing bowls – play the following figuration.

With the right hand – sound the 3rd bowl 16 times in quick succession by striking the side of the bowl with the index finger.

At the same time – sound the 1ˢᵗ and 2ⁿᵈ bowls – in the same way – in this manner –

12/12/12/12/12/12/12/12/.

Without pause – now sound the 3ʳᵈ bowl 24 times in quick succession.
At the same time – sound the 1ˢᵗ and 2ⁿᵈ bowls in this manner – *('·' signifies non-strike)*

1-2/1-2/1-2/1-2/1-2/1-2/1-2/1-2/.

Without pause – now sound the 3ʳᵈ bowl 40 times in quick succession.
At the same time – sound the 1ˢᵗ and 2ⁿᵈ bowls in this manner –

1--2-/1--2-/1--2-/1--2-/1--2-/1--2-/1--2-/1--2-/.

Without pause – now sound the 3ʳᵈ bowl 64 times in quick succession.

At the same time – sound the 1ˢᵗ and 2ⁿᵈ bowls in this manner –

1----2--/1----2--/1----2--/1----2--/1----2--/1----2--/1----2--/1----2--/
1----2--/.

Without pause – now sound the 3ʳᵈ bowl 64 times in quick succession.
At the same time – sound the 1ˢᵗ and 2ⁿᵈ bowls in this manner –

1-------2----/1-------2----/1-------2----/1-------2----/1-------2----
/1-------2----/1-------2----/1-------2----/.

Now – having allowed the bowls to ring until silent – gently sound the bowls once in
turn and set the chosen note/chord sounding on the shruti-box.
Sound the note/chord for 13 'breaths' of the shruti-box.

Sing – on the lowest note of the chord – 13 (or 21 – or 34 etc.) vowels to accompany
the shruti-box – exploring the various harmonics that the changing vowels produce.
In particular – you may wish to sing the vowels 'EE AH OO AY' – followed by 8
(or 13 – or 21 etc.) 'AUM' tones ('AH OO MM') followed by 5 (or 8 – or 13 etc.)
'MUA' tones ('MM OO AH')..

Cease toning and continue to sound the shruti-box for 21 (or 34 – or 55 etc.) of its
breaths..

After the shruti-box has ceased sounding – gently strike the bowls once in reverse order.

Rise from the half-lotus position and engage in the following –

Gesture A   With right hand held aloft – eyes and ears open – palm open to
the sky – and left hand towards the ground – palm open to the earth –

Turn 360° widdershins – once.

Gesture B   With left hand held aloft – eyes and ears open – palm open to
the sky – and right hand towards the ground – palm open to the earth –

Turn 360° sunwise – once.

Then alternate – in Fibonacci manner – i.e. –

Gesture A – widdershins twice

Gesture B – sunwise once

Gesture A – widdershins thrice

Gesture B – sunwise twice

Gesture A – widdershins five times

Gesture B – sunwise thrice

Gesture A – widdershins eight times

Gesture B – sunwise five times

Gesture A – widdershins 13 times

Gesture B – sunwise 8 times

(A single widdershins turn will prevent dizziness)

Now – sitting – on a folded pillow – half-lotus once more – and listening to your heart – (with a stethoscope if easier – place your left hand over the chest piece against your heart and your right hand upturned on your right knee) –

Breathe in for 2 heartbeats – breathe out for 3 heartbeats (x5)

Breathe in for 3 heartbeats – breathe out for 5 heartbeats (x5)

Breathe in for 5 heartbeats – breathe out for 8 heartbeats (x5)

Breathe in for 8 heartbeats – breathe out for 13 heartbeats (x5)

Breathe in for 13 heartbeats – breathe out for 21 heartbeats (x5)

Now – perform a mudra – keeping to the same mudra for one week – during the duration of which you should breathe in the following way – this time without listening to the heart – (as your hands will be engaged upon the mudra) – but still keeping to its pulse – (which you will have imbibed during the previous portion of the ceremony) –

Breathe in for 8 (or 13) heartbeats – holding the breath for 13 (or 21) heartbeats
Breathe out for 8 (or 13) heartbeats – holding the breath for 13 (or 21) heartbeats (x21)

Now tone once more around the shruti note/chord as indicated above – following this with a listening to the shruti-box's breathing for a time..

Now – upon the 3 singing bowls – play the figurations given above – but in reverse – i.e. begin with sounding the 3rd bowl 64 times etc.

Before extinguishing the candle – having prostrated yourself once more – five times – before rose and candle – say the following verse –

> 'Fire in the heart –
> The thinking heart –
> The thinking heart wills love.'

Having extinguished the candle – continue to gaze into the rose for a time.

This ceremony lasts – at its shortest – about 40 minutes – though higher Fibonacci numbers may be reached – at any point during the ceremony – at participant's discretion.

If the turning described above is not possible – it may be equally beneficial to twiddle one's thumbs in like manner – and to much higher numbers in the Fibonacci sequence!

Of course – variations on the above will be inculcated as required.

Evening

In the evening – reverse the numbers – i.e. turning 1,1 – 1,2 – 2,3 – 3,5 – 5,8 – 8,13 etc.
And breathing – in for 3, out for 2, - in for 5, out for 3, - in for 8, out for 5 etc.

Be sure to listen and to be receptive between these disparate gestures.

Communal Variation

When performing the Ceremony with 2 or more people – sit in a form approaching a circle – with roses and beeswax candles towards – spokelike – its centre – the ceremonial space being scented through the burning of one or more essential oils.

The Ceremonial Rose-Tree would be – if possible – an excellent centrepiece to proceedings – drawn in chalk if not able to be constructed.

It would be optimal if each participant had their own shruti box and singing bowls with which to partake in the ceremony. Gongs would be yet more delightful.

Ideally – The Communal Ceremony would end with a group improvisation whereby 3 - 5 of the company would choose – by the role of the die – beforehand – separate rhythmic motifs – which they would then play – (while the tone or chord for that day is sounding and upon which those present are toning) – on any percussion of their choice – the motifs always to be built from 5 discrete note values – lasting either 1, 2, 3, 5, 8 or 13 semiquavers in duration – always at Crotchet = 60.

Resources

A shruti box.
3 singing bowls.
A rose.
A beeswax candle.
A book of mudras.
A stethoscope.
An open heart.

Further points of research

The golden ratio – encouraging such a ratio to thrive between heart and breath – the Chladni stand and its ramifications with respect to 'tuning' – the harmonic series and the nature of coherence and form – the sustained tone and its seemingly infinite richness and expansiveness – alone and in combination.

The Opening and Closing of the Shruti Flower

96 notes and chords to accompany the practice of golden breathing –
toning and turning

1	a	33	cef	65	fgab
2	e	34	dfg	66	gabc
3	d	35	ega	67	dgc
4	f	36	ceg	68	egc
5	g	37	dfa	69	dbc
6	b	38	cfg	70	ebc
7	c	39	dga	71	eab
8	ab	40	cfa	72	fbc
9	ga	41	dgb	73	egb
10	cd	42	eac	74	fac
11	de	43	cga	75	fab
12	fg	44	dab	76	gbc
13	ce	45	cab	77	fgb
14	gb	46	cea	78	gac
15	eg	47	dfb	79	gab
16	fa	48	cfb	80	abc
17	dg	49	cgc	81	dc
18	cf	50	cefa	82	ec
19	gc	51	dfgb	83	eb
20	cg	52	cdef	84	fc
21	da	53	defg	85	fb
22	db	54	efga	86	ea
23	ca	55	cdefg	87	df
24	cb	56	defga	88	ac
25	cc	57	efgab	89	bc
26	cde	58	cdefga	90	ef
27	def	59	defgab	91	d
28	efg	60	cdefgab	92	a
29	fga	61	efgabc	93	b
30	cdf	62	fgabc	94	e
31	deg	63	cgabc	95	c
32	efa	64	egac	96	f

APPENDIX 2

CEREMONIAL ROSE-TREE

A living emblem of – beeswax – fire and rose – employed during the performance of much of the music of *The Lollipop Entity's* favour and fancy –

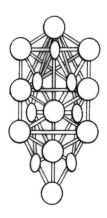

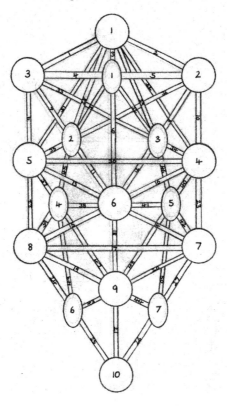

- the circles representing candles which – in their turn – represent –

1	Crown's coronal – coeur de lion – coronarial.
2	Wisdom's will's wing windward – wit's witness as wish.
3	Intelligence's in and ex tempore interfusional integrity – intentions interpretative – intercessional.
4	Love's luminescence and loss – lullabies lucid and lucent – lustrous lugholes leered luneward.
5	Discernment's dithyrambics disclosed – dissentient – distilled disputational.
6	Beauty's bitter bounty – boundaries bounce boundless.
7	Steadfastness's stellular stillness.
8	Splendour's spontaneous spandrel – spark – sparse and spangle.
9	Presence's precedence – precision and plenipotent prepossession.
10	Equanimity's equinoctial – equipollent and equidiurnal equilibrium.

- the ellipses representing roses which - in their turn - represent -

1	The Fool
2	Ornament
3	Forgetfulness
4	Laughter
5	The Erotic
6	Curiosity
7	Kindness

- the wooden - arterial branches - (intimately related to the 52 white notes of the piano - each note that is heard evoking these qualities in resonant interplay both with what is represented by candle and rose and with what is represented by the remaining 51 branches - each note to be thought of as a temporary vessel inhabited by other beings that - for the duration of their inhabitation - listen to us) - mediating between the candles and the roses - representing -

1	The making contact in compassionate strength.
2	The feeling that is steadily beneficent.
3	The perceiving as a ruler and as a friend.
4	The willing in purity and laudability.
5	The flawlessly concentrated mind in its knowing.
6	The soul inspiring as a beginner.
7	The being attentive as a protection and a restoring.
8	The initial attempting in eminence and quickening.
9	The sustained attempting in aliveness and amending.
10	The effort in superb self-subsistence.
11	The pleasurable interest in creating and finding.
12	The desire to do - to make nobly out of naught.
13	The deciding upon the unique shape of beauty.
14	The generosity in forgiving - as The One.
15	The passion both to subdue and to satisfy.
16	The perspicuity in bestowing - in making able.
17	The fortuity in prevailing - and so - sustaining.
18	The openness toward opening the inward eye - and to bringing what it sees.
19	The sympathy towards the delaying of the knowing.
20	The altruism in being the first to be restrained.
21	The joy in being the last to be enlarged.
22	The disinhibiting of the extended and the manifest.
23	The courage of the hidden - exalted.
24	The focusing of the strengthener transcended.
25	The sleep of the hearer of all as a keeping of faith.
26	The dream of the eminently humble.

27   The complexity of the seer as form giver.
28   The acquiescence of the withholder as decider.
29   The amity of the just as a bestowing of honours.
30   The reasoning of The Subtle One to be carefully judged.
31   The faith of the totally aware and benign.
32   The mindfulness of the gentle – immense.
33   The modesty of the magnificent – forbearing.
34   The discretion of the all-forgiving – nourishing.
35   The balance of mind in the rewards of thankfulness as a hearkening.
36   The composure of the mental properties as sublime life-giving.
37   The composure of mind as the magniloquence of the The Patient One.
38   The buoyancy of mental properties as all-preserving – rightly guided.
39   The buoyancy of mind as giver of strength – enduring.
40   The pliancy of mental properties as the ultimate contrapuntal – incomparable.
41   The pliancy of mind as the majestic way – showing and sharing.
42   The adaptability of mental properties as the bountiful propitiousness.
43   The adaptability of mind as a watching and preventing of harm.
44   The proficiency of mental properties as a responsiveness and enrichment.
45   The proficiency of mind as an all-embracing independence.
46   The rectitude of mental properties as a wise gathering.
47   The rectitude of mind as a loving – equitable.
48   The right speaking as a glorious light.
49   The right action as the raising clemency.
50   The right living as the witnessing to the owning of none and all by none and all.
51   The pitying as the truth of the mild.
52   The appreciating as a relenting advocacy.

– the colours of candles – roses and branches changing as each piece of music requires – the rose-tree's blooming – and its quiescence – that is – when the candles are to be lit and extinguished – being left to the discretion of the tender-witness of the rose-tree – the tender-witness also – at the beginning of each piece of music – setting a scented oil burning – there only ever being 7 oils burning at one time – the tender-witness – therefore – extinguishing the '1ˢᵗ' oil when the '8ᵗʰ' has begun to burn – the order of oils to be burned being randomly determined – for each piece of music – from among the following 52 oils –

allspice – ambrette seed – atlas cedarwood – bay – mint bergamot – black pepper – blue tansy – cade – Cananga – cannabis – catnip – cistus – copaiba balsam – Japanese cypress – davana – dalmatian sage – fennel – fir needle – galbanum – rose geranium – grapefruit – hemlock – hemp – ho wood – jatamansi – kunzea – laurel leaf – lavender – lemongrass – lime – linden blossom – myrtle – niaouli – opoponax – bitter orange – peppermint – pinyon pine – Ravensara – ravintsara – Rosalina – rosewood – saro – siberian fir – spearmint – black spruce – sweet myrrh – tangerine – common tea-tree – tobacco – tulsi – wintergreen – ylang ylang.

APPENDIX 3

FEN BUILDING

The *Lollipop Entity* and *The Lampedephorian* had – over many years – discussed the construction of a building in which to perform *The Lampedephoria* and other works.

At first – they had come to the conclusion that a setting somewhere amidst the East Anglian fenlands would be the most apt – though – in an inspired act of associative thinking – The *Lampedephorian* suggested that the knob of the door to such a building would be most appositely placed – (bearing in mind the number of white keys utilized – more or less equally – during *The Lampedephoria)* – at precisely 52°E and 0°N – thus placing the edifice slightly to the south of what had originally been conceived.

The dimensions having been established – the building's construction was begun – many adjustments to the surrounding landscape and conurbation being necessary.

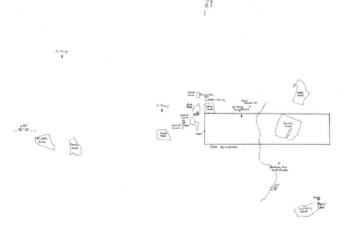

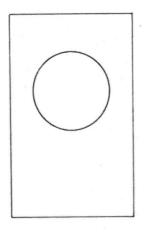

EAST FACING WALL – of gold and sandstone

Height – 4181 ft
Width – 2584 ft

Diameter of CLEAR GLASS WINDOW – 1597 ft
Centre of CLEAR GLASS WINDOW – 2584 ft by 1292 ft

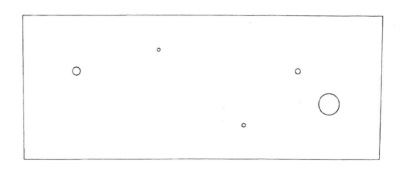

SOUTH FACING WALL – of copper and marble

Height – 4181 ft
Width – 10946 ft

Diameter of DARK PINK STAINED-GLASS WINDOW – 610 ft
Centre of DARK PINK STAINED-GLASS WINDOW – 1597 ft (e > w) by 1597 ft (v)
Diameter of PURPLE STAINED-GLASS WINDOW – 144 ft
Centre of PURPLE STAINED-GLASS WINDOW – 2584 ft (e > w) by 2584 ft(v)
Diameter of BLUE STAINED-GLASS WINDOW – 89 ft
Centre of BLUE STAINED-GLASS WINDOW – 4181 ft (e > w) by 987 ft (v)
Diameter of GREEN STAINED-GLASS WINDOW – 55 ft
Centre of GREEN STAINED-GLASS WINDOW – 6765 ft (e > w) by 987 ft (v)
Diameter of YELLOW STAINED-GLASS WINDOW – 233 ft
Centre of YELLOW STAINED-GLASS WINDOW – 1597 ft (e > w) by 2584 ft (v)

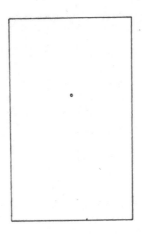

WEST FACING WALL – of silver and limestone

Height – 4181 ft
Width – 2584 ft

Diameter of CLEAR GLASS WINDOW – 34 ft
Centre of CLEAR GLASS WINDOW – 2584 ft by 1292 ft

DOOR – of lead and ebony oak

Height – 21 ft
Width – 13 ft

DOOR – (above which shall be inscribed – inside the building – the words – *'Rekindle All Hope (towards the fire of love in deed) – All You Who Enter Here')* – which shall have no means of being locked – to be placed 1597 ft across the width of the WEST WALL (w>s)

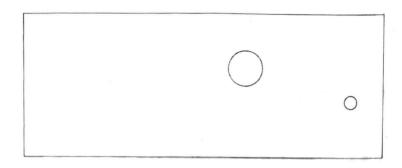

NORTH FACING WALL – of iron and flint

Diameter of ORANGE WINDOW – 377 ft

Centre of ORANGE WINDOW – 987 ft (w > e) by 1597 ft (v)

Diameter of RED WINDOW – 987 ft

Centre of RED WINDOW – 4181 ft (w > e) by 2584 ft (v)

ROOF

ROOF to be retractable such that it encloses the space for 226 – randomly chosen – days of the year – at all other times allowing full exposure to the elements.

INTERIOR

The already existent *Earl's Wood* – which shall be utterly rewilded – (boar – bear – wolf – lynx – etc.) – shall remain flourishing – within *The Fen Building* – as shall *The River Quin*.

The *Fen Building* shall also encompass the Church of *St Mary Magdalene*.

All nearby roads shall either be removed or diverted far from the site.

The space shall also contain a *FRODOBINE-YAWNSTEERS* grand piano – an extensively furnished (the world's largest – manufactured by CURIOSITY-rose-ZEAL – 33,333 pipes) organ – several large gongs and shruti boxes – telescope (non-electrical) and 3 bicycles.

Aside from the above – (and all the unforeseen life *within* the above) – the *Fen Building* shall be empty – and floored with *Amazonite Green Marble* throughout – aside from that region taken up by *Earl's Wood* – and excluding space made for a simple bridge over the *River Quin*.

APPENDIX 4

THE DIVINATIVITORY CARDS

The 78 images referred to by The Lollipop Entity on p515 may be used as *divinativitory cards* – that is – as a set of yantra/mandalas from which to glean *meteorontological* insights.

They are in 4 'suits'.

12 PAX IMMEMORIA.
16 – Actual – Bloodly Transubstantiations of Body – Flesh and Nerve, not Spirit.
22 Epiphaneia.
28 Changes in Solalterity.

Finding your own method of random selection – choose 5 of the 78 cards and lay them out in the form of a quincunx or pentangle – deciding – for yourself – which point shall be assigned to which number.

Subsequent to this – and to fully complement your engagement in divinativitory meditation upon the cards – listen to a randomly selected piece from the Lampedephoria.

Card 1 – *The Blessing you Fear.*

Card 2 – *The Blessing for which you have Hope.*

Card 3 – *The Shape of The Real as it is Unfolding at the present time.*

Card 4 – *The Shape of the Other that is to be Encountered.*

Card 5 – *The Card of the Approaching Blessing.*

MICHAELMAS 2023 – TOMBLAND – NORWICH

As above – so below

350 photographs
242 pieces of music
59 drawings
43 tales
42 moments
28 phases of the sun
22 divinativitory cards
21 works of art
16 tableaux of – Actual – Bloodly Transubstantiations of Body – Flesh and Nerve – not Spirit
12 inscriptions
9 countries
9 holes
1 ceremonial rose-tree
1 meditative ceremony
1 building
1 race
1 pack of 78 cards

1 dark-pink rose

The Artel Press
Liverpool